Twelve Classic One-Act Plays

DOVER · THRIFT · EDITIONS

Twelve Classic One-Act Plays

EDITED BY

MARY CAROLYN WALDREP

DOVER PUBLICATIONS, INC.
Mineola, New York

DOVER THRIFT EDITIONS

GENERAL EDITOR: MARY CAROLYN WALDREP
EDITOR OF THIS VOLUME: ALISON DAURIO

Bibliographical Note

This Dover edition, first published in 2010, is a new anthology of works from stan-
dard sources. See the Bibliographical Sources on page xi for more information. The
introductory Note was prepared specially for this edition.

Library of Congress Cataloging-in-Publication Data

Twelve classic one-act plays / edited by Mary Carolyn Waldrep.
    p. cm. — (Dover thrift edition)
  ISBN-13: 978-0-486-47490-8
  ISBN-10: 0-486-47490-9
  1. One-act plays. I. Waldrep, Mary Carolyn.

PN6120.O5T84 2010
808.82'41—dc22

                                                        20090534643

Manufactured in the United States by Courier Corporation
47490901
www.doverpublications.com

NOTE

Although never widely popular on Broadway, the one-act play has long been a staple of the experimental, regional, and non-professional theater. Drama, satire, comedy, farce, even tragedy, are all fodder for the one-act, and all have been successfully presented. In addition to meeting all the normal requirements of a well-wrought play, a one-act must be even more tightly constructed, with all unneccessary dialogue pared away.

The twelve plays chosen for this collection cover a wide variety of styles and moods, beginning with Aristophanes' satire, *The Birds,* to Louise Saunders' 1923 bauble, *The Knave of Hearts.* The playwrights represent some of the best, and best known in the field of drama.

The collection has been put together with the non-professional theater in mind. Mounting a production involves time, effort and expense. Often, the amateur theater does not have a permanent home and has limited rehearsal and performance time. Drawing an audience is also a problem, particularly in an area where there is competition from professional theaters.

Some groups have turned to the one-act play as a way of solving some of these problems. A festival of one-act plays has a number of advantages—a one-act play takes less rehearsal time, and can often easily be rehearsed off-site (I have even seen a one-act play successfully rehearsed in a studio apartment).

In addition, a festival of one-acts is an excellent vehicle for offering first time directors an opportunity of trying their hand. Since each play in a such a festival generally has its own separate cast, a large number of actors are generally involved in the production, and, it cannot be denied that, for amateur theater at least, the more people involved in a production, the larger the audience it will draw.

Finally, each of the twelve plays presented here can be performed freely, without paying any royalty at all, an advantage any theater group can appreciate.

Contents

Bibliographical Sources

Aristophanes, *The Birds* is an unabridged republication of the anonymous translation that originally appeared in *Aristophanes: The Eleven Comedies*, published by Horace Liveright, New York, 1928, on a subscription basis. The translator's footnotes have been edited for this edition.

Molière, *The Countess of Escarbagnas* reprinted from *The Dramatic Works of Molière*, translated by Charles Heron Wall and published by G. Bell and Sons, Ltd., London, in 1913.

Anton Chekhov, *The Proposal*, reprinted from *Plays by Anton Tchekoff*, translated by Julius West and published by Charles Scribner's Sons, New York, in 1916.

William Butler Yeats, *The Land of Heart's Desire*, originally published in 1894, revised in 1911. Reprinted from the 1921 edition of *Selected Poems*, published by The Macmillan Company, New York.

J. M. Synge, *Riders to the Sea*, published by John W. Luce & Company, Boston, in 1911.

August Strindberg, *The Stronger*, translated by Edith and Warner Oland, reprinted from *August Strindberg Plays*, published by John W. Luce and Company, Boston, in 1912.

Oscar Wilde, *A Florentine Tragedy*, published by John W. Luce and Company, Boston, in 1908.

James M. Barrie, *The Old Lady Shows Her Medals*, published by Hodder and Stoughton Ltd., London, in 1918.

Susan Glaspell, *Trifles*, reprinted from *Plays*, published by Small, Maynard & Company, Boston in 1920.

Eugene O'Neill, *The Moon of the Caribbees*, reprinted from *The Moon of the Caribbees and Six Other Plays of the Sea*, published by Boni & Liveright, New York, in 1919.

Edna St. Vincent Millay, *Aria da Capo*, published by Harper & Brothers, New York, in 1920.

Louise Saunders, *The Knave of Hearts*, reprinted from *The Atlantic Book of Modern Plays*, published by Atlantic Monthly Press, Boston, in 1921.

THE BIRDS
Aristophanes

CAST OF CHARACTERS

EUELPIDES
PISTHETÆRUS
EPOPS (THE HOOPOE)
TROCHILUS, Servant to Epops
PHŒNICOPTERUS
HERALDS
A PRIEST
A PROPHET
METON, a Geometrician
A COMMISSIONER
A DEALER IN DECREES

IRIS
A PARRICIDE
CINESIAS, a Dithyrambic Bard
AN INFORMER
PROMETHEUS
POSIDON
TRIBALLUS
HERACLES
SERVANT OF PISTHETÆRUS
MESSENGERS
CHORUS OF BIRDS

Scene: A wild, desolate tract of open country; broken rocks and brushwood occupy the centre of the stage.

EUELPIDES [*to his jay*].[1]   Do you think I should walk straight for yon tree?

PISTHETÆRUS [*to his crow*].   Cursed beast, what are you croaking to me?... to retrace my steps?

EUELPIDES.   Why, you wretch, we are wandering at random, we are exerting ourselves only to return to the same spot; 'tis labour lost.

PISTHETÆRUS.   To think that I should trust to this crow, which has made me cover more than a thousand furlongs!

EUELPIDES.   And that I to this jay, who has torn every nail from my fingers!

PISTHETÆRUS.   If only I knew where we were....

EUELPIDES.   Could you find your country again from here?

---

1. Euelpides is holding a jay and Pisthetærus a crow: they are the guides who are to lead them to the kingdom of the birds.

1

PISTHETÆRUS. No, I feel quite sure I could not, any more than could Execestides[1] find his.

EUELPIDES. Oh dear! oh dear!

PISTHETÆRUS. Aye, aye, my friend, 'tis indeed the road of "oh dears" we are following.

EUELPIDES. That Philocrates, the bird-seller, played us a scurvy trick, when he pretended these two guides could help us to find Tereus,[2] the Epops, who is a bird, without being born of one. He has indeed sold us this jay, a true son of Tharelides,[3] for an obolus, and this crow for three, but what can they do? Why, nothing whatever but bite and scratch!—What's the matter with you then, that you keep opening your beak? Do you want us to fling ourselves headlong down these rocks? There is no road that way.

PISTHETÆRUS. Not even the vestige of a track in any direction.

EUELPIDES. And what does the crow say about the road to follow?

PISTHETÆRUS. By Zeus, it no longer croaks the same thing it did.

EUELPIDES. And which way does it tell us to go now?

PISTHETÆRUS. It says that, by dint of gnawing, it will devour my fingers.

EUELPIDES. What misfortune is ours! we strain every nerve to get to the birds,[4] do everything we can to that end, and we cannot find our way! Yes, spectators, our madness is quite different from that of Sacas. He is not a citizen, and would fain be one at any cost; we, on the contrary, born of an honourable tribe and family and living in the midst of our fellow-citizens, we have fled from our country as hard as ever we could go. 'Tis not that we hate it; we recognize it to be great and rich, likewise that everyone has the right to ruin himself; but the crickets only chirrup among the fig-trees for a month or two, whereas the Athenians spend their whole lives in chanting forth judgments from their law-courts.[5] That is why we started off with a basket, a stewpot and some

---

1. A stranger who wanted to pass as an Athenian, although coming originally from a far-away country.

2. A king of Thrace, a son of Ares, who married Procné, the daughter of Pandion, King of Athens. He violated his sister-in-law, Philomela, and then cut out her tongue; she managed to convey to her sister how she had been treated. They agreed to kill Itys, whom Procné had borne to Tereus, and dished up the limbs of his son to the father; at the end of the meal Philomela appeared and threw the child's head upon the table. Tereus rushed with drawn sword upon the princesses, but all the actors in this scene were metamorphised. Tereus became an Epops [hoopoe], Procné a nightingale, Philomela a swallow, and Itys a goldfinch.

3. An Athenian who had some resemblance to a jay.

4. Literally, *to go to the crows*, a proverbial expression equivalent to our *going to the devil*.

5. They leave Athens because of their hatred of lawsuits and informers; this is the especial failing of the Athenians satirized in 'The Wasps.'

myrtle boughs[1] and have come to seek a quiet country in which to settle. We are going to Tereus, the Epops, to learn from him, whether, in his aerial flights, he has noticed some town of this kind.

PISTHETÆRUS.   Here! look!

EUELPIDES.   What's the matter?

PISTHETÆRUS.   Why, the crow has been pointing me to something up there for some time now.

EUELPIDES.   And the jay is also opening its beak and craning its neck to show me I know not what. Clearly, there are some birds about here. We shall soon know, if we kick up a noise to start them.

PISTHETÆRUS.   Do you know what to do? Knock your leg against this rock.

EUELPIDES.   And you your head to double the noise.

PISTHETÆRUS.   Well then use a stone instead; take one and hammer with it.

EUELPIDES.   Good idea! Ho there, within! Slave! slave!

PISTHETÆRUS.   What's that, friend! You say, "slave," to summon Epops! 'Twould be much better to shout, "Epops, Epops!"

EUELPIDES.   Well then, Epops! Must I knock again? Epops!

TROCHILUS.   Who's there? Who calls my master?

EUELPIDES.   Apollo the Deliverer! what an enormous beak![2]

TROCHILUS.   Good god! they are bird-catchers.

EUELPIDES.   The mere sight of him petrifies me with terror. What a horrible monster.

TROCHILUS.   Woe to you!

EUELPIDES.   But we are not men.

TROCHILUS.   What are you, then?

EUELPIDES.   I am the Fearling, an African bird.

TROCHILUS.   You talk nonsense.

EUELPIDES.   Well, then, just ask it of my feet.[3]

TROCHILUS.   And this other one, what bird is it?

PISTHETÆRUS.   I? I am a Cackling,[4] from the land of the pheasants.

EUELPIDES.   But you yourself, in the name of the gods! what animal are you?

TROCHILUS.   Why, I am a slave-bird.

1. Myrtle boughs were used in sacrifices, and the founding of every colony was started by a sacrifice.

2. The actors wore masks made to resemble the birds they were supposed to represent.

3. Fear had had disastrous effects upon Euelpides' internal economy, and this his feet evidenced.

4. The same mishap had occurred to Pisthetærus.

EUELPIDES. Why, have you been conquered by a cock?

TROCHILUS. No, but when my master was turned into a peewit, he begged me to become a bird too, to follow and to serve him.

EUELPIDES. Does a bird need a servant, then?

TROCHILUS. 'Tis no doubt because he was a man. At times he wants to eat a dish of loach from Phalerum; I seize my dish and fly to fetch him some. Again he wants some pea-soup; I seize a ladle and a pot and run to get it.

EUELPIDES. This is, then, truly a running-bird.[1] Come, Trochilus, do us the kindness to call your master.

TROCHILUS. Why, he has just fallen asleep after a feed of myrtle-berries and a few grubs.

EUELPIDES. Never mind; wake him up.

TROCHILUS. I an certain he will be angry. However, I will wake him to please you.

PISTHETÆRUS. You cursed brute! why, I am almost dead with terror!

EUELPIDES. Oh! my god! 'twas sheer fear that made me lose my jay.

PISTHETÆRUS. Ah! you great coward! were you so frightened that you let go your jay?

EUELPIDES. And did you not lose your crow, when you fell sprawling on the ground? Pray tell me that.

PISTHETÆRUS. No, no.

EUELPIDES. Where is it, then?

PISTHETÆRUS. It has flown away.

EUELPIDES. Then you did not let it go! Oh! you brave fellow!

EPOPS. Open the forest,[2] that I may go out!

EUELPIDES. By Heracles! what a creature! what plumage! What means this triple crest?

EPOPS. Who wants me?

EUELPIDES. The twelve great gods have used you ill, meseems.

EPOPS. Are you chaffing me about my feathers? I have been a man, strangers.

EUELPIDES. 'Tis not you we are jeering at.

EPOPS. At what, then?

EUELPIDES. Why, 'tis your beak that looks so odd to us.

EPOPS. This is how Sophocles outrages me in his tragedies. Know, I once was Tereus.[3]

1. The Greek word for *wren* is derived from the same root as the Greek verb *to run*.
2. No doubt there was some scenery to represent a forest.
3. Sophocles had written a tragedy about Tereus, in which, no doubt, the king finally appears as a hoopoe.

EUELPIDES. You were Tereus, and what are you now? a bird or a peacock?

EPOPS. I am a bird.

EUELPIDES. Then where are your feathers? For I don't see them.

EPOPS. They have fallen off.

EUELPIDES. Through illness?

EPOPS. No. All birds moult their feathers, you know, every winter, and others grow in their place. But tell me, who are you?

EUELPIDES. We? We are mortals.

EPOPS. From what country?

EUELPIDES. From the land of the beautiful galleys.[1]

EPOPS. Are you dicasts?[2]

EUELPIDES. No, if anything, we are anti-dicasts.

EPOPS. Is that kind of seed sown among you?[3]

EUELPIDES. You have to look hard to find even a little in our fields.

EPOPS. What brings you here?

EUELPIDES. We wish to pay you a visit.

EPOPS. What for?

EUELPIDES. Because you formerly were a man, like we are, formerly you had debts, as we have, formerly you did not want to pay them, like ourselves; furthermore, being turned into a bird, you have when flying seen all lands and seas. Thus you have all human knowledge as well as that of birds. And hence we have come to you to beg you to direct us to some cosy town, in which one can repose as if on thick coverlets.

EPOPS. And are you looking for a greater city than Athens?

EUELPIDES. No, not a greater, but one more pleasant to dwell in.

EPOPS. Then you are looking for an aristocratic country.

EUELPIDES. I? Not at all! I hold the son of Scellias in horror.[4]

EPOPS. But, after all, what sort of city would please you best?

EUELPIDES. A place where the following would be the most important business transacted.—Some friend would come knocking at the door quite early in the morning saying, "By Olympian Zeus, be at my house early, as soon as you have bathed, and bring your children too. I am giving a nuptial feast, so don't fail, or else don't cross my threshold when I am in distress."

---

1. Athens.

2. The Athenians were madly addicted to lawsuits.

3. As much as to say, *Then you have such things as anti-dicasts?* And Euelpides practically replies, *Very few.*

4. His name was Aristocrates; he was a general and commanded a fleet sent in aid of Corcyra.

EPOPS. Ah! that's what may be called being fond of hardships! And what say you?

PISTHETÆRUS. My tastes are similar.

EPOPS. And they are?

PISTHETÆRUS. I want a town where the father of a handsome lad will stop in the street and say to me reproachfully as if I had failed him, "Ah! Is this well done, Stilbonides! You met my son coming from the bath after the gymnasium and you neither spoke to him, nor embraced him, nor took him with you, nor ever once twitched his parts. Would anyone call you an old friend of mine?"

EPOPS. Ah! wag, I see you are fond of suffering. But there is a city of delights, such as you want. 'Tis on the Red Sea.

EUELPIDES. Oh, no. Not a sea-port, where some fine morning the Salaminian[1] galley can appear, bringing a writ-server along. Have you no Greek town you can propose to us?

EPOPS. Why not choose Lepreum in Elis for your settlement?

EUELPIDES. By Zeus! I could not look at Lepreum without disgust, because of Melanthius.[2]

EPOPS. Then, again, there is the Opuntian, where you could live.

EUELPIDES. I would not be Opuntian[3] for a talent. But come, what is it like to live with the birds? You should know pretty well.

EPOPS. Why, 'tis not a disagreeable life. In the first place, one has no purse.

EUELPIDES. That does away with much roguery.

EPOPS. For food the gardens yield us white sesamè, myrtle-berries, poppies and mint.

EUELPIDES. Why, 'tis the life of the newly-wed indeed.[4]

PISTHETÆRUS. Ha! I am beginning to see a great plan, which will transfer the supreme power to the birds, if you will but take my advice.

EPOPS. Take your advice? In what way?

PISTHETÆRUS. In what way? Well, firstly, do not fly in all directions with open beak; it is not dignified. Among us, when we see a thoughtless man, we ask, "What sort of bird is this?" and Teleas answers, "'Tis a man who has no brain, a bird that has lost his head, a creature you cannot catch, for it never remains in any one place."

---

1. The State galley, which carried the officials of the Athenian republic to their several departments and brought back those whose time had expired.
2. A tragic poet, who was a leper.
3. An allusion to Opuntius, who was one-eyed.
4. The newly-married ate a sesamè-cake, decorated with garlands of myrtle, poppies, and mint.

EPOPS.   By Zeus himself! your jest hits the mark. What then is to be done?
PISTHETÆRUS.   Found a city.
EPOPS.   We birds? But what sort of city should we build?
PISTHETÆRUS.   Oh, really, really! 'tis spoken like a fool! Look down.
EPOPS.   I am looking.
PISTHETÆRUS.   Now look upwards.
EPOPS.   I am looking.
PISTHETÆRUS.   Turn your head round.
EPOPS.   Ah! 'twill be pleasant for me, if I end in twisting my neck!
PISTHETÆRUS.   What have you seen?
EPOPS.   The clouds and the sky.
PISTHETÆRUS.   Very well! is not this the pole of the birds then?
EPOPS.   How their pole?
PISTHETÆRUS.   Or, if you like it, the land. And since it turns and passes
    through the whole universe, it is called, 'pole.'[1] If you build and
    fortify it, you will turn your pole into a fortified city.[2] In this way
    you will reign over mankind as you do over the grasshoppers and
    cause the gods to die of rabid hunger.
EPOPS.   How so?
PISTHETÆRUS.   The air is 'twixt earth and heaven. When we want to
    go to Delphi, we ask the Bœotians[3] for leave of passage; in the
    same way, when men sacrifice to the gods, unless the latter pay
    you tribute, you exercise the right of every nation towards strang-
    ers and don't allow the smoke of the sacrifices to pass through
    your city and territory.
EPOPS.   By earth! by snares! by network! I never heard of anything
    more cleverly conceived; and, if the other birds approve, I am
    going to build the city along with you.
PISTHETÆRUS.   Who will explain the matter to them?
EPOPS.   You must yourself. Before I came they were quite ignorant,
    but since I have lived with them I have taught them to speak.
PISTHETÆRUS.   But how can they be gathered together?
EPOPS.   Easily. I will hasten down to the coppice to waken my dear
    Procnè! as soon as they hear our voices, they will come to us hot
    wing.
PISTHETÆRUS.   My dear bird, lose no time, I beg. Fly at once into the
    coppice and awaken Procnè.
EPOPS.   Chase off drowsy sleep, dear companion. Let the sacred hymn
    gush from thy divine throat in melodious strains; roll forth in soft

---

1. From the Greek verb that means *to turn.*
2. The Greek words for *pole* and *city* only differ by a single letter.
3. Bœotia separated Attica from Phocis.

cadence your refreshing melodies to bewail the fate of Itys,[1] which has been the cause of so many tears to us both. Your pure notes rise through the thick leaves of the yew-tree right up to the throne of Zeus, where Phœbus listens to you, Phœbus with his golden hair. And his ivory lyre responds to your plaintive accents; he gathers the choir of the gods and from their immortal lips rushes a sacred chant of blessed voices.

[*The flute is played behind the scene.*]

PISTHETÆRUS.   Oh! by Zeus! what a throat that little bird possesses. He has filled the whole coppice with honey-sweet melody!

EUELPIDES.   Hush!

PISTHETÆRUS.   What's the matter?

EUELPIDES.   Will you keep silence?

PISTHETÆRUS.   What for?

EUELPIDES.   Epops is going to sing again.

EPOPS [*in the Coppice*].   Epopoi, poi, popoi, epopoi, popoi, here, here, quick, quick, quick, my comrades in the air; all you, who pillage the fertile lands of the husbandmen, the numberless tribes who gather and devour the barley seeds, the swift flying race who sing so sweetly. And you whose gentle twitter resounds through the fields with the little cry of tio, tio, tio, tio, tio, tio, tio, tio; and you who hop about the branches of the ivy in the gardens; the mountain birds, who feed on the wild olive berries or the arbutus, hurry to come at my call, trioto, trioto, totobrix; you also, who snap up the sharp-stinging gnats in the marshy vales, and you who dwell in the fine plain of Marathon, all damp with dew, and you, the francolin with speckled wings; you too, the halcyons, who flit over the swelling waves of the sea, come hither to hear the tidings; let all the tribes of long-necked birds assemble here; know that a clever old man has come to us, bringing an entirely new idea and proposing great reforms. Let all come to the debate here, here, here, here. Torotorotorotorotix, kikkobau, kikkobau, torotorotorotorolililix.

PISTHETÆRUS.   Can you see any bird?

EUELPIDES.   By Phœbus, no! and yet I am straining my eyesight to scan the sky.

PISTHETÆRUS.   'Twas really not worth Epops' while to go and bury himself in the thicket like a plover when a-hatching.

PHŒNICOPTERUS.   Torotina, torotina.

PISTHETÆRUS.   Hold, friend, here is another bird.

---

1. The son of Tereus and Procné.

EUELPIDES. I' faith, yes! 'tis a bird, but of what kind? Isn't it a peacock?

PISTHETÆRUS. Epops will tell us. What is this bird?

EPOPS. 'Tis not one of those you are used to seeing; 'tis a bird from the marshes.

PISTHETÆRUS. Oh! oh! but he is very handsome with his wings as crimson as flame.

EPOPS. Undoubtedly; indeed he is called flamingo.

EUELPIDES. Hi! I say! You!

PISTHETÆRUS. What are you shouting for?

EUELPIDES. Why, here's another bird.

PISTHETÆRUS. Aye, indeed; 'tis a foreign bird too. What is this bird from beyond the mountains with a look as solemn as it is stupid?

EPOPS. He is called the Mede.[1]

PISTHETÆRUS. The Mede! But, by Heracles! how, if a Mede, has he flown here without a camel?

EUELPIDES. Here's another bird with a crest.

PISTHETÆRUS. Ah! that's curious. I say, Epops, you are not the only one of your kind then?

EPOPS. This bird is the son of Philocles, who is the son of Epops;[2] so that, you see, I am his grandfather; just as one might say, Hipponicus,[3] the son of Callias, who is the son of Hipponicus.

PISTHETÆRUS. Then this bird is Callias! Why, what a lot of his feathers he has lost![4]

EPOPS. That's because he is honest; so the informers set upon him and the women too pluck out his feathers.

PISTHETÆRUS. By Posidon, do you see that many-coloured bird? What is his name?

EPOPS. This one? 'Tis the glutton.

PISTHETÆRUS. Is there another glutton besides Cleonymus? But why, if he is Cleonymus, has he not thrown away his crest?[5] But what is the meaning of all these crests? Have these birds come to contend for the double stadium prize?[6]

---

1. Aristophanes mixes up real birds with people and individuals, whom he represents in the form of birds; he is personifying the Medians here.

2. Philocles, a tragic poet, had written a tragedy on Tereus, which was a plagiarism of the play of the same name by Sophocles. Philocles is the son of Epops, because he got his inspiration from Sophocles' Tereus, and at the same time is father to Epops, since he produced another Tereus.

3. This Hipponicus is probably the orator whose ears Alcibiades boxed to gain a bet; he was a descendant of Callias, who was famous for his hatred of Pisistratus.

4. This Callias, who must not be confounded with the foe of Pisistratus, had ruined himself.

5. Cleonymus had cast away his shield.

6. A race in which the track had to be circled twice.

EPOPS. They are like the Carians, who cling to the crests of their mountains for greater safety.[1]

PISTHETÆRUS. Oh, Posidon! do you see what swarms of birds are gathering here?

EUELPIDES. By Phœbus! what a cloud! The entrance to the stage is no longer visible, so closely do they fly together.

PISTHETÆRUS. Here is the partridge.

EUELPIDES. Faith! there is the francolin.

PISTHETÆRUS. There is the poachard.

EUELPIDES. Here is the kingfisher. And over yonder?

EPOPS. 'Tis the barber.

EUELPIDES. What? a bird a barber

PISTHETÆRUS. Why, Sporgilus is one.[2] Here comes the owl.

EUELPIDES. And who is it brings an owl to Athens?[3]

PISTHETÆRUS. Here is the magpie, the turtle-dove, the swallow, the horned owl, the buzzard, the pigeon, the falcon, the ring-dove, the cuckoo, the red-foot, the red-cap, the purple-cap, the kestrel, the diver, the ousel, the osprey, the woodpecker.

EUELPIDES. Oh! oh! what a lot of birds! what a quantity of black-birds! how they scold, how they come rushing up! What a noise! what a noise! Can they be bearing us ill-will? Oh! there! there! they are opening their beaks and staring at us.

PISTHETÆRUS. Why, so they are.

CHORUS. Popopopopopopopoi. Where is he who called me? Where am I to find him?

EPOPS. I have been waiting for you this long while! I never fail in my word to my friends.

CHORUS. Tititititititi. What good thing have you to tell me?

EPOPS. Something that concerns our common safety, and that is just as pleasant as it is to the purpose. Two men, who are subtle reason-ers, have come here to seek me.

Chorus. Where? What? What are you saying?

EPOPS. I say, two old men have come from the abode of men to propose a vast and splendid scheme to us.

CHORUS. Oh! 'tis a horrible, unheard-of crime! What are you saying?

EPOPS. Nay! never let my words scare you.

CHORUS. What have you done then?

EPOPS. I have welcomed two men, who wish to live with us.

---

1. A people of Asia Minor; when pursued by the Ionians they took refuge in the mountains.
2. An Athenian barber.
3. The owl was dedicated to Athenè, and being respected at Athens, it had greatly multiplied. Hence the proverb, *taking owls to Athens*, similar to our English *taking coals to Newcastle*.

CHORUS.   And you have dared to do that!

EPOPS.   Aye, and am delighted at having done so.

CHORUS.   Where are they?

EPOPS.   In your midst, as I am.

CHORUS.   Ah! ah! we are betrayed; 'tis sacrilege! Our friend, he who picked up corn-seeds in the same plains as ourselves, has violated our ancient laws; he has broken the oaths that bind all birds; he has laid a snare for me, he has handed us over to the attacks of that impious race which, throughout all time, has never ceased to war against us. As for this traitorous bird, we will decide his case later, but the two old men shall be punished forthwith; we are going to tear them to pieces.

PISTHETÆRUS.   'Tis all over with us.

EUELPIDES.   You are the sole cause of all our trouble. Why did you bring me from down yonder?

PISTHETÆRUS.   To have you with me.

EUELPIDES.   Say rather to have me melt into tears.

PISTHETÆRUS.   Go to! you are talking nonsense.

EUELPIDES.   How so?

PISTHETÆRUS.   How will you be able to cry when once your eyes are pecked out?

CHORUS.   Io! io! forward to the attack, throw yourselves upon the foe, spill his blood; take to your wings and surround them on all sides. Woe to them! let us get to work with our beaks, let us devour them. Nothing can save them from our wrath, neither the mountain forests, nor the clouds that float in the sky, nor the foaming deep. Come, peck, tear to ribbons. Where is the chief of the cohort? Let him engage the right wing.

EUELPIDES.   This is the fatal moment. Where shall I fly to, unfortunate wretch that I am?

PISTHETÆRUS.   Stay! stop here!

EUELPIDES.   That they may tear me to pieces?

PISTHETÆRUS.   And how do you think to escape them?

EUELPIDES.   I don't know at all.

PISTHETÆRUS.   Come, I will tell you. We must stop and fight them. Let us arm ourselves with these stew-pots.

EUELPIDES.   Why with the stew-pots?

PISTHETÆRUS.   The owl will not attack us.[1]

EUELPIDES.   But do you see all those hooked claws?

---

1. An allusion to the Feast of Pots, when all sorts of vegetables were stewed together and offered for the dead to Bacchus and Athené. This Feast was peculiar to Athens. Hence Pisthetærus thinks that the owl will recognize they are Athenians by seeing the stew-pots, and as he is an Athenian bird, he will not attack them.

PISTHETÆRUS.   Seize the spit and pierce the foe on your side.

EUELPIDES.   And how about my eyes?

PISTHETÆRUS.   Protect them with this dish or this vinegar-pot.

EUELPIDES.   Oh! what cleverness! what inventive genius! You are a great general, even greater than Nicias,[1] where stratagem is concerned.

CHORUS.   Forward, forward, charge with your beaks! Come, no delay. Tear, pluck, strike, flay them, and first of all smash the stew-pot.

EPOPS.   Oh, most cruel of all animals, why tear these two men to pieces, why kill them? What have they done to you? They belong to the same tribe, to the same family as my wife.[2]

CHORUS.   Are wolves to be spared? Are they not our most mortal foes? So let us punish them.

EPOPS.   If they are your foes by nature, they are your friends in heart, and they come here to give you useful advice.

CHORUS.   Advice or a useful word from their lips, from them, the enemies of my forebears!

EPOPS.   The wise can often profit by the lessons of a foe, for caution is the mother of safety. 'Tis just such a thing as one will not learn from a friend and which an enemy compels you to know. To begin with, 'tis the foe and not the friend that taught cities to build high walls, to equip long vessels of war; and 'tis this knowledge that protects our children, our slaves and our wealth.

CHORUS.   Well then, I agree, let us first hear them, for 'tis best; one can even learn something in an enemy's school.

PISTHETÆRUS.   Their wrath seems to cool. Draw back a little.

EPOPS.   'Tis only justice, and you will thank me later.

CHORUS.   Never have we opposed your advice up to now.

PISTHETÆRUS.   They are in a more peaceful mood; put down your stew-pot and your two dishes; spit in hand, doing duty for a spear, let us mount guard inside the camp close to the pot and watch in our arsenal closely; for we must not fly.

EUELPIDES.   You are right. But where shall we be buried, if we die?

PISTHETÆRUS.   In the Ceramicus;[3] for, to get a public funeral, we shall tell the Strategi that we fell at Orneæ,[4] fighting the country's foes.

CHORUS.   Return to your ranks and lay down your courage beside your wrath as the Hoplites do. Then let us ask these men who

---

1. Nicias, the famous Athenian general.
2. Procné, the daughter of Pandion, King of Athens.
3. A space beyond the walls of Athens which contained the gardens of the Academy and the graves of citizens who had died for their country.
4. A town in Western Argolis, where the Athenians had been recently defeated. A somewhat similar word in Greek signifies *birds*.

they are, whence they come, and with what intent. Here, Epops,
answer me.

EPOPS.   Are you calling me? What do you want of me?

CHORUS.   Who are they? From what country?

EPOPS.   Strangers, who have come from Greece, the land of the
wise.

CHORUS.   And what fate has led them hither to the land of the
birds?

EPOPS.   Their love for you and their wish to share your kind of life;
to dwell and remain with you always.

CHORUS.   Indeed, and what are their plans?

EPOPS.   They are wonderful, incredible, unheard of.

CHORUS.   Why, do they think to see some advantage that determines
them to settle here? Are they hoping with our help to triumph
over their foes or to be useful to their friends?

EPOPS.   They speak of benefits so great it is impossible either to describe or conceive them; all shall be yours, all that we see here,
there, above and below us; this they vouch for.

CHORUS.   Are they mad?

EPOPS.   They are the sanest people in the world.

CHORUS.   Clever men?

EPOPS.   The slyest of foxes, cleverness its very self, men of the world,
cunning, the cream of knowing folk.

CHORUS.   Tell them to speak and speak quickly; why, as I listen to you,
I am beside myself with delight.

EPOPS.   Here, you there, take all these weapons and hang them up
inside close to the fire, near the figure of the god who presides
there and under his protection;[1] as for you, address the birds, tell
them why I have gathered them together.

PISTHETÆRUS.   Not I, by Apollo, unless they agree with me as the
little ape of an armourer agreed with his wife, not to bite me, nor
pull me by the parts, nor shove things up my...

CHORUS.   You mean the...[puts finger to bottom]. Oh! be quite at ease.

PISTHETÆRUS.   No, I mean my eyes.

CHORUS.   Agreed.

PISTHETÆRUS.   Swear it.

CHORUS.   I swear it and, if I keep my promise, let judges and spectators give me the victory unanimously.

PISTHETÆRUS.   It is a bargain.

CHORUS.   And if I break my word, may I succeed by one vote only.

---

1. Epops is addressing the two slaves, no doubt Xanthias and Manes, who are mentioned later
on.

HERALD.   Hearken, ye people! Hoplites, pick up your weapons and return to your firesides; do not fail to read the decrees of dismissal we have posted.

CHORUS.   Man is a truly cunning creature, but nevertheless explain. Perhaps you are going to show me some good way to extend my power, some way that I have not had the wit to find out and which you have discovered. Speak! 'tis to your own interest as well as to mine, for if you secure me some advantage, I will surely share it with you. But what object can have induced you to come among us? Speak boldly, for I shall not break the truce,—until you have told us all.

PISTHETÆRUS.   I am bursting with desire to speak; I have already mixed the dough of my address and nothing prevents me from kneading it.... Slave! bring the chaplet and water, which you must pour over my hands. Be quick![1]

EUELPIDES.   Is it a question of feasting? What does it all mean?

PISTHETÆRUS.   By Zeus, no! but I am hunting for fine, tasty words to break down the hardness of their hearts.—I grieve so much for you, who at one time were kings...

CHORUS.   We kings! Over whom?

PISTHETÆRUS.   ...of all that exists, firstly of me and of this man, even of Zeus himself. Your race is older than Saturn, the Titans and the Earth.

CHORUS.   What, older than the Earth!

PISTHETÆRUS.   By Phœbus, yes.

CHORUS.   By Zeus, but I never knew that before!

PISTHETÆRUS.   'Tis because you are ignorant and heedless, and have never read your Æsop. 'Tis he who tells us that the lark was born before all other creatures, indeed before the Earth; his father died of sickness, but the Earth did not exist then; he remained unburied for five days, when the bird in its dilemma decided, for want of a better place, to entomb its father in its own head.

EUELPIDES.   So that the lark's father is buried at Cephalæ.[2]

EPOPS.   Hence, if we existed before the Earth, before the gods, the kingship belongs to us by right of priority.

EUELPIDES.   Undoubtedly, but sharpen your beak well; Zeus won't be in a hurry to hand over his sceptre to the woodpecker.

PISTHETÆRUS.   It was not the gods, but the birds, who were formerly the masters and kings over men; of this I have a thousand proofs. First of all, I will point you to the cock, who governed the

---

1. It was customary, when speaking in public and also at feasts, to wear a chaplet; hence the question Euelpides puts.

2. A deme of Attica. In Greek the word also means *heads*, and hence the pun.

Persians before all other monarchs, before Darius and Megabyzus.[1]
'Tis in memory of his reign that he is called the Persian bird.

EUELPIDES. For this reason also, even today, he alone of all the birds
wears his tiara straight on his head, like the Great King.[2]

PISTHETÆRUS. He was so strong, so great, so feared, that even now, on
account of his ancient power, everyone jumps out of bed as soon
as ever he crows at daybreak. Blacksmiths, potters, tanners, shoe-
makers, bathmen, corn-dealers, lyre-makers and armourers, all put
on their shoes and go to work before it is daylight.

EUELPIDES. I can tell you something about that. 'Twas the cock's fault
that I lost a splendid tunic of Phrygian wool. I was at a feast in
town, given to celebrate the birth of a child; I had drunk pretty
freely and had just fallen asleep, when a cock, I suppose in a
greater hurry than the rest, began to crow. I thought it was dawn
and set out for Alimos.[3] I had hardly got beyond the walls, when
a footpad struck me in the back with his bludgeon; down I went
and wanted to shout, but he had already made off with my
mantle.

PISTHETÆRUS. Formerly also the kite was ruler and king over the
Greeks.

EPOPS. The Greeks?

PISTHETÆRUS. And when he was king, 'twas he who first taught them
to fall on their knees before the kites.[4]

EUELPIDES. By Zeus! 'tis what I did myself one day on seeing a kite;
but at the moment I was on my knees, and leaning backwards[5]
with mouth agape, I bolted an obolus and was forced to carry my
bag home empty.[6]

PISTHETÆRUS. The cuckoo was king of Egypt and of the whole of
Phœnicia. When he called out "cuckoo," all the Phœnicians hur-
ried to the fields to reap their wheat and their barley.[7]

EUELPIDES. Hence no doubt the proverb, "Cuckoo! cuckoo! go to
the fields, ye circumcised."[8]

---

1. One of Darius' best generals.
2. All Persians wore the tiara, but always on one side; the Great King alone wore it straight
on his head.
3. Noted as the birthplace of Thucydides, a deme of Attica of the tribe of Leontis.
4. The appearance of the kite in Greece betokened the return of springtime; it was therefore worshipped as a symbol of that season.
5. To look at the kite, who no doubt was flying high in the sky.
6. The Athenians were addicted to carrying small coins in their mouths. This obolus was
for the purpose of buying flour to fill the bag he was carrying
7. In Phœnicia and Egypt the cuckoo makes its appearance about harvest-time.
8. This was an Egyptian proverb, meaning, *When the cuckoo sings we go harvesting.* Both the
Phœnicians and the Egyptians practised circumcision.

PISTHETÆRUS.   So powerful were the birds, that the kings of Grecian cities, Agamemnon, Menelaus, for instance, carried a bird on the tip of their sceptres, who had his share of all presents.[1]

EUELPIDES.   That I didn't know and was much astonished when I saw Priam come upon the stage in the tragedies with a bird, which kept watching Lysicrates[2] to see if he got any present.

PISTHETÆRUS.   But the strongest proof of all is, that Zeus, who now reigns, is represented as standing with an eagle on his head as a symbol of his royalty;[3] his daughter has an owl, and Phœbus, as his servant, has a hawk.

EUELPIDES.   By Demeter, 'tis well spoken. But what are all these birds doing in heaven?

PISTHETÆRUS.   When anyone sacrifices and, according to the rite, offers the entrails to the gods, these birds take their share before Zeus. Formerly men always swore by the birds and never by the gods; even now Lampon[4] swears by the goose, when he wants to lie....Thus 'tis clear that you were great and sacred, but now you are looked upon as slaves, as fools, as Helots; stones are thrown at you as at raving madmen, even in holy places. A crowd of bird-catchers sets snares, traps, limed-twigs and nets of all sorts for you; you are caught, you are sold in heaps and the buyers finger you over to be certain you are fat. Again, if they would but serve you up simply roasted; but they rasp cheese into a mixture of oil, vinegar and laserwort, to which another sweet and greasy sauce is added, and the whole is poured scalding hot over your back, for all the world as if you were diseased meat.

CHORUS.   Man, your words have made my heart bleed; I have groaned over the treachery of our fathers, who knew not how to transmit to us the high rank they held from their forefathers. But 'tis a benevolent Genius, a happy Fate, that sends you to us; you shall be our deliverer and I place the destiny of my little ones and my own in your hands with every confidence. But hasten to tell me what must be done; we should not be worthy to live, if we did not seek to regain our royalty by every possible means.

PISTHETÆRUS.   First I advise that the birds gather together in one city and that they build a wall of great bricks, like that at Babylon,

---

1.   The staff, called a sceptre, generally terminated in a piece of carved work, representing a flower, a fruit, and most often a bird.

2.   A general accused of treachery. The bird watches Lysicrates, because, according to Pisthetærus, he had a right to a share of the presents.

3.   It is thus that Phidias represents his Olympian Zeus.

4.   One of the diviners sent to Sybaris (in Magna Græcia, S. Italy) with the Athenian colonists, who rebuilt the town under the new name of Thurium.

round the plains of the air and the whole region of space that divides earth from heaven.

EPOPS. Oh, Cebriones! oh, Porphyrion![1] what a terribly strong place!

PISTHETÆRUS. This, this being well done and completed, you demand back the empire from Zeus; if he will not agree, if he refuses and does not at once confess himself beaten, you declare a sacred war against him and forbid the gods henceforward to pass through your country with lust, as hitherto, for the purpose of fondling their Alcmenas, their Alopès, or their Semelès![2] if they try to pass through, you infibulate them with rings so that they can work no longer. You send another messenger to mankind, who will proclaim to them that the birds are kings, that for the future they must first of all sacrifice to them, and only afterwards to the gods; that it is fitting to appoint to each deity the bird that has most in common with it. For instance, are they sacrificing to Aphroditè, let them at the same time offer barley to the coot; are they immolating a sheep to Posidon, let them consecrate wheat in honour of the duck;[3] is a steer being offered to Heracles, let honey-cakes be dedicated to the gull;[4] is a goat being slain for King Zeus, there is a King-Bird, the wren, to whom the sacrifice of a male gnat is due before Zeus himself even.

EUELPIDES. This notion of an immolated gnat delights me! And now let the great Zeus thunder!

EPOPS. But how will mankind recognize us as gods and not as jays? Us, who have wings and fly?

PISTHETÆRUS. You talk rubbish! Hermes is a god and has wings and flies, and so do many other gods. First of all, Victory flies with golden wings, Eros is undoubtedly winged too, and Iris is compared by Homer to a timorous dove. If men in their blindness do not recognize you as gods and continue to worship the dwellers in Olympus, then a cloud of sparrows greedy for corn must

---

1. As if he were saying, "Oh, gods!" Like Lampon, he swears by the birds, instead of swearing by the gods.
2. Alcmena, wife of Amphitryon, King of Thebes and mother of Heracles.—Semelé, the daughter of Cadmus and Hermioné and mother of Bacchus; both seduced by Zeus.—Alopé, daughter of Cercyon, a robber, who reigned at Eleusis and was conquered by Perseus. Alopé was honoured with Posidon's caresses; by him she had a son named Hippothous, at first brought up by shepherds but who afterwards was restored to the throne of his grandfather by Theseus.
3. Because water is the duck's domain, as it is that of Posidon.
4. Because the gull, like Heracles, is voracious.

descend upon their fields and eat up all their seeds; we shall see then if Demeter will mete them out any wheat.

EUELPIDES.   By Zeus, she'll take good care she does not, and you will see her inventing a thousand excuses.

PISTHETÆRUS.   The crows too will prove your divinity to them by pecking out the eyes of their flocks and of their draught-oxen; and then let Apollo cure them, since he is a physician and is paid for the purpose.[1]

EUELPIDES.   Oh! don't do that! Wait first until I have sold my two young bullocks.

PISTHETÆRUS.   If on the other hand they recognize that you are God, the principle of life, that you are Earth, Saturn, Posidon, they shall be loaded with benefits.

EPOPS.   Name me one of these then.

PISTHETÆRUS.   Firstly, the locusts shall not eat up their vine-blossoms; a legion of owls and kestrels will devour them. Moreover, the gnats and the gall-bugs shall no longer ravage the figs; a flock of thrushes shall swallow the whole host down to the very last.

EPOPS.   And how shall we give wealth to mankind? This is their strongest passion.

PISTHETÆRUS.   When they consult the omens, you will point them to the richest mines, you will reveal the paying ventures to the diviner, and not another shipwreck will happen or sailor perish.

EPOPS.   No more shall perish? How is that?

PISTHETÆRUS.   When the auguries are examined before starting on a voyage, some bird will not fail to say, "Don't start! there will be a storm," or else, "Go! you will make a most profitable venture."

EUELPIDES.   I shall buy a trading-vessel and go to sea, I will not stay with you.

PISTHETÆRUS.   You will discover treasures to them, which were buried in former times, for you know them. Do not all men say, "None knows where my treasure lies, unless perchance it be some bird."

EUELPIDES.   I shall sell my boat and buy a spade to unearth the vessels.

EPOPS.   And how are we to give them health, which belongs to the gods?

PISTHETÆRUS.   If they are happy, is not that the chief thing towards health? The miserable man is never well.

EPOPS.   Old Age also dwells in Olympus. How will they get at it? Must they die in early youth?

---

1. In sacrifices.

PISTHETÆRUS. Why, the birds, by Zeus, will add three hundred years to their life.

EPOPS. From whom will they take them?

PISTHETÆRUS. From whom? Why, from themselves. Don't you know the cawing crow lives five times as long as a man?

EUELPIDES. Ah! ah! these are far better kings for us than Zeus!

PISTHETÆRUS. Far better, are they not? And firstly, we shall not have to build them temples of hewn stone, closed with gates of gold; they will dwell amongst the bushes and in the thickets of green oak; the most venerated of birds will have no other temple than the foliage of the olive tree; we shall not go to Delphi or to Ammon to sacrifice;[1] but standing erect in the midst of arbutus and wild olives and holding forth our hands filled with wheat and barley, we shall pray them to admit us to a share of the blessings they enjoy and shall at once obtain them for a few grains of wheat.

CHORUS. Old man, whom I detested, you are now to me the dearest of all; never shall I, if I can help it, fail to follow your advice. Inspirited by your words, I threaten my rivals the gods, and I swear that if you march in alliance with me against the gods and are faithful to our just, loyal and sacred bond, we shall soon have shattered their sceptre. 'Tis our part to undertake the toil, 'tis yours to advise.

EPOPS. By Zeus! 'tis no longer the time to delay and loiter like Nicias;[2] let us act as promptly as possible.... In the first place, come, enter my nest built of brushwood and blades of straw, and tell me your names.

PISTHETÆRUS. That is soon done; my name is Pisthetærus.

EPOPS. And his?

PISTHETÆRUS. Euelpides, of the deme of Thria.

EPOPS. Good! and good luck to you.

PISTHETÆRUS. We accept the omen.

EPOPS. Come in here.

PISTHETÆRUS. Very well, 'tis you who lead us and must introduce us.

EPOPS. Come then.

PISTHETÆRUS. Oh! my god! do come back here. Hi! tell us how we are to follow you. You can fly, but we cannot.

---

1. A celebrated temple to Zeus in an oasis of Libya.
2. Nicias was commander, along with Demosthenes, and later on Alcibiades, of the Athenian forces before Syracuse, in the ill-fated Sicilian Expedition, 415–413 B.C. He was much blamed for dilatoriness and indecision.

EPOPS. Well, well.

PISTHETÆRUS. Remember Æsop's fables. It is told there, that the fox fared very ill, because he had made an alliance with the eagle.

EPOPS. Be at ease. You shall eat a certain root and wings will grow on your shoulders.

PISTHETÆRUS. Then let us enter. Xanthias and Manes,[1] pick up our baggage.

CHORUS. Hi! Epops! do you hear me?

EPOPS. What's the matter?

CHORUS. Take them off to dine well and call your mate, the melodious Procnè, whose songs are worthy of the Muses; she will delight our leisure moments.

PISTHETÆRUS. Oh! I conjure you, accede to their wish; for this delightful bird will leave her rushes at the sound of your voice; for the sake of the gods, let her come here, so that we may contemplate the nightingale.

EPOPS. Let it be as you desire. Come forth, Procnè, show yourself to these strangers.

PISTHETÆRUS. Oh! great Zeus! what a beautiful little bird! what a dainty form! what brilliant plumage![2]

EUELPIDES. Do you know how dearly I should like to split her legs for her?

PISTHETÆRUS. She is dazzling all over with gold, like a young girl.[3]

EUELPIDES. Oh! how I should like to kiss her!

PISTHETÆRUS. Why, wretched man, she has two little sharp points on her beak.

EUELPIDES. I would treat her like an egg, the shell of which we remove before eating it; I would take off her mask and then kiss her pretty face.

EPOPS. Let us go in.

PISTHETÆRUS. Lead the way, and may success attend us.

CHORUS. Lovable golden bird, whom I cherish above all others, you, whom I associate with all my songs, nightingale, you have come, you have come, to show yourself to me and to charm me with your notes. Come, you, who play spring melodies upon the harmonious flute,[4] lead off our anapæsts.[5]

---

1. Servants of Pisthetærus and Euelpides.
2. The actor representing Procné was dressed out as a courtesan, but wore the mask of a bird.
3. Young unmarried girls wore golden ornaments; the apparel of married women was much simpler.
4. The actor representing Procné was a flute-player.
5. The parabasis.

Weak mortals, chained to the earth, creatures of clay as frail as the foliage of the woods, you unfortunate race, whose life is but darkness, as unreal as a shadow, the illusion of a dream, hearken to us, who are immortal beings, ethereal, ever young and occupied with eternal thoughts, for we shall teach you about all celestial matters; you shall know thoroughly what is the nature of the birds, what the origin of the gods, of the rivers, of Erebus, and Chaos; thanks to us, even Prodicus[1] will envy you your knowledge.

At the beginning there was only Chaos, Night, dark Erebus, and deep Tartarus. Earth, the air and heaven had no existence. Firstly, black-winged Night laid a germless egg in the bosom of the infinite deeps of Erebus, and from this, after the revolution of long ages, sprang the graceful Eros with his glittering golden wings, swift as the whirlwinds of the tempest. He mated in deep Tartarus with dark Chaos, winged like himself, and thus hatched forth our race, which was the first to see the light. That of the Immortals did not exist until Eros had brought together all the ingredients of the world, and from their marriage Heaven, Ocean, Earth and the imperishable race of blessed gods sprang into being. Thus our origin is very much older than that of the dwellers in Olympus. We are the offspring of Eros; there are a thousand proofs to show it. We have wings and we lend assistance to lovers. How many handsome youths, who had sworn to remain insensible, have not been vanquished by our power and have yielded themselves to their lovers when almost at the end of their youth, being led away by the gift of a quail, a waterfowl, a goose, or a cock.[2]

And what important services do not the birds render to mortals! First of all, they mark the seasons for them, springtime, winter, and autumn. Does the screaming crane migrate to Libya,—it warns the husbandman to sow, the pilot to take his ease beside his tiller hung up in his dwelling,[3] and Orestes[4] to weave a tunic, so that the rigorous cold may not drive him any more to strip other folk. When the kite reappears, he tells of the return of spring and of the period when the fleece of the sheep must be clipped. Is the swallow in sight? All hasten to sell their warm tunic and to buy some light clothing. We are your Ammon, Delphi, Dodona, your

---

1. A sophist of the island of Ceos, a disciple of Protagoras, as celebrated for his knowledge as for his eloquence.
2. Lovers often gave each other presents of birds. The cock and the goose are mentioned in jest.
3. i.e. that it gave notice of the approach of winter, when the Ancients did not venture to sea.
4. A notorious robber.

Phœbus Apollo.[1] Before undertaking anything, whether a business transaction, a marriage, or the purchase of food, you consult the birds by reading the omens, and you give this name of omen[2] to all signs that tell of the future. With you a word is an omen, you call a sneeze an omen, a meeting an omen, an unknown sound an omen, a slave or an ass an omen.[3] Is it not clear that we are a prophetic Apollo to you? If you recognize us as gods, we shall be your divining Muses, through us you will know the winds and the seasons, summer, winter, and the temperate months. We shall not withdraw ourselves to the highest clouds like Zeus, but shall be among you and shall give to you and to your children and the children of your children, health and wealth, long life, peace, youth, laughter, songs and feasts; in short, you will all be so well off, that you will be weary and satiated with enjoyment.

Oh, rustic Muse of such varied note, tio, tio, tio, tiotinx, I sing with you in the groves and on the mountain tops, tio, tio, tio, tio, tiotinx.[4] I pour forth sacred strains from my golden throat in honour of the god Pan,[5] tio, tio, tio, tiotinx, from the top of the thickly leaved ash, and my voice mingles with the mighty choirs who extol Cybelè on the mountain tops,[6] totototototototinx. 'Tis to our concerts that Phrynichus comes to pillage like a bee the ambrosia of his songs, the sweetness of which so charms the ear, tio, tio, tio, tio, tinx.

If there be one of you spectators who wishes to spend the rest of his life quietly among the birds, let him come to us. All that is disgraceful and forbidden by law on earth is on the contrary honourable among us, the birds. For instance, among you 'tis a crime to beat your father, but with us 'tis an estimable deed; it's considered fine to run straight at your father and hit him, saying, "Come, lift your spur if you want to fight."[7] The runaway slave, whom you brand, is only a spotted francolin with us.[8] Are you Phrygian like Spintharus?[9] Among us you would be the Phrygian bird, the goldfinch, of the race of Philemon.[10] Are you a slave and a Carian like

---

1. Meaning, "*We are your oracles.*" Dodona was an oracle in Epirus.
2. The Greek word for *omen* is the same as that for *bird*.
3. A satire on the passion of the Greeks for seeing an omen in everything.
4. An imitation of the nightingale's song.
5. God of the groves and wilds.
6. The 'Mother of the Gods'; roaming the mountains, she held dances, always attended by Pan and his accompanying rout of Fauns and Satyrs.
7. An allusion to cock-fighting; the birds are armed with brazen spurs.
8. An allusion to the spots on this bird, which resemble the scars left by a branding iron.
9. He was of Asiatic origin, but wished to pass for an Athenian.
10 Or Philamnon, King of Thrace; the Phrygians and the Thracians had a common origin.

Execestides? Among us you can create yourself forefathers;[1] you can always find relations. Does the son of Pisias want to betray the gates of the city to the foe? Let him become a partridge, the fitting offspring of his father; among us there is no shame in escaping as cleverly as a partridge.

So the swans on the banks of the Hebrus, tio, tio, tio, tio, tiotinx, mingle their voices to serenade Apollo, tio, tio, tio, tio, tiotinx, flapping their wings the while, tio, tio, tio, tio, tiotinx; their notes reach beyond the clouds of heaven; all the dwellers in the forest stand still with astonishment and delight; a calm rests upon the waters, and the Graces and the choirs in Olympus catch up the strain, tio, tio, tio, tio, tiotinx.

There is nothing more useful nor more pleasant than to have wings. To begin with, just let us suppose a spectator to be dying with hunger and to be weary of the choruses of the tragic poets; if he were winged, he would fly off, go home to dine and come back with his stomach filled. Some Patroclides in urgent need would not have to soil his cloak, but could fly off, satisfy his requirements, and, having recovered his breath, return. If one of you, it matters not who, had adulterous relations and saw the husband of his mistress in the seats of the senators, he might stretch his wings, fly thither, and, having appeased his craving, resume his place. Is it not the most priceless gift of all, to be winged? Look at Diitrephes![2] His wings were only wickerwork ones, and yet he got himself chosen Phylarch and then Hipparch; from being nobody, he has risen to be famous; 'tis now the finest gilded cock of his tribe.[3]

PISTHETÆRUS. Halloa! What's this? By Zeus! I never saw anything so funny in all my life.[4]

EUELPIDES. What makes you laugh?

PISTHETÆRUS. 'Tis your bits of wings. D'you know what you look like? Like a goose painted by some dauber-fellow.

EUELPIDES. And you look like a close-shaven blackbird.

PISTHETÆRUS. 'Tis ourselves asked for this transformation, and, as Æschylus has it, "These are no borrowed feathers, but truly our own."[5]

EPOPS. Come now, what must be done?

---

1. The Greek word here is also the name of a little bird.
2. A basket-maker who had become rich. — The Phylarchs were the headmen of the tribes. The Hipparchs were the leaders of the cavalry.
3. He had become a senator.
4. Pisthetærus and Euelpides now both return with wings.
5. Meaning, 'tis we who wanted to have these wings.

PISTHETÆRUS. First give our city a great and famous name, then sacrifice to the gods.

EUELPIDES. I think so too.

EPOPS. Let's see. What shall our city be called?

PISTHETÆRUS. Will you have a high-sounding Laconian name? Shall
we call it Sparta?

EUELPIDES. What! call my town Sparta? Why, I would not use esparto
for my bed,¹ even though I had nothing but bands of rushes.

PISTHETÆRUS. Well then, what name can you suggest?

EUELPIDES. Some name borrowed from the clouds, from these lofty
regions in which we dwell—in short, some well-known name.

PISTHETÆRUS. Do you like Nephelococcygia?²

EPOPS. Oh! capital! truly 'tis a brilliant thought!

EUELPIDES. Is it in Nephelococcygia that all the wealth of Theovenes³
and most of Aeschines'⁴ is?

PISTHETÆRUS. No, 'tis rather the plain of Phlegra,⁵ where the gods
withered the pride of the sons of the Earth with their shafts.

EUELPIDES. Oh! what a splendid city! But what god shall be its patron? for whom shall we weave the peplus?⁶

PISTHETÆRUS. Why not choose Athenè Polias?⁷

EUELPIDES. Oh! what a well-ordered town 'twould be to have a female
deity armed from head to foot, while Clisthenes⁸ was spinning!

PISTHETÆRUS. Who then shall guard the Pelargicon?⁹

EPOPS. One of ourselves, a bird of Persian strain, who is everywhere
proclaimed to be the bravest of all, a true chick of Ares.¹⁰

EUELPIDES. Oh! noble chick! What a well-chosen god for a rocky home!

PISTHETÆRUS. Come! into the air with you to help the workers who
are building the wall; carry up rubble, strip yourself to mix the
mortar, take up the hod, tumble down the ladder, an [*sic*] you like,
post sentinels, keep the fire smouldering beneath the ashes, go
round the walls, bell in hand,¹¹ and go to sleep up there yourself;

---

1. The Greek word signified the city of Sparta, and also a kind of broom used for weaving
rough matting, which served for the beds of the very poor.

2. A fanciful name constructed from a cloud and a cuckoo; thus a city of clouds and
cuckoos.

3. He was a boaster nicknamed *smoke,* because he promised a great deal and never kept
his word.

4. A great Athenian orator, second only to Demosthenes.

5. Because the war of the Titans against the gods was only a fiction of the poets.

6. A sacred cloth, with which the statue of Athené in the Acropolis was draped.

7. Meaning, to be patron-goddess of the city. Athené had a temple of this name.

8. An Athenian effeminate, frequently ridiculed by Aristophanes.

9. This was the name of the wall surrounding the Acropolis.

10. i.e. the fighting-cock.

11. To waken the sentinels, who might else have fallen asleep.

then dispatch two heralds, one to the gods above, the other to mankind on earth and come back here.

EUELPIDES. As for yourself, remain here, and may the plague take you for a troublesome fellow!

PISTHETÆRUS. Go, friend, go where I send you, for without you my orders cannot be obeyed. For myself, I want to sacrifice to the new god, and I am going to summon the priest who must preside at the ceremony. Slaves! slaves! bring forward the basket and the lustral water.

CHORUS. I do as you do, and I wish as you wish, and I implore you to address powerful and solemn prayers to the gods, and in addition to immolate a sheep as a token of our gratitude. Let us sing the Pythian chant in honour of the god, and let Chæris accompany our voices.

PISTHETÆRUS [to the flute-player]. Enough! but, by Heracles! what is this? Great gods! I have seen many prodigious things, but I never saw a muzzled raven.[1]

EPOPS. Priest! 'tis high time! Sacrifice to the new gods.

PRIEST. I begin, but where is he with the basket? Pray to the Vesta of the birds, to the kite, who presides over the hearth, and to all the god and goddess-birds who dwell in Olympus.

CHORUS. Oh! Hawk, the sacred guardian of Sunium, oh, god of the storks!

PRIEST. Pray to the swan of Delos, to Latona the mother of the quails, and to Artemis, the goldfinch.

PISTHETÆRUS. 'Tis no longer Artemis Colænis, but Artemis the goldfinch.[2]

PRIEST. And to Bacchus, the finch and Cybelè, the ostrich and mother of the gods and mankind.

CHORUS. Oh! sovereign ostrich, Cybelè, the mother of Cleocritus,[3] grant health and safety to the Nephelococcygians as well as to the dwellers in Chios...

PISTHETÆRUS. The dwellers in Chios! Ah! I am delighted they should be thus mentioned on all occasions.[4]

CHORUS. ...to the heroes, the birds, to the sons of heroes, to the porphyrion, the pelican, the spoon-bill, the redbreast, the grouse,

---

1. An allusion to the leather strap which flute-players wore to constrict the cheeks and add to the power of the breath. The performer here no doubt wore a raven's mask.

2. Hellanicus, the Mitylenian historian, tells that this surname of Artemis is derived from Colænus, King of Athens before Cecrops and a descendant of Hermes. In obedience to an oracle he erected a temple to the goddess, invoking her as Artemis Colaenis (the Artemis of Colænus).

3. This Cleocritus was long-necked and strutted like an ostrich.

4. The Chians were the most faithful allies of Athens, and hence their name was always mentioned in prayers, decrees, etc.

the peacock, the horned-owl, the teal, the bittern, the heron, the stormy petrel, the fig-pecker, the titmouse...

PISTHETÆRUS.   Stop! stop! you drive me crazy with your endless list. Why, wretch, to what sacred feast are you inviting the vultures and the sea-eagles? Don't you see that a single kite could easily carry off the lot at once? Begone, you and your fillets and all; I shall know how to complete the sacrifice by myself.

PRIEST.   It is imperative that I sing another sacred chant for the rite of the lustral water, and that I invoke the immortals, or at least one of them, provided always that you have some suitable food to offer him; from what I see here, in the shape of gifts, there is naught whatever but horn and hair.

PISTHETÆRUS.   Let us address our sacrifices and our prayers to the winged gods.

A POET.   Oh, Muse! celebrate happy Nephelococcygia in your hymns.

PISTHETÆRUS.   What have we here? Where did you come from, tell me? Who are you?

POET.   I am he whose language is sweeter than honey, the zealous slave of the Muses, as Homer has it.

PISTHETÆRUS.   You a slave! and yet you wear your hair long?

POET.   No, but the fact is all we poets are the assiduous slaves of the Muses, according to Homer.

PISTHETÆRUS.   In truth your little cloak is quite holy too through zeal! But, poet, what ill wind drove you here?

POET.   I have composed verses in honour of your Nephelococcygia, a host of splendid dithyrambs and parthenians,[1] worthy of Simonides himself.

PISTHETÆRUS.   And when did you compose them? How long since?

POET.   Oh! 'tis long, aye, very long, that I have sung in honour of this city.

PISTHETÆRUS.   But I am only celebrating its foundation with this sacrifice;[2] I have only just named it, as is done with little babies.

POET.   "Just as the chargers fly with the speed of the wind, so does the voice of the Muses take its flight. Oh! thou noble founder of the town of Ætna,[3] thou, whose name recalls the holy sacrifices, make us such gift as thy generous heart shall suggest."

PISTHETÆRUS.   He will drive us silly if we do not get rid of him by some present. Here! you, who have a fur as well as your tunic, take

---

1. Verses sung by maidens.
2. This ceremony took place on the tenth day after birth.
3. Hiero, tyrant of Syracuse.

it off and give it to this clever poet. Come, take this fur; you look to me to be shivering with cold.

POET. My Muse will gladly accept this gift; but engrave these verses of Pindar's on your mind.

PISTHETÆRUS. Oh! what a pest! 'Tis impossible then to be rid of him!

POET. "Straton wanders among the Scythian nomads, but has no linen garment. He is sad at only wearing an animal's pelt and no tunic." Do you conceive my bent?

PISTHETÆRUS. I understand that you want me to offer you a tunic. Hi! you [to EUELPIDES], take off yours; we must help the poet.... Come, you, take it and begone.

POET. I am going, and these are the verses that I address to this city: "Phœbus of the golden throne, celebrate this shivery, freezing city; I have travelled through fruitful and snow-covered plains. Tralala! Tralala!"[1]

PISTHETÆRUS. What are you chanting us about frosts? Thanks to the tunic, you no longer fear them. Ah! by Zeus! I could not have believed this cursed fellow could so soon have learnt the way to our city. Come, priest, take the lustral water and circle the altar.

PRIEST. Let all keep silence!

A PROPHET. Let not the goat be sacrificed.[2]

PISTHETÆRUS. Who are you?

PROPHET. Who am I? A prophet.

PISTHETÆRUS. Get you gone.

PROPHET. Wretched man, insult not sacred things. For there is an oracle of Bacis, which exactly applies to Nephelococcygia.

PISTHETÆRUS. Why did you not reveal it to me before I founded my city?

PROPHET. The divine spirit was against it.

PISTHETÆRUS. Well, 'tis best to know the terms of the oracle.

PROPHET. "But when the wolves and the white crows shall dwell together between Corinth and Sicyon...."

PISTHETÆRUS. But how do the Corinthians concern me?

PROPHET. 'Tis the regions of the air that Bacis indicated in this manner. "They must first sacrifice a white-fleeced goat to Pandora, and give the prophet, who first reveals my words, a good cloak and new sandals."

PISTHETÆRUS. Are the sandals there?

PROPHET. Read. "And besides this a goblet of wine and a good share of the entrails of the victim."

---

1. A parody of poetic pathos.
2. Which the priest was preparing to sacrifice.

PISTHETÆRUS.   Of the entrails—is it so written?

PROPHET.   Read. "If you do as I command, divine youth, you shall be an eagle among the clouds; if not, you shall be neither turtle-dove, nor eagle, nor woodpecker."

PISTHETÆRUS.   Is all that there?

PROPHET.   Read.

PISTHETÆRUS.   This oracle in no sort of way resembles the one Apollo dictated to me: "If an impostor comes without invitation to annoy you during the sacrifice and to demand a share of the victim, apply a stout stick to his ribs."

PROPHET.   You are drivelling.

PISTHETÆRUS.   "And don't spare him, were he an eagle from out of the clouds, were it Lampon himself[1] or the great Diopithes."[2]

PROPHET.   Is all that there?

PISTHETÆRUS.   Here, read it yourself, and go and hang yourself.

CHORUS.   Oh! unfortunate wretch that I am.

PISTHETÆRUS.   Away with you, and take your prophecies elsewhere.

METON.[3]   I have come to you.

PISTHETÆRUS.   Yet another pest! What have you come to do? What's your plan? What's the purpose of your journey? Why these splendid buskins?

METON.   I want to survey the plains of the air for you and to parcel them into lots.

PISTHETÆRUS.   In the name of the gods, who are you?

METON.   Who am I? Meton, known throughout Greece and at Colonus.[4]

PISTHETÆRUS.   What are these things?

METON.   Tools for measuring the air. In truth, the spaces in the air have precisely the form of a furnace. With this bent ruler I draw a line from top to bottom; from one of its points I describe a circle with the compass. Do you understand?

PISTHETÆRUS.   Not the very least.

METON.   With the straight ruler I set to work to inscribe a square within this circle; in its centre will be the market-place, into which all the straight streets will lead, converging to this centre like a star, which, although only orbicular, sends forth its rays in a straight line from all sides.

PISTHETÆRUS.   Meton, you new Thales...[5]

---

1. Noted Athenian diviner.
2. No doubt another Athenian diviner.
3. A celebrated geometrician and astronomer.
4. A deme contiguous to Athens.
5. Thales was no less famous as a geometrician than he was as a sage.

METON. What d'you want with me?

PISTHETÆRUS. I want to give you a proof of my friendship. Use your legs.

METON. Why, what have I to fear?

PISTHETÆRUS. 'Tis the same here as in Sparta. Strangers are driven away, and blows rain down as thick as hail.

METON. Is there sedition in your city?

PISTHETÆRUS. No, certainly not.

METON. What's wrong then?

PISTHETÆRUS. We are agreed to sweep all quacks and impostors far from our borders.

METON. Then I'm off.

PISTHETÆRUS. I fear 'tis too late. The thunder growls already. [Beats him.]

METON. Oh, woe! oh, woe!

PISTHETÆRUS. I warned you. Now, be off, and do your surveying somewhere else.

[Meton takes to his heels.]

AN INSPECTOR. Where are the Proxeni?[1]

PISTHETÆRUS. Who is this Sardanapalus?[2]

INSPECTOR. I have been appointed by lot to come to Nephelococcygia as inspector.[3]

PISTHETÆRUS. An inspector! and who sends you here, you rascal?

INSPECTOR. A decree of Taleas.[4]

PISTHETÆRUS. Will you just pocket your salary, do nothing, and be off?

INSPECTOR. I' faith! that I will; I am urgently needed to be at Athens to attend the assembly; for I am charged with the interests of Pharnaces.[5]

PISTHETÆRUS. Take it then, and be off. See, here is your salary. [Beats him.]

INSPECTOR. What does this mean?

PISTHETÆRUS. 'Tis the assembly where you have to defend Pharnaces.

INSPECTOR. You shall testify that they dare to strike me, the inspector.

---

1. Officers of Athens, whose duty was to protect strangers who came on political or other business, and see to their interests generally.

2. He addresses the inspector thus because of the royal and magnificent manners he assumes.

3. Magistrates appointed to inspect the tributary towns.

4. A much-despised citizen, already mentioned. He ironically supposes him invested with the powers of an Archon, which ordinarily were entrusted only to men of good repute.

5. A Persian satrap.—An allusion to certain orators, who, bribed with Asiatic gold, had often defended the interests of the foe in the Public Assembly.

PISTHETÆRUS.   Are you not going to clear out with your urns? 'Tis not to be believed; they send us inspectors before we have so much as paid sacrifice to the gods.

A DEALER IN DECREES.   "If the Nephelococcygian does wrong to the Athenian..."

PISTHETÆRUS.   Now whatever are these cursed parchments?

DEALER IN DECREES.   I am a dealer in decrees, and I have come here to sell you the new laws.

PISTHETÆRUS.   Which?

DEALER IN DECREES.   "The Nephelococcygians shall adopt the same weights, measures and decrees as the Olophyxians."[1]

PISTHETÆRUS.   And you shall soon be imitating the Ototyxians. [*Beats him.*]

DEALER IN DECREES.   Hullo! what are you doing?

PISTHETÆRUS.   Now will you be off with your decrees? For I am going to let *you* see some severe ones.

INSPECTOR [*returning*].   I summon Pisthetærus for outrage for the month of Munychion.[2]

PISTHETÆRUS.   Ha! my friend! are you still there?

DEALER IN DECREES.   "Should anyone drive away the magistrates and not receive them, according to the decree duly posted..."

PISTHETÆRUS.   What! rascal! you are there too?

INSPECTOR.   Woe to you! I'll have you condemned to a fine of ten thousand drachmæ.

PISTHETÆRUS.   And I'll smash your urns.[3]

INSPECTOR.   Do you recall that evening when you stooled against the column where the decrees are posted?

PISTHETÆRUS.   Here! here! let him be seized. [*The* INSPECTOR *runs off.*] Well! don't you want to stop any longer?

PRIEST.   Let us get indoors as quick as possible; we will sacrifice the goat inside.[4]

CHORUS.   Henceforth it is to me that mortals must address their sacrifices and their prayers. Nothing escapes my sight nor my might. My glance embraces the universe, I preserve the fruit in the flower by destroying the thousand kinds of voracious insects the

---

1. A Macedonian people in the peninsula of Chalcidicè. This name is chosen because of its similarity to the Greek word *to groan*. It is from another verb meaning the same thing, that Pisthetærus coins the name of Ototyxians, i.e. groaners, because he is about to beat the dealer.—The mother-country had the right to impose any law it chose upon its colonies.
2. Corresponding to our month of April.
3. Which the inspector had brought with him for the purpose of inaugurating the assemblies of the people or some tribunal.
4. So that the sacrifices might no longer be interrupted.

soil produces, which attack the trees and feed on the germ when it has scarcely formed in the calyx; I destroy those who ravage the balmy terrace gardens like a deadly plague; all these gnawing crawling creatures perish beneath the lash of my wing. I hear it proclaimed everywhere: "A talent for him who shall kill Diagoras of Melos,[1] and a talent for him who destroys one of the dead tyrants."[2] We likewise wish to make our proclamation: "A talent to him among you who shall kill Philocrates, the Struthian;[3] four, if he brings him to us alive. For this Philocrates skewers the finches together and sells them at the rate of an obolus for seven. He tortures the thrushes by blowing them out, so that they may look bigger, sticks their own feathers into the nostrils of black-birds, and collects pigeons, which he shuts up and forces them, fastened in a net, to decoy others." That is what we wish to proclaim. And if anyone is keeping birds shut up in his yard, let him hasten to let them loose; those who disobey shall be seized by the birds and we shall put them in chains, so that in their turn they may decoy other men.

Happy indeed is the race of winged birds who need no cloak in winter! Neither do I fear the relentless rays of the fiery dog-days; when the divine grasshopper, intoxicated with the sunlight, when noon is burning the ground, is breaking out into shrill melody, my home is beneath the foliage in the flowery meadows. I winter in deep caverns, where I frolic with the mountain nymphs, while in spring I despoil the gardens of the Graces and gather the white, virgin berry on the myrtle bushes. I want now to speak to the judges about the prize they are going to award; if they are favourable to us, we will load them with benefits far greater than those Paris[4] received. Firstly, the owls of Laurium,[5] which every judge desires above all things, shall never be wanting to you; you shall see them homing with you, building their nests

1. A disciple of Democrites; he passed over from superstition to atheism.
2. By this jest Aristophanes means to imply that tyranny is dead, and that no one aspires to despotic power, though this silly accusation was constantly being raised by the demagogues and always favourably received by the populace.
3. A poulterer.—Struthian, used in jest to designate him, as if from the name of his 'deme,' is derived from the Greek for sparrow. The birds' foe is thus grotesquely furnished with an ornithological surname.
4. From Aphroditè (Venus), to whom he had awarded the apple, prize of beauty, in the contest of the "goddesses three."
5. Laurium was an Athenian deme containing valuable silver mines, the revenues of which were largely employed in the maintenance of the fleet and payment of the crews. The "owls of Laurium," means pieces of money; Athenian coinage was stamped with a representation of an owl, the bird of Athenè.

in your money-bags and laying coins. Besides, you shall be housed like the gods, for we shall erect gables[1] over your dwellings; if you hold some public post and want to do a little pilfering, we will give you the sharp claws of a hawk. Are you dining in town, we will provide you with crops.[2] But, if your award is against us, don't fail to have metal covers fashioned for yourselves, like those they place over statues;[3] else, look out! for the day you wear a white tunic all the birds will soil it with their droppings.

PISTHETÆRUS. Birds! the sacrifice is propitious. But I see no messenger coming from the wall to tell us what is happening. Ah! here comes one running himself out of breath as though he were running the Olympic stadium.

MESSENGER. Where, where is he? Where, where, where is he? Where, where, where is he? Where is Pisthetærus, our leader?

PISTHETÆRUS. Here am I.

MESSENGER. The wall is finished.

PISTHETÆRUS. That's good news.

MESSENGER. 'Tis a most beautiful, a most magnificent work of art. The wall is so broad, that Proxenides, the Braggartian, and Theogenes could pass each other in their chariots, even if they were drawn by steeds as big as the Trojan horse.

PISTHETÆRUS. 'Tis wonderful!

MESSENGER. Its length is one hundred stadia; I measured it myself.

PISTHETÆRUS. A decent length, by Posidon! And who built such a wall?

MESSENGER. Birds—birds only; they had neither Egyptian brickmaker, nor stonemason, nor carpenter; the birds did it all themselves; I could hardly believe my eyes. Thirty thousand cranes came from Libya with a supply of stones,[4] intended for the foundations. The water-rails chiselled them with their beaks. Ten thousand storks were busy making bricks; plovers and other water fowl carried water into the air.

PISTHETÆRUS. And who carried the mortar?

MESSENGER. Herons, in hods.

---

1. A pun, impossible to keep in English, on the two meanings of this word in Greek, which signifies both an eagle and the gable of a house or pediment of a temple.
2. That is, birds' crops, into which they could stow away plenty of good things.
3. The Ancients appear to have placed metal discs over statues standing in the open air, to save them from injury from the weather, etc.
4. So as not to be carried away by the wind when crossing the sea, cranes are popularly supposed to ballast themselves with stones, which they carry in their beaks.

PISTHETÆRUS.   But how could they put the mortar into hods?

MESSENGER.   Oh! 'twas a truly clever invention; the geese used their feet like spades; they buried them in the pile of mortar and then emptied them into the hods.

PISTHETÆRUS.   Ah! to what use cannot feet be put?[1]

MESSENGER.   You should have seen how eagerly the ducks carried bricks. To complete the tale, the swallows came flying to the work, their beaks full of mortar and their trowel on their back, just the way little children are carried.

PISTHETÆRUS.   Who would want paid servants after this? But, tell me, who did the woodwork?

MESSENGER.   Birds again, and clever carpenters too, the pelicans, for they squared up the gates with their beaks in such a fashion that one would have thought they were using axes; the noise was just like a dockyard. Now the whole wall is tight everywhere, securely bolted and well guarded; it is patrolled, bell in hand; the sentinels stand everywhere and beacons burn on the towers. But I must run off to clean myself; the rest is your business.

CHORUS.   Well! what do you say to it? Are you not astonished at the wall being completed so quickly?

PISTHETÆRUS.   By the gods, yes, and with good reason. 'Tis really not to be believed. But here comes another messenger from the wall to bring us some further news! What a fighting look he has!

SECOND MESSENGER.   Oh! oh! oh! oh! oh! oh!

PISTHETÆRUS.   What's the matter?

SECOND MESSENGER.   A horrible outrage has occurred; a god sent by Zeus has passed through our gates and has penetrated the realms of the air without the knowledge of the jays, who are on guard in the daytime.

PISTHETÆRUS.   'Tis an unworthy and criminal deed. What god was it?

SECOND MESSENGER.   We don't know that. All we know is, that he has got wings.

PISTHETÆRUS.   Why were not guards sent against him at once?

SECOND MESSENGER.   We have dispatched thirty thousand hawks of the legion of mounted archers.[2] All the hook-clawed birds are moving against him, the kestrel, the buzzard, the vulture, the great-horned owl; they cleave the air, so that it resounds with the flapping of their wings; they are looking everywhere for the god, who cannot be far away; indeed, if I mistake not, he is coming from yonder side.

---

1. Pisthetærus modifies the Greek proverbial saying, "To what use cannot hands be put?"
2. A corps of Athenian cavalry was so named.

PISTHETÆRUS. All arm themselves with slings and bows! This way, all
   our soldiers; shoot and strike! Some one give me a sling!

CHORUS. War, a terrible war is breaking out between us and the
   gods! Come, let each one guard Air, the son of Erebus,[1] in
   which the clouds float. Take care no immortal enters it without your knowledge. Scan all sides with your glance. Hark!
   methinks I can hear the rustle of the swift wings of a god
   from heaven.

PISTHETÆRUS. Hi! you woman! where are you flying to? Halt, don't
   stir! keep motionless! not a beat of your wing!—Who are you and
   from what country? You must say whence you come.[2]

IRIS. I come from the abode of the Olympian gods.

PISTHETÆRUS. What's your name, ship or cap?[3]

IRIS. I am swift Iris.

PISTHETÆRUS. Paralus or Salaminia?[4]

IRIS. What do you mean?

PISTHETÆRUS. Let a buzzard rush at her and seize her.[5]

IRIS. Seize me! But what do all these insults betoken?

PISTHETÆRUS. Woe to you!

IRIS. 'Tis incomprehensible.

PISTHETÆRUS. By which gate did you pass through the wall, wretched
   woman?

IRIS. By which gate? Why, great gods, I don't know.

PISTHETÆRUS. You hear how she holds us in derision. Did you present
   yourself to the officers in command of the jays? You don't answer.
   Have you a permit, bearing the seal of the storks?

IRIS. Am I awake?

PISTHETÆRUS. Did you get one?

IRIS. Are you mad?

PISTHETÆRUS. No head-bird gave you a safe-conduct?

IRIS. A safe-conduct to me, you poor fool!

PISTHETÆRUS. Ah! and so you slipped into this city on the sly and
   into these realms of air-land that don't belong to you.

IRIS. And what other roads can the gods travel?

---

1. Chaos, Night, Tartarus, and Erebus alone existed in the beginning; Eros was born from
Night and Erebus, and he wedded Chaos and begot Earth, Air, and Heaven; so runs the
fable.

2. Iris appears from the top of the stage and arrests her flight in mid-career.

3. Ship, because of her wings, which resemble oars; cap, because she no doubt wore the
head-dress [as a messenger of the gods] with which Hermes is generally depicted.

4. The names of the two sacred galleys which carried Athenian officials on State business.

5. A buzzard is named in order to raise a laugh, the Greek name also meaning, etymologically,
provided with three testicles, vigorous in love.

PISTHETÆRUS. By Zeus! I know nothing about that, not I. But they won't pass this way. And you still dare to complain! Why, if you were treated according to your deserts, no Iris would ever have more justly suffered death.

IRIS. I am immortal.

PISTHETÆRUS. You would have died nevertheless.—Oh! 'twould be truly intolerable! What! should the universe obey us and the gods alone continue their insolence and not understand that they must submit to the law of the strongest in their due turn? But tell me, where are you flying to?

IRIS. I? The messenger of Zeus to mankind, I am going to tell them to sacrifice sheep and oxen on the altars and to fill their streets with the rich smoke of burning fat.

PISTHETÆRUS. Of which gods are you speaking?

IRIS. Of which? Why, of ourselves, the gods of heaven.

PISTHETÆRUS. You, gods?

IRIS. Are there others then?

PISTHETÆRUS. Men now adore the birds as gods, and 'tis to them, by Zeus, that they must offer sacrifices, and not to Zeus at all!

IRIS. Oh! fool! fool! Rouse not the wrath of the gods, for 'tis terrible indeed. Armed with the brand of Zeus, Justice would annihilate your race; the lightning would strike you as it did Licymnius and consume both your body and the porticos of your palace.[1]

PISTHETÆRUS. Here! that's enough tall talk. Just you listen and keep quiet! Do you take me for a Lydian or a Phrygian[2] and think to frighten me with your big words? Know, that if Zeus worries me again, I shall go at the head of my eagles, who are armed with lightning, and reduce his dwelling and that of Amphion to cinders.[3] I shall send more than six hundred porphyrions clothed in leopards' skins[4] up to heaven against him; and formerly a single Porphyrion gave him enough to do. As for you, his messenger, if you annoy me, I shall begin by stretching your legs asunder and so conduct myself, Iris though you be, that despite my age, you will be astonished. I will show you something that will make you three times over.

IRIS. May you perish, you wretch, you and your infamous words!

PISTHETÆRUS. Won't you be off quickly? Come, stretch your wings or look out for squalls!

---

1. Iris' reply is a parody of the tragic style.—'Lycimnius' is the title of a tragedy by Euripides, which is about a ship that is struck by lightning.

2. i.e. for a poltroon, like the slaves, most of whom came to Athens from these countries.

3. A parody of a passage in the lost tragedy of 'Niobe' of Æschylus.

4. Because this bird has a spotted plumage.—Porphyrion is also the name of one of the Titans who tried to storm heaven.

IRIS. If my father does not punish you for your insults...

PISTHETÆRUS. Ha!... but just you be off elsewhere to roast younger folk than us with your lightning.

CHORUS. We forbid the gods, the sons of Zeus, to pass through our city and the mortals to send them the smoke of their sacrifices by this road.

PISTHETÆRUS. 'Tis odd that the messenger we sent to the mortals has never returned.

HERALD. Oh! blessed Pisthetærus, very wise, very illustrious, very gracious, thrice happy, very... Come, prompt me, somebody, do.

PISTHETÆRUS. Get to your story!

HERALD. All peoples are filled with admiration for your wisdom, and they award you this golden crown.

PISTHETÆRUS. I accept it. But tell me, why do the people admire me?

HERALD. Oh you, who have founded so illustrious a city in the air, you know not in what esteem men hold you and how many there are who burn with desire to dwell in it. Before your city was built, all men had a mania for Sparta; long hair and fasting were held in honour, men went dirty like Socrates and carried staves. Now all is changed. Firstly, as soon as 'tis dawn, they all spring out of bed together to go and seek their food, the same as you do; then they fly off towards the notices and finally devour the decrees. The bird-madness is so clear, that many actually bear the names of birds. There is a halting victualler, who styles himself the par-tridge; Menippus calls himself the swallow; Opuntius the one-eyed crow; Philocles the lark; Theogenes the fox-goose; Lycurgus the ibis; Chærephon the bat; Syracosius the magpie; Midias the quail;[1] indeed he looks like a quail that has been hit heavily over the head. Out of love for the birds they repeat all the songs which concern the swallow, the teal, the goose or the pigeon; in each verse you see wings, or at all events a few feathers. This is what is happening down there. Finally, there are more than ten thousand folk who are coming here from earth to ask you for feathers and hooked claws; so, mind you supply yourself with wings for the immigrants.

PISTHETÆRUS. Ah! by Zeus, 'tis not the time for idling. Go as quick as possible and fill every hamper, every basket you can find with

---

1. All these surnames bore some relation to the character or the build of the individual to whom the poet applies them.—Chærephon, Socrates' disciple, was of white and ash-en hue.—Opuntius was one-eyed.—Syracosius was a braggart.—Midias had a passion for quail-fights, and, besides, resembled that bird physically.

wings. Manes[1] will bring them to me outside the walls, where I will welcome those who present themselves.

CHORUS. This town will soon be inhabited by a crowd of men.

PISTHETÆRUS. If fortune favours us.

CHORUS. Folk are more and more delighted with it.

PISTHETÆRUS. Come, hurry up and bring them along.

CHORUS. Will not man find here everything that can please him— wisdom, love, the divine Graces, the sweet face of gentle peace?

PISTHETÆRUS. Oh! you lazy servant! won't you hurry yourself?

CHORUS. Let a basket of wings be brought speedily. Come, beat him as I do, and put some life into him; he is as lazy as an ass.

PISTHETÆRUS. Aye, Manes is a great craven.

CHORUS. Begin by putting this heap of wings in order; divide them in three parts according to the birds from whom they came; the singing, the prophetic[2] and the aquatic birds; then you must take care to distribute them to the men according to their character.

PISTHETÆRUS [to MANES]. Oh! by the kestrels! I can keep my hands off you no longer; you are too slow and lazy altogether.

A PARRICIDE.[3] Oh! might I but become an eagle, who soars in the skies! Oh! might I fly above the azure waves of the barren sea![4]

PISTHETÆRUS. Ha! 'twould seem the news was true; I hear someone coming who talks of wings.

PARRICIDE. Nothing is more charming than to fly; I burn with desire to live under the same laws as the birds; I am bird-mad and fly towards you, for I want to live with you and to obey your laws.

PISTHETÆRUS. Which laws? The birds have many laws.

PARRICIDE. All of them; but the one that pleases me most is, that among the birds it is considered a fine thing to peck and strangle one's father.

PISTHETÆRUS. Aye, by Zeus! according to us, he who dares to strike his father, while still a chick, is a brave fellow.

PARRICIDE. And therefore I want to dwell here, for I want to strangle my father and inherit his wealth.

PISTHETÆRUS. But we have also an ancient law written in the code of the storks, which runs thus, "When the stork father has reared his young and has taught them to fly, the young must in their turn support the father."

---

1. Pisthetærus' servant, already mentioned.
2. From the inspection of which auguries were taken, e.g. the eagles, the vultures, the crows.
3. Or rather, a young man who contemplated parricide.
4. A parody of verses in Sophocles 'Œnomaus.'

PARRICIDE. 'Tis hardly worth while coming all this distance to be compelled to keep my father!

PISTHETÆRUS. No, no, young friend, since you have come to us with such willingness, I am going to give you these black wings, as though you were an orphan bird; furthermore, some good advice, that I received myself in infancy. Don't strike your father, but take these wings in one hand and these spurs in the other; imagine you have a cock's crest on your head and go and mount guard and fight; live on your pay and respect your father's life. You're a gallant fellow! Very well, then! Fly to Thrace and fight.[1]

PARRICIDE. By Bacchus! 'Tis well spoken; I will follow your counsel.

PISTHETÆRUS. 'Tis acting wisely, by Zeus.

CINESIAS.[2] "On my light pinions I soar off to Olympus; in its capricious flight my Muse flutters along the thousand paths of poetry in turn..."

PISTHETÆRUS. This is a fellow will need a whole shipload of wings.

CINESIAS. "...and being fearless and vigorous, it is seeking fresh outlet."

PISTHETÆRUS. Welcome, Cinesias, you lime-wood man![3] Why have you come here a-twisting your game leg in circles?

CINESIAS. "I want to become a bird, a tuneful nightingale."

PISTHETÆRUS. Enough of that sort of ditty. Tell me what you want.

CINESIAS. Give me wings and I will fly into the topmost airs to gather fresh songs in the clouds, in the midst of the vapours and the fleecy snow.

PISTHETÆRUS. Gather songs in the clouds?

CINESIAS. 'Tis on them the whole of our latter-day art depends. The most brilliant dithyrambs are those that flap their wings in void space and are clothed in mist and dense obscurity. To appreciate this, just listen.

PISTHETÆRUS. Oh! no, no, no!

CINESIAS. By Hermes! but indeed you shall. "I shall travel through thine ethereal empire like a winged bird, who cleaveth space with his long neck..."

PISTHETÆRUS. Stop! easy all, I say![4]

CINESIAS. "...as I soar over the seas, carried by the breath of the winds..."

---

1. The Athenians were then besieging Amphipolis in the Thracian Chalcidicè.
2. There was a real Cinesias—a dythyrambic poet, born at Thebes.
3. One scholarly interpretation has it that Cinesias, who was tall and slight of build, wore a kind of corset of lime-wood to support his waist.
4. The Greek word used here was the word of command employed to stop the rowers.

PISTHETÆRUS.   By Zeus! but I'll cut your breath short.

CINESIAS.   "...now rushing along the tracks of Notus, now nearing Boreas across the infinite wastes of the ether." [PISTHETÆRUS *beats him.*] Ah! old man, that's a pretty and clever idea truly!

PISTHETÆRUS.   What! are you not delighted to be cleaving the air?[1]

CINESIAS.   To treat a dithyrambic poet, for whom the tribes dispute with each other, in this style![2]

PISTHETÆRUS.   Will you stay with us and form a chorus of winged birds as slender as Leotrophides[3] for the Cecropid tribe?

CINESIAS.   You are making game of me, 'tis clear; but know that I shall never leave you in peace if I do not have wings wherewith to traverse the air.

AN INFORMER.   What are these birds with downy feathers, who look so pitiable to me? Tell me, oh swallow with the long dappled wings.[4]

PISTHETÆRUS.   Oh! but 'tis a perfect invasion that threatens us. Here comes another of them, humming along.

INFORMER.   Swallow with the long dappled wings, once more I summon you.

PISTHETÆRUS.   It's his cloak I believe he's addressing; 'faith, it stands in great need of the swallows' return.[5]

INFORMER.   Where is he who gives out wings to all comers?

PISTHETÆRUS.   'Tis I, but you must tell me for what purpose you want them.

INFORMER.   Ask no questions. I want wings, and wings I must have.

PISTHETÆRUS.   Do you want to fly straight to Pellenè?[6]

INFORMER.   I? Why, I am an accuser of the islands,[7] an informer...

PISTHETÆRUS.   A fine trade, truly!

INFORMER.   ...a hatcher of lawsuits. Hence I have great need of wings to prowl round the cities and drag them before justice.

PISTHETÆRUS.   Would you do this better if you had wings?

---

1. Cinesias makes a bound each time that Pisthetærus strikes him.

2. The tribes of Athens, or rather the rich citizens belonging to them, were wont on feast-days to give representations of dithyrambic choruses as well as of tragedies and comedies.

3. Another dithyrambic poet, a man of extreme leanness.

4. The informer is dissatisfied at only seeing birds of sombre plumage and poor appearance. He would have preferred to denounce the rich.

5. The informer was clothed with a ragged cloak, the tatters of which hung down like wings, in fact, a cloak that could not protect him from the cold and must have made him long for the swallows' return, i.e. the spring.

6. A town in Achaia, where woollen cloaks were made

7. His trade was to accuse the rich citizens of the subject islands, and drag them before the Athenian courts.

INFORMER.   No, but I should no longer fear the pirates; I should return with the cranes, loaded with a supply of lawsuits by way of ballast.

PISTHETÆRUS.   So it seems, despite all your youthful vigour, you make it your trade to denounce strangers?

INFORMER.   Well, and why not? I don't know how to dig.

PISTHETÆRUS.   But, by Zeus! there are honest ways of gaining a living at your age without all this infamous trickery.

INFORMER.   My friend, I am asking you for wings, not for words.

PISTHETÆRUS.   'Tis just my words that give you wings.

INFORMER.   And how can you give a man wings with your words?

PISTHETÆRUS.   'Tis thus that all first start.

INFORMER.   All?

PISTHETÆRUS.   Have you not often heard the father say to young men in the barbers' shops, "It's astonishing how Diitrephes' advice has made my son fly to horse-riding."—"Mine," says another, "has flown towards tragic poetry on the wings of his imagination."

INFORMER.   So that words give wings?

PISTHETÆRUS.   Undoubtedly; words give wings to the mind and make a man soar to heaven. Thus I hope that my wise words will give you wings to fly to some less degrading trade.

INFORMER.   But I do not want to.

PISTHETÆRUS.   What do you reckon on doing then?

INFORMER.   I won't belie my breeding; from generation to generation we have lived by informing. Quick, therefore, give me quickly some light, swift hawk or kestrel wings, so that I may summon the islanders, sustain the accusation here, and haste back there again on flying pinions.

PISTHETÆRUS.   I see. In this way the stranger will be condemned even before he appears.

INFORMER.   That's just it.

PISTHETÆRUS.   And while he is on his way here by sea, you will be flying to the islands to despoil him of his property.

INFORMER.   You've hit it, precisely; I must whirl hither and thither like a perfect humming-top.

PISTHETÆRUS.   I catch the idea. Wait, i' faith, I've got some fine Corcyræan wings.[1] How do you like them?

INFORMER.   Oh! woe is me! Why, 'tis a whip!

PISTHETÆRUS.   No, no; these are the wings, I tell you, that set the top a-spinning.

INFORMER.   Oh! oh! oh!

---

1.   That is, whips—Corcyra being famous for these articles.

PISTHETÆRUS. Take your flight, clear off, you miserable cur, or you
    will soon see what comes of quibbling and lying. Come, let us
    gather up our wings and withdraw.

CHORUS. In my ethereal flights I have seen many things new and
    strange and wondrous beyond belief. There is a tree called
    Cleonymus belonging to an unknown species; it has no heart, is
    good for nothing and is as tall as it is cowardly. In springtime it
    shoots forth calumnies instead of buds and in autumn it strews the
    ground with bucklers in place of leaves.[1]

    Far away in the regions of darkness, where no ray of light ever
    enters, there is a country, where men sit at the table of the heroes
    and dwell with them always—save always in the evening. Should
    any mortal meet the hero Orestes at night, he would soon be
    stripped and covered with blows from head to foot.[2]

PROMETHEUS. Ah! by the gods! if only Zeus does not espy me!
    Where is Pisthetærus?

PISTHETÆRUS. Ha! what is this? A masked man!

PROMETHEUS. Can you see any god behind me?

PISTHETÆRUS. No, none. But who are you, pray?

PROMETHEUS. What's the time, please?

PISTHETÆRUS. The time? Why, it's past noon. Who are you?

PROMETHEUS. Is it the fall of day? Is it no later than that?[3]

PISTHETÆRUS. Oh! 'pon my word! but you grow tiresome.

PROMETHEUS. What is Zeus doing? Is he dispersing the clouds or
    gathering them?[4]

PISTHETÆRUS. Take care, lest I lose all patience.

PROMETHEUS. Come, I will raise my mask.

PISTHETÆRUS. Ah! my dear Prometheus!

PROMETHEUS. Stop! stop! speak lower!

PISTHETÆRUS. Why, what's the matter, Prometheus?

PROMETHEUS. H'sh, h'sh! Don't call me by my name; you will be my
    ruin, if Zeus should see me here. But, if you want me to tell you
    how things are going in heaven, take this umbrella and shield me,
    so that the gods don't see me.

PISTHETÆRUS. I can recognize Prometheus in this cunning trick.
    Come, quick then, and fear nothing; speak on.

PROMETHEUS. Then listen.

---

1. Cleonymus is a standing butt of Aristophanes' wit, both as an informer and a notorious
    poltroon.
2. In allusion to the cave of the bandit Orestes; the poet terms him a hero only because of
    his heroic name Orestes.
3. Prometheus wants night to come and so reduce the risk of being seen from Olympus.
4. The clouds would prevent Zeus seeing what was happening below him.

PISTHETÆRUS.   I am listening, proceed!

PROMETHEUS.   It's all over with Zeus.

PISTHETÆRUS.   Ah! and since when, pray?

PROMETHEUS.   Since you founded this city in the air. There is not a man who now sacrifices to the gods; the smoke of the victims no longer reaches us. Not the smallest offering comes! We fast as though it were the festival of Demeter.[1] The barbarian gods, who are dying of hunger, are bawling like Illyrians[2] and threaten to make an armed descent upon Zeus, if he does not open markets where joints of the victims are sold.

PISTHETÆRUS.   What! there are other gods besides you, barbarian gods who dwell above Olympus?

PROMETHEUS.   If there were no barbarian gods, who would be the patron of Execestides?[3]

PISTHETÆRUS.   And what is the name of these gods?

PROMETHEUS.   Their name? Why, the Triballi.[4]

PISTHETÆRUS.   Ah, indeed! 'tis from that no doubt that we derive the word 'tribulation.'

PROMETHEUS.   Most likely. But one thing I can tell you for certain, namely, that Zeus and the celestial Triballi are going to send deputies here to sue for peace. Now don't you treat, unless Zeus restores the sceptre to the birds and gives you Basileia[5] in marriage.

PISTHETÆRUS.   Who is this Basileia?

PROMETHEUS.   A very fine young damsel, who makes the lightning for Zeus; all things come from her, wisdom, good laws, virtue, the fleet, calumnies, the public paymaster and the triobolus.

PISTHETÆRUS.   Ah! then she is a sort of general manageress to the god.

PROMETHEUS.   Yes, precisely. If he gives you her for your wife, yours will be the almighty power. That is what I have come to tell you; for you know my constant and habitual goodwill towards men.

PISTHETÆRUS.   Oh, yes! 'tis thanks to you that we roast our meat.[6]

PROMETHEUS.   I hate the gods, as you know.

PISTHETÆRUS.   Aye, by Zeus, you have always detested them.

---

1. The third day of the festival of Demeter was a fast.

2. A semi-savage people, addicted to violence and brigandage.

3. Who, being reputed a stranger despite his pretension to the title of a citizen, could only have a strange god for his patron or tutelary deity.

4. The Triballi were a Thracian people; it was a term commonly used in Athens to describe coarse men, obscene debauchees and greedy parasites.

5. i.e. the *supremacy* of Greece, the real object of the war.

6. Prometheus had stolen the fire from the gods to gratify mankind.

PROMETHEUS.   Towards them I am a veritable Timon;[1] but I must return in all haste, so give me the umbrella; if Zeus should see me from up there, he would think I was escorting one of the Canephori.[2]

PISTHETÆRUS.   Wait, take this stool as well.

CHORUS.   Near by the land of the Sciapodes[3] there is a marsh, from the borders whereof the odious Socrates evokes the souls of men. Pisander[4] came one day to see his soul, which he had left there when still alive. He offered a little victim, a camel, slit his throat and, following the example of Ulysses, stepped one pace backwards.[5] Then that bat of a Chærephon[6] came up from hell to drink the camel's blood.

POSIDON.[7]   This is the city of Nephelococcygia, Cloud-cuckoo-town, whither we come as ambassadors. [To TRIBALLUS.] Hi! what are you up to? you are throwing your cloak over the left shoulder. Come, fling it quick over the right! And why, pray, does it draggle in this fashion? Have you ulcers to hide like Læspodias?[8] Oh! democracy![9] whither, oh! whither are you leading us? Is it possible that the gods have chosen such an envoy?

TRIBALLUS.   Leave me alone.

POSIDON.   Ugh! the cursed savage! you are by far the most barbarous of all the gods.—Tell me, Heracles, what are we going to do?

HERACLES.   I have already told you that I want to strangle the fellow who has dared to block us in.

POSIDON.   But, my friend, we are envoys of peace.

HERACLES.   All the more reason why I wish to strangle him.

---

1. A celebrated misanthrope, contemporary to Aristophanes.

2. The Canephori were young maidens, chosen from the first families of the city, who carried baskets wreathed with myrtle at the feast of Athenè, while at those of Bacchus and Demeter they appeared with gilded baskets.—The daughters of 'Metics,' or resident aliens, walked behind them, carrying an umbrella and a stool.

3. According to Ctesias, the Sciapodes were a people who dwelt on the borders of the Atlantic. Their feet were larger than the rest of their bodies, and to shield themselves from the sun's rays they held up one of their feet as an umbrella.—By giving the Socratic philosophers the name of Sciapodes here Aristophanes wishes to convey that they are walking in the dark and busying themselves with the greatest nonsense.

4. This Pisander was a notorious coward; for this reason the poet jestingly supposes that he had lost his soul, the seat of courage.

5. In the evocation of the dead, Book XI of the Odyssey.

6. Chærephon was given this same title by the Herald earlier in this comedy.—Aristophanes supposes him to have come from hell because he is lean and pallid.

7. Posidon appears on the stage accompanied by Heracles and a Triballian god.

8. An Athenian general.—Neptune is trying to give Triballus some notions of elegance and good behaviour.

9. Aristophanes supposes that democracy is in the ascendant in Olympus as it is in Athens.

PISTHETÆRUS.　Hand me the cheese-grater; bring me the silphium for sauce; pass me the cheese and watch the coals.[1]

HERACLES.　Mortal! we who greet you are three gods.

PISTHETÆRUS.　Wait a bit till I have prepared my silphium pickle.

HERACLES.　What are these meats?[2]

PISTHETÆRUS.　These are birds that have been punished with death for attacking the people's friends.

HERACLES.　And you are seasoning them before answering us?

PISTHETÆRUS.　Ah! Heracles! welcome, welcome! What's the matter?[3]

HERACLES.　The gods have sent us here as ambassadors to treat for peace.

A SERVANT.　There's no more oil in the flask.

PISTHETÆRUS.　And yet the birds must be thoroughly basted with it.[4]

HERACLES.　We have no interest to serve in fighting you; as for you, be friends and we promise that you shall always have rain-water in your pools and the warmest of warm weather. So far as these points go we are armed with plenary authority.

PISTHETÆRUS.　We have never been the aggressors, and even now we are as well disposed for peace as yourselves, provided you agree to one equitable condition, namely, that Zeus yield his sceptre to the birds. If only this is agreed to, I invite the ambassadors to dinner.

HERACLES.　That's good enough for me. I vote for peace.

POSIDON.　You wretch! you are nothing but a fool and a glutton. Do you want to dethrone your own father?

PISTHETÆRUS.　What an error! Why, the gods will be much more powerful if the birds govern the earth. At present the mortals are hidden beneath the clouds, escape your observation, and commit perjury in your name; but if you had the birds for your allies, and a man, after having sworn by the crow and Zeus, should fail to keep his oath, the crow would dive down upon him unawares and pluck out his eye.

POSIDON.　Well thought of, by Posidon![5]

HERACLES.　My notion too.

PISTHETÆRUS.　[*to the* TRIBALLIAN] And you, what's your opinion?

TRIBALLUS.　Nabaisatreu.[6]

1.　He is addressing his servant, Manes.
2.　Heracles softens at sight of the food.—Heracles is the glutton of the comic poets.
3.　He pretends not to have seen them at first, being so much engaged with his cookery.
4.　He pretends to forget the presence of the ambassadors.
5.　Posidon jestingly swears by himself.
6.　The barbarian god utters some gibberish which Pisthetærus interprets as consent.

PISTHETÆRUS. D'you see? he also approves. But hear another thing in which we can serve you. If a man vows to offer a sacrifice to some god, and then procrastinates, pretending that the gods can wait, and thus does not keep his word, we shall punish his stinginess.

POSIDON. Ah! ah! and how?

PISTHETÆRUS. While he is counting his money or is in the bath, a kite will relieve him, before he knows it, either in coin or in clothes, of the value of a couple of sheep, and carry it to the god.

HERACLES. I vote for restoring them the sceptre.

POSIDON. Ask the Triballian.

HERACLES. Hi! Triballian, do you want a thrashing?

TRIBALLUS. Saunaka baktarikrousa.

HERACLES. He says, "Right willingly."

POSIDON. If that be the opinion of both of you, why, I consent too.

HERACLES. Very well! we accord the sceptre.

PISTHETÆRUS. Ah! I was nearly forgetting another condition. I will leave Herè to Zeus, but only if the young Basileia is given me in marriage.

POSIDON. Then you don't want peace. Let us withdraw.

PISTHETÆRUS. It matters mighty little to me. Cook, look to the gravy.

HERACLES. What an odd fellow this Posidon is! Where are you off to? Are we going to war about a woman?

POSIDON. What else is there to do?

HERACLES. What else? Why, conclude peace.

POSIDON. Oh! the ninny! do you always want to be fooled? Why, you are seeking your own downfall. If Zeus were to die, after having yielded them the sovereignty, you would be ruined, for you are the heir of all the wealth he will leave behind.

PISTHETÆRUS. Oh! by the gods! how he is cajoling you. Step aside, that I may have a word with you. Your uncle is getting the better of you, my poor friend.[1] The law will not allow you an obolus of the paternal property, for you are a bastard and not a legitimate child.

HERACLES. I a bastard! What's that you tell me?

PISTHETÆRUS. Why, certainly; are you not born of a stranger woman? Besides, is not Athenè recognized as Zeus' sole heiress? And no daughter would be that, if she had a legitimate brother.

HERACLES. But what if my father wished to give me his property on his death-bed, even though I be a bastard?

---

1. Heracles, the god of strength, was far from being remarkable in the way of cleverness.

PISTHETÆRUS.   The law forbids it, and this same Posidon would be the first to lay claim to his wealth, in virtue of being his legitimate brother. Listen; thus runs Solon's law: "A bastard shall not inherit, if there are legitimate children; and if there are no legitimate children, the property shall pass to the nearest kin."

HERACLES.   And I get nothing whatever of the paternal property?

PISTHETÆRUS.   Absolutely nothing. But tell me, has your father had you entered on the registers of his phratria?[1]

HERACLES.   No, and I have long been surprised at the omission.

PISTHETÆRUS.   What ails you, that you should shake your fist at heaven? Do you want to fight it? Why, be on my side, I will make you a king and will feed you on bird's milk and honey.

HERACLES.   Your further condition seems fair to me. I cede you the young damsel.

POSIDON.   But I, I vote against this opinion.

PISTHETÆRUS.   Then all depends on the Triballian. [*To the* TRIBBALLIAN.] What do you say?

TRIBALLUS.   Big bird give daughter pretty and queen.

HERACLES.   You say that you give her?

POSIDON.   Why no, he does not say anything of the sort, that he gives her; else I cannot understand any better than the swallows.

PISTHETÆRUS.   Exactly so. Does he not say she must be given to the swallows?

POSIDON.   Very well! you two arrange the matter; make peace, since you wish it so; I'll hold my tongue.

HERACLES.   We are of a mind to grant you all that you ask. But come up there with us to receive Basileia and the celestial bounty.

PISTHETÆRUS.   Here are birds already cut up, and very suitable for a nuptial feast.

HERACLES.   You go and, if you like, I will stay here to roast them.

PISTHETÆRUS.   You to roast them! you are too much the glutton; come along with us.

HERACLES.   Ah! how well I would have treated myself!

PISTHETÆRUS.   Let someone bring me a beautiful and magnificent tunic for the wedding.

---

1.   The poet attributes to the gods the same customs as those which governed Athens, and according to which no child was looked upon as legitimate unless his father had entered him on the registers of his phratria. The phratria was a division of the tribe and consisted of thirty families.

CHORUS.[1]   At Phanæ,[2] near the Clepsydra,[3] there dwells a people who
have neither faith nor law, the Englottogastors,[4] who reap, sow, pluck
the vines and the figs[5] with their tongues; they belong to a barbaric
race, and among them the Philippi and the Gorgiases[6] are to be found;
'tis these Englottogastorian Philippi who introduced the custom all
over Attica of cutting out the tongue separately at sacrifices.[7]

A MESSENGER.   Oh, you, whose unbounded happiness I cannot express in words, thrice happy race of airy birds, receive your king
in your fortunate dwellings. More brilliant than the brightest star
that illumes the earth, he is approaching his glittering golden
palace; the sun itself does not shine with more dazzling glory. He
is entering with his bride at his side,[8] whose beauty no human
tongue can express; in his hand he brandishes the lightning, the
winged shaft of Zeus; perfumes of unspeakable sweetness pervade
the ethereal realms. 'Tis a glorious spectacle to see the clouds of
incense wafting in light whirlwinds before the breath of the
Zephyr! But here he is himself. Divine Muse! let thy sacred lips
begin with songs of happy omen.

CHORUS.   Fall back! to the right! to the left! advance![9] Fly around this
happy mortal, whom Fortune loads with her blessings. Oh! oh! what
grace! what beauty! Oh, marriage so auspicious for our city! All
honour to this man! 'tis through him that the birds are called to such
glorious destinies. Let your nuptial hymns, your nuptial songs, greet
him and his Basileia! 'Twas in the midst of such festivities that the
Fates formerly united Olympian Herè to the King who governs the
gods from the summit of his inaccessible throne. Oh! Hymen! oh!
Hymenæus! Rosy Eros with the golden wings held the reins and
guided the chariot; 'twas he, who presided over the union of Zeus
and the fortunate Herè. Oh! Hymen! oh! Hymenæus!

PISTHETÆRUS.   I am delighted with your songs, I applaud your verses.
Now celebrate the thunder that shakes the earth, the flaming
lightning of Zeus and the terrible flashing thunderbolt.

1.   The chorus continues to tell what it has seen on its flights.
2.   The harbour of the island of Chios; but this name [from the Greek verb, to denounce] is
used here in the sense of being the land of informers.
3.   i.e. near the orators' platform, in the Public Assembly, or because there stood the water-
clock, by which speeches were limited.
4.   A coined name, made up of the words tongue, and stomach, and meaning those who fill
their stomach with what they gain with their tongues, to wit, the orators.
5.   The Greek word for fig forms part of the Greek word for informer.
6.   Both rhetoricians.
7.   Because they consecrated it specially to the god of eloquence.
8.   Basileia, whom he brings back from heaven.
9.   Terms used in regulating a dance.

CHORUS.   Oh, thou golden flash of the lightning! oh, ye divine shafts of flame, that Zeus has hitherto shot forth! Oh, ye rolling thunders, that bring down the rain! 'Tis by the order of *our* king that ye shall now stagger the earth! Oh, Hymen! 'tis through thee that he commands the universe and that he makes Basileia, whom he has robbed from Zeus, takeher seat at his side. Oh! Hymen! oh! Hymenæus!

PISTHETÆRUS.   Let all the winged tribes of our fellow-citizens follow the bridal couple to the palace of Zeus[1] and to the nuptial couch! Stretch forth your hands, my dear wife! Take hold of me by my wings and let us dance; I am going to lift you up and carry you through the air.

CHORUS.   Oh, joy! Io Pæan! Tralala! victory is thing, oh, thou greatest of the gods!

CURTAIN

---

1. Where Pisthetærus is henceforth to reign.

THE COUNTESS
OF ESCARBAGNAS
Molière

CAST OF CHARACTERS

THE COUNT, son to the Countess
THE VISCOUNT, in love with Julia
MR. THIBAUDIER, councillor, in love with the Countess
MR. HARPIN, receiver of taxes, also in love with the Countess
MR. BOBINET, tutor to the Count
JEANNOT, servant to Mr. Thibaudier
CRIQUET, servant to the Countess
THE COUNTESS OF ESCARBAGNAS
JULIA, in love withthe Viscount
ANDRÉE, maid to the Countess

Scene: Angoulême.

SCENE I

JULIA, THE VISCOUNT.

VISCOUNT. What! you are here already?
JULIA. Yes, and you ought to be ashamed of yourself, Cléante; it is not
  right for a lover to be the last to come to the rendezvous.
VISCOUNT. I should have been here long ago if there were no importu-
  nate people in the world. I was stopped on my way by an old bore
  of rank, who asked me news of the court, merely to be able himself to detail to me the most absurd things that can well be imag-
  ined about it. You know that those great newsmongers are the
  curse of provincial towns, and that they have no greater anxiety
  than to spread everywhere abroad all the tittle-tattle they pick up.
  This one showed me, to begin with, two large sheets of paper full
  to the very brim with the greatest imaginable amount of rubbish,

which, he says, comes from the safest quarters. Then, as if it were a wonderful thing, he read full length and with great mystery all the stupid jokes in the Dutch Gazette, which he takes for gospel. He thinks that France is being brought to ruin by the pen of that writer, whose fine wit, according to him, is sufficient to defeat armies. After that he raved about the ministry, spoke of all its faults, and I thought he would never have done. If one is to believe him, he knows the secrets of the cabinet better than those who compose it. The policy of the state is an open book to him, and no step is taken without his seeing through it. He shows you the secret machinations of all that takes place, whither the wisdom of our neighbours tends, and controls at his will and pleasure all the affairs of Europe. His knowledge of what goes on extends as far as Africa and Asia, and he is informed of all that is discussed in the privy council of Prester John and the Great Mogul.

JULIA. You make the best excuse you can, and so arrange it that it may pass off well and be easily received.

VISCOUNT. I assure you, dear Julia, that this is the real reason of my being late. But if I wanted to say anything gallant, I could tell you that the rendezvous to which you bring me here might well excuse the sluggishness of which you complain. To compel me to pay my addresses to the lady of this house is certainly reason enough for me to fear being here the first. I ought not to have to bear the misery of it, except when she whom it amuses is present. I avoid finding myself alone with that ridiculous countess with whom you shackle me. In short, as I come only for your sake, I have every reason to stay away until you are here.

JULIA. Oh! you will never lack the power of giving a bright colour to your faults. However, if you had come half an hour sooner, we should have enjoyed those few moments. For when I came, I found that the countess was out, and I have no doubt that she is gone all over the town to claim for herself the honour of the comedy you gave me under her name.

VISCOUNT. But, pray, when will you put an end to this, and make me buy less dearly the happiness of seeing you?

JULIA. When our parents agree, which I scarcely dare hope for. You know as well as I do that the dissensions which exist between our two families deprive us of the possibility of seeing each other anywhere else, and that neither my brothers nor my father are likely to approve of our engagement.

VISCOUNT. Yes; but why not profit better by the opportunity which their enmity gives us, and why oblige me to waste under a ridiculous deception, the moments I pass near you?

JULIA. It is the better to hide our love; and, besides, to tell you the truth, this deception you speak of is to me a very amusing comedy, and I hardly think that the one you give me today will amuse me as much. Our Countess of Escarbagnas, with her perpetual infatuation for "quality," is as good a personage as can be put on the stage. The short journey she has made to Paris has brought her back to Angoulême more crazy than ever. The air of the court has given a new charm to her extravagance, and her folly grows and increases every day.

VISCOUNT. Yes; but you do not take into consideration that what amuses you drives me to despair; and that one cannot dissimulate long when one is under the sway of love as true as that which I feel for you. It is cruel to think, dear Julia, that this amusement of yours should deprive me of the few moments during which I could speak to you of my love, and last night I wrote on the subject some verses that I cannot help repeating to you, so true is it that the mania of reciting one's verses is inseparable from the title of a poet:

> "Iris, too long thou keepst on torture's rack
> One who obeys thy laws, yet whisp'ring chides
> In that thou bidst me boast a joy I lack,
> And hush the sorrow that my bosom hides.
>
> Must thy dear eyes, to which I yield my arms,
> From my sad sighs draw wanton pleasure still?
> Is't not enough to suffer for thy charms
> That I must grieve at thy capricious will?
>
> This double martyrdom a pain affords
> Too keen to bear at once; thy deeds, thy words,
> Work on my wasting heart a cruel doom.
>
> Love bids it burn; constraint its life doth chill.
> If pity soften not thy wayward will,
> Love, feigned and real, will lead me to the tomb."

JULIA. I see that you make yourself out much more ill-used than you need; but it is the way with you poets to tell falsehoods in cold blood, and to pretend that those you love are much more cruel than they are, in order to make them correspond to the fancies you may take into your heads. Yet, I should like you, if you will, to give me those verses in writing.

VISCOUNT.   No, it is enough that I have repeated them to you, and I ought to stop there. A man may be foolish enough to make verses, but that is different from giving them to others.

JULIA.   It is in vain for you to affect a false modesty; your wit is well known, and I do not see why you should hide what you write.

VISCOUNT.   Ah! we must tread here with the greatest circumspection. It is a dangerous thing to set up for a wit. There is inherent to it a certain touch of absurdity which is catching, and we should be warned by the example of some of our friends.

JULIA.   Nonsense, Cléante; I see that, in spite of all you say, you are longing to give me your verses; and I feel sure that you would be very unhappy if I pretended not to care for them.

VISCOUNT.   I unhappy? Oh! dear no, I am not so much of a poet for you to think that I.... but here is the Countess of Escarbagnas; I'll go by this door, so as not to meet her, and will see that everything is got ready for the play I have promised you.

SCENE II

THE COUNTESS, JULIA; ANDRÉE AND CRIQUET IN THE BACKGROUND.

COUNTESS.   What, Madam, are you alone? Ah! what a shame! All alone! I thought my people had told me that the Viscount was here.

JULIA.   It is true that he came, but it was sufficient for him to know that you were not at home; he would not stop after that.

COUNTESS.   What! did he see you?

JULIA.   Yes.

COUNTESS.   And did he not stop to talk with you?

JULIA.   No, Madam; he wished to show you how very much he is struck by your charms.

COUNTESS.   Still, I shall call him to account for that. However much any one may be in love with me, I wish them to pay to our sex the homage that is due to it. I am not one of those unjust women who approve of the rudeness their lovers display towards other fair ones.

JULIA.   You must in no way be surprised at his conduct. The love he has for you shows itself in all his actions, and prevents him from caring for anybody but you.

COUNTESS.   I know that I can give rise to a strong passion; I have for that enough of beauty, youth, and rank, thank Heaven; but it is no reason why those who love me should not keep within the bounds of propriety towards others. [*Seeing* CRIQUET.] What are you doing there, little page? Is there not an ante-room for you to

be in until you are called? It is a strange thing that in the provinces we cannot meet with a servant who knows his place! To
whom do you think I am speaking? Why do you not move? Will
you go outside, little knave that you are!

SCENE III

THE COUNTESS, JULIA, ANDRÉE.

COUNTESS.   Come hither, girl.

ANDRÉE.   What do you wish me to do, Ma'am?

COUNTESS.   To take off my head-dress. Gently, you awkward girl: how
roughly you touch my head with your heavy hands!

ANDRÉE.   I do it as gently as I can, Ma'am.

COUNTESS.   No doubt; but what you call gently is very rough treat-
ment for my head. You have almost put my neck out of joint.
Now, take also this muff; go and put it with the rest into the
closet; don't leave anything about. Well! where is she going to
now? What is the stupid girl doing?

ANDRÉE.   I am going to take this into the closet, as you told me,
Ma'am.

COUNTESS.   Ah! heavens! [To JULIA] Pray, excuse her rudeness,
Madam. [To ANDRÉE] I told you my closet, great ass; that is the
place where I keep my dresses.

ANDRÉE.   Please, Ma'am, is a cupboard called a closet at court?

COUNTESS.   Yes, dunce; it is thus that a place where clothes are kept
is called.

ANDRÉE.   I will remember it, Ma'am, as well as the word furniture
warehouse for your attic.

SCENE IV

THE COUNTESS, JULIA.

COUNTESS.   What trouble it gives me to have to teach such simpletons.

JULIA.   I think them very fortunate to be under your discipline,
Madam.

COUNTESS.   She is my nurse's daughter, whom I have made lady's-
maid; the post is quite new to her, as yet.

JULIA.   It shows a generous soul, Madam, and it is glorious thus to
form people.

COUNTESS.   Come, some seats, I say! Here, little page! little page! little
page-boy! Truly, this is too bad not to have a page to give us
chairs! My maids! my page! my page! my maids! Ho! somebody!
I really think that they must be all dead, and that we shall have to
find seats for ourselves.

SCENE V

The Countess, Julia, Andrée.

ANDRÉE. What is it you want, Ma'am?

COUNTESS. You do make people scream after you, you servants!

ANDRÉE. I was putting your muff and head-dress away in the cup.... in the closet, I mean.

COUNTESS. Call in that rascal of a page.

ANDRÉE. I say, Criquet!

COUNTESS. Cease that "Criquet" of yours, stupid, and call out "Page."

ANDRÉE. Page then, and not Criquet, come and speak to missis. I think he must be deaf. Criq.... Page! page!

SCENE VI

The Countess, Julia, Andrée, Criquet.

CRIQUET. What is it you want?

COUNTESS. Where were you, you rascal?

CRIQUET. In the street, Ma'am.

COUNTESS. Why in the street?

CRIQUET. You told me to go outside.

COUNTESS. You are a rude little fellow, and you ought to know that outside among people of quality, means the ante-room. Andrée, mind you ask my equerry to flog this little rogue. He is an incorrigible little wretch.

ANDRÉE. Whom do you mean by your equerry, Ma'am? Is it Mr. Charles you call by that name?

COUNTESS. Be silent, impertinent girl! You can hardly open your mouth without making some rude remark. [*To* CRIQUET] Quick, some seats; [*to* ANDREÉ] and you, light two wax candles in my silver candlesticks; it is getting late. What is it now? why do you look so scared?

ANDRÉE. Ma'am....

COUNTESS. Well—Ma'am—what is the matter?

ANDRÉE. It is that...

COUNTESS. What?

ANDRÉE. I have no wax candles, but only dips.

COUNTESS. The simpleton! And where are the wax candles I bought a few days ago?

ANDRÉE. I have seen none since I have been here.

COUNTESS. Get out from my presence, rude girl. I will send you back to your home again. Bring me a glass of water.

SCENE VII

THE COUNTESS AND JULIA [*making much ceremony before they sit down*].

COUNTESS. Madam!
JULIA. Madam!
COUNTESS. Ah! Madam!
JULIA. Ah! Madam!
COUNTESS. Madam, I beg of you!
JULIA. Madam, I beg of you!
COUNTESS. Oh! Madam!
JULIA. Oh! Madam!
COUNTESS. Pray, Madam!
JULIA. Pray, Madam!
COUNTESS. Now really, Madam!
JULIA. Now really, Madam!
COUNTESS. I am in my own house, Madam! We are agreed as to that. Do you take me for a provincial, Madam?
JULIA. Oh! Heaven forbid, Madam!

SCENE VIII

THE COUNTESS, JULIA, ANDRÉE [*who brings a glass of water*], CRIQUET.

COUNTESS [*to* ANDRÉE]. Get along with you, you hussy. I drink with a salver. I tell you that you must go and fetch me a salver.
ANDRÉE. Criquet, what's a salver?
CRIQUET. A salver?
ANDRÉE. Yes.
CRIQUET. I don't know.
COUNTESS [*to* ANDRÉE]. Will you move, or will you not?
ANDRÉE. We don't either of us know what a salver is.
COUNTESS. Know, then, that it is a plate on which you put the glass.

SCENE IX

THE COUNTESS, JULIA.

COUNTESS. Long live Paris! It is only there that one is well waited upon; there a glance is enough.

SCENE X

THE COUNTESS, JULIA, ANDRÉE [*who brings a glass of water, with a plate on the top of it*], CRIQUET.

COUNTESS. Is that what I asked you for, dunderhead? It is under that you must put the plate.

ANDRÉE.   That is easy to do. [*She breaks the glass in trying to put it on the plate.*]

COUNTESS.   You stupid girl! You shall really pay for the glass; you shall, I promise you!

ANDRÉE.   Very well, Ma'am, I will pay you for it.

COUNTESS.   But did you ever see such an awkward loutish girl? such a...

ANDRÉE.   I say, Ma'am, if I am to pay for the glass, I won't be scolded into the bargain.

COUNTESS.   Get out of my sight.

SCENE XI

THE COUNTESS, JULIA.

COUNTESS.   Really, Madam, small towns are strange places. In them there is no respect of persons, and I have just been making a few calls at houses where they drove me almost to despair; so little regard did they pay to my rank.

JULIA.   Where could you expect them to have learnt manners? They have never been to Paris.

COUNTESS.   Still, they might learn, if they would only listen to one; but what I think too bad is that they will persist in saying that they know as much as I do—I who have spent two months in Paris, and have seen the whole court.

JULIA.   What absurd people!

COUNTESS.   They are unbearable in the impertinent equality with which they treat people. For, in short, there ought to be a certain subordination in things; and what puts me out of all patience is that a town upstart, whether with two days' gentility to boast of or with two hundred years', should have impudence enough to say that he is as much of a gentleman as my late husband, who lived in the country, kept a pack of hounds, and took the title of Count in all the deeds that he signed.

JULIA.   They know better how to live in Paris, in those large hotels you must remember with such pleasure! That Hotel of Mouchy, Madam; that Hotel of Lyons, that Hotel of Holland, what charming places to live in![1]

COUNTESS.   It is true that those places are very different from what we have here. You see there people of quality who do not hesitate to show you all the respect and consideration which you look for. One is not under the obligation of rising from one's seat, and if

---

1. Instead of naming the hotels [= mansions] of the great noblemen, Julia names the hotels [= inns] of the time. She thus shows where the countess had studied the aristocracy.

one wants to see a review or the great ballet of Psyche, your wishes are at once attended to.

JULIA.   I should think, Madam, that during your stay in Paris you made many a conquest among the people of quality.

COUNTESS.   You can readily believe, Madam, that of all the famous court gallants not one failed to come to my door and pay his respects to me. I keep in my casket some of the letters sent me, and can prove by them what offers I have refused. There is no need for me to tell you their names; you know what is meant by court gallants.

JULIA.   I wonder, Madam, how, after all those great names, which I can easily guess, you can descend to Mr. Thibaudier, a councillor, and Mr. Harpin, a collector of taxes. The fall is great, I must say. For your viscount, although nothing but a country viscount, is still a viscount, and can take a journey to Paris if he has not been there already. But a councillor and a tax-gatherer are but poor lovers for a great countess like you.

COUNTESS.   They are men whom one treats kindly in the country, in order to make use of when the need arises. They serve to fill up the gaps of gallantry, and to swell the ranks of one's lovers. It is a good thing not to leave a lover the sole master of one's heart, lest, for want of rivals, his love go to sleep through over-confidence.

JULIA.   I confess, Madam, that no one can help profiting wonderfully by all you say. Your conversation is a school, to which I do not fail to come every day in order to learn something new.

SCENE XII

The COUNTESS, JULIA, ANDRÉE, CRIQUET.

CRIQUET [to the COUNTESS].   Here is Jeannot, Mr. Thibaudier's man, who wants to see you, Ma'am.

COUNTESS.   Ah! you little wretch, this is another of your stupidities. A well-bred lackey would have spoken in a whisper to the gentlewoman in attendance; the latter would have come to her mistress and have whispered in her ear: "Here is the footman of Mr. So-and-so, who wants to speak to you, Madam." To which the mistress would have answered, "Show him in."

SCENE XIII

The COUNTESS, JULIA, ANDRÉE, CRIQUET, JEANNOT.

CRIQUET.   Come along in, Jeannot.

COUNTESS.   Another blunder. [To JEANNOT.] What do you want, page? What have you there?

JEANNOT. It is Mr. Thibaudier, Ma'am, who wishes you good morning, and, before he comes, sends you some pears out of his garden, with this small note.

SCENE XIV

THE COUNTESS, CRIQUET, JEANNOT.

COUNTESS [*giving some money to* JEANNOT]. Here, my boy; here is something for your trouble.

JEANNOT. Oh no, thank you, Ma'am.

COUNTESS. Take it, I say.

JEANNOT. My master told me not take anything from you Ma'am.

COUNTESS. Never mind, take it all the same.

JEANNOT. Excuse me, Ma'am.

CRIQUET. Take it, Jeannot. If you don't want it, you can give it me.

COUNTESS. Tell your master that I thank him.

CRIQUET [*to* JEANNOT, *who is going*]. Give it to me, Jeannot.

JEANNOT. Yes, you catch me.

CRIQUET. It was I who made you take it.

JEANNOT. I should have taken it without your help.

COUNTESS. What pleases me in this Mr. Thibaudier is that he knows how to behave with people of my quality, and that he is very respectful.

SCENE XV

THE VISCOUNT, THE COUNTESS, JULIA, CRIQUET.

VISCOUNT. I come to tell you, Madam, that the theatricals will soon be ready, and that we can go into the hall in a quarter of an hour.

COUNTESS. Mind, I will have no crowd after me. [*To* CRIQUET] Tell the porter not to let anybody come in.

VISCOUNT. If so, Madam, I give up our theatricals. I could take no interest in them unless the spectators are numerous. Believe me, if you want to enjoy it thoroughly, tell your people to let the whole town in.

COUNTESS. Page, a seat. [*To the* VISCOUNT, *after he is seated*] You have come just in time to accept a self-sacrifice I am willing to make to you. Look, I have here a note from Mr. Thibaudier, who sends me some pears. I give you leave to read it aloud; I have not opened it yet.

VISCOUNT [*after he has read the note to himself*]. This note is written in the most fashionable style, Madam, and is worthy of all your attention. [*Reads aloud.*] "Madam, I could not have made you the present I send you if my garden did not bring me more fruit than my love...."

COUNTESS. You see clearly by this that nothing has taken place between us.

VISCOUNT. "The pears are not quite ripe yet, but they will all the better match the hardness of your heart, the continued disdain of which promises me nothing soft and sweet. Allow me, Madam, without risking an enumeration of your charms, which would be endless, to conclude with begging you to consider that I am as good a Christian as the pears which I send you, for I render good for evil; which is to say, to explain myself more plainly, that I present you with good Christian pears in return for the choke-pears which your cruelty makes me swallow every day.

YOUR UNWORTHY SLAVE,
"THIBAUDIER."

Madam, this letter is worth keeping.

COUNTESS. There may be a few words in it that are not of the Academy, but I observe in it a certain respect which pleases me greatly.

JULIA. You are right, Madam, and even if the viscount were to take it amiss, I should love a man who would write so to me.

SCENE XVI

MR. THIBAUDIER, THE VISCOUNT, THE COUNTESS, JULIA, CRIQUET.

COUNTESS. Come here, Mr. Thibaudier; do not be afraid of coming in. Your note was well received, and so were your pears; and there is a lady here who takes your part against your rival.

THIBAUDIER. I am much obliged to her, Madam, and if ever she has a lawsuit in our court, she may be sure that I shall not forget the honour she does me in making herself the advocate of my flame near your beauty.

JULIA. You have no need of an advocate, Sir, and your cause has justice on its side.

THIBAUDIER. This, nevertheless, Madam, the right has need of help, and I have reason to apprehend the being supplanted by such a rival, and the beguiling of the lady by the rank of the viscount.

VISCOUNT. I had hopes before your note came, Sir, but now, I confess fears for my love.

THIBAUDIER. Here are likewise a few little couplets which I have composed to your honour and glory, Madam.

VISCOUNT. Ah! I had no idea that Mr. Thibaudier was a poet; these few little couplets will be my ruin.

COUNTESS. He means two strophes. [To CRIQUET.] Page, give a seat to Mr. Thibaudier. [Aside to CRIQUET, who brings a chair] A folding-chair, little animal! Mr. Thibaudier, sit down there, and read your strophes to us.

THIBAUDIER [*reads*].

> "A person of quality
>   Is my fair dame;
> She has got beauty,
>   Fierce is my flame;
>   Yet I must blame
> Her pride and cruelty."

VISCOUNT.   I am lost after that.

COUNTESS.   The first line is excellent: "A person of quality."

JULIA.   I think it is a little too long; but a liberty may be taken to express a noble thought.

COUNTESS [*to* MR. THIBAUDIER]. Let us have the other.

THIBAUDIER [*reads*].

> "I know not if you doubt that my love be sincere,
>   Yet this I know, that my heart every moment
>   Longs to leave its sorry apartment
> To visit yours, with fond respect and fear.
> After all this, having my love in hand,
> And my honour, of superfine brand,
>   You ought, in turn, I say,
>   Content to be a countess gay,
>   To cast that tigress' skin away,
>   Which hides your charms both night and day."

VISCOUNT.   I am undone by Mr. Thibaudier.

COUNTESS.   Do not make fun of it; for the verses are good although they are country verses.

VISCOUNT.   I, Madam, make fun of it! Though he is my rival, I think his verses admirable. I do not call them, like you, two strophes merely; but two epigrams, as good as any of Martial's.

COUNTESS.   What! Does Martial make verses? I thought he only made gloves.

THIBAUDIER.   It is not that Martial, Madam, but an author who lived thirty or forty years ago.[1]

VISCOUNT.   Mr. Thibaudier has read the authors, as you see. But, Madam, we shall see if my comedy, with its interludes and dances, will counteract in your mind the progress which the two strophes have made.

COUNTESS.   My son the count must be one of the spectators, for he came this morning from my country-seat, with his tutor, whom I see here.

---

1.   The Martial who *did not write verses*, sold perfumery, and was valet-de-chambre to the king's brother. Martial, the Roman epigrammatist, lived in the first century after Christ.

SCENE XVII

THE COUNTESS, JULIA, THE VISCOUNT, MR. THIBAUDER, MR BOBINET,
CRIQUET.

COUNTESS.   Mr. Bobinet, I say, Mr. Bobinet, come forward.

BOBINET.   I give the good evening to all this honourable company.
What does Madam the Countess of Escarbagnas want of her
humble servant Bobinet?

COUNTESS.   At what time, Mr. Bobinet, did you leave Escarbagnas
with the Count my son?

BOBINET.   At a quarter to nine, my lady, according to your orders.

COUNTESS.   How are my two other sons, the Marquis and the
Commander?

BOBINET.   They are, Heaven be thanked, in perfect health.

COUNTESS.   Where is the Count?

BOBINET.   In your beautiful room, with a recess in it, Madam.

COUNTESS.   What is he doing, Mr. Bobinet?

BOBINET.   Madam, he is composing an essay upon one of the epistles
of Cicero, which I have just given him as a subject.

COUNTESS.   Call him in, Mr. Bobinet.

BOBINET.   Be it according to your command, Madam. [*Exit*]

SCENE XVIII

THE COUNTESS, JULIA, THE VISCOUNT, MR. THIBAUDIER.

THIBAUDIER [*to the* COUNTESS].   That Mr. Bobinet, Madam, looks very
wise, and I think that he is a man of *esprit*.

SCENE XIX

THE COUNTESS, JULIA, THE VISCOUNT, THE COUNT, MR. BOBINET, MR.
THIBAUDIER

BOBINET.   Come, my Lord, show what progress you make under
the good precepts that are given you. Bow to the honourable
company.

COUNTESS [*showing* JULIA].   Come, Count, salute this lady; bow low
to the viscount; salute the councillor.

THIBAUDIER.   I am delighted, Madam, that you should grant me the
favour of embracing his lordship. One cannot love the trunk
without loving the branches.

COUNTESS.   Goodness gracious, Mr. Thibaudier, what a comparison
to use!

JULIA.   Really, Madam, his lordship the count has perfect manners.

VISCOUNT. This is a young gentleman who is thriving well.

JULIA. Who could have believed that your ladyship had so big a child.

COUNTESS. Alas! when he was born, I was so young that I still played with dolls.

JULIA. He is your brother and not your son.

COUNTESS. Be very careful of his education, Mr. Bobinet.

BOBINET. I shall never, Madam, neglect anything towards the cultivation of the young plant which your goodness has entrusted to my care, and I will try to inculcate in him the seeds of all the virtues.

COUNTESS. Mr. Bobinet, just make him recite some choice piece from what you teach him.

BOBINET. Will your lordship repeat your lesson of yesterday morning?

COUNT. *Omne viro soli quod convenit esto virile,*
Omne viri....

COUNTESS. Fie! Mr. Bobinet; what silly stuff is that you teach him?

BOBINET. It is Latin, Madam, and the first rule of Jean Despautère.

COUNTESS. Truly, that Jean Despautère is an impudent fellow, and I beg you to teach my son more honest Latin than this is in future.

BOBINET. If you will allow him to say it all through, Madam, the gloss will explain the meaning.

COUNTESS. There is no need; it explains itself sufficiently.

SCENE XX

THE COUNTESS, JULIA, THE VISCOUNT, MR. THIBAUDIER, THE COUNT, MR. BOBINET, CRIQUET.

CRIQUET. The actors send me to tell you that they are ready.

COUNTESS. Let us take our seats. [*Showing* JULIA.] Mr. Thibaudier, take this lady under your care.

[CRIQUET *places all the chairs on one side of the stage. The* COUNTESS, JULIA, *and the* VISCOUNT *sit down, and* MR. THIBAUDIER *sits down at the* COUNTESS'S *feet.*]

VISCOUNT. It is important for you to observe that this comedy was made only to unite the different pieces of music and dancing which compose the entertainment, and that....

COUNTESS. Ah! never mind, let us see it; we have enough good sense to understand things.

VISCOUNT. Begin then at once, and see that no troublesome intruder comes to disturb our pleasure.

[*The violins begin an overture.*]

SCENE XXI

THE COUNTESS, JULIA, THE VISCOUNT, THE COUNT, MR. HARPIN,
MR. THIBAUDIER, MR. BOBINET, CRIQUET.

HARPIN. By George! This is fine, and I rejoice to see what I see.

COUNTESS. How! Mr. Receiver, what do you mean by this behaviour? Is it right to come and interrupt a comedy in that fashion?

HARPIN. By Jove, Madam, I am delighted at this adventure, and it shows me what I ought to think of you, and what I ought to believe of the assurances you gave me of the gift of your heart, and likewise of all your oaths of fidelity.

COUNTESS. But, really, one should not come thus in the middle of a play and disturb an actor who is speaking.

HARPIN. Hah! zounds, the real comedy here is the one you are playing, and I care little if I disturb you.

COUNTESS. Really, you do not know what you are saying.

HARPIN. Yes, d——it, I know perfectly well; and....

[MR. BOBINET, *frightened, takes up the* COUNT, *and runs away;* CRIQUET *follows him.*]

COUNTESS. Fie, Sir! How wrong it is to swear in that fashion!

HARPIN. Ah! 'sdeath! If there is anything bad here, it is not my swearing, but your actions; and it would be much better for you to swear by heaven and hell than to do what you do with the viscount.

VISCOUNT. I don't know, Sir, of what you have to complain; and if....

HARPIN [*to the* VISCOUNT]. I have nothing to say to you, Sir; you do right to push your fortune; that is quite natural; I see nothing strange in it, and I beg your pardon for interrupting your play. But neither can you find it strange that I complain of her proceedings; and we both have a right to do what we are doing.

VISCOUNT. I have nothing to say to that, and I do not know what cause of complaint you can have against her ladyship the Countess of Escarbagnas.

COUNTESS. When one suffers from jealousy, one does not give way to such outbursts, but one comes peaceably to complain to the person beloved.

HARPIN. I complain peaceably!

COUNTESS. Yes; one does not come and shout on the stage what should be said in private.

HARPIN. I came purposely to complain on the stage. 'Sdeath! it is the place that suits me best, and I should be glad if this were a real theatre so that I might expose you more publicly.

COUNTESS. Is there need for such an uproar because the viscount gives a play in my honour? Just look at Mr. Thibaudier, who loves me; he acts more respectfully than you do.

HARPIN. Mr. Thibaudier does as he pleases; I don't know how far Mr. Thibaudier has got with you, but Mr. Thibaudier is no example for me. I don't like to pay the piper for other people to dance.

COUNTESS. But, Mr. Receiver, you don't consider what you are saying. Women of rank are not treated thus, and those who hear you might believe that something strange had taken place between us.

HARPIN. Confound it all, Madam; let us cast aside all this foolery.

COUNTESS. What do you mean by foolery?

HARPIN. I mean that I do not think it strange that you should yield to the viscount's merit; you are not the first woman in the world who plays such a part, and who has a receiver of taxes of whom the love and purse are betrayed for the first new comer who takes her fancy. But do not think it extraordinary that I do not care to be the dupe of an infidelity so common to coquettes of the period, and that I come before good company to say that I break with you, and that I, the receiver of taxes, will no more be taxed on your account.

COUNTESS. It is really wonderful how angry lovers have become the fashion! We see nothing else anywhere. Come, come, Mr. Receiver, cast aside your anger, and come and take a seat to see the play.

HARPIN. I sit down? 'sdeath! not I! [*Showing* MR. THIBAUDIER.] Look for a fool at your feet, my lady Countess; I give you up to my lord the viscount, and it is to him that I will send the letters I have received from you. My scene is ended, my part is played. Good night to all!

THIBAUDIER. We shall meet somewhere else, and I will show you that I am a man of the sword as well as of the pen.

HARPIN. Right, my good Mr. Thibaudier. [*Exit.*]

COUNTESS. Such insolence confounds me!

VISCOUNT. The jealous, Madam, are like those who lose their cause; they have leave to say anything. Let us listen to the play now.

SCENE XXII

THE COUNTESS, THE VISCOUNT, JULIA, MR. THIBAUDIER, JEANNOT.

JEANNOT [*to the* VISCOUNT]. Sir, here is a note which I have been asked to give to you immediately.

VISCOUN [*reads*]. "As you may have some measures to take, I send you notice at once that the quarrel between your family and that of

Julia's has just been settled, and that the condition of this agreement is your marriage with Julia. Good night!" [*To* JULIA] Truly, Madam, our part is also played.

[*The* VISCOUNT, *the* COUNTESS, *and* MR. THIBAUDIER *all rise.*]

JULIA.   Ah! Cléante, what happiness is this! Our love could scarcely hope for such a happy end.

COUNTESS.   What is it you mean?

VISCOUNT.   It means, Madam, that I marry Julia; and if you will believe me, in order to make the play complete at all points, you will marry Mr. Thibaudier, and give Andrée to his footman, whom he will make his valet-de-chambre.

COUNTESS.   What! you deceive thus a person of my rank!

VISCOUNT.   No offence to you, Madam, but plays require such things.

COUNTESS.   Yes, Mr. Thibaudier, I will marry you to vex everybody.

THIBAUDIER.   You do me too much honour, Madam.

VISCOUNT.   Allow us, Madam, in spite of our vexation, to see the end of the play.

CURTAIN

THE PROPOSAL
Anton Chekhov

CAST OF CHARACTERS

STEPAN STEPANOVITCH CHUBUKOV, a landowner
NATALYA STEPANOVNA, his daughter, twenty-five years old
IVAN VASSILEVITCH LOMOV, a neighbour of CHUBUKOV, a large and hearty, but very suspicious landowner

Scene: CHUBUKOV'S *country-house.*

[*A drawing-room in* CHUBUKOV'S *house.* LOMOV *enters, wearing a dress-jacket and white gloves.* CHUBUKOV *rises to meet him.*]

CHUBUKOV.   My dear fellow, whom do I see! Ivan Vassilevitch! I am extremely glad! [*Squeezes his hand.*] Now this is a surprise, my darling.... How are you?

LOMOV.   Thank you. And how may you be getting on?

CHUBUKOV.   We just get along somehow, my angel, thanks to your prayers, and so on. Sit down, please do.... Now, you know, you shouldn't forget all about your neighbours, my darling. My dear fellow, why are you so formal in your get-up? Evening dress, gloves, and so on. Can you be going anywhere, my treasure?

LOMOV.   No, I've come only to see you, honoured Stepan Stepanovitch.

CHUBUKOV.   Then why are you in evening dress, my precious? As if you're paying a New Year's Eve visit!

LOMOV.   Well, you see, it's like this. [*Takes his arm*] I've come to you, honoured Stepan Stepanovitch, to trouble you with a request. Not once or twice have I already had the privilege of applying to you for help, and you have always, so to speak ... I must ask your pardon, I am getting excited. I shall drink some water, honoured Stepan Stepanovitch. [*Drinks.*]

CHUBUKOV [*aside*].   He's come to borrow money! Shan't give him any! [*Aloud.*] What is it, my beauty?

66

LOMOV. You see, Honour Stepanitch ... I beg pardon, Stepan Honouritch ... I mean, I'm awfully excited, as you will please notice.... In short, you alone can help me, though I don't deserve it, of course ... and haven't any right to count on your assistance....

CHUBUKOV. Oh, don't go round and round it, darling! Spit it out! Well?

LOMOV. One moment ... this very minute. The fact is, I've come to ask the hand of your daughter, NATALYA STEPANOVNA, in marriage.

CHUBUKOV [*joyfully*]. By Jove! Ivan Vassilevitch! Say it again—I didn't hear it all!

LOMOV. I have the honour to ask ...

CHUBUKOV [*interrupting*]. My dear fellow ... I'm so glad, and so on.... Yes, indeed, and all that sort of thing. [*Embraces and kisses* LOMOV] I've been hoping for it for a long time. It's been my continual desire. [*Sheds a tear*] And I've always loved you, my angel, as if you were my own son. May God give you both His help and His love and so on, and I did so much hope ...What am I behaving in this idiotic way for? I'm off my balance with joy, absolutely off my balance! Oh, with all my soul ... I'll go and call Natasha, and all that.

LOMOV [*greatly moved*]. Honoured Stepan Stepanovitch, do you think I may count on her consent?

CHUBUKOV. Why, of course, my darling, and ... as if she won't consent! She's in love; egad, she's like a love-sick cat, and so on.... Shan't be long! [*Exit.*]

LOMOV. It's cold ... I'm trembling all over, just as if I'd got an examination before me. The great thing is, I must have my mind made up. If I give myself time to think, to hesitate, to talk a lot, to look for an ideal, or for real love, then I'll never get married.... Brr! ... It's cold! Natalya Stepanovna is an excellent housekeeper, not bad-looking, well-educated.... What more do I want? But I'm getting a noise in my ears from excitement. [*Drinks*] And it's impossible for me not to marry.... In the first place, I'm already 35—a critical age, so to speak. In the second place, I ought to lead a quiet and regular life.... I suffer from palpitations, I'm excitable and always getting awfully upset.... At this very moment my lips are trembling, and there's a twitch in my right eyebrow.... But the very worst of all is the way I sleep. I no sooner get into bed and begin to go off when suddenly something in my left side—gives a pull, and I can feel it in my shoulder and head.... I jump up like a lunatic, walk about a bit, and lie down again, but as soon as I begin to get off to sleep there's another pull! And this may happen twenty times....

[NATALYA STEPANOVNA *comes in.*]

NATALYA STEPANOVNA. Well, there! It's you, and papa said, "Go; there's a merchant come for his goods." How do you do, Ivan Vassilevitch!

LOMOV. How do you do, honoured Natalya Stepanovna?

NATALYA STEPANOVNA. You must excuse my apron and nélige ... we're shelling peas for drying. Why haven't you been here for such a long time? Sit down. [*They seat themselves*] Won't you have some lunch?

LOMOV. No, thank you, I've had some already.

NATALYA STEPANOVNA. Then smoke.... Here are the matches.... The weather is splendid now, but yesterday it was so wet that the workmen didn't do anything all day. How much hay have you stacked? Just think, I felt greedy and had a whole field cut, and now I'm not at all pleased about it because I'm afraid my hay may rot. I ought to have waited a bit. But what's this? Why, you're in evening dress! Well, I never! Are you going to a ball, or what?— though I must say you look better. Tell me, why are you got up like that?

LOMOV [*excited*]. You see, honoured Natalya Stepanovna ... the fact is, I've made up my mind to ask you to hear me out.... Of course you'll be surprised and perhaps even angry, but a ... [*Aside.*] It's awfully cold!

NATALYA STEPANOVNA. What's the matter? [*Pause*] Well?

LOMOV. I shall try to be brief. You must know, honoured Natalya Stepanovna, that I have long, since my childhood, in fact, had the privilege of knowing your family. My late aunt and her husband, from whom, as you know, I inherited my land, always had the greatest respect for your father and your late mother. The Lomovs and the Chubukovs have always had the most friendly, and I might almost say the most affectionate, regard for each other. And, as you know, my land is a near neighbour of yours. You will remember that my Oxen Meadows touch your birchwoods.

NATALYA STEPANOVNA. Excuse my interrupting you. You say, "my Oxen Meadows...." But are they yours?

LOMOV. Yes, mine.

NATALYA STEPANOVNA. What are you talking about? Oxen Meadows are ours, not yours!

LOMOV. No, mine, honoured Natalya Stepanovna.

NATALYA STEPANOVNA. Well, I never knew that before. How do you make that out?

LOMOV. How? I'm speaking of those Oxen Meadows which are wedged in between your birchwoods and the Burnt Marsh.

NATALYA STEPANOVNA.   Yes, yes.... They're ours.

LOMOV.   No, you're mistaken, honoured Natalya Stepanovna, they're mine.

NATALYA STEPANOVNA.   Just think, Ivan Vassilevitch! How long have they been yours?

LOMOV.   How long? As long as I can remember.

NATALYA STEPANOVNA.   Really, you won't get me to believe that!

LOMOV.   But you can see from the documents, honoured Natalya Stepanovna. Oxen Meadows, it's true, were once the subject of dispute, but now everybody knows that they are mine. There's nothing to argue about. You see, my aunt's grandmother gave the free use of these Meadows in perpetuity to the peasants of your father's grandfather, in return for which they were to make bricks for her. The peasants belonging to your father's grandfather had the free use of the Meadows for forty years, and had got into the habit of regarding them as their own, when it happened that ...

NATALYA STEPANOVNA.   No, it isn't at all like that! Both my grandfather and great-grandfather reckoned that their land extended to Burnt Marsh—which means that Oxen Meadows were ours. I don't see what there is to argue about. It's simply silly!

LOMOV.   I'll show you the documents, Natalya Stepanovna!

NATALYA STEPANOVNA.   No, you're simply joking, or making fun of me.... What a surprise! We've had the land for nearly three hundred years, and then we're suddenly told that it isn't ours! Ivan Vassilevitch, I can hardly believe my own ears.... These Meadows aren't worth much to me. They only come to five dessiatins, and are worth perhaps 300 roubles, but I can't stand unfairness. Say what you will, but I can't stand unfairness.

LOMOV.   Hear me out, I implore you! The peasants of your father's grandfather, as I have already had the honour of explaining to you, used to bake bricks for my aunt's grandmother. Now my aunt's grandmother, wishing to make them a pleasant ...

NATALYA STEPANOVNA.   I can't make head or tail of all this about aunts and grandfathers and grandmothers! The Meadows are ours, and that's all.

LOMOV.   Mine.

NATALYA STEPANOVNA.   Ours! You can go on proving it for two days on end, you can go and put on fifteen dress-jackets, but I tell you they're ours, ours, ours! I don't want anything of yours and I don't want to give up anything of mine. So there!

LOMOV.   Natalya Ivanovna, I don't want the Meadows, but I am acting on principle. If you like, I'll make you a present of them.

NATALYA STEPANOVNA.   I can make you a present of them myself, because they're mine! Your behaviour, Ivan Vassilevitch, is strange, to say the least! Up to this we have always thought of you as a good neighbour, a friend: last year we lent you our threshing-machine, although on that account we had to put off our own threshing till November, but you behave to us as if we were gipsies. Giving me my own land, indeed! No, really, that's not at all neighbourly! In my opinion, it's even impudent, if you want to know....

LOMOV.   Then you make out that I'm a land-grabber? Madam, never in my life have I grabbed anybody else's land, and I shan't allow anybody to accuse me of having done so.... [*Quickly steps to the carafe and drinks more water.*] Oxen Meadows are mine!

NATALYA STEPANOVNA.   It's not true, they're ours!

LOMOV.   Mine!

NATALYA STEPANOVNA.   It's not true! I'll prove it! I'll send my mowers out to the Meadows this very day!

LOMOV.   What?

NATALYA STEPANOVNA.   My mowers will be there this very day!

LOMOV.   I'll give it to them in the neck!

NATALYA STEPANOVNA.   You dare!

LOMOV [*clutches at his heart*].   Oxen Meadows are mine! You understand? Mine!

NATALYA STEPANOVNA.   Please don't shout! You can shout yourself hoarse in your own house, but here I must ask you to restrain yourself!

LOMOV.   If it wasn't, madam, for this awful, excruciating palpitation, if my whole inside wasn't upset, I'd talk to you in a different way! [*Yells*] Oxen Meadows are mine!

NATALYA STEPANOVNA.   Ours!

LOMOV.   Mine!

NATALYA STEPANOVNA.   Ours!

LOMOV.   Mine!

[*Enter* CHUBUKOV.]

CHUBUKOV.   What's the matter? What are you shouting at?

NATALYA STEPANOVNA.   Papa, please tell to this gentleman who owns Oxen Meadows, we or he?

CHUBUKOV [*to* LOMOV].   Darling, the Meadows are ours!

LOMOV.   But, please, Stepan Stepanitch, how can they be yours? Do be a reasonable man! My aunt's grandmother gave the Meadows for the temporary and free use of your grandfather's peasants. The peasants used the land for forty years and got as accustomed to it as if it was their own, when it happened that ...

CHUBUKOV.   Excuse me, my precious…. You forget just this, that the peasants didn't pay your grandmother and all that, because the Meadows were in dispute, and so on. And now everybody knows that they're ours. It means that you haven't seen the plan.

LOMOV.   I'll prove to you that they're mine!

CHUBUKOV.   You won't prove it, my darling.

LOMOV.   I shall!

CHUBUKOV.   Dear one, why yell like that? You won't prove anything just by yelling. I don't want anything of yours, and don't intend to give up what I have. Why should I? And you know, my beloved, that if you propose to go on arguing about it, I'd much sooner give up the meadows to the peasants than to you. There!

LOMOV.   I don't understand! How have you the right to give away somebody else's property?

CHUBUKOV.   You may take it that I know whether I have the right or not. Because, young man, I'm not used to being spoken to in that tone of voice, and so on: I, young man, am twice your age, and ask you to speak to me without agitating yourself, and all that.

LOMOV.   No, you just think I'm a fool and want to have me on! You call my land yours, and then you want me to talk to you calmly and politely! Good neighbours don't behave like that, Stepan Stepanitch! You're not a neighbour, you're a grabber!

CHUBUKOV.   What's that? What did you say?

NATALYA STEPANOVNA.   Papa, send the mowers out to the Meadows at once!

CHUBUKOV.   What did you say, sir?

NATALYA STEPANOVNA.   Oxen Meadows are ours, and I shan't give them up, shan't give them up, shan't give them up!

LOMOV.   We'll see! I'll have the matter taken to court, and then I'll show you!

CHUBUKOV.   To court? You can take it to court, and all that! You can! I know you; you're just on the look-out for a chance to go to court, and all that…. You pettifogger! All your people were like that! All of them!

LOMOV.   Never mind about my people! The Lomovs have all been honourable people, and not one has ever been tried for embezzlement, like your grandfather!

CHUBUKOV.   You Lomovs have had lunacy in your family, all of you!

NATALYA STEPANOVNA.   All, all, all!

CHUBUKOV.   Your grandfather was a drunkard, and your younger aunt, Nastasya Mihailovna, ran away with an architect, and so on…

LOMOV.   And your mother was hump-backed. [Clutches at his heart.] Something pulling in my side…. My head…. Help! Water!

CHUBUKOV.   Your father was a guzzling gambler!

NATALYA STEPANOVNA.   And there haven't been many backbiters to equal your aunt!

LOMOV.   My left foot has gone to sleep.... You're an intriguer.... Oh, my heart! ... And it's an open secret that before the last elections you bri ... I can see stars.... Where's my hat?

NATALYA STEPANOVNA.   It's low! It's dishonest! It's mean!

CHUBUKOV.   And you're just a malicious, double-faced intriguer! Yes!

LOMOV.   Here's my hat.... My heart! ... Which way? Where's the door? Oh! ... I think I'm dying.... My foot's quite numb.... [*Goes to the door.*]

CHUBUKOV [*following him*].   And don't set foot in my house again!

NATALYA STEPANOVNA. Take it to court! We'll see!

[LOMOV *staggers out.*]

CHUBUKOV.   Devil take him! [*Walks about in excitement.*]

NATALYA STEPANOVNA.   What a rascal! What trust can one have in one's neighbours after that!

CHUBUKOV.   The villain! The scarecrow!

NATALYA STEPANOVNA.   The monster! First he takes our land and then he has the impudence to abuse us.

CHUBUKOV.   And that blind hen, yes, that turnip-ghost has the confounded cheek to make a proposal, and so on! What? A proposal!

NATALYA STEPANOVNA.   What proposal?

CHUBUKOV.   Why, he came here so as to propose to you.

NATALYA STEPANOVNA.   To propose? To me? Why didn't you tell me so before?

CHUBUKOV.   So he dresses up in evening clothes. The stuffed sausage! The wizen-faced frump!

NATALYA STEPANOVNA.   To propose to me? Ah! [*Falls into an easy-chair and wails.*] Bring him back! Back! Ah! Bring him here.

CHUBUKOV.   Bring whom here?

NATALYA STEPANOVNA.   Quick, quick! I'm ill! Fetch him! [*Hysterics.*]

CHUBUKOV.   What's that? What's the matter with you? [*Clutches at his head*] Oh, unhappy man that I am! I'll shoot myself! I'll hang myself! We've done for her!

NATALYA STEPANOVNA.   I'm dying! Fetch him!

CHUBUKOV.   Tfoo! At once. Don't yell!

[*Runs out. A pause.* NATALYA STEPANOVNA *wails.*]

NATALYA STEPANOVNA.   What have they done to me! Fetch him back! Fetch him! [*A pause.*]

[CHUBUKOV *runs in.*]

CHUBUKOV. He's coming, and so on, devil take him! Ouf! Talk to
him yourself; I don't want to....

NATALYA STEPANOVNA [*wails*]. Fetch him!

CHUBUKOV [*yells*]. He's coming, I tell you. Oh, what a burden, Lord, to
be the father of a grown–up daughter! I'll cut my throat! I will, indeed!
We cursed him, abused him, drove him out, and it's all you ... you!

NATALYA STEPANOVNA. No, it was you!

CHUBUKOV. I tell you it's not my fault. [LOMOV *appears at the door*] Now
you talk to him yourself [*Exit.*]

[*LOMOV enters, exhausted.*]

LOMOV. My heart's palpitating awfully.... My foot's gone to sleep....
There's something keeps pulling in my side....

NATALYA STEPANOVNA. Forgive us, Ivan Vassilevitch, we were all a
little heated.... I remember now: Oxen Meadows really are
yours.

LOMOV. My heart's beating awfully.... My Meadows.... My eyebrows
are both twitching....

NATALYA STEPANOVNA. The Meadows are yours, yes, yours.... Do sit
down.... [*They sit.*] We were wrong....

LOMOV. I did it on principle.... My land is worth little to me, but the
principle ...

NATALYA STEPANOVNA. Yes, the principle, just so.... Now let's talk of
something else.

LOMOV. The more so as I have evidence. My aunt's grandmother gave
the land to your father's grandfather's peasants ...

NATALYA STEPANOVNA. Yes, yes, let that pass.... [*Aside.*] I wish I knew
how to get him started.... [*Aloud*]. Are you going to start shooting
soon?

LOMOV. I'm thinking of having a go at the blackcock, honoured
Natalya Stepanovna, after the harvest. Oh, have you heard? Just
think, what a misfortune I've had! My dog Guess, whom you
know, has gone lame.

NATALYA STEPANOVNA. What a pity! Why?

LOMOV. I don't know.... Must have got twisted, or bitten by some
other dog.... [*Sighs*] My very best dog, to say nothing of the expense. I gave Mironov 125 roubles for him.

NATALYA STEPANOVNA. It was too much, Ivan Vassilevitch.

LOMOV. I think it was very cheap. He's a first-rate dog.

NATALYA STEPANOVNA. Papa gave 85 roubles for his Squeezer, and
Squeezer is heaps better than Guess!

LOMOV. Squeezer better than Guess? What an idea! [*Laughs.*] Squeezer better than Guess!

NATALYA STEPANOVNA. Of course he's better! Of course, Squeezer is young, he may develop a bit, but on points and pedigree he's better than anything that even Volchanetsky has got.

LOMOV. Excuse me, Natalya Stepanovna, but you forget that he is overshot, and an overshot always means the dog is a bad hunter!

NATALYA STEPANOVNA. Overshot, is he? The first time I hear it!

LOMOV. I assure you that his lower jaw is shorter than the upper.

NATALYA STEPANOVNA. Have you measured?

LOMOV. Yes. He's all right at following, of course, but if you want him to get hold of anything ...

NATALYA STEPANOVNA. In the first place, our Squeezer is a thoroughbred animal, the son of Harness and Chisels, while there's no getting at the pedigree of your dog at all.... He's old and as ugly as a worn-out cab-horse.

LOMOV. He is old, but I wouldn't take five Squeezers for him.... Why, how can you? ... Guess is a dog; as for Squeezer, well, it's too funny to argue.... Anybody you like has a dog as good as Squeezer ... you may find them under every bush almost. Twenty-five roubles would be a handsome price to pay for him.

NATALYA STEPANOVNA. There's some demon of contradiction in you today, Ivan Vassilevitch. First you pretend that the Meadows are yours; now, that Guess is better than Squeezer. I don't like people who don't say what they mean, because you know perfectly well that Squeezer is a hundred times better than your silly Guess. Why do you want to say it isn't?

LOMOV. I see, Natalya Stepanovna, that you consider me either blind or a fool. You must realize that Squeezer is overshot!

NATALYA STEPANOVNA. It's not true.

LOMOV. He is!

NATALYA STEPANOVNA. It's not true!

LOMOV. Why shout, madam?

NATALYA STEPANOVNA. Why talk rot? It's awful! It's time your Guess was shot, and you compare him with Squeezer!

LOMOV. Excuse me; I cannot continue this discussion: my heart is palpitating.

NATALYA STEPANOVNA. I've noticed that those hunters argue most who know least.

LOMOV. Madam, please be silent.... My heart is going to pieces.... [*Shouts*] Shut up!

NATALYA STEPANOVNA. I shan't shut up until you acknowledge that Squeezer is a hundred times better than your Guess!

LOMOV. A hundred times worse! Be hanged to your Squeezer! His
    head ... eyes ... shoulder ...
NATALYA STEPANOVNA. There's no need to hang your silly Guess; he's
    half-dead already!
LOMOV [*weeps*]. Shut up! My heart's bursting!
NATALYA STEPANOVNA. I shan't shut up.

[*Enter* CHUBUKOV.]

CHUBUKOV. What's the matter now?
NATALYA STEPANOVNA. Papa, tell us truly, which is the better dog, our
    Squeezer or his Guess.
LOMOV. Stepan Stepanovitch, I implore you to tell me just one thing:
    is your Squeezer overshot or not? Yes or no?
CHUBUKOV. And suppose he is? What does it matter? He's the best
    dog in the district for all that, and so on.
LOMOV. But isn't my Guess better? Really, now?
CHUBUKOV. Don't excite yourself, my precious one.... Allow me....
    Your Guess certainly has his good points.... He's pure-bred, firm
    on his feet, has well-sprung ribs, and all that. But, my dear man, if
    you want to know the truth, that dog has two defects: he's old and
    he's short in the muzzle.
LOMOV. Excuse me, my heart.... Let's take the facts.... You will remember
    that on the Marusinsky hunt my Guess ran neck-and-neck with the
    Count's dog, while your Squeezer was left a whole verst behind.
CHUBUKOV. He got left behind because the Count's whipper-in hit
    him with his whip.
LOMOV. And with good reason. The dogs are running after a fox,
    when Squeezer goes and starts worrying a sheep!
CHUBUKOV. It's not true! ... My dear fellow, I'm very liable to lose
    my temper, and so, just because of that, let's stop arguing. You
    started because everybody is always jealous of everybody else's
    dogs. Yes, we're all like that! You too, sir, aren't blameless! You
    no sooner notice that some dog is better than your Guess than
    you begin with this, that ... and the other ... and all that.... I
    remember everything!
LOMOV. I remember too!
CHUBUKOV [*teasing him*]. I remember, too.... What do you remember?
LOMOV. My heart ... my foot's gone to sleep.... I can't ...
NATALYA STEPANOVNA [*teasing*]. My heart.... What sort of a hunter are
    you? You ought to go and lie on the kitchen oven and catch
    blackbeetles, not go after foxes! My heart!
CHUBUKOV. Yes really, what sort of a hunter are you, anyway? You
    ought to sit at home with your palpitations, and not go tracking

animals. You could go hunting, but you only go to argue with
people and interfere with their dogs and so on. Let's change
the subject in case I lose my temper. You're not a hunter at all,
anyway!

LOMOV.   And are you a hunter? You only go hunting to get in with the
Count and to intrigue.... Oh, my heart! ...You're an intriguer!

CHUBUKOV.   What? I an intriguer? [*Shouts*] Shut up!

LOMOV.   Intriguer!

CHUBUKOV.   Boy! Pup!

LOMOV.   Old rat! Jesuit!

CHUBUKOV.   Shut up or I'll shoot you like a partridge! You fool!

LOMOV.   Everybody knows that—oh my heart!—your late wife used
to beat you.... My feet ... temples ... sparks.... I fall, I fall!

CHUBUKOV.   And you're under the slipper of your housekeeper!

LOMOV.   There, there, there ... my heart's burst! My shoulder's
come off.... Where is my shoulder? I die. [*Falls into an armchair*] A doctor! [*Faints.*]

CHUBUKOV.   Boy! Milksop! Fool! I'm sick! [*Drinks water*] Sick!

NATALYA STEPANOVNA.   What sort of a hunter are you? You can't even
sit on a horse! [*To her father*] Papa, what's the matter with him?
Papa! Look, papa! [*Screams.*] Ivan Vassilevitch! He's dead!

CHUBUKOV.   I'm sick! ... I can't breathe! ... Air!

NATALYA STEPANOVNA.   He's dead. [*Pulls* LOMOV's *sleeve*] Ivan
Vassilevitch! Ivan Vassilevitch! What have you done to me? He's
dead. [*Falls into an armchair*] A doctor, a doctor! [*Hysterics.*]

CHUBUKOV.   Oh! ...What is it? What's the matter?

NATALYA STEPANOVNA [*wails*].   He's dead ... dead!

CHUBUKOV.   Who's dead? [*Looks at* LOMOV] So he is! My word!
Water! A doctor! [*Lifts a tumbler to* LOMOV's *mouth*] Drink this! ...
No, he doesn't drink.... It means he's dead, and all that.... I'm the
most unhappy of men! Why don't I put a bullet into my brain?
Why haven't I cut my throat yet? What am I waiting for? Give me
a knife! Give me a pistol! [LOMOV *moves*] He seems to be coming
round.... Drink some water! That's right....

LOMOV.   I see stars ... mist.... Where am I?

CHUBUKOV.   Hurry up and get married and—well, to the devil with
you! She's willing! [*He puts* LOMOV's *hand into his daughter's*] She's
willing and all that. I give you my blessing and so on. Only leave
me in peace!

LOMOV [*getting up*].   Eh? What? To whom?

CHUBUKOV.   She's willing! Well? Kiss and be damned to you!

NATALYA STEPANOVNA [*wails*].   He's alive...Yes, yes, I'm willing....

CHUBUKOV. Kiss each other!

LOMOV. Eh? Kiss whom? [*They kiss.*] Very nice, too. Excuse me, what's it all about? Oh, now I understand ... my heart ... stars ... I'm happy. Natalya Stepanovna.... [*Kisses her hand*] My foot's gone to sleep....

NATALYA STEPANOVNA. I ... I'm happy too....

CHUBUKOV. What a weight off my shoulders.... Ouf!

NATALYA STEPANOVNA. But ... still you will admit now that Guess is worse than Squeezer.

LOMOV. Better!

NATALYA STEPANOVNA. Worse!

CHUBUKOV. Well, that's a way to start your family bliss! Have some champagne!

LOMOV. He's better!

NATALYA STEPANOVNA. Worse! worse! worse!

CHUBUKOV [*trying to shout her down*]. Champagne! Champagne!

CURTAIN

THE LAND OF HEART'S DESIRE

William Butler Yeats

CAST OF CHARACTERS

MAURTEEN BRUIN
BRIDGET BRUIN
SHAWN BRUIN
MARY BRUIN
FATHER HART
A FAERY CHILD

The Scene is laid in the Barony of Kilmacowen, in the County of Sligo, and at a remote time.

Scene: A room with a hearth on the floor in the middle of a deep alcove to the right. There are benches in the alcove and a table; and a crucifix on the wall. The alcove is full of a glow of light from the fire. There is an open door facing the audience to the left, and to the left of this a bench. Through the door one can see the forest. It is night, but the moon or a late sunset glimmers through the trees and carries the eye far off into a vague, mysterious world. MAURTEEN BRUIN, SHAWN BRUIN, and BRIDGET BRUIN sit in the alcove at the table or about the fire. They are dressed in the costume of some remote time, and near them sits an old priest, FATHER HART. He may be dressed as a friar. There is food and drink upon the table. MARY BRUIN stands by the door reading a book. If she looks up she can see through the door into the wood.

BRIDGET. Because I bid her clean the pots for supper,
    She took that old book down out of the thatch,
    She has been doubled over it ever since.
    We should be deafened by her groans and moans,
    Had she to work as some do, Father Hart,
    Get up at dawn like me and mend and scour;
    Or ride abroad in the boisterous night like you,
    The pyx and blessed bread under your arm.

SHAWN. Mother, you are too cross.

BRIDGET. You've married her,
    And fear to vex her and so take her part.

MAURTEEN [to FATHER HART]. It is but right that youth should
    side with youth;
    She quarrels with my wife a bit at times,
    And is too deep just now in the old book!
    (But do not blame her greatly; she will grow
    As quiet as a puff-ball in a tree
    When but the moons of marriage dawn and die
    For half a score of times.)[1]

FATHER HART. Their hearts are wild,
    As be the hearts of birds, till children come.

BRIDGET. She would not mind the kettle, milk the cow,
    Or even lay the knives and spread the cloth.

SHAWN. Mother, if only—

MAURTEEN. Shawn, this is half empty;
    Go, bring up the best bottle that we have.

FATHER HART. I never saw her read a book before,
    What can it be?

MAURTEEN [to SHAWN]. What are you waiting for?
    You must not shake it when you draw the cork;
    It's precious wine, so take your time about it. [SHAWN goes.]
    [To PRIEST.] (There was a Spaniard wrecked at Ocris Head,
    When I was young, and I have still some bottles.)
    He cannot bear to hear her blamed; the book
    Has lain up in the thatch these fifty years,
    My father told me my grandfather wrote it,
    And killed a heifer for the binding of it—
    (But supper's spread, and we can talk and eat.)
    It was little good he got out of the book,
    Because it filled his house with rambling fiddlers,
    And rambling ballad-makers and the like.
    The griddle-bread is there in front of you.
    Colleen, what is the wonder in that book,
    That you must leave the bread to cool? Had I
    Or had my father read or written books,
    There was no stocking stuffed with yellow guineas
    To come when I am dead to Shawn and you.

---

1. Amateurs perform this more often than any other play of mine, and I urge them to omit
all lines that I have enclosed in heavy round brackets ().—W.B.Y.

FATHER HART. You should not fill your head with foolish dreams.
    What are you reading?
MARY. How a Princess Edane,
    A daughter of a King of Ireland, heard
    A voice singing on a May Eve like this,
    And followed, half awake and half asleep,
    Until she came into the Land of Faery,
    Where nobody gets old and godly and grave,
    Where nobody gets old and crafty and wise,
    Where nobody gets old and bitter of tongue.
    And she is still there, busied with a dance,
    Deep in the dewy shadow of a wood,
    (Or where stars walk upon a mountain-top.)
MAURTEEN. Persuade the colleen to put down the book;
    My grandfather would mutter just such things,
    And he was no judge of a dog or a horse,
    And any idle boy could blarney him;
    Just speak your mind.
FATHER HART. Put it away, my colleen.
    (God spreads the heavens above us like great wings,
    And gives a little round of deeds and days,
    And then come the wrecked angels and set snares,
    And bait them with light hopes and heavy dreams,
    Until the heart is puffed with pride and goes
    Half shuddering and half joyous from God's peace;)
    And it was some wrecked angel, blind with tears,
    Who flattered Edane's heart with merry words.
    My colleen, I have seen some other girls
    Restless and ill at ease, but years went by
    And they grew like their neighbours and were glad
    In minding children, working at the churn,
    And gossiping of weddings and of wakes;
    (For life moves out of a red flare of dreams
    Into a common light of common hours,
    Until old age bring the red flare again.)
MAURTEEN. That's true—but she's too young to know it's true.
BRIDGET. She's old enough to know that it is wrong
    To mope and idle.
MAURTEEN. I've little blame for her;
    She's dull when my big son is in the fields,
    And that and maybe this good woman's tongue
    Have driven her to hide among her dreams
    Like children from the dark under the bed-clothes.
BRIDGET. She'd never do a turn if I were silent.

MAURTEEN.   And maybe it is natural upon May Eve
   To dream of the good people. But tell me, girl,
   If you've the branch of blessed quicken wood
   That women hang upon the post of the door
   That they may send good luck into the house?
   Remember they may steal new-married brides
   After the fall of twilight on May Eve,
   Or what old women mutter at the fire
   Is but a pack of lies.
FATHER HART.   It may be truth.
   We do not know the limit of those powers
   God has permitted to the evil spirits
   For some mysterious end. You have done right [*to* MARY].
   It's well to keep old innocent customs up.

[MARY BRUIN *has taken a bough of quicken wood from a seat and hung it on a nail in the door-post. A girl child strangely dressed, perhaps in faery green, comes out of the wood and takes it away.*]

MARY.   I had no sooner hung it on the nail
   Before a child ran up out of the wind;
   She has caught it in her hand and fondled it;
   (Her face is pale as water before dawn.)
FATHER HART.   Whose child can this be?
MAURTEEN.   No one's child at all.
   She often dreams that some one has gone by,
   When there was nothing but a puff of wind.
MARY.   They have taken away the blessed quicken wood,
   They will not bring good luck into the house;
   Yet I am glad that I was courteous to them,
   For are not they, likewise, children of God?
FATHER HART.   Colleen, they are the children of the fiend,
   And they have power until the end of Time,
   When God shall fight with them a great pitched battle
   And hack them into pieces.
MARY.   He will smile,
   Father, perhaps, and open His great door.
FATHER HART.   Did but the lawless angels see that door,
   They would fall, slain by everlasting peace
   And when such angels knock upon our doors,
   Who goes with them must drive through the same storm.

[*A thin old arm comes round the door-post and knocks and beckons. It is clearly seen in the silvery light.* MARY BRUIN *goes to door and stands in it for a moment.* MAURTEEN BRUIN *is busy filling* FATHER HART'S *plate.* BRIDGET BRUIN *stirs the fire.*]

MARY [*coming to table*].   There's somebody out there that beckoned me
      And raised her hand as though it held a cup,
      And she was drinking from it, so it may be
      That she is thirsty.

[*She takes milk from the table and carries it to the door.*]

FATHER HART.   That will be the child
      That you would have it was no child at all.
BRIDGET.   (And maybe, Father, what he said was true;
      For there is not another night in the year
      So wicked as tonight.
MAURTEEN.   Nothing can harm us
      While the good Father's underneath our roof.
MARY.   A little queer old woman dressed in green.
BRIDGET.   The good people beg for milk and fire,
      Upon May Eve—woe to the house that gives,
      For they have power upon it for a year.
MAURTEEN.   Hush, woman, hush!
BRIDGET.   She's given milk away.
      I knew she would bring evil on the house.
MAURTEEN.   Who was it?
MARY.   Both the tongue and face were strange.
MAURTEEN.   Some strangers came last week to Clover Hill;
      She must be one of them.)
BRIDGET.   I am afraid.
FATHER HART.   The Cross will keep all evil from the house
      While it hangs there.
MAURTEEN.   Come, sit beside me, colleen,
      And put away your dreams of discontent,
      For I would have you light up my last days,
      Like the good glow of the turf; and when I die
      You'll be the wealthiest hereabout, for, colleen,
      I have a stocking full of yellow guineas
      Hidden away where nobody can find it.
BRIDGET.   You are the fool of every pretty face,
      And I must spare and pinch that my son's wife
      May have all kinds of ribbons for her head.
MAURTEEN.   Do not be cross; she is a right good girl!
      (The butter is by your elbow, Father Hart.
      My colleen, have not Fate and Time and Change
      Done well for me and for old Bridget there?)
      We have a hundred acres of good land,

And sit beside each other at the fire.
 I have this reverend Father for my friend,
I look upon your face and my son's face—
We've put his plate by yours—and here he comes,
And brings with him the only thing we have lacked,
Abundance of good wine. [SHAWN *comes in.*] Stir up the fire,
And put new turf upon it till it blaze;
To watch the turf-smoke coiling from the fire,
And feel content and wisdom in your heart,
This is the best of life; (when we are young
We long to tread a way none trod before,
But find the excellent old way through love,
And through the care of children, to the hour
For bidding Fate and Time and Change good-bye.)

[MARY *stands for a moment in the door and then takes a sod of turf from
the fire and goes out through the door.* SHAWN *follows her and meets her
coming in.*]

SHAWN.   What is it draws you to the chill o' the wood?
    There is a light among the stems of the trees
    That makes one shiver.
MARY.   A little queer old man
    Made me a sign to show he wanted fire
    To light his pipe.
BRIDGET.   You've given milk and fire,
    Upon the unluckiest night of the year, and brought,
    For all you know, evil upon the house.
    Before you married you were idle and fine
    And went about with ribbons on your head;
    And now—no, Father, I will speak my mind,
    She is not a fitting wife for any man—
SHAWN.   Be quiet, Mother!
MAURTEEN.   You are much too cross.
MARY.   What do I care if I have given this house,
    Where I must hear all day a bitter tongue,
    Into the power of faeries!
BRIDGET.   You know well
    How calling the good people by that name,
    Or talking of them overmuch at all,
    May bring all kinds of evil on the house.
MARY.   Come, faeries, take me out of this dull house!
    Let me have all the freedom I have lost;

Work when I will and idle when I will!
Faeries, come take me out of this dull world,
For I would ride with you upon the wind.
(Run on the top of the dishevelled tide,)
And dance upon the mountains like a flame.

FATHER HART. You cannot know the meaning of your words.

MARY. Father, I am right weary of four tongues:
A tongue that is too crafty and too wise,
A tongue that is too godly and too grave,
A tongue that is more bitter than the tide,
And a kind tongue too full of drowsy love,
Of drowsy love and my captivity.

[SHAWN BRUIN *leads her to a seat at the left of the door.*]

SHAWN. Do not blame me; I often lie awake
Thinking that all things trouble your bright head.
How beautiful it is—your broad pale forehead
Under a cloudy blossoming of hair!
Sit down beside me here—these are too old,
And have forgotten they were ever young.

MARY. O, you are the great door-post of this house,
And I the branch of blessed quicken wood,
And if I could I'd hang upon the post,
Till I had brought good luck into the house.

[*She would put her arms about him, but looks shyly at the priest and lets her arms fall.*]

FATHER HART. My daughter, take his hand; by love alone
God binds us to Himself and to the hearth,
That shuts us from the waste beyond His peace
From maddening freedom and bewildering light.

SHAWN. Would that the world were mine to give it you,
And not its quiet hearths alone, but even
All that bewilderment of light and freedom.
If you would have it.

MARY. I would take the world
And break it into pieces in my hands
To see you smile watching it crumble away.

SHAWN. Then I would mould a world of fire and dew,
With no one bitter, grave, or over wise,
And nothing marred or old to do you wrong,
And crowd the enraptured quiet of the sky
With candles burning to your lonely face.

MARY. Your looks are all the candles that I need.

SHAWN.   Once a fly dancing in a beam of the sun,
    Or the light wind blowing out of the dawn,
    Could fill your heart with dreams none other knew,
    But now the indissoluble sacrament
    Has mixed your heart that was most proud and cold
    With my warm heart for ever; the sun and moon
    Must fade and heaven be rolled up like a scroll;
    But your white spirit still walk by my spirit.

[*A Voice singing in the wood.*]

MAURTEEN.   There's some one singing. Why, it's but a child.
    It sang, "The lonely of heart is withered away."
    A strange song for a child, but she sings sweetly,
    Listen, Listen!

[*Goes to door.*]

MARY.   O, cling close to me,
    Because I have said wicked things tonight.
THE VOICE.   The wind blows out of the gates of the day,
    The wind blows over the lonely of heart,
    And the lonely of heart is withered away!"
    While the faeries dance in a place apart,
    Shaking their milk-white feet in a ring,
    Tossing their milk-white arms in the air;
    For they hear the wind laugh and murmur and sing
    Of a land where even the old are fair,
    And even the wise are merry of tongue;
    But I heard a reed of Coolaney say,
    "When the wind has laughed and murmured and sung
    The lonely of heart is withered away!"
MAURTEEN.   Being happy, I would have all others happy,
    So I will bring her in out of the cold.

[*He brings in the faery child.*]

THE CHILD.   (I tire of winds and waters and pale lights.
MAURTEEN.   And that's no wonder, for when night has fallen)
    The wood's a cold and a bewildering place;
    But you are welcome here.
THE CHILD.   I am welcome here.
    (For when I tire of this warm little house,)
    There is one here that must away, away.
MAURTEEN.   O, listen to her dreamy and strange talk.
    Are you not cold?

THE CHILD.   I will crouch down beside you,
    For I have run a long, long way this night.
BRIDGET.   You have a comely shape.
MAURTEEN.   Your hair is wet.
BRIDGET.   I'll warm your chilly feet.
MAURTEEN.   You have come indeed
    A long, long way—for I have never seen
    Your pretty face—and must be tired and hungry,
    Here is some bread and wine.
THE CHILD.   The wine is bitter.
    Old mother, have you no sweet food for me?
BRIDGET.   I have some honey. [*She goes into the next room.*]
MAURTEEN.   You have coaxing ways,
    The mother was quite cross before you came.

[BRIDGET *returns with the honey and fills a porringer with milk.*]

BRIDGET.   She is the child of gentle people; look
    At her white hands and at her pretty dress.
    I've brought you some new milk, but wait a while
    And I will put it to the fire to warm,
    For things well fitted for poor folk like us
    Would never please a high-born child like you.
THE CHILD.   From dawn, when you must blow the fire ablaze,
    You work your fingers to the bone, old mother.
    The young may lie in bed and dream and hope,
    But you must work your fingers to the bone
    Because your heart is old.
BRIDGET.   The young are idle.
THE CHILD.   Your memories have made you wise, old father,
    The young must sigh through many a dream and hope,
    But you are wise because your heart is old.

[BRIDGET *gives her more bread and honey.*]

MAURTEEN.   O, who would think to find so young a girl
    Loving old age and wisdom?
THE CHILD.   No more, mother.
MAURTEEN.   What a small bite! The milk is ready now. [*Hands it
    to her.*]
    What a small sip!
THE CHILD.   Put on my shoes, old mother.
    Now I would like to dance, now I have eaten,
    The reeds are dancing by Coolaney lake,

And I would like to dance until the reeds
And the white waves have danced themselves asleep.
[BRIDGET *puts on the shoes, and the* CHILD *is about to dance, but suddenly sees the crucifix and shrieks and covers her eyes.*]
What is that ugly thing on the black cross?
FATHER HART.   You cannot know how naughty your words are!
    That is our Blessed Lord.
THE CHILD.   Hide it away.
BRIDGET.   I have begun to be afraid again.
THE CHILD.   Hide it away.
MAURTEEN.   That would be wickedness!
BRIDGET.   That would be sacrilege!
THE CHILD.   The tortured thing!
      Hide it away!
MAURTEEN.   Her parents are to blame.
FATHER HART.   That is the image of the Son of God.
THE CHILD [*caressing him*].   Hide it away, hide it away!
MAURTEEN.   No, no.
FATHER HART.   Because you are so young and like a bird,
    That must take fright at every stir of the leaves,
    I will go take it down.
THE CHILD.   Hide it away!
    And cover it out of sight and out of mind!

[FATHER HART *takes crucifix from wall and carries it towards inner room.*]

FATHER HART.   Since you have come into this barony,
    I will instruct you in our blessed faith;
    And being so keen-witted you'll soon learn.
    [*To the others.*]
    We must be tender to all budding things,
    Our Maker let no thought of Calvary
    Trouble the morning stars in their first song.

[*Puts crucifix in inner room.*]

THE CHILD.   Here is level ground for dancing; I will dance.
    [*Sings.*] "The wind blows out of the gates of the day,
    The wind blows over the lonely of heart,
    And the lonely of heart is withered away."

[*She dances.*]

MARY [*to* SHAWN].   Just now when she came near I thought I heard
    Other small steps beating upon the floor,

And a faint music blowing in the wind,
Invisible pipes giving her feet the tune.
SHAWN.   I heard no steps but hers.
MARY.   I hear them now,
The unholy powers are dancing in the house.
MAURTEEN.   Come over here, and if you promise me,
Not to talk wickedly of holy things,
I will give you something.
THE CHILD.   Bring it me, old father.
MAURTEEN.   Here are some ribbons that I bought in the town
For my son's wife—but she will let me give them
To tie up that wild hair the winds have tumbled.
THE CHILD.   Come, tell me, do you love me?
MAURTEEN.   Yes, I love you.
THE CHILD.   Ah, but you love this fireside. Do you love me?
FATHER HART.   When the Almighty puts so great a share
Of His own ageless youth into a creature,
To look is but to love.
THE CHILD.   But you love Him?
BRIDGET.   She is blaspheming.
THE CHILD.   And do you love me too?
MARY.   I do not know.
THE CHILD.   You love that young man there,
Yet I could make you ride upon the winds,
(Run on the top of the dishevelled tide,)
And dance upon the mountains like a flame.
MARY.   Queen of Angels and kind saints defend us!
Some dreadful thing will happen. A while ago
She took away the blessed quicken wood.
FATHER HART.   You fear because of her unmeasured prattle;
She knows no better. Child, how old are you?
THE CHILD.   When winter sleep is abroad my hair grows thin,
My feet unsteady. When the leaves awaken
My mother carries me in her golden arms;
I'll soon put on my womanhood and marry
The spirits of wood and water, but who can tell
When I was born for the first time? I think
I am much older than the eagle cock
(That blinks and blinks on Ballygawley Hill,)
And he is the oldest thing under the moon.
FATHER HART.   O she is of the faery people.
THE CHILD.   One called,
I sent my messengers for milk and fire,
She called again, and after that I came.

[ALL *except* SHAWN *and* MARY BRUIN *gather behind the priest for protection.*]

SHAWN [*rising*].   Though you have made all these obedient,
    You have not charmed my sight, and won from me
    A wish or gift to make you powerful;
    I'll turn you from the house.
FATHER HART.   No, I will face her.
THE CHILD.   Because you took away the crucifix
    I am so mighty that there's none can pass
    Unless I will it, where my feet have danced
    Or where I've whirled my fingertops.

[SHAWN *tries to approach her and cannot.*]

MAURTEEN.   Look, look!
    There something stops him—look how he moves his hands
    As though he rubbed them on a wall of glass!
FATHER HART.   I will confront this mighty spirit alone.
    Be not afraid, the Father is with us,
    (The Holy Martyrs and the Innocents,
    The adoring Magi in their coats of mail,)
    And He who died and rose on the third day,
    And all the nine angelic hierarchies.

[*The* CHILD *kneels upon the settle beside* MARY *and puts her arms about her.*]

    Cry, daughter, to the Angels and the Saints.
THE CHILD.   You shall go with me, newly-married bride,
    And gaze upon a merrier multitude.
    (White-armed Nuala, Aengus of the Birds,
    Feacra of the hurtling foam, and him
    Who is the ruler of the Western Host,
    Finvarra, and their Land of Heart's Desire,)
    Where beauty has no ebb, decay no flood,
    But joy is wisdom, Time an endless song.
    I kiss you and the world begins to fade.
SHAWN.   Awake out of that trance—and cover up
    Your eyes and ears.
FATHER HART.   She must both look and listen,
    For only the soul's choice can save her now.
    Come over to me, daughter; stand beside me;
    Think of this house and of your duties in it.
THE CHILD.   Stay and come with me, newly-married bride,
    For if you hear him you grow like the rest,
    Bear children, cook, and bend above the churn,
    And wrangle over butter, fowl, and eggs,

Until at last, grown old and bitter of tongue,
You're crouching there and shivering at the grave.

FATHER HART.   Daughter, I point you out the way to Heaven.

THE CHILD.   But I can lead you, newly-married bride,
Where nobody gets old and crafty and wise,
Where nobody gets old and godly and grave,
Where nobody gets old and bitter of tongue,
And where kind tongues bring no captivity;
For we are but obedient to the thoughts
That drift into the mind at a wink of the eye.

FATHER HART.   By the dear Name of the One crucified,
I bid you, Mary Bruin, come to me.

THE CHILD.   I keep you in the name of your own heart.

FATHER HART.   Because I put away the crucifix
That I am nothing, and my power is nothing,
I'll bring it here again.

MAURTEEN [*clinging to him*].   No!

BRIDGET.   Do not leave us.

FATHER HART.   O, let me go before it is too late;
It is my sin alone that brought it all.

[*Singing outside.*]

THE CHILD.   I hear them sing, "Come, newly-married bride,
Come, to the woods and waters and pale lights."

MARY.   I will go with you.

FATHER HART.   She is lost, alas!

THE CHILD [*standing by the door*].   But clinging mortal hope must
fall from you,
For we who ride the winds, run on the waves,
And dance upon the mountains are more light
Than dew-drops on the banner of the dawn.

MARY.   O, take me with you.

SHAWN.   Beloved, I will keep you.
I've more than words, I have these arms to hold you,
Nor all the faery host, do what they please,
Can ever loosen you from these arms.

MARY.   Dear face! Dear voice!

THE CHILD.   Come, newly-married bride.

MARY.   I always loved her world—and yet—and yet—

THE CHILD.   White bird, white bird, come with me, little bird.

MARY.   She is calling me!

THE CHILD.   Come with me, little bird.

[*Distant dancing figures appear in the wood.*]

MARY.   I can hear songs and dancing.
SHAWN.   Stay with me.
MARY.   I think that I would stay—and yet—and yet—
THE CHILD.   Come, little bird, with crest of gold.
MARY [*very soft*].   And yet—
THE CHILD.   Come, little bird with silver feet!

[MARY BRUIN *dies, and the* CHILD *goes.*]

SHAWN.   She is dead!
BRIDGET.   Come from that image; body and soul are gone;
        You have thrown your arms about a drift of leaves,
        Or bole of an ash tree changed into her image.
FATHER HART.   Thus do the spirits of evil snatch their prey,
        Almost out of the very hand of God;
        And day by day their power is more and more,
        And men and women leave old paths, for pride
        Comes knocking with thin knuckles on the heart.

[*Outside there are dancing figures, and it may be a white bird, and many voices singing.*]

        "The wind blows out of the gates of the day,
        The wind blows over the lonely of heart,
        And the lonely of heart is withered away;
        (While the faeries dance in a place apart,
        Shaking their milk-white feet in a ring,
        Tossing their milk-white arms in the air;
        For they hear the wind laugh and murmur and sing
        Of a land where even the old are fair,
        And even the wise are merry of tongue;
        But I heard a reed of Coolaney say—
        'When the wind has laughed and murmured and sung,
        The lonely of heart is withered away.'")

CURTAIN

RIDERS TO THE SEA
J. M. Synge

CAST OF CHARACTERS

MAURYA, an old woman
BARTLEY, her son
CATHLEEN, her daughter
NORA, a younger daughter
MEN AND WOMEN

Scene: An island off the West of Ireland. (Cottage kitchen, with nets, oil-skins, spinning-wheel, some new boards standing by the wall, etc. CATHLEEN, *a girl of about twenty, finishes kneading cake, and puts it down in the pot-oven by the fire; then wipes her hands, and begins to spin at the wheel.* NORA, *a young girl, puts her head in at the door.)*

NORA [*in a low voice*]. Where is she?
CATHLEEN. She's lying down, God help her, and may be sleeping, if she's able.

[NORA *comes in softly, and takes a bundle from under her shawl.*]

CATHLEEN [*spinning the wheel rapidly*]. What is it you have?
NORA. The young priest is after bringing them. It's a shirt and a plain stocking were got off a drowned man in Donegal.

[CATHLEEN *stops her wheel with a sudden movement, and leans out to listen.*]

NORA. We're to find out if it's Michael's they are, some time herself will be down looking by the sea.
CATHLEEN. How would they be Michael's, Nora? How would he go the length of that way to the far north?
NORA. The young priest says he's known the like of it. "If it's Michael's they are," says he, "you can tell herself he's got a clean burial by the grace of God, and if they're not his, let no one say a word about them, for she'll be getting her death," says he, "with crying and lamenting."

[*The door which* NORA *half closed is blown open by a gust of wind.*]

CATHLEEN [*looking out anxiously*]. Did you ask him would he stop
   BARTLEY going this day with the horses to the Galway fair?
NORA. "I won't stop him," says he, "but let you not be afraid.
   Herself does be saying prayers half through the night, and the
   Almighty God won't leave her destitute," says he, "with no
   son living."
CATHLEEN. Is the sea bad by the white rocks, Nora?
NORA. Middling bad, God help us. There's a great roaring in the west,
   and it's worse it'll be getting when the tide's turned to the wind. [*She
   goes over to the table with the bundle.*] Shall I open it now?
CATHLEEN. Maybe she'd wake up on us, and come in before we'd
   done. [*Coming to the table.*] It's a long time we'll be, and the two
   of us crying.
NORA [*goes to the inner door and listens*]. She's moving about on the
   bed. She'll be coming in a minute.
CATHLEEN. Give me the ladder, and I'll put them up in the turf-
   loft, the way she won't know of them at all, and maybe when
   the tide turns she'll be going down to see would he be floating
   from the east.

[*They put the ladder against the gable of the chimney;* CATHLEEN *goes up
a few steps and hides the bundle in the turf-loft.* MAURYA *comes from the
inner room.*]

MAURYA [*looking up at* CATHLEEN *and speaking querulously*]. Isn't it
   turf enough you have for this day and evening?
CATHLEEN. There's a cake baking at the fire for a short space [*throwing down the turf*] and Bartley will want it when the tide turns if
   he goes to Connemara.

[NORA *picks up the turf and puts it round the pot-oven.*]

MAURYA [*sitting down on a stool at the fire*]. He won't go this day with
   the wind rising from the south and west. He won't go this day, for
   the young priest will stop him surely.
NORA. He'll not stop him, mother, and I heard Eamon Simon and
   Stephen Pheety and Colum Shawn saying he would go.
MAURYA. Where is he itself?
NORA. He went down to see would there be another boat sailing in
   the week, and I'm thinking it won't be long till he's here now, for
   the tide's turning at the green head, and the hooker's tacking from
   the east.
CATHLEEN. I hear some one passing the big stones.

NORA [*looking out*].   He's coming now, and he in a hurry.

BARTLEY [*comes in and looks round the room; speaking sadly and quietly*].   Where is the bit of new rope, Cathleen, was bought in Connemara?

CATHLEEN [*coming down*].   Give it to him, NORA; it's on a nail by the white boards. I hung it up this morning, for the pig with the black feet was eating it.

NORA [*giving him a rope*].   Is that it, Bartley?

MAURYA.   You'd do right to leave that rope, Bartley, hanging by the boards. [BARTLEY *takes the rope.*] It will be wanting in this place, I'm telling you, if Michael is washed up tomorrow morning, or the next morning, or any morning in the week, for it's a deep grave we'll make him by the grace of God.

BARTLEY [*beginning to work with the rope*].   I've no halter the way I can ride down on the mare, and I must go now quickly. This is the one boat going for two weeks or beyond it, and the fair will be a good fair for horses, I heard them saying below.

MAURYA.   It's a hard thing they'll be saying below if the body is washed up and there's no man in it to make the coffin, and I after giving a big price for the finest white boards you'd find in Connemara.

[*She looks round at the boards.*]

BARTLEY.   How would it be washed up, and we after looking each day for nine days, and a strong wind blowing a while back from the west and south?

MAURYA.   If it wasn't found itself, that wind is raising the sea, and there was a star up against the moon, and it rising in the night. If it was a hundred horses, or a thousand horses you had itself, what is the price of a thousand horses against a son where there is one son only?

BARTLEY [*working at the halter, to* CATHLEEN].   Let you go down each day, and see the sheep aren't jumping in on the rye, and if the jobber comes you can sell the pig with the black feet if there is a good price going.

MAURYA.   How would the like of her get a good price for a pig?

BARTLEY [*to* CATHLEEN].   If the west wind holds with the last bit of the moon let you and Nora get up weed enough for another cock for the kelp. It's hard set we'll be from this day with no one in it but one man to work.

MAURYA.   It's hard set we'll be surely the day you're drownd'd with the rest. What way will I live and the girls with me, and I an old woman looking for the grave?

[BARTLEY *lays down the halter, takes off his old coat, and puts on a newer one of the same flannel.*]

BARTLEY [*to* NORA].   Is she coming to the pier?

NORA [*looking out*].   She's passing the green head and letting fall her sails.

BARTLEY [*getting his purse and tobacco*].   I'll have half an hour to go down, and you'll see me coming again in two days, or in three days, or maybe in four days if the wind is bad.

MAURYA [*turning round to the fire, and putting her shawl over her head*].   Isn't it a hard and cruel man won't hear a word from an old woman, and she holding him from the sea?

CATHLEEN.   It's the life of a young man to be going on the sea, and who would listen to an old woman with one thing and she saying it over?

BARTLEY [*taking the halter*].   I must go now quickly. I'll ride down on the red mare, and the gray pony'll run behind me. The blessing of God on you.

[*He goes out.*]

MAURYA [*crying out as he is in the door*].   He's gone now, God spare us, and we'll not see him again. He's gone now, and when the black night is falling I'll have no son left me in the world.

CATHLEEN.   Why wouldn't you give him your blessing and he looking round in the door? Isn't it sorrow enough is on every one in this house without your sending him out with an unlucky word behind him, and a hard word in his ear?

[MAURYA *takes up the tongs and begins raking the fire aimlessly without looking round.*]

NORA [*turning towards her*].   You're taking away the turf from the cake.

CATHLEEN [*crying out*].   The Son of God forgive us, Nora, we're after forgetting his bit of bread.

[*She comes over to the fire.*]

NORA.   And it's destroyed he'll be going till dark night, and he after eating nothing since the sun went up.

CATHLEEN [*turning the cake out of the oven*].   It's destroyed he'll be, surely. There's no sense left on any person in a house where an old woman will be talking for ever.

[MAURYA *sways herself on her stool.*]

CATHLEEN [*cutting off some of the bread and rolling it in a cloth, to* MAURYA].   Let you go down now to the spring well and give him this and he passing. You'll see him then and the dark word will be broken, and you can say, "God speed you," the way he'll be easy in his mind.

MAURYA [*taking the bread*].   Will I be in it as soon as himself?

CATHLEEN.   If you go now quickly.

MAURYA [*standing up unsteadily*].   It's hard set I am to walk.

CATHLEEN [*looking at her anxiously*].   Give her the stick, Nora, or maybe she'll slip on the big stones.

NORA.   What stick?

CATHLEEN.   The stick Michael brought from Connemara.

MAURYA [*taking a stick Nora gives her*].   In the big world the old people do be leaving things after them for their sons and children, but in this place it is the young men do be leaving things behind for them that do be old.

[*She goes out slowly. NORA goes over to the ladder.*]

CATHLEEN.   Wait, NORA, maybe she'd turn back quickly. She's that sorry, God help her, you wouldn't know the thing she'd do.

NORA.   Is she gone round by the bush?

CATHLEEN [*looking out*].   She's gone now. Throw it down quickly, for the Lord knows when she'll be out of it again.

NORA [*getting the bundle from the loft*].   The young priest said he'd be passing tomorrow, and we might go down and speak to him below if it's Michael's they are surely.

CATHLEEN [*taking the bundle*].   Did he say what way they were found?

NORA [*coming down*].   "There were two men," says he, "and they rowing round with poteen before the cocks crowed, and the oar of one of them caught the body, and they passing the black cliffs of the north."

CATHLEEN [*trying to open the bundle*].   Give me a knife, NORA; the string's perished with the salt water, and there's a black knot on it you wouldn't loosen in a week.

NORA [*giving her a knife*].   I've heard tell it was a long way to Donegal.

CATHLEEN [*cutting the string*].   It is surely. There was a man in here a while ago—the man sold us that knife—and he said if you set off walking from the rocks beyond, it would be seven days you'd be in Donegal.

NORA.   And what time would a man take, and he floating?

[CATHLEEN *opens the bundle and takes out a bit of a stocking. They look at them eagerly.*]

CATHLEEN [*in a low voice*].   The Lord spare us, NORA! Isn't it a queer hard thing to say if it's his they are surely?

NORA. I'll get his shirt off the hook the way we can put the one flannel on the other. [*She looks through some clothes hanging in the corner.*] It's not with them, Cathleen, and where will it be?

CATHLEEN. I'm thinking Bartley put it on him in the morning, for his own shirt was heavy with the salt in it [*pointing to the corner.*] There's a bit of a sleeve was of the same stuff. Give me that and it will do.

[NORA *brings it to her and they compare the flannel.*]

CATHLEEN. It's the same stuff, Nora; but if it is itself, aren't there great rolls of it in the shops of Galway, and isn't it many another man may have a shirt of it as well as Michael himself?

NORA [*who has taken up the stocking and counted the stitches, crying out*]. It's Michael, Cathleen, it's Michael; God spare his soul and what will herself say when she hears this story, and Bartley on the sea?

CATHLEEN [*taking the stocking*]. It's a plain stocking.

NORA. It's the second one of the third pair I knitted, and I put up three score stitches, and I dropped four of them.

CATHLEEN [*counts the stitches*]. It's that number is in it [*crying out.*] Ah, Nora, isn't it a bitter thing to think of him floating that way to the far north, and no one to keen him but the black hags that do be flying on the sea?

NORA [*swinging herself round, and throwing out her arms on the clothes*]. And isn't it a pitiful thing when there is nothing left of a man who was a great rower and fisher, but a bit of an old shirt and a plain stocking?

CATHLEEN [*after an instant*]. Tell me is herself coming, Nora? I hear a little sound on the path.

NORA [*looking out*]. She is, Cathleen. She's coming up to the door.

CATHLEEN. Put these things away before she'll come in. Maybe it's easier she'll be after giving her blessing to Bartley, and we won't let on we've heard anything the time he's on the sea.

NORA [*helping CATHLEEN to close the bundle*]. We'll put them here in the corner.

[*They put them into a hole in the chimney corner.* CATHLEEN *goes back to the spinning-wheel.*]

NORA. Will she see it was crying I was?

CATHLEEN. Keep your back to the door the way the light'll not be on you.

[NORA *sits down at the chimney corner, with her back to the door.* MAURYA *comes in very slowly, without looking at the girls, and goes over to her stool at the other side of the fire. The cloth with the bread is still in her hand. The girls look at each other, and* NORA *points to the bundle of bread.*]

CATHLEEN [*after spinning for a moment*]. You didn't give him his bit of bread?

[*MAURYA begins to keen softly, without turning round.*]

CATHLEEN. Did you see him riding down?

[MAURYA *goes on keening.*]

CATHLEEN [*a little impatiently*]. God forgive you; isn't it a better thing to raise your voice and tell what you seen, than to be making lamentation for a thing that's done? Did you see Bartley, I'm saying to you.

MAURYA [*with a weak voice*]. My heart's broken from this day.

CATHLEEN [*as before*]. Did you see Bartley?

MAURYA. I seen the fearfulest thing.

CATHLEEN [*leaves her wheel and looks out*]. God forgive you; he's riding the mare now over the green head, and the gray pony behind him.

MAURYA [*starts, so that her shawl falls back from her head and shows her white tossed hair. With a frightened voice*]. The gray pony behind him.

CATHLEEN [*coming to the fire*]. What is it ails you, at all?

MAURYA [*speaking very slowly*]. I've seen the fearfulest thing any person has seen, since the day Bride Dara seen the dead man with the child in his arms.

CATHLEEN AND NORA. Uah.

[*They crouch down in front of the old woman at the fire.*]

NORA. Tell us what it is you seen.

MAURYA. I went down to the springwell, and I stood there saying a prayer to myself. Then Bartley came along, and he riding on the red mare with the gray pony behind him [*she puts up her hands, as if to hide something from her eyes.*] The Son of God spare us, Nora!

CATHLEEN. What is it you seen?

MAURYA. I seen Michael himself.

CATHLEEN [*speaking softly*]. You did not, mother; it wasn't Michael you seen, for his body is after being found in the far north, and he's got a clean burial by the grace of God.

MAURYA [*a little defiantly*]. I'm after seeing him this day, and he riding and galloping. Bartley came first on the red mare; and I tried to say "God speed you," but something choked the words in my throat. He went by quickly; and, "the blessing of God on you," says he, and I could say nothing. I looked up then, and I crying, at the gray pony, and there was Michael upon it—with fine clothes on him, and new shoes on his feet.

CATHLEEN [*begins to keen*].   It's destroyed we are from this day. It's destroyed, surely.

NORA.   Didn't the young priest say the Almighty God wouldn't leave her destitute with no son living?

MAURYA [*in a low voice, but clearly*].   It's little the like of him knows of the sea.... Bartley will be lost now, and let you call in Eamon and make me a good coffin out of the white boards, for I won't live after them. I've had a husband, and a husband's father, and six sons in this house—six fine men, though it was a hard birth I had with every one of them and they coming to the world—and some of them were found and some of them were not found, but they're gone now, the lot of them.... There were Stephen, and Shawn, were lost in the great wind, and found after in the Bay of Gregory of the Golden Mouth, and carried up the two of them on the one plank, and in by that door.

[*She pauses for a moment, the girls start as if they heard something through the door that is half-open behind them.*]

NORA [*in a whisper*].   Did you hear that, Cathleen? Did you hear a noise in the northeast?

CATHLEEN [*in a whisper*].   There's some one after crying out by the seashore.

MAURYA [*continues without hearing anything*].   There was Sheamus and his father, and his own father again, were lost in a dark night, and not a stick or sign was seen of them when the sun went up. There was Patch after was drowned out of a curagh that turned over. I was sitting here with Bartley, and he a baby, lying on my two knees, and I seen two women, and three women, and four women coming in, and they crossing themselves, and not saying a word. I looked out then, and there were men coming after them, and they holding a thing in the half of a red sail, and water dripping out of it—it was a dry day, Nora—and leaving a track to the door.

[*She pauses again with her hand stretched out towards the door. It opens softly and old women begin to come in, crossing themselves on the threshold, and kneeling down in front of the stage with red petticoats over their heads.*]

MAURYA [*half in a dream, to* CATHLEEN].   Is it Patch, or Michael, or what is it at all?

CATHLEEN. Michael is after being found in the far north, and when he is found there how could he be here in this place?

MAURYA. There does be a power of young men floating round in the sea, and what way would they know if it was Michael they had, or another man like him, for when a man is nine days in the sea, and the wind blowing, it's hard set his own mother would be to say what man was it.

CATHLEEN. It's Michael, God spare him, for they're after sending us a bit of his clothes from the far north.

[*She reaches out and hands* MAURYA *the clothes that belonged to* MICHAEL. MAURYA *stands up slowly, and takes them in her hands.* NORA *looks out.*]

NORA. They're carrying a thing among them and there's water dripping out of it and leaving a track by the big stones.

CATHLEEN [*in a whisper to the women who have come in*]. Is it Bartley it is?

ONE OF THE WOMEN. It is surely, God rest his soul.

[*Two younger women come in and pull out the table. Then men carry in the body of* BARTLEY, *laid on a plank, with a bit of a sail over it, and lay it on the table.*]

CATHLEEN [*to the women, as they are doing so*]. What way was he drowned?

ONE OF THE WOMEN. The gray pony knocked him into the sea, and he was washed out where there is a great surf on the white rocks.

[MAURYA *has gone over and knelt down at the head of the table. The women are keening softly and swaying themselves with a slow movement.* CATHLEEN *and* NORA *kneel at the other end of the table. The men kneel near the door.*]

MAURYA [*raising her head and speaking as if she did not see the people around her*]. They're all gone now, and there isn't anything more the sea can do to me.... I'll have no call now to be up crying and praying when the wind breaks from the south, and you can hear the surf is in the east, and the surf is in the west, making a great stir with the two noises, and they hitting one on the other. I'll have no call now to be going down and getting Holy Water in the dark nights after Samhain, and I won't care what way the sea is when the other women will be keening. [*To* NORA.] Give me the Holy Water, Nora, there's a small sup still on the dresser.

[NORA *gives it to her.*]

MAURYA [*drops* MICHAEL'S *clothes across* BARTLEY'S *feet, and sprinkles the Holy Water over him*].   It isn't that I haven't prayed for you, Bartley, to the Almighty God. It isn't that I haven't said prayers in the dark night till you wouldn't know what I'd be saying; but it's a great rest I'll have now, and it's time surely. It's a great rest I'll have now, and great sleeping in the long nights after Samhain, if it's only a bit of wet flour we do have to eat, and maybe a fish that would be stinking.

[*She kneels down again, crossing herself, and saying prayers under her breath.*]

CATHLEEN [*to an old man*].   Maybe yourself and Eamon would make a coffin when the sun rises. We have fine white boards herself bought, God help her, thinking Michael would be found, and I have a new cake you can eat while you'll be working.

THE OLD MAN [*looking at the boards*].   Are there nails with them?

CATHLEEN.   There are not, Colum; we didn't think of the nails.

ANOTHER MAN.   It's a great wonder she wouldn't think of the nails, and all the coffins she's seen made already.

CATHLEEN.   It's getting old she is, and broken.

[*MAURYA stands up again very slowly and spreads out the pieces of MICHAEL'S clothes beside the body, sprinkling them with the last of the Holy Water.*]

NORA [*in a whisper to* CATHLEEN].   She's quiet now and easy; but the day Michael was drowned you could hear her crying out from this to the spring well. It's fonder she was of Michael, and would any one have thought that?

CATHLEEN [*slowly and clearly*].   An old woman will be soon tired with anything she will do, and isn't it nine days herself is after crying and keening, and making great sorrow in the house?

MAURYA [*puts the empty cup mouth downwards on the table, and lays her hands together on* BARTLEY'S *feet*].   They're all together this time, and the end is come. May the Almighty God have mercy on Bartley's soul, and on Michael's soul, and on the souls of Sheamus and Patch, and Stephen and Shawn [*bending her head*]; and may He have mercy on my soul, Nora, and on the soul of everyone is left living in the world.

[*She pauses, and the keen rises a little more loudly from the women, then sinks away.*]

MAURYA [*continuing*].   Michael has a clean burial in the far north, by the grace of the Almighty God. Bartley will have a fine coffin out of the white boards, and a deep grave surely. What more can we want than that? No man at all can be living for ever, and we must be satisfied.

[*She kneels down again, and the curtain falls slowly.*]

CURTAIN

THE STRONGER
August Strindberg

CAST OF CHARACTERS

MME X., an actress, married
MLLE Y., an actress, unmarried
A WAITRESS

Scene—The corner of a ladies' cafe. Two little iron tables, a red velvet sofa, several chairs. Enter MME X., *dressed in winter clothes, carrying a Japanese basket on her arm.*

[MLLE Y. *sits with a half empty beer bottle before her, reading an illustrated paper, which she changes later for another.*]

MME X. Good afternoon, Amelie. You're sitting here alone on Christmas eve like a poor bachelor!

MLLE Y. [*Looks up, nods, and resumes her reading.*]

MME X. Do you know it really hurts me to see you like this, alone, in a cafe, and on Christmas eve, too. It makes me feel as I did one time when I saw a bridal party in a Paris restaurant, and the bride sat reading a comic paper, while the groom played billiards with the witnesses. Huh, thought I, with such a beginning, what will follow, and what will be the end? He played billiards on his wedding eve! [MLLE Y. *starts to speak*]. And she read a comic paper, you mean? Well, they are not altogether the same thing.

[*A* WAITRESS *enters, places a cup of chocolate before* MME X. *and goes out.*]

MME X. You know what, Amelie! I believe you would have done better to have kept him! Do you remember, I was the first to say "Forgive him?" Do you remember that? You would be married now and have a home. Remember that Christmas when you went out to visit your fiance's parents in the country? How you gloried in the happiness of home life and really longed to quit

103

the theatre forever? Yes, Amelie dear, home is the best of all, the theatre next and children—well, you don't understand that.

MLLE Y.   [*Looks up scornfully.*]

[MME X. *sips a few spoonfuls out of the cup, then opens her basket and shows Christmas presents.*]

MME X.   Now you shall see what I bought for my piggywigs. [*Takes up a doll.*] Look at this! This is for Lisa, ha! Do you see how she can roll her eyes and turn her head, eh? And here is Maja's popgun.[*Loads it and shoots at* MLLE Y.]

MLLE Y.   [*Makes a startled gesture.*]

MME X.   Did I frighten you? Do you think I would like to shoot you, eh? On my soul, if I don't think you did! If you wanted to shoot *me* it wouldn't be so surprising, because I stood in your way—and I know you can never forget that—although I was absolutely innocent. You still believe I intrigued and got you out of the Stora theatre, but I didn't. I didn't do that, although you think so. Well, it doesn't make any difference what I say to you. You still believe I did it. [*Takes up a pair of embroidered slippers.*] And these are for my better half. I embroidered them myself—I can't bear tulips, but he wants tulips on everything.

MLLE Y.   [*Looks up ironically and curiously.*]

MME X [*putting a hand in each slipper*].   See what little feet Bob has! What? And you should see what a splendid stride he has! You've never seen him in slippers! [MLLE Y. *laughs aloud.*] Look! [*She makes the slippers walk on the table.* MLLE Y. *laughs loudly.*] And when he is grumpy he stamps like this with his foot. "What! Damn those servants who can never learn to make coffee. Oh, now those creatures haven't trimmed the lamp wick properly!" And then there are draughts on the floor and his feet are cold. "Ugh, how cold it is; the stupid idiots can never keep the fire going." [*She rubs the slippers together, one sole over the other.*]

MLLE Y.   [*Shrieks with laughter.*]

MME X.   And then he comes home and has to hunt for his slippers which Marie has stuck under the chiffonier—oh, but it's sinful to sit here and make fun of one's husband this way when he is kind and a good little man. You ought to have had such a husband, Amelie. What are you laughing at? What? What? And you see he's true to me. Yes, I'm sure of that, because he told me himself—what are you laughing at?—that when I was touring in Norway that that brazen Frêdêrique came and wanted to seduce him! Can you fancy anything so infamous? [*Pause.*] I'd have torn her eyes

out if she had come to see him when I was at home. [*Pause.*] It
was lucky that Bob told me about it himself and that it didn't
reach me through gossip. [*Pause.*] But would you believe it,
Frêdêrique wasn't the only one! I don't know why, but the
women are crazy about my husband. They must think he has influence about getting them theatrical engagements, because he is
connected with the government. Perhaps you were after him
yourself. I didn't use to trust you any too much. But now I know
he never bothered his head about you, and you always seemed to
have a grudge against him someway.

[*Pause. They look at each other in a puzzled way.*]

MME X.   Come and see us this evening, Amelie, and show us that
you're not put out with us—not put out with me at any rate. I
don't know, but I think it would be uncomfortable to have you
for an enemy. Perhaps it's because I stood in your way [*rallentando*]
or—I really—don't know why—in particular.

[*Pause. Mlle Y. stares at MME X curiously.*]

MME X. [*thoughtfully*].   Our acquaintance has been so queer. When I
saw you for the first time I was afraid of you, so afraid that I didn't
dare let you out of my sight; no matter when or where, I always
found myself near you—I didn't dare have you for an enemy, so I
became your friend. But there was always discord when you came
to our house, because I saw that my husband couldn't endure you,
and the whole thing seemed as awry to me as an ill-fitting
gown—and I did all I could to make him friendly toward you, but
with no success until you became engaged. Then came a violent
friendship between you, so that it looked all at once as though
you both dared show your real feelings only when you were secure—and then—how was it later? I didn't get jealous—strange
to say! And I remember at the christening, when you acted as
godmother, I made him kiss you—he did so, and you became so
confused—as it were; I didn't notice it then—didn't think about
it later, either—have never thought about it until—now! [*Rises
suddenly.*] Why are you silent? You haven't said a word this whole
time, but you have let me go on talking! You have sat there, and
your eyes have reeled out of me all these thoughts which lay like
raw silk in its cocoon—thoughts—suspicious thoughts, perhaps.
Let me see—why did you break your engagement? Why do you
never come to our house any more? Why won't you come to see
us tonight?

[MLLE Y. *appears as if about to speak.*]

MME X. Hush, you needn't speak—I understand it all! It was because—and because—and because! Yes, yes! Now all the ac-
counts balance. That's it. Fie, I won't sit at the same table with
you. [*Moves her things to another table.*] That's the reason I had to
embroider tulips—which I hate—on his slippers, because you
are fond of tulips; that's why [*Throws slippers on the floor*] we go
to Lake Mälarn in the summer, because you don't like salt
water; that's why my boy is named Eskil—because it's your
father's name; that's why I wear your colors, read your authors,
eat your favorite dishes, drink your drinks—chocolate, for instance; that's why—oh—my God—it's terrible, when I think
about it; it's terrible. Everything, everything came from you to
me, even your passions. Your soul crept into mine, like a worm
into an apple, ate and ate, bored and bored, until nothing was
left but the rind and a little black dust within. I wanted to get
away from you, but I couldn't; you lay like a snake and charmed
me with your black eyes; I felt that when I lifted my wings they
only dragged me down; I lay in the water with bound feet, and
the stronger I strove to keep up the deeper I worked myself
down, down, until I sank to the bottom, where you lay like a
giant crab to clutch me in your claws—and there I am lying
now.

I hate you, hate you, hate you! And you only sit there silent—silent and indifferent; indifferent whether it's new moon
or waning moon, Christmas or New Year's, whether others are
happy or unhappy; without power to hate or to love; as quiet
as a stork by a rat hole—you couldn't scent your prey and cap-
ture it, but you could lie in wait for it! You sit here in your
corner of the café—did you know it's called "The Rat Trap" for
you?—and read the papers to see if misfortune hasn't befallen
some one, to see if some one hasn't been given notice at the
theatre, perhaps; you sit here and calculate about your next
victim and reckon on your chances of recompense like a pilot in
a shipwreck. Poor Amelie, I pity you, nevertheless, because I
know you are unhappy, unhappy like one who has been
wounded, and angry because you are wounded. I can't be angry
with you, no matter how much I want to be—because you
come out the weaker one. Yes, all that with Bob doesn't trouble
me. What is that to me, after all? And what difference does it
make whether I learned to drink chocolate from you or some
one else. [*Sips a spoonful from her cup.*]

Besides, chocolate is very healthful. And if you taught me how to dress—tant mieux!—that has only made me more attractive to my husband; so you lost and I won there. Well, judging by certain signs, I believe you have already lost him; and you certainly intended that I should leave him—do as you did with your fiancé and regret as you now regret; but, you see, I don't do that—we mustn't be too exacting. And why should I take only what no one else wants?

Perhaps, take it all in all, I am at this moment the stronger one. You received nothing from me, but you gave me much. And now I seem like a thief since you have awakened and find I possess what is your loss. How could it be otherwise when everything is worthless and sterile in your hands? You can never keep a man's love with your tulips and your passions—but I can keep it. You can't learn how to live from your authors, as I have learned. You have no little Eskil to cherish, even if your father's name was Eskil. And why are you always silent, silent, silent? I thought that was strength, but perhaps it is because you have nothing to say! Because you never think about anything! [*Rises and picks up slippers.*]

Now I'm going home—and take the tulips with me—*your* tulips! You are unable to learn from another; you can't bend—therefore, you broke like a dry stalk. But I won't break! Thank you, Amelie, for all your good lessons. Thanks for teaching my husband how to love. Now I'm going home to love him. [*Goes.*]

CURTAIN

A FLORENTINE TRAGEDY

Oscar Wilde

CAST OF CHARACTERS

GUIDO BARDI, A Florentine prince
SIMONE, a merchant
BIANCA, his wife

Scene: Florence in the early sixteenth century.

[*Enter the husband.*]

SIMONE.   My good wife, you come slowly; were it not better to run to meet your lord? Here, take my cloak. Take this pack first. 'Tis heavy. I have sold nothing: Save a furred robe unto the Cardinal's son, who hopes to wear it when his father dies, and hopes that will be soon. But who is this? Why you have here some friend. Some kinsman doubtless, newly returned from foreign lands and fallen upon a house without a host to greet him? I crave your pardon, kinsman. For a house lacking a host is but an empty thing and void of honour; a cup without its wine, a scabbard without steel to keep it straight, a flowerless garden widowed of the sun. Again I crave your pardon, my sweet cousin.

BIANCA.   This is no kinsman and no cousin neither.

SIMONE.   No kinsman, and no cousin! You amaze me. Who is it then who with such courtly grace deigns to accept our hospitalities?

GUIDO.   My name is Guido Bardi.

SIMONE.   What! The son of that great Lord of Florence whose dim towers like shadows silvered by the wandering moon I see from out my casement every night! Sir Guido Bardi, you are welcome here, twice welcome. For I trust my honest wife, most honest if uncomely to the eye, hath not with foolish chatterings wearied you, as is the wont of women.

GUIDO.   Your gracious lady, whose beauty is a lamp that pales the stars and robs Diana's quiver of her beams has welcomed me with

such sweet courtesies that if it be her pleasure, and your own, I
will come often to your simple house. And when your business
bids you walk abroad I will sit here and charm her loneliness lest
she might sorrow for you overmuch. What say you, good
Simone!

SIMONE. My noble Lord, you bring me such high honour that my
tongue like a slave's tongue is tied, and cannot say the word it
would. Yet not to give you thanks were to be too unmannerly. So,
I thank you, from my heart's core. It is such things as these that
knit a state together, when a Prince so nobly born and of such fair
address, forgetting unjust Fortune's differences, comes to an honest burgher's honest home as a most honest friend.

And yet, my Lord, I fear I am too bold. Some other night we
trust that you will come here as a friend; tonight you come to buy
my merchandise. Is it not so? Silks, velvets, what you will, I doubt
not but I have some dainty wares will woo your fancy. True, the
hour is late, but we poor merchants toil both night and day to
make our scanty gains. The tolls are high, and every city levies its
own toll, and prentices are unskilful, and wives even lack sense
and cunning, though Bianca here has brought me a rich customer
tonight. Is it not so, Bianca?

But I waste time. Where is my pack? Where is my pack, I
say? Open it, my good wife. Unloose the cords. Kneel down upon
the floor. You are better so. Nay not that one, the other. Despatch,
despatch! Buyers will grow impatient oftentimes. We dare not
keep them waiting. Ay! 'tis that, give it to me; with care. It is most
costly. Touch it with care. And now, my noble Lord—Nay, pardon,
I have here a Lucca damask, the very web of silver and the roses so
cunningly wrought that they lack perfume merely to cheat the
wanton sense. Touch it, my Lord. Is it not soft as water, strong as
steel? And then the roses! Are they not finely woven? I think the
hillsides that best love the rose, at Bellosguardo or at Fiesole, throw
no such blossoms on the lap of spring, or if they do their blossoms
droop and die. Such is the fate of all the dainty things that dance
in wind and water. Nature herself makes war on her own loveli-
ness and slays her children like Medea. Nay but, my Lord, look
closer still. Why in this damask here it is summer always, and no
winter's tooth will ever blight these blossoms. For every ell I paid
a piece of gold. Red gold, and good, the fruit of careful thrift.

GUIDO. Honest Simone, enough, I pray you. I am well content, tomorrow I will send my servant to you, who will pay
twice your price.

SIMONE.   My generous Prince! I kiss your hands. And now I do remember another treasure hidden in my house which you must
see. It is a robe of state: woven by a Venetian: the stuff, cut-velvet:
the pattern, pomegranates: each separate seed wrought of a pearl:
the collar all of pearls, as thick as moths in summer streets at
night, and whiter than the moons that madmen see through
prison bars at morning. A male ruby burns like a lighted coal
within the clasp. The Holy Father has not such a stone, nor could
the Indies show a brother to it. The brooch itself is of most curious art, Cellini never made a fairer thing to please the great
Lorenzo. You must wear it. There is none worthier in our city
here, and it will suit you well. Upon one side a slim and horned
satyr leaps in gold to catch some nymphs of silver. Upon the
other stands Silence with a crystal in her hand, no bigger than the
smallest ear of corn, that wavers at the passing of a bird, and yet
so cunningly wrought that one would say it breathed, or held its
breath.

　　Worthy Bianca, would not this noble and most costly
robe suit young Lord Guido well?

　　Nay, but entreat him; he will refuse you nothing, though the
price be as a prince's ransom. And your profit shall not be less
than mine.

BIANCA.   Am I your prentice? Why should I chaffer for your velvet
robe?

GUIDO.   Nay, fair Bianca, I will buy the robe, and all things that the
honest merchant has I will buy also. Princes must be ran-
somed, and fortunate are all high lords who fall into the white
hands of so fair a foe.

SIMONE.   I stand rebuked. But you will buy my wares? Will you not
buy them? Fifty thousand crowns would scarce repay me. But
you, my Lord, shall have them for forty thousand. Is that price too
high? Name your own price. I have a curious fancy to see you in
this wonder of the loom amidst the noble ladies of the court, a
flower among flowers.

　　They say, my Lord, these high-born dames do so affect your
Grace that where you go they throng like flies around you, each
seeking for your favour. I have heard also of husbands that wear
horns, and wear them bravely, a fashion most fantastical.

GUIDO.   Simone, your reckless tongue needs curbing; and besides, You
do forget this gracious lady here whose delicate ears are surely not
attuned to such coarse music.

SIMONE.   True: I had forgotten, nor will offend again. Yet, my sweet
Lord, you'll buy the robe of state. Will you not buy it?

But forty thousand crowns. 'Tis but a trifle, to one who is Giovanni Bardi's heir.

GUIDO.   Settle this thing tomorrow with my steward Antonio Costa. He will come to you. And you shall have a hundred thousand crowns if that will serve your purpose.

SIMONE.   A hundred thousand! Said you a hundred thousand? Oh! be sure that will for all time, and in everything make me your debtor. Ay! from this time forth my house, with everything my house contains is yours, and only yours.

A hundred thousand! My brain is dazed. I shall be richer far than all the other merchants. I will buy vineyards and lands and gardens. Every loom from Milan down to Sicily shall be mine, and mine the pearls that the Arabian seas store in their silent caverns.

Generous Prince, this night shall prove the herald of my love, which is so great that whatsoe'er you ask it will not be denied you.

GUIDO.   What if I asked for white Bianca here?

SIMONE.   You jest, my Lord, she is not worthy of so great a Prince. She is but made to keep the house and spin. Is it not so, good wife? It is so. Look! Your distaff waits for you. Sit down and spin. Women should not be idle in their homes, for idle fingers make a thoughtless heart. Sit down, I say.

BIANCA.   What shall I spin?

SIMONE.   Oh! spin some robe which, dyed in purple, sorrow might wear for her own comforting: or some long-fringed cloth in which a new-born and unwelcome babe might wail unheeded; or a dainty sheet which, delicately perfumed with sweet herbs, might serve to wrap a dead man. Spin what you will; I care not, I.

BIANCA.   The brittle thread is broken, the dull wheel wearies of its ceaseless round, the duller distaff sickens of its load; I will not spin tonight.

SIMONE.   It matters not. Tomorrow you shall spin, and every day shall find you at your distaff. So Lucretia was found by Tarquin. So, perchance, Lucretia waited for Tarquin. Who knows? I have heard strange things about men's wives. And now, my Lord, what news abroad? I heard today at Pisa that certain of the English merchants there would sell their woollens at a lower rate than the just laws allow, and have entreated the Signory to hear them.

Is this well? Should merchant be to merchant as a wolf? And should the stranger living in our land seek by enforced privilege or craft to rob us of our profits?

GUIDO.   What should I do with merchants or their profits? Shall I go and wrangle with the Signory on your count? And wear the gown in which you buy from fools, or sell to sillier bidders?

Honest Simone, wool-selling or wool-gathering is for you. My wits have other quarries.

BIANCA.   Noble Lord, I pray you pardon my good husband here, his soul stands ever in the market-place, and his heart beats but at the price of wool. Yet he is honest in his common way. [*To* SIMONE.] And you, have you no shame? A gracious Prince comes to our house, and you must weary him with most misplaced assurance. Ask his pardon.

SIMONE.   I ask it humbly. We will talk tonight of other things. I hear the Holy Father has sent a letter to the King of France bidding him cross that shield of snow, the Alps, and make a peace in Italy, which will be worse than a war of brothers, and more bloody than civil rapine or intestine feuds.

GUIDO.   Oh! we are weary of that King of France, who never comes, but ever talks of coming. What are these things to me? There are other things closer, and of more import, good Simone.

BIANCA [*To* SIMONE.]   I think you tire our most gracious guest. What is the King of France to us? As much as are your English merchants with their wool.

SIMONE.   Is it so then? Is all this mighty world narrowed into the confines of this room with but three souls for poor inhabitants? Ay! there are times when the great universe, like cloth in some unskilful dyer's vat, shrivels into a handbreadth, and perchance that time is now! Well! let that time be now. Let this mean room be as that mighty stage whereon kings die, and our ignoble lives become the stakes God plays for.

I do not know why I speak thus. My ride has wearied me. And my horse stumbled thrice, which is an omen that bodes not good to any. Alas! my Lord, How poor a bargain is this life of man, and in how mean a market are we sold! When we are born our mothers weep, but when we die there is none weeps for us. No, not one. [*Passes to back of stage.*]

BIANCA.   How like a common chapman does he speak! I hate him, soul and body. Cowardice has set her pale seal on his brow. His hands whiter than poplar leaves in windy springs, shake with some palsy; and his stammering mouth blurts out a foolish froth of empty words like water from a conduit.

GUIDO.   Sweet Bianca, he is not worthy of your thought or mine. The man is but a very honest knave full of fine phrases for life's merchandise, selling most dear what he must hold most cheap, a windy brawler in a world of words. I never met so eloquent a fool.

BIANCA.   Oh, would that Death might take him where he stands!

SIMONE [*turning round*]. Who spake of Death? Let no one speak of Death. What should Death do in such a merry house, with but a wife, a husband, and a friend to give it greeting? Let Death go to houses where there are vile, adulterous things, chaste wives who growing weary of their noble lords draw back the curtains of their marriage beds, and in polluted and dishonoured sheets feed some unlawful lust. Ay! 'tis so strange, and yet so. *You* do not know the world. *You* are too single and too honourable. I know it well. And would it were not so, but wisdom comes with winters. My hair grows grey, and youth has left my body. Enough of that. Tonight is ripe for pleasure, and indeed, I would be merry as beseems a host who finds a gracious and unlooked-for guest waiting to greet him. [*Takes up a lute.*] But what is this, my Lord? Why, you have brought a lute to play to us. Oh! play, sweet Prince. And, if I am too bold, pardon, but play.

GUIDO. I will not play tonight. Some other night, Simone. [*To* BIANCA] You and I together, with no listeners but the stars, or the more jealous moon.

SIMONE. Nay, but my Lord! Nay, but I do beseech you. For I have heard that by the simple fingering of a string, or delicate breath breathed along hollowed reeds, or blown into cold mouths of cunning bronze, those who are curious in this art can draw poor souls from prison-houses. I have heard also how such strange magic lurks within these shells that at their bidding casements open wide And innocence puts vine-leaves in her hair, and wantons like a mænad. Let that pass. Your lute I know is chaste. And therefore play: ravish my ears with some sweet melody; my soul is in a prison-house, and needs music to cure its madness. Good Bianca, entreat our guest to play.

BIANCA. Be not afraid. Our well-loved guest will choose his place and moment: that moment is not now. You weary him with your uncouth insistence.

GUIDO. Honest Simone, some other night. Tonight I am content with the low music of Bianca's voice, who, when she speaks, charms the too amorous air. And makes the reeling earth stand still, or fix his cycle round her beauty.

SIMONE. You flatter her. She has her virtues as most women have, but beauty in a gem she may not wear. It is better so, perchance.

Well, my dear Lord, if you will not draw melodies from your lute To charm my moody and o'er-troubled soul you'll drink with me at least? [*Sees table.*] Your place is laid. Fetch me a stool, Bianca. Close the shutters. Set the great bar across. I would not

have the curious world with its small prying eyes to peer upon
our pleasure.

Now, my lord, give us a toast from a full brimming cup. [*Starts
back.*] What is this stain upon the cloth? It looks as purple as a
wound upon Christ's side. Wine merely is it? I have heard it
said when wine is spilt blood is spilt also, but that's a foolish tale.
My Lord, I trust my grape is to your liking? The wine of Naples is
fiery like its mountains. Our Tuscan vineyards yield a more whole-
some juice.

GUIDO.   I like it well, honest Simone; and, with your good leave, will
toast the fair Bianca when her lips have like red rose-leaves floated
on this cup and left its vintage sweeter. Taste, Bianca. [BIANCA
drinks.] Oh, all the honey of Hyblean bees, matched with this
draught were bitter! Good Simone, you do not share the feast.

SIMONE.   It is strange, my Lord, I cannot eat or drink with you, tonight. Some humour, or some fever in my blood, at other seasons
temperate, or some thought that like an adder creeps from point
to point, that like a madman crawls from cell to cell, poisons my
palate and makes appetite a loathing, not a longing. [*Goes aside.*]

GUIDO.   Sweet Bianca, this common chapman wearies me with
words. I must go hence. Tomorrow I will come. Tell me the
hour.

BIANCA.   Come with the youngest dawn! Until I see you all my life
is vain.

GUIDO.   Ah! loose the falling midnight of your hair, and in those
stars, your eyes, let me behold mine image, as in mirrors. Dear
Bianca, though it be but a shadow, keep me there, nor gaze at
anything that does not show some symbol of my semblance. I am
jealous of what your vision feasts on.

BIANCA.   Oh! be sure your image will be with me always. Dear, love
can translate the very meanest thing into a sign of sweet remem-
brances. But come before the lark with its shrill song has waked
a world of dreamers. I will stand upon the balcony.

GUIDO.   And by a ladder wrought out of scarlet silk and sewn with
pearls will come to meet me. White foot after foot, like snow
upon a rose-tree.

BIANCA.   As you will. You know that I am yours for love or Death.

GUIDO.   Simone, I must go to mine own house.

SIMONE.   So soon? Why should you? The great Duomo's bell has not
yet tolled its midnight, and the watchmen who with their hollow
horns mock the pale moon lie drowsy in their towers. Stay
awhile. I fear we may not see you here again, and that fear saddens
my too simple heart.

GUIDO. Be not afraid, Simone. I will stand most constant in my friendship, but tonight I go to mine own home, and that at once. Tomorrow, sweet Bianca.

SIMONE. Well, well, so be it. I would have wished for fuller converse with you, my new friend, my honourable guest, but that it seems may not be. And besides I do not doubt your father waits for you, wearying for voice or footstep. You, I think, are his one child? He has no other child. You are the gracious pillar of his house, the flower of a garden full of weeds. Your father's nephews do not love him well. So run folk's tongues in Florence. I meant but that; men say they envy your inheritance and look upon your vineyard with fierce eyes as Ahab looked on Naboth's goodly field. But that is but the chatter of a town where women talk too much.

  Goodnight, my Lord. Fetch a pine torch, Bianca. The old staircase is full of pitfalls, and the churlish moon grows, like a miser, niggard of her beams. And hides her face behind a muslin mask as harlots do when they go forth to snare some wretched soul in sin. Now, I will get your cloak and sword. Nay, pardon, my good Lord, it is but meet that I should wait on you who have so honoured my poor burgher's house, drunk of my wine, and broken bread, and made yourself a sweet familiar. Oftentimes my wife and I will talk of this fair night and its great issues.

  Why, what a sword is this! Ferrara's temper, pliant as a snake, and deadlier, I doubt not. With such steel one need fear nothing in the moil of life. I never touched so delicate a blade. I have a sword too, somewhat rusted now. We men of peace are taught humility, and to bear many burdens on our backs, and not to murmur at an unjust world. And to endure unjust indignities. We are taught that, and like the patient Jew find profit in our pain.

  Yet I remember how once upon the road to Padua a robber sought to take my pack-horse from me, I slit his throat and left him. I can bear dishonour, public insult, many shames, shrill scorn, and open contumely, but he who filches from me something that is mine, Ay! though it be the meanest trencher-plate from which I feed mine appetite—oh! he perils his soul and body in the theft and dies for his small sin. From what strange clay we men are moulded!

GUIDO. Why do you speak like this?

SIMONE. I wonder, my Lord Guido, if my sword is better tempered than this steel of yours? Shall we make trial? Or is my state too low for you to cross your rapier against mine, in jest, or earnest?

GUIDO.   Naught would please me better than to stand fronting you
with naked blade in jest, or earnest. Give me mine own
sword. Fetch yours. Tonight will settle the great issue whether the
Prince's or the merchant's steel is better tempered. Was not that
your word? Fetch your own sword. Why do you tarry, sir?

SIMONE.   My Lord, of all the gracious courtesies that you have show-
ered on my barren house this is the highest. Bianca, fetch my
sword. Thrust back that stool and table. We must have an open
circle for our match at arms, And good Bianca here shall hold the
torch lest what is but a jest grow serious.

BIANCA [*to* GUIDO].   Oh! kill him, kill him!

SIMONE.   Hold the torch, Bianca.

[*They begin to fight.*]

SIMONE.   Have at you! Ah! Ha! would you? [*He is wounded by* GUIDO.]
A scratch, no more. The torch was in mine eyes. Do not look sad,
Bianca. It is nothing. Your husband bleeds, 'tis nothing. Take a
cloth, bind it about mine arm. Nay, not so tight. More softly, my
good wife. And be not sad, I pray you be not sad. No; take it
off. What matter if I bleed? [*Tears bandage off.*] Again! again! [SIMONE
disarms GUIDO] My gentle Lord, you see that I was right. My
sword is better tempered, finer steel, but let us match our daggers.

BIANCA [*to* GUIDO].   Kill him! kill him!

SIMONE.   Put out the torch, Bianca. [BIANCA *puts out torch.*] Now, my
good Lord, now to the death of one, or both of us, or all three it
may be. [*They fight.*] There and there. Ah, devil! do I hold thee in
my grip?

[SIMONE *overpowers* GUIDO *and throws him down over table.*]

GUIDO.   Fool! take your strangling fingers from my throat. I am my
father's only son; the state has but one heir, and that false enemy
France waits for the ending of my father's line to fall upon our city.

SIMONE.   Hush! your father when he is childless will be happier. As
for the state, I think our state of Florence needs no adulterous
pilot at its helm. Your life would soil its lilies.

GUIDO.   Take off your hands. Take off your damned hands. Loose me,
I say!

SIMONE.   Nay, you are caught in such a cunning vice that nothing
will avail you, and your life narrowed into a single point of
shame ends with that shame and ends most shamefully.

GUIDO.   Oh! let me have a priest before I die!

SIMONE.   What wouldst thou have a priest for? Tell thy sins to God,
whom thou shalt see this very night and then no more for ever.

Tell thy sins to Him who is most just, being pitiless, most pitiful being just. As for myself. . . .

GUIDO.   Oh! help me, sweet Bianca! help me, Bianca, thou knowest I am innocent of harm.

SIMONE.   What, is there life yet in those lying lips? Die like a dog with lolling tongue! Die! Die! And the dumb river shall receive your corse and wash it all unheeded to the sea.

GUIDO.   Lord Christ receive my wretched soul tonight!

SIMONE.   Amen to that. Now for the other.

[*He dies.* SIMONE *rises and looks at* BIANCA. *She comes towards him as one dazed with wonder and with outstretched arms.*]

BIANCA.   Why did you not tell me you were so strong?

SIMONE.   Why did you not tell me you were beautiful?

[*He kisses her on the mouth.*]

CURTAIN

THE OLD LADY
SHOWS HER MEDALS
James M. Barrie

CAST OF CHARACTERS

MRS. DOWEY
MRS. MICKLEHAM
MRS. TULLY
MRS. HAGGERTY
THE REV. MR. WILKINSON
PRIVATE K. DOWEY OF THE BLACK WATCH

Scene I: MRS. DOWEY'S *living-room in a London basement, in the afternoon.*
Scene II: The same. Five days later, at night.
Scene III: The same. A month or two later in the early morning.

SCENE I

A basement in a drab locality in London; the kitchen, sitting-room and bed-room of MRS. DOWEY, *the charwoman. It is a poor room, as small as possible but clean and tidy; not at all bare, but containing many little articles and adorn-ments. The window at the back shows the area wall and a few steps up to the street, the level of which can just be seen. The door to the area is* L.C. *The door to a small scullery is in the right wall rather up stage, below which is a small kitchen grate. In the left wall is a piece of furniture with the appearance of a cheap wardrobe, but which is, in fact, a bed which can be let down. Below this is a small chest of drawers. There is a shabby deal table, its length across the stage, set* R.C., *with two wooden chairs above it and one at each end.*
The time is about 5 p.m.

The curtain rises on MRS. DOWEY *entertaining three other charwomen to tea. She is on the right of the table. On her left, above the table, is* MRS. MICKLEHAM, *on whose left is* MRS. TULLY. MRS. HAGGERTY, *the un-popular one, is at the left end of the table.*

118

There is no tablecloth, but there is tea, bread and butter, a dish of shrimps, of which only two are left, jam, and winkles—even a small sponge cake The loaf and two cut slices are near the hostess. The remaining shrimps, it is noted, are within easy reach of MRS. HAGGERTY.

There is a cheerful fire, and the kettle steams on the hob.

All the ladies are elderly, typical, without exaggeration, of their profession. MRS. MICKLEHAM, *whose cap and shawl are on a chair above the bed, is the plump one.* MRS. HAGGERTY, *whose things are on the chair up* R., *is small and rather pathetic.* MRS. TULLY, *apt to be aggressive, wears her shabby hat, an old coat over the back of her chair.* MRS. DOWEY *has a pale brave face; a Scotswoman who has made a fine struggle against poverty in London.*

It is wartime, and the conversation fluctuates between military strategy and dress fashions.

MRS. DOWEY *stands* R., *re-filling the teapot with hot water.*

MRS. DOWEY [*crossing back to the table*]. Another cup of tea, Mrs. Mickleham? [MRS. MICKLEHAM *waves the offer away.*] Mrs. Haggerty?

MRS. HAGGERTY.   No, I thank you, I've had so much tea I'm fair running over.

[*Looks of disapproval.*]

MRS. DOWEY.   Another winkle?

MRS. HAGGERTY.   If I took one more winkle it'd have to swim for it.

MRS. DOWEY [*to* MRS. TULLY]. The shrimps are with you, Sarah. There's two yet.

MRS. TULLY.   Two shrimps yet? There's twelve yet.

MRS. HAGGERTY [*feeling this is meant for her*]. How d'you make that out, ma'am?

MRS. TULLY [*who has been nursing a grievance*]. There's these two, Mrs. Haggerty, and there's the five *you* had, and the four Mrs. Mickleham had, and the *one* I had.

MRS. MICKLEHAM.   But they're eaten.

MRS. TULLY [*after a glance at* MRS. HAGGERTY]. In Germany, Mrs. Mickleham, when a shrimp is eaten, is that the end of the shrimp?

[MRS. MICKLEHAM *nods approval of this thrust.*]

MRS. HAGGERTY.   It may be so.

MRS. TULLY.   I suppose I ought to know, me that has a son a prisoner in Germany. [*Rather bumptiously.*] Being the only lady present that has that proud misfortune.

[*They are humiliated for a moment. Then:*]

Mrs. Dowey.   My son's fighting in France.
Mrs. Mickleham.   Mine is wounded in two places.
Mrs. Haggerty.   Mine is at *Salonikkey.*

[*The others look at her, and she is annoyed.*]

Mrs. Dowey [*firmly but not unkindly*].   You'll excuse us, Mrs. Haggerty,
but the correct pronunciation is Salo*nikey.*
Mrs. Haggerty.   I don't think. [*With a little more spirit than usual.*]
And I speak as one that has War Savings Certificates.
Mrs. Tully.   We all have them.

[*They disdain* Mrs. Haggerty, *and she whimpers.*]

Mrs. Dowey [*to restore cheerfulness*].   Oh, it's a terrible war. [*General
chorus of: "It is." "You may say so."*] The men is splendid, but I'm
none so easy about the staff. That's your weak point, Mrs.
Mickleham.
Mrs. Mickleham [*instantly on the defensive*].   What none of you grasp
is that this is a h'artillery war. Now ...
Mrs. Haggerty.   I say the word is Salo*nikkey.*

[*Having surreptitiously eaten the final shrimps, she is strengthened. But the
others only display disgust at her ignorance.*]

Mrs. Tully.   We'll change the subjeck. [*She takes a magazine from the
front of her dress.*] Have you seen this week's "Fashion Chat"? [*All
very attentive.*] The plain smock has come in again with the silk
lacing, giving that charming cheek effect.
Mrs. Dowey.   Oho! I must say I was always partial to the straight
line—though trying to them as is of too friendly a figure. [*Her
eye considers briefly* Mrs. Mickleham's *want of "line."* Mrs.
Mickleham *is resentfully conscious of this and listens earnestly to*
Mrs. Tully's *next.*]
Mrs. Tully [*reading*].   "Lady Dolly Kinley was seen conversing across
the railings in a dainty *de jou.*"
Mrs. Mickleham [*eating it*].   Was she now?
Mrs. Tully.   "She is equally popular as maid, wife, mother, and muni-
tion worker." [*Great approval.*] "Lady Pops Babington was married
in a tight tulle."
Mrs. Haggerty [*fortified by stolen sugar*].   What was her going-away
dress?
Mrs. Tully [*rolling it out*].   "A champagny cream velvet with dreamy
corsage. She's married to Colonel the Honourable Chingford.—
'Snubs' they called him at Eton."

MRS. HAGGERTY.   Very likely he'll be sent to Salo*nikk*ey.

MRS. MICKLEHAM.   Wherever he's sent, she'll have the same tremors as the rest of us. She'll be as keen to get the letters wrote in pencil as you or me.

MRS. TULLY.   Them pencil letters!

MRS. DOWEY [*timidly*].   And women in enemy lands gets those pencil letters—and then stops getting them, the same as ourselves—let's sometimes think of that.

[*The ladies gasp. Chairs are pushed back.*]

MRS. TULLY.   I've heard of females that have no male relations, and so have no man-party at the war. I've heard of them—but I don't mix with them.

MRS. MICKLEHAM.   What can the likes of us have to say to them? It's not *their* war.

MRS. DOWEY.   They are to be pitied.

MRS. MICKLEHAM.   But the place for them, Mrs. Dowey, is within doors with the blinds down.

MRS. DOWEY [*hurriedly*].   Ay, that's the place for them.

MRS. MICKLEHAM.   I saw one of them today, buying a flag. I thought it was very impudent of her.

MRS. DOWEY [*meekly*].   So it was.

MRS. MICKLEHAM [*preening herself and looking at the others*].   I had a letter from my son Percy today.

MRS. TULLY [*not to be outdone*].   Alfred sent me his photo.

MRS. HAGGERTY.   Letters from Salo*nikk*ey is less common.

[*A general display of pride except from* MRS. DOWEY, *who doggedly sets her lips.*]

MRS. DOWEY.   Kenneth writes to me every week. [*Exclamations of incredulity. She rises, and crosses* L.] I'll show you. [*She takes a packet of letters, tied up, from the chest of drawers.*] Look at this. All his.

[MRS. HAGGERTY *who, behind her hostess's back has just taken and eaten another piece of sugar, whimpers.*]

MRS. MICKLEHAM.   My word!

MRS. TULLY.   Alfred has little time for writing, being a bombardier.

MRS. DOWEY [L.C.].   Do your letters begin "Dear Mother"?

MRS. TULLY.   Generally.

MRS. MICKLEHAM.   Invariable.

MRS. HAGGERTY.   Every time.

MRS. DOWEY.   Kenneth's begin—"*Dearest* mother."

[*Speechless, their eyes follow her as she goes up to* R.C. *and fetches a little tray from a small table.*]

MRS. TULLY.   A short man, I should say, judging by yourself.

MRS. DOWEY [*coming down to* R. *end of the table*].   Six feet two—and a half.

[*The others are depressed.*]

MRS. HAGGERTY.   A kilty, did you tell me?

MRS. DOWEY [*smiling*].   Most certainly. He's in the famous Black Watch.

MRS. HAGGERTY [*tearful*].   The Surrey Rifles is the famousest.

MRS. MICKLEHAM [*pushing her plate away and leaning forward*].   There, you and the King disagree, Mrs. Haggerty. The King's choice is the Buffs—same as my Percy's.

MRS. TULLY [*sitting back, complacent*].   Give me the R.H.A., and you can keep the rest.

MRS. DOWEY [*putting plates and cups on the tray*].   I'm sure I've nothing to say against the Surreys [*this to* MRS. HAGGERTY]—nor the R.H.A. [*to* MRS. TULLY]—nor the Buffs [*to* MRS. MICKLEHAM. *She lifts the filled tray*]—but they're all three just breeches regiments, I understand.

MRS. HAGGERTY.   We can't all be kilties.

MRS. DOWEY [*with satisfaction*].   That's verra true. [*She takes the tray up to the little table.*]

MRS. TULLY [*trying again*].   Has your Kenneth great hairy legs?

MRS. DOWEY [*coming back to* R. *of the table*].   Enormous.

[*The depression deepens.*]

MRS. HAGGERTY [*rising, speaks across the table*].   At any rate, it's Salonikkey. [*She goes up to the window at the back and glances out, then sees some one is descending the steps.*] Ho ho!

[*The others turn to look at her.*]

MRS. TULLY.   Who is it, Mrs. Haggerty?

MRS. HAGGERTY [*moving* R.].   It's the Reverent gent.

[*There is instant movement. They rise,* MRS. DOWEY *moves down* R. MRS. MICKLEHAM *to above her chair,* MRS. TULLY *to* L. *of the table. All tidy themselves, smooth hair, etc.*]

[*There is a knock at the door, but the visitor enters at once. It is the* REV. MR. WILKINSON, *a curate. He is a very good fellow, to whom every little incident in which he figures is of astounding importance. He imparts any information with an air of profound secrecy.*]

WILKINSON [*up* L.].   Quite a party! [MRS. TULLY *offers a chair, dusting it with her apron, forestalling* MRS. DOWEY, *who had moved to do the same.* MR. WILKINSON *waves the chair aside.*] Thank you—not at all. [*Glowing with the surprise in store.*] Friends, I have news!

[*All are instantly anxious.* MRS. HAGGERTY *moves down a step.*]

MRS. MICKLEHAM [*coming to back of the table*].   News?
MRS. HAGGERTY.   From the Front?
MRS. TULLY [*a step towards* MR. WILKINSON].   My Alfred, sir ?
WILKINSON [*with a calming gesture*].   I tell you at once, all's well. [*General relief.*] The news—[*with an air*] is for Mrs. Dowey.
MRS. DOWEY [*who is really a lonely soul, is thunder-struck*].   News? For me?
WILKINSON [*with triumph*].   Your son, Mrs. Dowey—he has got five days' leave! [*She wets her lips, unable to speak, and lays the letters on* L. *end of the table. The others all look at her, pleased, if a little envious.*] Now, now! Good news doesn't kill.
MRS. TULLY [*sincerely*].   We're glad, Mrs. Dowey.
MRS. DOWEY [*moving a pace* L., *speaks directly to* MR. WILKINSON].   You're—sure?
WILKINSON.   Quite sure. He has arrived!
MRS. DOWEY.   He's in London?
WILKINSON.   He is. I have spoken to him.
MRS. MICKLEHAM [*to* MRS. DOWEY].   You lucky!
MRS. DOWEY [*to* WILKINSON].   Where?
WILKINSON [*up to* MRS. TULLY].   Ladies, it's quite a romance! I was in the—[*he glances round cautiously before continuing*] in the Church Army quarters in Central Street, trying to get on the track of one or two of our missing men, when—suddenly, I can't account for it—my eyes alighted on a Highlander seated rather drearily on a bench with his kit at his feet.
MRS. HAGGERTY [*anxiously, approaching* R. *end of the table*].   A big man?
WILKINSON.   A great brawny fellow. [MRS. HAGGERTY *sighs and turns away.*] "My friend," I said at once, "welcome back to Blighty!" I make a point of calling it Blighty. "I wonder," I said, "if there is anything I can do for you?" He shook his head. "What regiment?" I asked. "Black Watch, Fifth Battalion," he said. "Name?" I asked. [*A slight pause.*] Dowey!" says he. [*Triumphantly.*] "Kenneth Dowey," I said, "I know your mother."
MRS. HAGGERTY.   I declare! I do declare!
MRS. DOWEY [*quietly, again wetting her lips*].   What did he say to that?

WILKINSON.   He was incredulous. Indeed, he seemed to think I was balmy. But I offered to bring him straight to you. I told him how much you had talked to me about him.

MRS. DOWEY [*almost in a whisper*].   Bring him here?

MRS. MICKLEHAM.   I wonder he needed to be brought.

WILKINSON.   He had just arrived, and was bewildered in the great city. He listened to me in his taciturn Scotch way, and then he gave a curious laugh.

MRS. TULLY.   Laugh?

WILKINSON [*turning to her*].   The Scottish, Mrs. Tully, express their emotions differently from us. With them, tears signify a rollicking mood, while merriment denotes that they are plunged in gloom. When I had finished, he said, "Let's go and see the old lady."

MRS. DOWEY [*picking up the letters without glancing down, backs a step*].   Is he—coming ?

WILKINSON.   He *has* come! He is up there!

MRS. MICKLEHAM [*goes to the window*].   My word!

[*The other two guests follow her.*]

WILKINSON [*moving towards* MRS. DOWEY].   I told him I thought I had better break the joyful news to you.

MRS. DOWEY [*in a low, urgent voice*].   Get them away. [*She goes down* L. *to the chest of drawers.*]

WILKINSON [*turning up to the others*].   Ladies, I think this happy occasion scarcely requires *us*. [*They nod acquiescence.*] I don't mean to stay, myself.

[MRS. MICKLEHAM *goes to the chair above the bed for her cap and shawl and pail.*]

MRS. TULLY [*putting on her coat and cap*].   I would thank none for their company if my Alfred was at the door. [*She goes up to the door with the pail.*] A noble five days to you, Mrs. Dowey.

[MRS. HAGGERTY *has fetched her things from the chair above the fire.*]

MRS. HAGGERTY [*to* R. *of* MRS. TULLY].   The same from me.

MRS. TULLY [*to* WILKINSON].   Shall I send him down, sir?

WILKINSON.   Yes, do! Do!

[*Exit* MRS. TULLY *and* MRS. HAGGERTY.]

MRS. MICKLEHAM.   Look at the poor joyous thing, sir. She has his letters in her hand.

[*She exits after the others.*]

WILKINSON [*coming down a little*].   A good son to have written to you
so often, Mrs. Dowey. [*The letters slip from her hand to the floor. He
picks them up and gives them back.*] There! There!

[DOWEY *is seen descending the steps outside. He enters up* L. *He is a big
grim fellow in field service kit, with kilt, bonnet, overcoat, scarf, etc., of the
Black Watch. They are muddy. He carries pack and rifle. He is a dour-
looking fellow at present.*]

WILKINSON [*Up to* L. *of* DOWEY, *who is up* C.].   Dowey, there she is,
waiting for you with your letters in her hand.

DOWEY [*grimly*].   That's great!

[MR. WILKINSON *goes off consciously and stealthily, without looking behind
him. He closes the door and is seen to ascend the steps, and off.* DOWEY *surveys*
MRS. DOWEY, *lowering the butt of his rifle. She backs a pace or two, timidly.*]

DOWEY.   Do you recognize your loving son, Missis? [*He puts his rifle
against the chair above the bed and comes to* C., *on the left of the table.*]
I'm pleased I wrote to ye so often. [*Roughly.*] Let's see them.
[*Stepping to her, he takes the letters from her hand, and returns* C. *She
moves a pace nearer him. He pulls off the ribbon and examines the letters.*] Nothing but blank paper! Is this your writing on the envelopes? [*She can only nod.*] The covey told me you were a charwoman, so I suppose you picked the envelopes out of waste-paper
baskets, and then changed the address—them being written in
pencil. [*She nods again.*] Hah !

[*He strides above the table to the fire. She follows him quickly below the table,
on his* L.]

MRS. DOWEY.   Don't you burn them letters, Mister!

DOWEY [*staying his hand*].   They're not real letters.

MRS. DOWEY.   They're all I have.

DOWEY [*ironically*].   I thought you had a son?

MRS. DOWEY [*turning her face from him a little*].   I never had a son, nor a
husband, nor anything. I just call myself Missis to give me a standing.

DOWEY [*amazed*].   Well, it's past my understanding. [*He throws the letters on the table.*] What made you do it?

MRS. DOWEY.   It was everybody's war except mine. I wanted it to be
my war too.

DOWEY.   You'll need to be plainer...

MRS. DOWEY.   Well—I——

DOWEY [*crossing back above the table*].   And yet I'm d——d if I care to
hear, you lying old trickster !

[*He goes to the rifle* L. *and picks it up.*]

MRS. DOWEY [*following him, to* L. *end of the table*].   You're not going already?

DOWEY.   Yes. I just came to give you a piece of my mind.

MRS. DOWEY [*with a little begging gesture*].   You haven't given it to me yet.

[*He gives a short, hard laugh. His rifle butt thuds on the floor.*]

DOWEY.   You have a cheek! [*He stares at her.*]

MRS. DOWEY.   You wouldn't—drink some tea? [*She goes* R. *towards the fire.*]

DOWEY [*following her to* L. *end of the table*].   Me! I tell you I came here for the one purpose of blazing away at you!

MRS. DOWEY [*putting the kettle on the hob*].   You could drink the tea while you was blazing away. [*With a nod at the table.*] There's shrimps.

DOWEY [*interested*].   Is there? [*About to take one, then checks.*] Not me. You're just a common rogue. [*He sits in* MRS. TULLY'S *chair, about a yard* L. *of the table.*] Now then, out with it! [*He roars.*] Sit down! [*She returns to* R. *of the table.*] Although it's on your knees you should be to me.

MRS. DOWEY.   I'm willing.

DOWEY.   Stop it! [*She sits, and fingers the letters.*] Go on, you accomplished liar.

MRS. DOWEY.   It's true that my name is Dowey.

DOWEY.   It's enough to make me change mine.

MRS. DOWEY.   I've been charring and charring and charring as far back as I mind. I've been in London this twenty years.

DOWEY [*moving restlessly*].   We'll skip your early days. I've an appointment.

MRS. DOWEY.   And then, when I was old, the war broke out.

DOWEY.   How could it affect you ?

MRS. DOWEY [*rising, she speaks with slow hesitation*].   Oh, Mister, that's the thing. It didn't affect me. It affected everybody *but* me. The neighbours looked down on me. Even the posters on the walls, of the woman saying, "Go, my boy," leered at me. I sometimes cried by myself in the dark. [*She moves tentatively to the hob.*] You won't have a cup of tea?

DOWEY.   No.

MRS. DOWEY.   Sudden-like, the idea came to me to pretend I had a son.

DOWEY.   You nasty old limmer! But what in the name of old Nick made you choose me out of the whole British Army ?

MRS. DOWEY [*with a sly chuckle, she approaches him*].   Maybe, Mister, it was because I liked you best.

DOWEY [*sitting up, sharply*].   Now, now, woman!

MRS. DOWEY.   I read one day in the papers, "In which he was assisted by Private K. Dowey, 5th Battalion, Black Watch."

DOWEY [*flattered*].   Did you, now? Well, I expect that's the only time I was ever in the papers.

MRS. DOWEY [*quickly*].   But I didn't choose you for that alone.

DOWEY.   Eh?

MRS. DOWEY.   I read a history of the Black Watch first to make sure it was the best regiment in the world.

DOWEY [*complacently*].   Anybody could have told you that. [*He rises, to the table, on her* L. *Almost unconsciously he picks up a loaf.*] I like the voice of you—[*unthinkingly, he is cutting a slice*] it drummles on like a Scotch burn.

MRS. DOWEY.   Brosen Water runs by where I was born. [*He notices the shrimps. She observes this.*] Maybe it learned me to speak, Mister.

[*He looks at her sharply. Then, evasively:*]

DOWEY. Oh, havers!   [*He takes and skins a shrimp.*]

MRS. DOWEY [*sitting* R. *end of the table*].   I read about the Black Watch's ghostly piper, that plays proudly when the men of the Black Watch do well, and still prouder when they fall.

DOWEY [*pleased, still busy with the shrimp*].   Ay, there's some foolish story of the kind. [*He looks at her.*] But you couldn't have been living here at the time, or they would have guessed. [*He carelessly butters the slice.*] I suppose you changed your place of residence?

MRS. DOWEY.   Ay! It cost eleven and six-pence.

DOWEY [*puts down the slice and takes another shrimp*].   How did you guess that the "K" in my name stood for Kenneth?

MRS. DOWEY.   Does it? [*He nods.*] An angel whispered it to me in my sleep.

DOWEY [*picks up the buttered slice and comes down below the table*].   That's the only angel in the whole black business. [*He crosses to the fireplace.*] You little thought I would turn up. [*He swings round sharply.*] Or did you?

MRS. DOWEY [*rising, moves above the table, not looking at him*].   I was wearying for a sight of you—[*she looks down at the table*] Kenneth.

DOWEY [*who was about to take a bite, checks*].   What word was that?

MRS. DOWEY [*humbly correcting herself*].   —Mister.

DOWEY [*sarcastically*].   I hope you're pleased with me now you see me. [*He takes a bite of bread.*]

MRS. DOWEY [*earnestly*].   I'm very pleased.

[DOWEY *sits* R. *of the table. She pushes the jam-pot to him.*]

DOWEY.   No, thank you.

[*Disappointed,* MRS. DOWEY *turns away* L. *An idea strikes her and she goes* L. *to the chest of drawers and brings out the cash-box, returning to* C.]

MRS. DOWEY.   Look, I have five War Savings Certificates.
DOWEY [*munching*].   That's nought to me.
MRS. DOWEY.   I'll soon have six.
DOWEY [*dourly*].   What care I?
MRS. DOWEY.   You're hard.
DOWEY.   I am.

[*She goes back* L. *and returns the cash-box to the drawer; then comes back to* L. *of the table.*]

MRS.DOWEY.   Does your folk live in Scotland?
DOWEY [*unconsciously spreading jam on the bread*]. Glasgow.
MRS. DOWEY.   Both living?
DOWEY.   Umpha.
MRS. DOWEY.   Is your mother terrible proud of you?
DOWEY.   Naturally.
MRS. DOWEY.   You'll be going to them?
DOWEY.   After I've had a skite in London first.
MRS. DOWEY [*with a little sniff*].   So she's in London?
DOWEY.   Who?
MRS. DOWEY.   Your young lady.
DOWEY.   Are you jealyous ?
MRS. DOWEY [*haughtily*].   Not me!
DOWEY [*reaching out for more jam*].   You needna. *She's* a young thing.
MRS. DOWEY [*sarcastic*].   You surprise me. A beauty, no doubt?
DOWEY.   Famous. [*Swallowing a mouthful.*] She's a titled person. Her picture's in all the papers. She is equally popular as maid, wife, mother, and munition worker.
MRS. DOWEY [*remembering*].   Oh!
DOWEY.   She's sent me a lot of things—especially cakes, and a worsted waistcoat—with a loving message on the enclosed card.
MRS. DOWEY [*coming to above* L. *end of the table*].   Do you know her?
DOWEY. Only in the illustrations. But she may have seen me.
MRS. DOWEY.   You'll try one of my cakes. [*She goes towards the scullery.*]
DOWEY.   Not me.

[MRS. DOWEY *goes into the scullery, returning at once with a plate of small cakes. They should be of unusual appearance. She puts them on the table within his reach.*]

MRS. DOWEY.   They're my own making.

DOWEY [*looking sharply at them*].   Well I'm d——d!

MRS. DOWEY.   How?

DOWEY.   That's exactly the same kind of cake that her ladyship sends me.

MRS DOWEY [*in her glory*].   Is the waistcoat right? [*He pushes away his plate.*] I hope the Black Watch colours pleased you, Mister.

DOWEY [*rising*].   Wha-at? Was it you?

MRS. DOWEY [*for the moment a little scared again*].   I dared not give my own name, you see, and everyone's familiar with hers.

DOWEY [*backing a little* R.].   "Woman! Is there no getting rid of you?

MRS. DOWEY [*her courage returning*].   Are you angry?

DOWEY.   Oh, hell! Give me some tea. [*He sits at the table again.*]

[MRS. DOWEY *hurries happily into the scullery, returning at once with duplicate teapot with tea ready made, and a cup and saucer. The latter she puts on the table. The teapot she takes to the hob. Business of pouring hot water in. During this* DOWEY *has been eating.*]

MRS. DOWEY [*putting the teapot in front of him*].   Kenneth!

DOWEY [*this time he does not notice the use of his name*].   What?

MRS. DOWEY.   Nothing. Just—Kenneth. [*She fetches a large cup from the table up stage.*]

DOWEY [*between bites*].   Now don't you be thinking, Missis, for one moment that you've got me.

MRS. DOWEY [*busy with milk and sugar*].   No, no.

DOWEY [*spreading jam*].   I have a theatre tonight, followed by a randy-dandy.

MRS DOWEY.   Have you? [*She pours out his tea.*] Kenneth, this is a queer first meeting. [*She hands him a cup.*]

DOWEY.   It is. [*Stirring the tea.*] And it's also a last meeting. [*He pours tea into the saucer.*] Ave atque vale. [*He drinks.*] That means, hail and farewell.

MRS. DOWEY [*sitting on* R. *chair above the table*].   Are you a scholar?

DOWEY.   Being Scottish, there's almost nothing I don't know.

MRS. DOWEY.   What was your trade?

DOWEY [*reaching out for the loaf*].   Carter—glazier, orra man, and rough jobs.

MRS. DOWEY.   You're a proper man to look at.

DOWEY [*cutting another slice*].   I'm generally admired.

MRS. DOWEY [*rising*].   She's an enviable woman.

DOWEY. Who?

MRS. DOWEY.   Your mother. [*Up to the small table.*]

DOWEY.   Eh? Oh! That was just protecting myself from you. [*She turns, a small cup and saucer in her hand, and looks at him, very still.*] I have neither father nor mother nor wife nor grandmamma. [*She brings the cup down to the table. He continues bitterly.*] This party never even knew who his proud parents were.

MRS. DOWEY [*excited*].   Is that true?

DOWEY.   It's Gospel.

MRS. DOWEY.   Heavens be praised! [*She pours herself a cup of tea.*]

DOWEY.   Eh? None of that! I was a fool to tell you. But don't think you can take advantage of it. Pass the cake.

MRS. DOWEY [*bringing cake to him, peeps at his legs*].   Hairy legs!

DOWEY [*jocularly, covering his legs with his coat*].   Mind your manners. [*Drinking to her.*] But here's to you.

MRS. DOWEY [*raising her cup*].   Here's to you. [*She drinks, then, slyly.*] And our next meeting.

DOWEY.   I canna guess where that's to be.

MRS. DOWEY.   Maybe in Berlin.

DOWEY.   Gosh! If I ever get there, I believe I'll find you waiting for me!

MRS. DOWEY.   With your tea ready!

DOWEY.   Ay, and good tea too!

MRS. DOWEY [*sitting, as before*].   Kenneth, we'll come back by Paris.

DOWEY [*gaily*].   I knew ye'd say that! All the leddies hankers to get to Paris!

MRS. DOWEY [*wistfully*].   I want, before I die, to have a gown of Paris make, with dreamy corsage!

DOWEY.   We have a song about that. [*Half singing.*]

> Oh, Mistress Gill is very ill
> And nothing can improve her,
> But to see the Tuylleries
> And waddle through the Louvre.

[*Both laugh hilariously.*]

MRS. DOWEY.   Kenneth, you must learn me that. [*Singing.*]

> Mistress Dowey's very ill
> And nothing can improve her—

DOWEY [*breaking in*].

> But dressed up in a dreamy gown
> To waddle through the Louvre!

[*Both laugh heartily again. Then he suddenly realizes she is getting round him.*] Now, now, now! What nonsense is this? [*He rises, going below the table and up L. for his rifle.*] Well, thank you for my tea. I must be stepping.

Mrs. Dowey [*rising, goes* L. *to his* R.].   Where are you living?

Dowey [*scratching his head*].   That's the question. But there's a place called the Hut where some of the Fifth Battalion are. They'll take me in. [*Bitterly.*] Beggars can't be choosers.

Mrs. Dowey.   Beggars?

Dowey.   I've never been here before. If you knew what it is to be in such a place without a friend! I was crazy with glee when I got my leave, at the thought of seeing London at last, but after wandering its streets for four hours I'd have been glad to be back in the trenches.

Mrs. Dowey.   That's my position too, Kenneth. [*He nods.*] Twenty years have I been here. Folks is kind, but it's a foreign land to me.

Dowey [*kindly*].   I'm sorry for you. [*Shouldering his kit.*] But I see no way out for either of us. [*He turns away to pick up his rifle.*]

Mrs. Dowey [*longingly*].   Do you not?

Dowey [*checking, turns to look at her*].   Are you at it again?

Mrs. Dowey.   Kenneth, I've heard that the thing a man on leave longs for more than anything is a bed with sheets and a bath.

Dowey [*grimly*].   You never heard anything truer.

Mrs. Dowey.   Go into that scullery, Kenneth. [*He looks at her sharply, then crosses* R.] And lift the table-top and tell me what you see.

[*He gives her another look at the door, disappears for a moment and returns.*]

Dowey.   It's a kind of bath.

Mrs. Dowey.   You could do yourself pretty there, half at a time.

Dowey.   Me?

Mrs. Dowey.   There's a woman through the wall that would be very willing to give me a shake-down till your leave's up.

Dowey [*snorting*].   Oh, is there?

Mrs. Dowey.   Kenneth—look!

[*Turning* L., *she lets down the bed, then steps back for his approval.*]

Dowey [*striding over to* L.C., *examines this wonder*].   Hullo! That's the dodge we need in the trenches.

Mrs. Dowey.   That's your bed, Kenneth.

Dowey [*moved*].   Mine! [*He grins queerly at her.*] You queer old body! You spunky little divert, you! What can make you so keen to be burdened by a lump like me? [Mrs. Dowey *chuckles.*] I warn you I'm the commonest kind of man. I've been a kick-about all my life, and I'm no great shakes at the war.

Mrs. Dowey [*sitting on* R. *end of the bed*]. Yes, you are. How many Germans have you killed?

DOWEY [*to* L. *end of the table*].   Just two for certain, and there was no
   glory in it. It was just because they wanted my shirt.

MRS. DOWEY.   Your shirt?

DOWEY.   'Well, they said it was *their* shirt.

MRS. DOWEY.   Have you took prisoners?

DOWEY.   I once took half a dozen, but that was a poor affair, too.

MRS. DOWEY.   How could you take half a dozen?

DOWEY [*hitching up his pack, casually*].   Just in the usual way. I sur-
   rounded them.

MRS. DOWEY [*rising*].   Kenneth, you're just my ideal.

DOWEY.   You're easy pleased. [*He crosses to the bed and feels it. Then,
   loosening his kit.*] Old lady, if you really want me—I'll bide. [*He sets
   down his pack.*]

MRS. DOWEY [*in a transport of joy*].   Oh! Oh! Oh!

DOWEY.   But mind you, I don't accept you as a relation. [*Together they
   raise and replace the bed.*]   For your personal glory you can go on
   pretending to the neighbours, but the best I can say for you is that
   you're on your probation. I'm a cautious character, and we must
   see how you turn out.

MRS. DOWEY.   Yes, Kenneth.

DOWEY.   And now, I think, for that bath. [*He goes* R. *towards the scullery
   and turns.*] My theatre begins at six-thirty. A cove I met on the
   bus is going with me.

MRS. DOWEY [*following him to* C.].   You're sure you'll come back?

DOWEY.   I leave my kit in pledge.

MRS. DOWEY.   You won't liquor up too freely, Kenneth?

DOWEY [*coming a pace towards her, with a chuckle*].   You're the first to
   care whether I did or not. [*He pats her arm.*] I promise. Tod! I'm
   beginning to look forward to being awakened in the morning by
   hearing you cry, "Get up, you lazy swine!" I've often envied men
   that had womenfolk with a right to say that. [*He goes* R. *again to
   the scullery door. Checks, and turns.*] By Sal and Tal!

MRS. DOWEY [*a shade apprehensive*].   What is it, Kenneth?

DOWEY [*returning to* R.C.].   The theatre. It would be showier if I took
   a lady. [*He surveys her critically.*]

MRS. DOWEY.   Kenneth, tell me this instant what you mean. Don't
   keep me on the jumps.

DOWEY [*crosses down to her* L.—*same business*].   No, it couldn't be
   done.

MRS. DOWEY.   Was it—me you were thinking of?

DOWEY [*striding back to her* R.].   Ay, just for the moment. But you have
   no [*with a gesture*]—style.

Mrs. Dowey [*humbly*].   Not in this, of course—but if you saw me in my merino! [*He is attentive.*] Kenneth, it's grand! It has a wee bit lace in the front!

Dowey [*drops down and sits on* L. *end of the table*].   Let's see it. [Mrs. Dowey *hurries to the chest of drawers and takes from the lower drawer the black merino, and brings it* C.] Looks none so bad. [*He fingers it.*] Have you a bit chiffon for the neck? [*She nods eagerly.*] It's not the Kaiser, nor bombs, nor keeping the home fires burning, nor Tipperary, that the men in the trenches think about. [*He shakes his head.*] It's—chiffon. [*Dubiously.*] Any jewellery?

Mrs. Dowey.   I have a brooch.

Dowey.   Umpha.

Mrs. Dowey [*the boastful creature*].   And I have a muff—and gloves.

Dowey.   Ay, ay [*Candidly.*] Do you think you could give your face a less homely look?

Mrs. Dowey.   I'm sure I could.

Dowey.   Ay, ay. Then you can try. [*He goes up above the table and turns.*] But mind you, I promise nothing. It all depends—on the *effect*.

[*As he goes off into the scullery,* Mrs. Dowey *puts the dress on the chair* L. *of the table.* Dowey *shuts the door, and the rush of the hot-water tap is heard.* Mrs. Dowey *goes* R., *takes up the letters and throws them contemptuously into the fire. She then rushes to the pail down* R., *takes out the scrubbing-brush and swab, throwing these on the floor. She fills the pail from the kettle on the hob, and brings it to* L. *end of the table. She is about to wash, but checks. She goes down* L., *takes a small mirror from above the chest of drawers, and props it on the table against the pail. She examines her face and hair. Licking her palms, she smooths down her hair....*]

The *curtain* falls for a few moments.

SCENE II
[*Five days later.*]

The curtain rises on the same scene, but the dishes are gone from the table. The gas is lit, the blinds are drawn. There are chairs at each end of the table, and chairs above and below the fireplace. Dowey's *kit is up* L. *against the chair, his overcoat on the chair-back. The bed is let down. In the chest of drawers are—in the lower drawer her black dress, and in the centre drawer her merino. At this point, the top drawer contains only the cash-box and Certificates, and a small bag of lavender.*

MRS. MICKLEHAM *sits above the fire and* MRS. TULLY *is below. They are still in their charwomen clothes, but tidier. Sleeves are pulled down, aprons clean, skirts are not tucked up, and they wear hats. A very lively conversation is in progress.*

MRS. MICKLEHAM [*speaking before the curtain rises*].   I soon told him off. "Yes," I says, "you've got to make your peace terms." [*The curtain rises.*] To which, says he, "Then state your peace terms, ma'am," he says. To which, I make reply, "Reparation, restitution, and guarantys." [MRS. TULLY *nods with vigorous approval.*] What do you think will happen, Sarah, after the war? Will we go back to being as we were?

MRS. TULLY.   If you mean us in the charring line—[*she rises, and kneeling, pokes the fire and brushes the grate*]—speaking for myself, not *me*. The war has wakened me up, Amelia, to an understanding of my own importance that is truly astonishing.

MRS. MICKLEHAM.   Same here. Instead of being the poor worms the likes of you and me thought we was, we turn out to be valiable parts of a great and 'aughty empire.

MRS. TULLY [*replaces poker, straightens up, and stands back to the fire*].   When we have the vote, Amelia, will the men go on having it too?

MRS. MICKLEHAM [*graciously conceding*].   At first. But after a   bit— [MRS. HAGGERTY *enters in bonnet and shawl. The other two exchange a disgusted glance.*] [*Privately.*] Oh, here's that submarine again.

MRS. HAGGERTY.   Aren't they back, yet? [*She comes down to* L. *of the table.*]

MRS. MICKLEHAM.   No, we've been waiting this half-hour. They're at the theatre again.

MRS. HAGGERTY.   I just popped in with an insignificant present for him, as his leave's up. [*She moves above and to* R. *end of the table.*]

MRS. TULLY [*stiffly*].   The same errand brought us.

[MRS. HAGGERTY *takes the chair from* R. *of the table and draws it to some little distance on* MRS. MICKLEHAM'S L.]

MRS. HAGGERTY.   Though not in your set, Mrs. Mickleham, may I sit down? [*This is a timid attempt at a sneer.*]

MRS. MICKLEHAM [*distantly*].   It's not our house.

[MRS. HAGGERTY *sits. An awkward pause.*]

MRS. HAGGERTY.   It's a terrible war.

[*Pause.*]

MRS. TULLY. Is that so?

[*Pause.*]

MRS. HAGGERTY [*draws her chair a trifle nearer*]. I wonder what will happen when it ends?

[*Pause.*]

MRS. MICKLEHAM.   I've no idea. [*She edges her chair nearer the fire, away from the intruder.*]

[MRS. TULLY *sits.*]

MRS. HAGGERTY [*after another pause*].   My present is cigarettes.
MRS. MICKLEHAM [*annoyed*].   So's mine.
MRS. TULLY [*ditto*].   Mine too. [*Casually.*] Mine has gold tips.
MRS. MICKLEHAM [*equally casual*].   So has mine.
MRS. HAGGERTY [*evidently without gold tips, whimpering*].   What care I? Mine—is Exquissitos.

[*The others titter.*]

MRS. MICKLEHAM.   Excuse us, Mrs. Haggerty—if that's your name— but the word is Exquisytos.
MRS. HAGGERTY [*stiffly*].   Much obliged. [*She is inclined to weep.*]
MRS. MICKLEHAM [*rising*].   I think I heard a taxi. [*She goes up to the window.*]
MRS. TULLY [*following her*].   It'll be her third this week.
MRS. HAGGERTY [*as the others peer out through the blind, she turns her chair*].   What is she in?
MRS. MICKLEHAM.   A new astrakhan coat he gave her, with Venus sleeves.
MRS. HAGGERTY.   Has she sold her "Dainty Moments" coat?
MRS. MICKLEHAM [*coming down to above the table*].   Not her. She has them both at the theatre. The one she's wearing, and the other she's carrying flung careless-like over her arm.

[MRS. TULLY *comes down to the fireplace.*]

MRS. HAGGERTY [*to* MRS. MICKLEHAM].   I saw her strutting with him yesterday as if the two of them made a procession. [MRS. MICKLEHAM *ignores this and returns to the window.*] [*To* MRS. HAGGERTY.] She was in her merino, of course.

[MRS. TULLY *turns away to the fireplace.*]

MRS. MICKLEHAM. Hsh! They're coming! [MRS. HAGGERTY *rises, replaces the chair and goes up to the window.*] She'll guess we're here as the light's on. Strike me dead if she's not come mincing in hooked on his arm! [*She crosses down to* L. *of the table.*]

[*Enter* Mrs. Dowey *and* Dowey *as foretold. They leave the door open. Undoubtedly she is putting on airs. The astrakhan is over her merino, and she is in gloves, muff, and bonnet. A cloak is over her arm and she carries a small bag containing a champagne cork. It is not a comic get-up, but quiet and in good taste, though the effect is quaint.* Dowey's *clothes are now clean and his buttons, badges, etc., are bright.*]

Mrs. Dowey.   Kenneth! We have visitors!

Dowey.   Your servant, ladies! [*He closes the door.*]

Mrs. Tully.   Evening! We're not meaning to stay.

Mrs. Dowey.   You're very welcome. [*Rather ostentatiously.*] Just wait till I get out of my muff [*she places it on the table with the bag*]—and my astrakhan—and my cloak [*she places these on back of the chair L. of the table*]—and my Excelsior.... [*This last is the bonnet, which she takes* L. *to the chest of drawers.*]

Mrs. Mickleham.   You've given her a glory time, Mr. Dowey.

Dowey [*throws his bonnet on the table, crossing to the fire, and warming his hands—below* Mrs. Tully].   It's her that has given it to me, ma'am.

[Mrs. Mickleham *moves above the table.*]

Mrs. Dowey [*returning to* L. *of the table, giggling*].   He! he! he! He just pampers me! The Lord forgive us, but being his last night, we had a sit-down supper at a restaurant! I swear, we had champagny wine! [*The others are a little stiff.* Mrs. Dowey *takes the cork out of the bag and holds it up.*] And to them as doubts my words. There's the cork.

Mrs. Mickleham [*stiffly*].   I'm sure.

Mrs. Tully [*approaching, and speaking across the table*].   I would thank you, Mrs. Dowey, not to speak against my Alfred.

Mrs. Dowey.   Me! [*She replaces the cork in her handbag.*]

Dowey [*crossing up between* Mrs. Tully *and* Mrs. Haggerty].   Come, come, ladies! If you say another word I'll kiss the lot of you.

[*Pleased confusion.* Mrs. Tully *retires coyly down* R. Mrs. Haggerty *moves up* c., *while* Mrs. Mickleham *comes* L.C.]

Mrs. Dowey [*during the above*].   Kenneth! [*Above the table.*]

Mrs. Mickleham.   Really! Them sodgers!

Mrs. Tully.   The Kilties is the worst!

Mrs. Mickleham.   I'm sure we don't grudge you your treats, Mrs. Dowey, and sorry we are that this is the end.

Dowey.   Yes, it's the end. Leave's up. [*He glances at* Mrs. Dowey.] I must be off in ten minutes....

[MRS. DOWEY *makes a sudden bolt into the scullery. The others turn and look sympathetically at the door.* DOWEY *turns and goes to the fireplace, his face averted.*]

MRS. MICKLEHAM.   Poor soul. [*They look at* DOWEY.] We must run! [*She crosses to* L. *end of the table, producing the cigarettes from her underskirt pocket.*] You'll be having some last words to say to her.

DOWEY [*facing them with a worried expression*].   I kept her out long on purpose, so as not to have much time to say them in.

MRS. TULLY [*putting her chair back against the wall down* R.].   It's the best way. [*She produces her cigarettes and goes up to* DOWEY.] Just a mere nothing to wish you well, Mr. Dowey. [*She gives him the cigarettes, a little breathless, then goes up towards the door* L.C.]

MRS. MICKLEHAM [*crosses to him below the table, gives him cigarettes*].   A scraping, as one might say. [*She turns and joins* MRS. TULLY, *below and on her* L.]

MRS. HAGGERTY [*comes down to* R. *end of the table*].   The heart is warm, though it may not be gold-tipped. [*She gives him the cigarettes, and retreats* L. *to* R. *of* MRS. TULLY.]

DOWEY [*crossing quickly above and to* L. *of the table, touched*].   You bricks! [*He extends his hand.*] Shake! [*He shakes hands first with* MRS. HAGGERTY, *then* MRS. TULLY, *lastly with* MRS. MICKLEHAM. *They retire to the door in that order,* MRS. HAGGERTY *opening it.*] [*As he crosses* L. *to the chair.*] If you see a soger man up there wi' this sort of thing [*turning, indicates the kilt*], he's the one that's going back with me. [*He puts the cigarettes in his overcoat.*] Tell him not to come down, but to give me till the last moment, and then to whistle. [*He puts on his Tartan scarf.*]

MRS. TULLY.   I understand. Good luck. [*She exits to* R.]

MRS. MICKLEHAM.   Good luck ! [*She exits to* R.]

MRS. HAGGERTY [*pointing to his kilt*].   That's your style! [*She exits to* R.]

[DOWEY *puts on his coat, buttons it up, closes the door up* L., *and stands. Then he tries to grin, but fails. Mutters, "Hell!" Then crosses determinedly to scullery door, and putting his head inside, calls:*]

DOWEY.   Old lady! [*He backs two paces* L.]

[MRS. DOWEY *comes out of the scullery. She is in her merino only, and once more a timid thing.*]

MRS. DOWEY.   Is it—time ?

DOWEY.   Not yet. I've left word with Dickson that he's to whistle when go I must.

MRS. DOWEY [*crosses slowly and sits on the bed* L.].   All's ended.

DOWEY [*who is troubled himself. He crosses to* L. *end of the table*].   Now, now! You promised to be gay.

MRS. DOWEY [*looks up at him and tries to smile*].   Ay, Kenneth.

DOWEY.   It's bad for me. But it's worse for you.

MRS. DOWEY.   The men have their medals to win, you see.

DOWEY.   The women have their medals too. And they wear them in their hearts, where you wear yours. [*He sits on end of the table, and tries to be brusque.*] Come here! [*She starts to rise.*] No, I'll come to you. [*He crosses to* R. *end of the bed, looking down at her.*] My God! You're a woman!

MRS. DOWEY.   I had near forgot it.

DOWEY.   Have you noticed you have never called me "son"?

MRS. DOWEY.   Have I noticed? I was feared, Kenneth. You said I was on probation.

DOWEY.   And so you were. Son! It's a little word, but you've made me value it. Well, the probation's ended.

MRS. DOWEY.   Will I do?

DOWEY [*with a mischievous return to an earlier manner*].   Woman, don't be so forward! Wait till I've proposed.

MRS. DOWEY.   Propose for a mother?

DOWEY.   What for no? [*Kneeling.*] Mrs. Dowey, have I your permission to ask you the most important question an orphan can ask of a nice old lady?

MRS. DOWEY [*giggling*].   None of your sauce, Kenneth!

DOWEY.   For a long time, Mrs. Dowey, you cannot have been unaware of my sonnish feelings for you....

MRS. DOWEY.   Wait till I get my mop to you!

DOWEY.   And if you're not willing to be my mother, I swear I'll never ask another ...

[*She pulls his head down, embraces him, and strokes his hair. Her sadness has come back.*]

MRS. DOWEY.   You're just trying to make me gay.

DOWEY.   I wish you could do the same for me. [*She smiles bravely.*] Was I a well-behaved infant, Mother?

MRS. DOWEY.   Not you, sonny! You were a rampaging rogue!

DOWEY [*sitting back on his heels*].   Was I slow in learning to walk?

MRS. DOWEY.   The quickest in our street! [*The chuckle dies on her lips. She rises, moving L.*] Was that—the whistle?

DOWEY.   No, no! [*He rises.*] See here, in taking me over you have, in a manner of speaking, joined the Black Watch. [*She puts her hands up to her eyes.*] So you've got to be as proud as—as that ghostly piper. [*He comes to attention.*] 'SHUN! [*She "Shun's."*] That's the style! [*He goes to her.*] You've to be true to this little flag, you see. [*He indicates the little flag in her bodice.*]

MRS. DOWEY.   I am true to it, Kenneth.

DOWEY.   You're great. [*He crosses up above the bed for the pack.*] I've sent your name in as being my nearest of kin. Your allowance will be coming to you weekly in the usual way.

MRS. DOWEY.   Eh, is it wicked, Kenneth?

DOWEY [*hitching on his pack*].   I'll take the responsibility for it in both worlds. You see, I want you to be safeguarded in case anything hap ...

MRS. DOWEY.   Kenneth! [*Her head down, her hand out.*]

DOWEY.   'SHUN! [*She obeys.*] Have no fear, I'll come back, covered with mud and medals. [*Trying to be brusque.*] And mind you have that cup of tea waiting for me. Come here ! [*He comes to below the bed. She approaches him, and he sits, pulling her down on his knee. She chuckles.*] What fun we'll have writing to each other. Real letters this time!

MRS. DOWEY.   Ay!

DOWEY.   It would be a good plan if you began the first letter as soon as I've gone.

MRS. DOWEY.   I will.

DOWEY.   I hope that Lady Dolly will go on sending me cakes.

MRS. Dowey.   You may be sure.

DOWEY [*takes off his Tartan scarf and puts it round her neck*].   You must have been a bonny thing when you were young.

MRS. DOWEY [*pushing him away playfully*].   Away with you!

DOWEY.   It sets you fine.

MRS. Dowey.   Blue was always my colour.

[*The whistle is heard.* MRS. DOWEY *rises, and goes to the chair L. of the table, her face averted.* DOWEY *rises.*]

DOWEY.   'SHUN! [*She obeys. He goes to her, turns her round and places his hands affectionately on her shoulders.*] Old lady, when I'm out there in the trenches, I'll have something to think of I never had before—home. This room, you with your mop and pail, are what Blighty means to me now.

She pulls his head down and kisses him on the forejhead. Then pulls herself together and runs into the scullery, closing the door. [*Quick change here.*] DOWEY *gives his pack a hitch, goes for bonnet and puts it on, and slings his rifle. An idea strikes him, and he crosses quickly to R., takes pen, ink, and paper from the shelf above the fire and places them ready for* MRS. DOWEY *on the table. The whistle is repeated. He glances at the window.* DOWEY *goes to the scullery door, opens it softly and peeps in. We gather that Mrs. Dowey is on her knees, for he takes off his bonnet reverently, pauses, and then, turning away, goes out at the door up* L. C. *as—*

The curtain falls.

SCENE III

When the curtain rises, it is early morning, a month or two later. The blinds are up and the early sunshine streams in.

On the table are certain articles, namely, DOWEY'S *bonnet, on the* L. *of this a small packet of letters tied with ribbon, and the champagne cork. In the centre is the cash-box containing the Certificates.*

During this scene, low distant music of pipers playing the Black Watch Lament, The Flowers of the Forest, *is heard.*

MRS. DOWEY *is kneeling at the chest of drawers, taking from a lower drawer her best dress. She rises with it, brushing it carefully with her hand, and takes it over to the table. She lays it down, brushes the bonnet and places this on the dress. She then polishes the champagne cork with her apron and places it by the bonnet.*

The Lament ceases as she does this.

Next, she opens the cash-box and examines the Certificates. Closing it, she places this, too, on the dress.

Faintly, the Lament re-commences. She takes up the letters, presses them for a moment to her bosom, and puts them on the dress. Then she lifts all, and crossing, takes them over to the dr[awer and lays them in.

She then takes the Tartan scarf from a top drawer and spreads it over the things in the lower one. Lastly, she takes a bag of lavender from the upper drawer and places this on the scarf, after smelling it.

The Lament *ceases.*

MRS. DOWEY *closes the drawer gently. Then, turning to her pail and brushes down* L., *she picks them up, and goes slowly, bravely, off to her work through the door up* L.C.

Slow curtain.

TRIFLES
Susan Glaspell

CAST OF CHARACTERS

GEORGE HENDERSON, *County Attorney*
HENRY PETERS, *Sheriff*
LEWIS HALE, *A Neighboring Farmer*
MRS. PETERS
MRS. HALE

Scene: The kitchen in the now abandoned farmhouse of John Wright, a gloomy kitchen, and left without having been put in order—unwashed pans under the sink, a loaf of bread outside the bread-box, a dish-towel on the table—other signs of incompleted work. At the rear the outer door opens and the SHERIFF *comes in followed by the* COUNTY ATTORNEY *and* HALE. *The* SHERIFF *and* HALE *are in middle life, the* COUNTY ATTORNEY *is a young man; all are much bundled up and go at once to the stove. They are followed by the two women—the* SHERIFF's *wife first; she is a slight wiry woman, a thin nervous face.* MRS. HALE *is larger and would ordinarily be called more comfortable looking, but she is disturbed now and looks fearfully about as she enters. The women have come in slowly, and stand close together near the door.*

COUNTY ATTORNEY [*rubbing his hands*]. This feels good. Come up to the fire, ladies.
MRS. PETERS [*after taking a step forward*]. I'm not—cold.
SHERIFF [*unbuttoning his overcoat and stepping away from the stove as if to mark the beginning of official business*]. Now, Mr. Hale, before we move things about, you explain to Mr. Henderson just what you saw when you came here yesterday morning.
COUNTY ATTORNEY. By the way, has anything been moved? Are things just as you left them yesterday?
SHERIFF [*looking about*]. It's just the same. When it dropped below zero last night I thought I'd better send Frank out this morning to make a fire for us—no use getting pneumonia with a big case

on, but I told him not to touch anything except the stove—and you know Frank.

COUNTY ATTORNEY.   Somebody should have been left here yesterday.

SHERIFF.   Oh—yesterday. When I had to send Frank to Morris Center for that man who went crazy—I want you to know I had my hands full yesterday. I knew you could get back from Omaha by today and as long as I went over everything here myself—

COUNTY ATTORNEY.   Well, Mr. Hale, tell just what happened when you came here yesterday morning.

HALE.   Harry and I had started to town with a load of potatoes. We came along the road from my place and as I got here I said, "I'm going to see if I can't get John Wright to go in with me on a party telephone." I spoke to Wright about it once before and he put me off, saying folks talked too much anyway, and all he asked was peace and quiet—I guess you know about how much he talked himself; but I thought maybe if I went to the house and talked about it before his wife, though I said to Harry that I didn't know as what his wife wanted made much difference to John—

COUNTY ATTORNEY.   Let's talk about that later, Mr. Hale. I do want to talk about that, but tell now just what happened when you got to the house.

HALE.   I didn't hear or see anything; I knocked at the door, and still it was all quiet inside. I knew they must be up, it was past eight o'clock. So I knocked again, and I thought I heard somebody say, "Come in." I wasn't sure, I'm not sure yet, but I opened the door—this door [*indicating the door by which the two women are still standing*] and there in that rocker—[*pointing to it*] sat Mrs. Wright.

[*They all look at the rocker.*]

COUNTY ATTORNEY.   What—was she doing?

HALE.   She was rockin' back and forth. She had her apron in her hand and was kind of—pleating it.

COUNTY ATTORNEY.   And how did she—look?

HALE.   Well, she looked queer.

COUNTY ATTORNEY.   How do you mean—queer?

HALE.   Well, as if she didn't know what she was going to do next. And kind of done up.

COUNTY ATTORNEY.   How did she seem to feel about your coming?

HALE.   Why, I don't think she minded—one way or other. She didn't pay much attention. I said, "How do, Mrs. Wright, it's cold, ain't it?" And she said, "Is it?"—and went on kind of pleating at her apron. Well, I was surprised; she didn't ask me to come up to the stove, or to set down, but just sat there, not even looking at me, so I said, "I want to see John." And then she—laughed. I guess you would call it a laugh. I thought of Harry and the team outside, so I said a little sharp: "Can't I see John?" "No," she says, kind o' dull like. "Ain't he home?" says I. "Yes," says she, "he's home." "Then why can't I see him?" I asked her, out of patience. "'Cause he's dead," says she. "*Dead?*" says I. She just nodded her head, not getting a bit excited, but rockin' back and forth. "Why—where is he?" says I, not knowing what to say. She just pointed upstairs— like that [*himself pointing to the room above*]. I got up, with the idea of going up there. I walked from there to here—then I says, "Why, what did he die of?" "He died of a rope round his neck," says she, and just went on pleatin' at her apron. Well, I went out and called Harry. I thought I might—need help. We went upstairs and there he was lyin'—

COUNTY ATTORNEY.   I think I'd rather have you go into that upstairs, where you can point it all out. Just go on now with the rest of the story.

HALE.   Well, my first thought was to get that rope off. It looked . . . [*stops, his face twitches*] . . . but Harry, he went up to him, and he said, "No; he's dead all right, and we'd better not touch anything." So we went back down stairs. She was still sitting that same way. "Has anybody been notified?" I asked. "No," says she, unconcerned. "Who did this, Mrs. Wright?" said Harry. He said it business-like—and she stopped pleatin' of her apron. "I don't know," she says. "You don't *know?*" says Harry. "No," says she. "Weren't you sleepin' in the bed with him?" says Harry. "Yes," says she, "but I was on the inside." "Somebody slipped a rope round his neck and strangled him and you didn't wake up?" says Harry. "I didn't wake up," she said after him. We must 'a looked as if we didn't see how that could be, for after a minute she said, "I sleep sound." Harry was going to ask her more questions but I said maybe we ought to let her tell her story first to the coroner, or the sheriff, so Harry went fast as he could to Rivers' place, where there's a telephone.

COUNTY ATTORNEY.   And what did Mrs. Wright do when she knew that you had gone for the coroner?

HALE.   She moved from that chair to this one over here [*pointing to a small chair in the corner*] and just sat there with her hands held together and looking down. I got a feeling that I ought to make

some conversation, so I said I had come in to see if John wanted
to put in a telephone, and at that she started to laugh, and then
she stopped and looked at me—scared. [*The* COUNTY ATTORNEY,
who has had his notebook out, makes a note.] I dunno, maybe it wasn't
scared. I wouldn't like to say it was. Soon Harry got back, and
then Dr. Lloyd came, and you, Mr. Peters, and so I guess that's all
I know that you don't.

COUNTY ATTORNEY [*looking around*].   I guess we'll go upstairs first—
and then out to the barn and around there. [*To the* SHERIFF.] You're
convinced that there was nothing important here—nothing that
would point to any motive.

SHERIFF.   Nothing here but kitchen things.

[*The* COUNTY ATTORNEY, *after again looking around the kitchen, opens the
door of a cupboard closet. He gets up on a chair and looks on a shelf. Pulls
his hand away, sticky.*]

COUNTY ATTORNEY. Here's a nice mess.

[*The women draw nearer.*]

MRS. PETERS [*to the other woman*].   Oh, her fruit; it did freeze. [*To the*
LAWYER.] She worried about that when it turned so cold. She said
the fire'd go out and her jars would break.

SHERIFF.   Well, can you beat the women! Held for murder and wor-
ryin' about her preserves.

COUNTY ATTORNEY.   I guess before we're through she may have
something more serious than preserves to worry about.

HALE.   Well, women are used to worrying over trifles.

[*The two women move a little closer together.*]

COUNTY ATTORNEY [*with the gallantry of a young politician*].   And yet,
for all their worries, what would we do without the ladies? [*The
women do not unbend. He goes to the sink, takes a dipperful of water
from the pail and pouring it into a basin, washes his hands. Starts to wipe
them on the roller-towel, turns it for a cleaner place.*] Dirty towels!
[*Kicks his foot against the pans under the sink.*] Not much of a housekeeper, would you say, ladies?

MRS. HALE [*stiffly*].   There's a great deal of work to be done on a
farm.

COUNTY ATTORNEY.   To be sure. And yet [*with a little bow to her*] I
know there are some Dickson county farmhouses which do not
have such roller towels.

[*He gives it a pull to expose its full length again.*]

MRS. HALE. Those towels get dirty awful quick. Men's hands aren't always as clean as they might be.

COUNTY ATTORNEY. Ah, loyal to your sex, I see. But you and Mrs. Wright were neighbors. I suppose you were friends, too.

MRS. HALE [*shaking her head*]. I've not seen much of her of late years. I've not been in this house—it's more than a year.

COUNTY ATTORNEY. And why was that? You didn't like her?

MRS. HALE. I liked her all well enough. Farmers' wives have their hands full, Mr. Henderson. And then—

COUNTY ATTORNEY. Yes—?

MRS. HALE [*looking about*]. It never seemed a very cheerful place.

COUNTY ATTORNEY. No—it's not cheerful. I shouldn't say she had the homemaking instinct.

MRS. HALE. Well, I don't know as Wright had, either.

COUNTY ATTORNEY. You mean that they didn't get on very well?

MRS. HALE. No, I don't mean anything. But I don't think a place'd be any cheerfuller for John Wright's being in it.

COUNTY ATTORNEY. I'd like to talk more of that a little later. I want to get the lay of things upstairs now.

[*He goes to the left, where three steps lead to a stair door.*]

SHERIFF. I suppose anything Mrs. Peters does'll be all right. She was to take in some clothes for her, you know, and a few little things. We left in such a hurry yesterday.

COUNTY ATTORNEY. Yes, but I would like to see what you take, Mrs. Peters, and keep an eye out for anything that might be of use to us.

MRS. PETERS. Yes, Mr. Henderson.

[*The women listen to the men's steps on the stairs, then look about the kitchen.*]

MRS. HALE. I'd hate to have men coming into my kitchen, snooping around and criticising.

[*She arranges the pans under sink which the* LAWYER *had shoved out of place.*]

MRS. PETERS. Of course it's no more than their duty.

MRS. HALE. Duty's all right, but I guess that deputy sheriff that came out to make the fire might have got a little of this on. [*Gives the roller towel a pull.*] Wish I'd thought of that sooner. Seems mean to talk about her for not having things slicked up when she had to come away in such a hurry.

MRS. PETERS [*who has gone to a small table in the left rear corner of the room, and lifted one end of a towel that covers a pan*].   She had bread set.

[*Stands still.*]

MRS. HALE [*eyes fixed on a loaf of bread beside the breadbox, which is on a low shelf at the other side of the room. Moves slowly toward it*].   She was going to put this in there. [*Picks up loaf, then abruptly drops it. In a manner of returning to familiar things.*] It's a shame about her fruit. I wonder if it's all gone. [*Gets up on the chair and looks.*] I think there's some here that's all right, Mrs. Peters.   Yes—here; [*Holding it toward the window*] this is cherries, too. [*Looking again.*] I declare I believe that's the only one. [*Gets down, bottle in her hand. Goes to the sink and wipes it off on the outside.*] She'll feel awful bad after all her hard work in the hot weather. I remember the afternoon I put up my cherries last summer.

[*She puts the bottle on the big kitchen table, center of the room. With a sigh, is about to sit down in the rocking-chair. Before she is seated realizes what chair it is; with a slow look at it, steps back. The chair which she has touched rocks back and forth.*]

MRS. PETERS.   Well, I must get those things from the front room closet. [*She goes to the door at the right, but after looking into the other room, steps back.*] You coming with me, Mrs. Hale? You could help me carry them.

[*They go in the other room; reappear,* MRS. PETERS *carrying a dress and skirt,* MRS. HALE *following with a pair of shoes.*

MRS. PETERS.   My, it's cold in there.

[*She puts the clothes on the big table, and hurries to the stove.*]

MRS. HALE [*examining the skirt*].   Wright was close. I think maybe that's why she kept so much to herself. She didn't even belong to the Ladies Aid. I suppose she felt she couldn't do her part, and then you don't enjoy things when you feel shabby. She used to wear pretty clothes and be lively, when she was Minnie Foster, one of the town girls singing in the choir. But that—oh, that was thirty years ago. This all you was to take in?

MRS. PETERS.   She said she wanted an apron. Funny thing to want, for there isn't much to get you dirty in jail, goodness knows. But I suppose just to make her feel more natural. She said they was in the top drawer in this cupboard. Yes, here. And then her little shawl that always hung behind the door. [*Opens stair door and looks.*] Yes, here it is. [*Quickly shuts door leading upstairs.*]

MRS. HALE [*abruptly moving toward her*].   Mrs. Peters?

MRS. PETERS.   Yes, Mrs. Hale?

MRS. HALE.   Do you think she did it?

MRS. PETERS [*in a frightened voice*].   Oh, I don't know.

MRS. HALE.   Well, I don't think she did. Asking for an apron and her little shawl. Worrying about her fruit.

MRS. PETERS [*starts to speak, glances up, where footsteps are heard in the room above. In a low voice.*].   Mr. Peters says it looks bad for her. Mr. Henderson is awful sarcastic in a speech and he'll make fun of her sayin' she didn't wake up.

MRS. HALE.   Well, I guess John Wright didn't wake when they was slipping that rope under his neck.

MRS. PETERS.   No, it's strange. It must have been done awful crafty and still. They say it was such a—funny way to kill a man, rigging it all up like that.

MRS. HALE.   That's just what Mr. Hale said. There was a gun in the house. He says that's what he can't understand.

MRS. PETERS.   Mr. Henderson said coming out that what was needed for the case was a motive; something to show anger, or—sudden feeling.

MRS. HALE [*who is standing by the table*].   Well, I don't see any signs of anger around here. [*She puts her hand on the dish towel which lies on the table, stands looking down at table, one half of which is clean, the other half messy.*] It's wiped to here. [*Makes a move as if to finish work, then turns and looks at loaf of bread outside the breadbox. Drops towel. In that voice of coming back to familiar things.*] Wonder how they are finding things upstairs. I hope she had it a little more red-up up there. You know, it seems kind of *sneaking*. Locking her up in town and then coming out here and trying to get her own house to turn against her!

MRS. PETERS.   But Mrs. Hale, the law is the law.

MRS. HALE.   I s'pose 'tis. [*Unbuttoning her coat.*] Better loosen up your things, Mrs. Peters. You won't feel them when you go out.

[MRS. PETERS *takes off her fur tippet, goes to hang it on hook at back of room, stands looking at the under part of the small corner table.*]

MRS. PETERS.   She was piecing a quilt. [*She brings the large sewing basket and they look at the bright pieces.*]

MRS. HALE.   It's log cabin pattern. Pretty, isn't it? I wonder if she was goin' to quilt it or just knot it?

Footsteps have been heard coming down the stairs. The SHERIFF *enters followed by* HALE *and the* COUNTY ATTORNEY.]

SHERIFF.   They wonder if she was going to quilt it or just knot it!

[*The men laugh, the women look abashed.*]

COUNTY ATTORNEY [*rubbing his hands over the stove*].   Frank's fire didn't do much up there, did it? Well, let's go out to the barn and get that cleared up.

[*The men go outside.*]

MRS. HALE [*resentfully*].   I don't know as there's anything so strange, our takin' up our time with little things while we're waiting for them to get the evidence. [*She sits down at the big table smoothing out a block with decision.*] I don't see as it's anything to laugh about.

MRS. PETERS [*apologetically*].   Of course they've got awful important things on their minds. [*Pulls up a chair and joins* MRS. HALE *at the table.*]

MRS. HALE [*examining another block*].   Mrs. Peters, look at this one. Here, this is the one she was working on, and look at the sewing! All the rest of it has been so nice and even. And look at this! It's all over the place! Why, it looks as if she didn't know what she was about!

[*After she had said this they look at each other, then start to glance back at the door. After an instant* MRS. HALE *has pulled at a knot and ripped the sewing.*

MRS. PETERS.   Oh, what are you doing, Mrs. Hale?

MRS. HALE [*mildly*].   Just pulling out a stitch or two that's not sewed very good. [*Threading a needle.*] Bad sewing always made me fidgety.

MRS. PETERS [*nervously*].   I don't think we ought to touch things.

MRS. HALE.   I'll just finish up this end. [*Suddenly stopping and leaning forward.*] Mrs. Peters?

MRS. PETERS.   Yes, Mrs. Hale?

MRS. HALE.   What do you suppose she was so nervous about?

MRS. PETERS.   Oh—I don't know. I don't know as she was nervous. I sometimes sew awful queer when I'm just tired. [MRS. HALE *starts to say something, looks at* MRS. PETERS, *then goes on sewing.*] Well I must get these things wrapped up. They may be through sooner than we think. [*Putting apron and other things together.*] I wonder where I can find a piece of paper, and string.

MRS. HALE.   In that cupboard, maybe.

MRS. PETERS [*looking in cupboard.*]   Why, here's a bird-cage. [*Holds it up.*] Did she have a bird, Mrs. Hale?

MRS. HALE. Why, I don't know whether she did or not—I've not been here for so long. There was a man around last year selling canaries cheap, but I don't know as she took one; maybe she did. She used to sing real pretty herself.

MRS. PETERS [*glancing around*]. Seems funny to think of a bird here. But she must have had one, or why would she have a cage? I wonder what happened to it.

MRS. HALE. I s'pose maybe the cat got it.

MRS. PETERS. No, she didn't have a cat. She's got that feeling some people have about cats—being afraid of them. My cat got in her room and she was real upset and asked me to take it out.

MRS. HALE. My sister Bessie was like that. Queer, ain't it?

MRS. PETERS [*examining the cage*]. Why, look at this door. It's broke. One hinge is pulled apart.

MRS. HALE [*looking too*]. Looks as if someone must have been rough with it.

MRS. PETERS. Why, yes. [*She brings the cage forward and puts it on the table.*

MRS. HALE. I wish if they're going to find any evidence they'd be about it. I don't like this place.

MRS. PETERS. But I'm awful glad you came with me, Mrs. Hale. It would be lonesome for me sitting here alone.

MRS. HALE. It would, wouldn't it? [*Dropping her sewing.*] But I tell you what I do wish, Mrs. Peters. I wish I had come over sometimes when *she* was here. I—[*Looking around the room*]— wish I had.

MRS. PETERS. But of course you were awful busy, Mrs. Hale—your house and your children.

MRS. HALE. I could've come. I stayed away because it weren't cheer-ful—and that's why I ought to have come. I—I've never liked this place. Maybe because it's down in a hollow and you don't see the road. I dunno what it is, but it's a lonesome place and always was, I wish I had come over to see Minnie Foster sometimes. I can see now—[*Shakes her head.*]

MRS. PETERS. Well, you mustn't reproach yourself, Mrs. Hale. Somehow we just don't see how it is with other folks until— something comes up.

MRS. HALE. Not having children makes less work—but it makes a quiet house, and Wright out to work all day, and no company when he did come in. Did you know John Wright, Mrs. Peters?

MRS. PETERS. No; I've seen him in town. They say he was a good man.

MRS. HALE.   Yes—good; he didn't drink, and kept his word as well as most, I guess, and paid his debts. But he was a hard man, Mrs. Peters. Just to pass the time of day with him—[*Shivers.*] Like a raw wind that gets to the bone. [*Pauses, her eye falling on the cage.*] I should think she would 'a wanted a bird. But what do you suppose went with it?

MRS. PETERS.   I don't know, unless it got sick and died. [*She reaches over and swings the broken door, swings it again, both women watch it.*

MRS. HALE.   You weren't raised round here, were you? [MRS. PETERS *shakes her head.*] You didn't know—her?

MRS. PETERS.   Not till they brought her yesterday.

MRS. HALE.   She—come to think of it, she was kind of like a bird herself—real sweet and pretty, but kind of timid and—fluttery. How—she—did—change. [*Silence; then as if struck by a happy thought and relieved to get back to every day things.*] Tell you what, Mrs. Peters, why don't you take the quilt in with you? It might take up her mind.

MRS. PETERS.   Why, I think that's a real nice idea, Mrs. Hale. There couldn't possibly be any objection to it, could there? Now, just what would I take? I wonder if her patches are in here—and her things.

[*They look in the sewing basket.*]

MRS. HALE.   Here's some red. I expect this has got sewing things in it. [*Brings out a fancy box.*] What a pretty box. Looks like something somebody would give you. Maybe her scissors are in here. [*Opens box. Suddenly puts her hand to her nose.*] Why—[MRS. PETERS *bends nearer, then turns her face away.*] There's something wrapped up in this piece of silk.

MRS. PETERS.   Why, this isn't her scissors.

MRS. HALE [*lifting the silk*].   Oh, Mrs. Peters—its—

[MRS. PETERS *bends closer.*]

MRS. PETERS.   It's the bird.

MRS. HALE [*jumping up*].   But, Mrs. Peters—look at it! Its neck! Look at its neck! It's all—other side *to.*

MRS. PETERS.   Somebody—wrung—its—neck.

[*Their eyes meet. A look of growing comprehension, of horror. Steps are heard outside.* MRS. HALE *slips box under quilt pieces, and sinks into her chair.* Enter SHERIFF *and* COUNTY ATTORNEY. MRS. PETERS *rises.*

COUNTY ATTORNEY[*as one turning from serious things to little pleasantries*].   Well, ladies, have you decided whether she was going to quilt it or knot it?

MRS. PETERS. We think she was going to—knot it.

COUNTY ATTORNEY. Well, that's interesting, I'm sure. [*Seeing the bird-cage.*] Has the bird flown?

MRS. HALE [*putting more quilt pieces over the box*]. We think the—cat got it.

COUNTY ATTORNEY [*preoccupied*]. Is there a cat?

[MRS. HALE *glances in a quick covert way at* MRS. PETERS.]

MRS. PETERS. Well, not *now.* They're superstitious, you know. They leave.

COUNTY ATTORNEY [*to* SHERIFF PETERS, *continuing an interrupted conversation*]. No sign at all of anyone having come from the outside. Their own rope. Now let's go up again and go over it piece by piece. [*They start upstairs.*] It would have to have been someone who knew just the—

[MRS. PETERS *sits down. The two women sit there not looking at one another, but as if peering into something and at the same time holding back. When they talk now it is in the manner of feeling their way over strange ground, as if afraid of what they are saying, but as if they can not help saying it.*

MRS. HALE. She liked the bird. She was going to bury it in that pretty box.

MRS. PETERS [*in a whisper*]. When I was a girl—my kitten—there was a boy took a hatchet, and before my eyes—and before I could get there—[*Covers her face an instant.*] If they hadn't held me back I would have—[*catches herself, looks upstairs where steps are heard, falters weakly*]—hurt him.

MRS. HALE [*with a slow look around her*]. I wonder how it would seem never to have had any children around. [*Pause.*] No, Wright wouldn't like the bird—a thing that sang. She used to sing. He killed that, too.

MRS. PETERS [*moving uneasily*]. We don't know who killed the bird.

MRS. HALE. I knew John Wright.

MRS. PETERS. It was an awful thing was done in this house that night, Mrs. Hale. Killing a man while he slept, slipping a rope around his neck that choked the life out of him.

MRS. HALE. His neck. Choked the life out of him. [*Her hand goes out and rests on the bird-cage.*

MRS. PETERS [*with rising voice.*]. We don't know who killed him. We don't *know.*

MRS. HALE [*her own feeling not interrupted*]. If there'd been years and years of nothing, then a bird to sing to you, it would be awful—still, after the bird was still.

MRS. PETERS [*something within her speaking*].   I know what stillness is. When we homesteaded in Dakota, and my first baby died—after he was two years old, and me with no other then—

MRS. HALE [*moving*].   How soon do you suppose they'll be through, looking for the evidence?

MRS. PETERS.   I know what stillness is. [*Pulling herself back.*] The law has got to punish crime, Mrs. Hale.

MRS. HALE [*not as if answering that*].   I wish you'd seen Minnie Foster when she wore a white dress with blue ribbons and stood up there in the choir and sang. [*A look around the room.*] Oh, I *wish* I'd come over here once in a while! That was a crime! That was a crime! Who's going to punish that?

MRS. PETERS [*looking upstairs*].   We mustn't—take on.

MRS. HALE.   I might have known she needed help! I know how things can be—for women, I tell you, it's queer, Mrs. Peters. We live close together and we live far apart. We all go through the same things—it's all just a different kind of the same thing. [*Brushes her eyes, noticing the bottle of fruit, reaches out for it.*] If I was you I wouldn't tell her her fruit was gone. Tell her it *ain't*. Tell her it's all right. Take this in to prove it to her. She—she may never know whether it was broke or not.

MRS. PETERS [*takes the bottle, looks about for something to wrap it in; takes petticoat from the clothes brought from the other room, very nervously begins winding this around the bottle. In a false voice.*].   My, it's a good thing the men couldn't hear us. Wouldn't they just laugh! Getting all stirred up over a little thing like a—dead canary. As if that could have anything to do with—with—wouldn't they *laugh*!

[*The men are heard coming down stairs.*]

MRS. HALE. [*under her breath.*]   Maybe they would—maybe they wouldn't.

COUNTY ATTORNEY.   No, Peters, it's all perfectly clear except a reason for doing it. But you know juries when it comes to women. If there was some definite thing. Something to show—something to make a story about—a thing that would connect up with this strange way of doing it—

[*The women's eyes meet for an instant. Enter* HALE *from outer door.*]

HALE.   Well, I've got the team around. Pretty cold out there.

COUNTY ATTORNEY.   I'm going stay here a while by myself. [*To the* SHERIFF.] You can send Frank out for me, can't you? I want to go over everything. I'm not satisfied that we can't do better.

SHERIFF. Do you want to see what Mrs. Peters is going to take in?

[*The* LAWYER *goes to the table, picks up the apron, laughs.*]

COUNTY ATTORNEY. Oh, I guess they're not very dangerous things the ladies have picked out. [*Moves a few things about, disturbing the quilt pieces which cover the box. Steps back.*] No, Mrs. Peters doesn't need supervising. For that matter, a sheriff's wife is married to the law. Ever think of it that way, Mrs. Peters?

MRS. PETERS. Not—just that way.

SHERIFF [*chuckling*]. Married to the law. [*Moves toward the other room.*] I just want you to come in here a minute, George. We ought to take a look at these windows.

COUNTY ATTORNEY [*scoffingly*]. Oh, windows!

SHERIFF. We'll be right out, Mr. Hale.

[HALE *goes outside. The* SHERIFF *follows the* COUNTY ATTORNEY *into the other room. Then* MRS. HALE *rises, hands tight together, looking intensely at* MRS. PETERS, *whose eyes make a slow turn, finally meeting* MRS. HALE'S. *A moment* MRS. HALE *holds her, then her own eyes point the way to where the box is concealed. Suddenly* MRS. PETERS *throws back quilt pieces and tries to put the box in the bag she is wearing. It is too big. She opens box, starts to take bird out, cannot touch it, goes to pieces, stands there helpless. Sound of a knob turning in the other room.* MRS. HALE *snatches the box and puts it in the pocket of her big coat. Enter* COUNTY ATTORNEY *and* SHERIFF.]

COUNTY ATTORNEY [*facetiously*]. Well, Henry, at least we found out that she was not going to quilt it. She was going to—what is it you call it, ladies?

MRS. HALE [*her hand against her pocket*]. We call it—knot it, Mr. Henderson.

CURTAIN

THE MOON OF THE CARIBBEES
Eugene O'Neill

CAST OF CHARACTERS

SEAMEN OF THE BRITISH TRAMP STEAMER, GLENCAIRN

YANK
DRISCOLL
OLSON
DAVIS
COCKY
SMITTY
PAUL

LAMPS, *the lamptrimmer*
CHIPS, *the carpenter*
OLD TOM, *the donkeyman*

FIREMEN ON THE GLENCAIRN

BIG FRANK
DICK
MAX
PADDY

WEST INDIAN NEGRESSES

BELLA
SUSIE
VIOLET
PEARL

THE FIRST MATE

Two other seamen—SCOTTY AND IVAN—and several other members of the stokehole-engine-room crew.

Scene: A forward section of the main deck of the British tramp steamer Glencairn, at anchor off an island in the West Indies. The full moon, half-way up the sky, throws a clear light on the deck. The sea is calm and the ship motionless.

154

On the left two of the derrick booms of the foremast jut out at an angle of forty-five degrees, black against the sky. In the rear the dark outline of the port bulwark is sharply defined against a distant strip of coral beach, white in the moonlight, fringed with coco palms whose tops rise clear of the horizon. On the right is the forecastle with an open doorway in the center leading to the seamen's and firemen's compartments. On either side of the doorway are two closed doors opening on the quarters of the Bo'sun, the ship's carpenter, the messroom steward, and the donkeyman—what might be called the petty officers of the ship. Near each bulwark there is also a short stairway, like a section of fire escape, leading up to the forecastle head [the top of the forecastle]—the edge of which can be seen on the right.

In the center of the deck, and occupying most of the space, is the large, raised square of the number one hatch, covered with canvas, battened down for the night.

A melancholy negro chant, faint and far-off, drifts, crooning, over the water.

Most of the seamen and firemen are reclining or sitting on the hatch. PAUL *is leaning against the port bulwark, the upper part of his stocky figure outlined against the sky.* SMITTY *and* COCKY *are sitting on the edge of the forecastle head with their legs dangling over. Nearly all are smoking pipes or cigarettes. The majority are dressed in patched suits of dungaree. Quite a few are in their bare feet and some of them, especially the firemen, have nothing on but a pair of pants and an undershirt. A good many wear caps.*

There is the low murmur of different conversations going on in the separate groups as the curtain rises. This is followed by a sudden silence in which the singing from the land can be plainly heard.

DRISCOLL [*a powerfully built Irishman who is on the edge of the hatch, front—irritably*].   Will ye listen to them naygurs? I wonder now, do call that keenin' a song?

SMITTY [*a young Englishman with a blond mustache. He is sitting on the forecastle head looking out over the water with his chin supported on his hands*].   It doesn't make a chap feel very cheerful, does it? [*He sighs.*]

COCKY [*a wizened runt of a man with a straggling gray mustache—slapping* SMITTY *on the back*].   Cheero, ole dear! Down't be ser dawn in the marf, Duke. She loves yer.

SMITTY [*gloomily*].   Shut up, Cocky! [*He turns away from* COCKY *and falls to dreaming again, staring toward the spot on shore where the singing seems to come from.*]

BIG FRANK [*a huge fireman sprawled out on the right of the hatch—waving a hand toward the land*].   They bury somebody—py chiminy Christmas, I tink so from way it sound.

YANK [*a rather good-looking rough who is sitting beside* DRISCOLL].   What d'yuh mean, bury? They don't plant 'em down here, Dutchy. They eat 'em to save fun'ral expenses. I guess this guy went down the wrong way an' they got indigestion.

COCKY.   Indigestion! Ho yus, not 'arf! Down't yer know as them blokes 'as two stomacks like a bleedin' camel?

DAVIS [*a short, dark man seated on the right of hatch*].   An' you seen the two, I s'pect, ain't you?

COCKY [*scornfully*].   Down't be showin' yer igerance be tryin' to make a mock o' me what has seen more o' the world than yeself ever will.

MAX [*a Swedish fireman—from the rear of hatch*].   Spin dat yarn, Cocky.

COCKY.   It's Gawd's troof, what I tole yer. I 'eard it from a bloke what was captured pris'ner by 'em in the Solomon Islands. Shipped wiv 'im one voyage. 'Twas a rare treat to 'ear 'im tell what 'appened to 'im among 'em. [*musingly*] 'E was a funny bird, 'e was—'ailed from Mile End, 'e did.

DRISCOLL [*with a snort*].   Another lyin' Cockney, the loike av yourself!

LAMPS [*a fat Swede who is sitting on a camp stool in front of his door talking with* CHIPS].   Where you meet up with him, Cocky?

CHIPS [*a lanky Scotchman—derisively*].   In New Guinea, I'll lay my oath!

COCKY [*defiantly*].   Yus! It was in New Guinea, time I was shipwrecked there. [*There is a perfect storm of groans and laughter at this speech.*]

YANK [*getting up*].   Yuh know what we said yuh'd get if yuh sprung any of that lyin' New Guinea dope on us again, don't yuh? Close that trap if yuh don't want a duckin' over the side.

COCKY.   Ow, I was on'y tryin' to edicate yer a bit. [*He sinks into dignified silence.*]

YANK [*nodding toward the shore*].   Don't yuh know this is the West Indies, yuh crazy mut? They're ain't no cannibals here. They're only common niggers.

DRISCOLL [*irritably*].   Whativir they are, the divil take their cryin'. It's enough to give a man the jigs listenin' to 'em.

YANK [*with a grin*].   What's the matter, Drisc? Yuh're as sore as a boil about somethin'.

DRISCOLL.   I'm dyin' wid impatience to have a dhrink; an' that blarsted bumboat naygur woman took her oath she'd bring back rum enough for the lot av us whin she came back on board tonight.

BIG FRANK [*overhearing this—in a loud eager voice*].   You say the bumboat voman vill bring booze?

DRISCOLL [*sarcastically*]. That's right—tell the Old Man about ut, an' the Mate, too. [*All of the crew have edged nearer to* DRISCOLL *and are listening to the conversation with an air of suppressed excitement.* DRISCOLL *lowers his voice impressively and addresses them all.*] She said she cud snake ut on board in the bottoms av thim baskets av fruit they're goin' to bring wid 'em to sell to us for'ard.

THE DONKEYMAN [*an old gray-headed man with a kindly, wrinkled face. He is sitting on a camp stool in front of his door, right front*]. She'll be bringin' some black women with her this time—or times has changed since I put in here last.

DRISCOLL. She said she wud—two or three—more, maybe, I dunno. [*This announcement is received with great enthusiasm by all hands.*]

COCKY. Wot a bloody lark!

OLSON. Py yingo, we have one hell of a time!

DRISCOLL [*warningly*]. Remimber ye must be quiet about ut, ye scuts—wid the dhrink, I mane—ivin if the bo'sun is ashore. The Old Man ordered her to bring no booze on board or he wudn't buy a thing off av her for the ship.

PADDY [*a squat, ugly Liverpool Irishman*]. To the divil wid him!

BIG FRANK [*turning on him*]. Shud up, you tamn fool, Paddy! You vant make trouble? [*To* DRISCOLL] You und me, ve keep dem quiet, Drisc.

DRISCOLL. Right ye are, Dutchy. I'll split the skull av the first wan av ye starts to foight. [*Three bells are heard striking.*]

DAVIS. Three bells. When's she comin', Drisc?

DRISCOLL. She'll be here any minute now, surely. [*to* PAUL, *who has returned to his position by the bulwark after hearing* DRISCOLL'S *news.*] D'you see 'em comin', Paul?

PAUL. I don't see anyting like bumboat. [*They all set themselves to wait, lighting pipes, cigarettes, and making themselves comfortable. There is a silence broken only by the mournful singing of the negroes on shore.*]

SMITTY [*slowly—with a trace of melancholy*]. I wish they'd stop that song. It makes you think of—well—things you ought to forget. Rummy go, what?

COCKY [*slapping him on the back*]. Cheero, ole love! We'll be 'avin our rum in arf a mo', Duke. [*He comes down to the deck, leaving* SMITTY *alone on the forecastle head.*]

BIG FRANK. Sing someting, Drisc. Den ve don't hear dot yelling.

DAVIS. Give us a chanty, Drisc.

PADDY. Wan all av us knows.

MAX. We all sing in on chorus.

OLSON. "Rio Grande," Drisc.

BIG FRANK. No, ve don't know dot. Sing "Viskey Johnny."

CHIPS. "Flyin' Cloud."

COCKY. Now! Guv us "Maid o' Amsterdam."

LAMPS. "Santa Anna" iss good one.

DRISCOLL. Shut your mouths, all av you. [*Scornfully.*] A chanty it ut ye want? I'll bet me whole pay day there's not wan in the crowd 'ceptin' Yank here, an' Ollie, an' meself, an' Lamps an' Cocky, maybe, wud be sailors enough to know the main from mizzen on a windjammer. Ye've heard the names av chanties but divil a note av the tune or a loine av the words do ye know. There's hardly a rale deep-water sailor lift on the seas, more's the pity.

YANK. Give us "Blow The Man Down." We all know some of that. [*A chorus of assenting voices: Yes!—Righto!—Let 'er drive! Start 'er, Drisc! etc.*]

DRISCOLL. Come in then, all av ye. [*He sings:*] As I was a-roamin' down Paradise Street—

ALL. Wa-a-ay, blow the man down!

DRISCOLL. As I was a-roamin' down Paradise Street—

ALL. Give us some time to blow the man down!

CHORUS Blow the man down, boys, oh, blow the man down!
        Wa-a-ay, blow the man down!
        As I was a-roamin' down Paradise Street—
        Give us some time to blow the man down!

DRISCOLL. A pretty young maiden I chanced for to meet.

ALL. Wa-a-ay, blow the man down!

DRISCOLL. A pretty young maiden I chanced for to meet.

ALL. Give us some time to blow the man down!

CHORUS. Blow the man down, boys, oh, blow the man down!
        Wa-a-ay, blow the man down!
        A pretty young maiden I chanced for to meet.
        Give us some time to blow the man down!

PAUL [*just as* DRISCOLL *is clearing his throat preparatory to starting the next verse*]. Hay, Drisc! Here she come, I tink. Some bumboat comin' dis way. [*They all rush to the side and look toward the land.*]

YANK. There's five or six of them in it—and they paddle like skirts.

DRISCOLL [*wildly elated*]. Hurroo, ye scuts! 'Tis thim right enough. [*He does a few jig steps on the deck.*]

OLSON [*after a pause during which all are watching the approaching boat*]. Py yingo, I see six in boat, yes, sir.

DAVIS. I kin make out the baskets. See 'em there amidships?

BIG FRANK. Vot kind booze dey bring—viskey?

DRISCOLL. Rum, foine West Indy rum wid a kick in ut loike a mule's hoind leg.

LAMPS. Maybe she don't bring any; maybe skipper scare her.

DRISCOLL. Don't be throwin' cold water, Lamps. I'll skin her black hoide off av her if she goes back on her worrd.

YANK. Here they come. Listen to 'em gigglin'. [*Calling.*] Oh, you kiddo! [*The sound of women's voices can be heard talking and laughing.*]

DRISCOLL [*calling*]. Is ut you, Mrs. Old Black Joe?

A WOMAN'S VOICE. Ullo, Mike! [*There is loud feminine laughter at this retort.*]

DRISCOLL. Shake a leg an' come abord thin.

THE WOMAN'S VOICE. We're a-comin'.

DRISCOLL. Come on, Yank. You an' me'd best be goin' to give 'em a hand wid their truck. 'Twill put em in good spirits.

COCKY [*as they start off left*]. Ho, you ain't 'arf a fox, Drisc. Down't drink it all afore we sees it.

DRISCOLL [*over his shoulder*]. You'll be havin' yours, me sonny bye, don't fret. [*He and YANK go off left.*]

COCKY [*licking his lips*]. Gawd blimey, I can do wiv a wet.

DAVIS. Me, too!

CHIPS. I'll bet there ain't none of us'll let any go to waste.

BIG FRANK. I could trink a whole barrel mineself, py chiminy Christmas!

COCKY. I 'opes all the gels ain't as bloomin' ugly as 'er. Looked like a bloody organ-grinder's monkey, she did. Gawd, I couldn't put up wiv the likes of 'er!

PADDY. Ye'll be lucky if any of thim looks at ye, ye squint-eyed runt.

COCKY [*angrily*]. Ho, yus? You ain't no bleedin' beauty prize yeself, me man. A 'airy ape, I calls yer.

PADDY [*walking toward him—truculently*]. Whot's thot? Say ut again if ye dare.

COCKY [*his hand on his sheath knife—snarling*]. 'Airy ape! That's wot I says! [*PADDY tries to reach him but the others keep them apart.*]

BIG FRANK [*pushing PADDY back*]. Vot's the matter mit you, Paddy. Don't you hear vat Driscoll say—no fighting?

PADDY [*grumblingly*]. I don't take no back talk from that deck-scrubbin' shrimp.

COCKY. Blarsted coal-puncher! [*DRISCOLL appears wearing a broad grin of satisfaction. The fight is immediately forgotten by the crowd who gather around him with exclamations of eager curiosity: How is it, Drisc? Any luck? Vot she bring, Drisc? Where's the gels? etc.*]

DRISCOLL [*with an apprehensive glance back at the bridge*]. Not so loud, for the love av hivin! [*The clamor dies down.*] Yis, she has ut wid her. She'll be here in a minute wid a pint bottle or two for each wan av ye—three shillin's a bottle. So don't be impashunt.

COCKY [*indignantly*].   Three bob! The bloody cow!

SMITTY [*with an ironic smile*].   Grand larceny, by God! [*They all turn and look up at him, surprised to hear him speak.*]

OLSON.   Py yingo, we don't pay so much.

BIG FRANK.   Tamn black tief!

PADDY.   We'll take ut away from her and give her nothin'.

THE CROWD [*growling*].   Dirty thief! Dot's right! Give her nothin'! Not a bloomin' 'apenny! etc.

DRISCOLL [*grinning*].   Ye can take ut or lave ut, me sonny byes. [*He casts a glance in the direction of the bridge and then reaches inside his shirt and pulls out a pint bottle.*] 'Tis foine rum, the rale stuff. [*He drinks.*] I slipped this wan out av wan av the baskets whin they wasn't lookin'. [*He hands the bottle to* OLSON, *who is nearest him.*] Here ye are, Ollie. Take a small sup an' pass ut to the nixt. 'Tisn't much but 'twill serve to take the black taste out av your mouths if ye go aisy wid ut. An' there's buckets more av ut comin'. [*The bottle passes from hand to hand, each man taking a sip and smacking his lips with a deep "Aa-ah" of satisfaction.*]

DAVIS.   Where's she now, Drisc?

DRISCOLL.   Up havin' a worrd wid the skipper, makin' arrangements about the money, I s'pose.

DAVIS.   An' where's the other gels?

DRISCOLL.   Wid her. There's foive av thim she took aboard—two swate little slips av things, near as white as you an' me are, for that gray-whiskered auld fool, an' the mates—an' the engineers too, maybe. The rist av thim'll be comin' for'ard whin she comes.

COCKY.   'E ain't 'arf a funny ole bird, the skipper. Gawd blimey! 'Member when we sailed from 'ome 'ow 'e stands on the bridge lookin' like a bloody ole sky pilot? An' 'is missus dawn on the bloomin' dock 'owlin' fit to kill 'erself? An' 'is kids 'owlin' an' wavin' their 'andkerchiefs? [*With great moral indignation.*] An' 'ere 'e is makin' up to a bleedin' nigger! There's a captain for yer! Gawd blimey! Bloody crab, I calls 'im!

DRISCOLL.   Shut up, ye insect! Sure, it's not you should be talkin', an' you wid a woman an' childer weepin' for ye in iviry divil's port in the wide worrld, if we can believe your own tale av ut.

COCKY [*still indignant*].   I ain't no bloomin' captain, I ain't. I ain't got no missus—reg'lar married, I means. I ain't—

BIG FRANK [*putting a huge paw over* COCKY'S *mouth*].   You ain't going talk so much, you hear? [COCKY *wriggles away from him.*] Say, Drisc, how ve pay dis voman for booze? Ve ain't got no cash.

DRISCOLL.   It's aisy enough. Each girl'll have a slip av paper wid her
an' whin you buy anythin' u write ut down and the price beside
ut and sign your your name. If ye can't write have some one who
can do ut for ye. An' rimimber this: Whin ye buy a bottle av
dhrink or [*with a wink*] somethin' else forbid, ye must write down
tobaccy or fruit or somethin' the loike av that. Whin she laves the
skiper'll pay what's owin' on the paper an' take ut out av your pay.
Is ut clear to ye now?

ALL.   Yes—Clear as day—Aw right, Drisc—Righto—Sure. etc.

DRISCOLL.   An' don't forgit what I said about bein' quiet wid the
dhrink, or the Mate'll be down on our necks an' spile the fun. [*A
chorus of assent*]

DAVIS [*looking aft*].   Ain't this them comin'? [*They all look in that direction. The silly laughter of a woman is heard.*]

DRISCOLL.   Look at Yank, wud ye, wid his arrm around the middle av
wan av thim. That lad's not wastin' any toime.

[*The four women enter from the left, giggling and whispering to each other.
The first three carry baskets on their heads. The youngest and best-looking
comes last. YANK has his arm about her waist and is carrying her basket in
his other hand. All four are distinct negro types. They wear light-colored,
loose-fitting clothes and have bright bandana handkerchiefs on their heads.
They put down their baskets on the hatch and sit down beside them. The men
crowd around, grinning.*]

BELLA [*she is the oldest, stoutest, and homeliest of the four—grinning back at
them*].   Ullo, boys.

THE OTHER GIRLS.   Ullo, boys.

THE MEN.   Hello, yourself—Evenin'—Hello—How are you? etc.

BELLA [*genially*].   Hope you had a nice voyage. My name's Bella, this
here's Susie, yander's Violet, and her there [*pointing to the girl with
YANK*] is Pearl. Now we all knows each other.

PADDY [*roughly*].   Never mind the girls. Where's the dhrink?

BELLA [*tartly*].   You're a hawg, ain't you? Don't talk so loud or you
don't git any—you nor no man. Think I wants the ole captain to
put me off the ship, do you?

YANK.   Yes, nix on hollerin', you! D'yuh wanta queer all of us?

BELLA [*casting a quick glance over her shoulder*].   Here! Some of you big
strapping boys sit back of us on the hatch there so's them officers can't see what we're doin'. [*DRISCOLL and several of the others
sit and stand in back of the girls on the hatch. BELLA turns to
DRISCOLL.*] Did you tell 'em they gotter sign for what they
gits—and *how* to sign?

DRISCOLL.   I did—what's your name again—oh, yis—Bella, darlin'.

BELLA. Then it's all right; but you boys has gotter go inside the fo'castle when you gits your bottle. No drinkin' out here on deck. I ain't takin' chances. [*An impatient murmur of assent goes up from the crowd.*] Ain't that right, Mike?

DRISCOLL. Right as rain, darlin'. [BIG FRANK *leans over and says something to him in a low voice.* DRISCOLL *laughs and slaps his thigh.*] Listen, Bella, I've somethin' to ask ye for my little friend here who's bashful. Ut has to do wid the ladies so I'd best be whisperin' ut to ye meself to kape them from blushin'. [*He leans over and asks her a question.*]

BELLA [*firmly*]. Four shillin's.

DRISCOLL [*laughing*]. D'you hear that, all av ye? Four shillin's ut is.

PADDY [*angrily*]. To hell wid this talkin! I want a dhrink.

BELLA. Is everything all right, Mike?

DRISCOLL [*after a look back at the bridge*]. Sure. Let her droive!

BELLA. All right, girls. [*The girls reach down in their baskets in under the fruit which is on top and each pulls out a pint bottle. Four of the men crowd and take the bottles.*] Fetch a light, Lamps, that's a good boy. [LAMPS *goes to his room and returns with a candle. This is passed from one girl to another as the men sign the sheets of paper for their bottles.*] Don't you boys forget to mark down cigarettes or tobacco or fruit, remember! Three shillin's is the price. Take it into the fo'castle. For Gawd's sake, don't stand out here drinkin' in the moonlight. [*The four go into the forecastle. Four more take their places.* PADDY *plants himself in front of* PEARL *who is sitting by* YANK *with his arm still around her.*]

PADDY [*gruffly*]. Gimme thot! [*She holds out a bottle which he snatches from her hand. He turns to go away.*]

YANK [*sharply*]. Here, you! Where d'yuh get that stuff? You ain't signed for that yet.

PADDY [*sullenly*]. I can't write me name.

YANK. Then I'll write it for yuh. [*He takes the paper from* PEARL *and writes.*] There ain't goin' to be no welchin' on little Bright Eyes here—not when I'm around, see? Ain't I right, kiddo?

PEARL [*with a grin*]. Yes, suh.

BELLA [*seeing all four are served*]. Take it into the fo'castle, boys. [PADDY *defiantly raises his bottle and gulps down a drink in the full moonlight.* BELLA *sees him.*] Look at 'im! Look at the dirty swine! [PADDY *slouches into the forecastle.*] Wants to git me in trouble. That settles it! We all got to git inside, boys, where we won't git caught. Come on, girls.

[*The girls pick up their baskets and follow* BELLA. YANK *and* PEARL *are the last to reach the doorway. She lingers behind him, her eyes fixed on* SMITTY, *who is still sitting on the forecastle head, his chin on his hands, staring off into vacancy.*]

PEARL [*waving a hand to attract his attention*].   Come ahn in, pretty boy. Ah likes you.

SMITTY [*coldly*].   Yes; I want to buy a bottle, please. [*He goes down the steps and follows her into the forecastle. No one remains on deck but* THE DONKEYMAN, *who sits smoking his pipe in front of his door. There is the subdued babble of voices from the crowd inside but the mournful cadence of the song from the shore can again be faintly heard.* SMITTY *reappears and closes the door to the forecastle after him. He shudders and shakes his shoulders as if flinging off something which disgusted him. Then he lifts the bottle which is in his hand to his lips and gulps down a long drink.* THE DONKEYMAN *watches him impassively.* SMITTY *sits down on the hatch facing him. Now that the closed door has shut off nearly all the noise the singing from shore comes clearly over the moonlit water.*]

SMITTY [*listening to it for a moment*].   Damn that song of theirs. [*He takes another big drink.*] What do you say, Donk?

THE DONKEYMAN [*quietly*].   Seems nice an' sleepy-like.

SMITTY [*with a hard laugh*].   Sleepy! If I listened to it long—sober—I'd never go to sleep.

THE DONKEYMAN.   'Tain't sich bad music, is it? Sounds kinder pretty to me—low an' mournful—same as listenin' to the organ outside o' church of a Sunday.

SMITTY [*with a touch of impatience*].   I didn't mean it was bad music. It isn't. It's the beastly memories the damn thing brings up—for some reason. [*He takes another pull at the bottle.*]

THE DONKEYMAN.   Ever hear it before?

SMITTY.   No; never in my life. It's just a something about the rotten thing which makes me think of—well—oh, the devil! [*He forces a laugh.*]

THE DONKEYMAN [*spitting placidly*].   Queer things, mem'ries. I ain't ever been bothered much by 'em.

SMITTY [*looking at him fixedly for a moment—with quiet scorn*].   No, you wouldn't be.

THE DONKEYMAN.   Not that I ain't had my share o' things goin' wrong; but I puts 'em out o' me mind, like, an' fergets 'em.

SMITTY.   But suppose you couldn't put them out of your mind? Suppose they haunted you when you were awake and when you were asleep—what then?

THE DONKEYMAN [*quietly*].   I'd git drunk, same's you're doin'.

SMITTY [*with a harsh laugh*].   Good advice. [*He takes another drink. He is beginning to show the effects of the liquor. His face is flushed and he talks rather wildly.*] We're poor little lambs who have lost our way,

eh, Donk? Damned from here to eternity, what? God have mercy
on such as we! True, isn't it, Donk?

THE DONKEYMAN.   Maybe; I dunno. [*After a slight pause*] Whatever set
you goin' to sea? You ain't made for it.

SMITTY [*laughing wildly*].   My old friend in the bottle here, Donk.

THE DONKEYMAN.   I done my share o' drinkin' in my time. [*Regretfully.*]
Them was good times, those days. Can't hold up under drink no
more. Doctor told me I'd got to stop or die. [*He spits contentedly.*]
So I stops.

SMITTY [*with a foolish smile*].   Then I'll drink one for you. Here's your
health, old top! [*He drinks.*]

THE DONKEYMAN [*after a pause*].   S'pose there's a gel mixed up in it
someplace, ain't there?

SMITTY [*stiffly*].   What makes you think so?

THE DONKEYMAN.   Always is when a man lets music bother 'im. [*After
a few puffs at his pipe*] An' she said she threw you over 'cause you
was drunk; an' you said you was drunk 'cause she threw you over.
[*He spits leisurely.*] Queer thing, love, ain't it?

SMITTY [*rising to his feet with drunken dignity*].   I'll trouble you not to
pry into my affairs, Donkeyman.

THE DONKEYMAN [*unmoved*].   That's everybody's affair, what I said. I
been through it many's the time. [*Genially.*] I always hit 'em a
whack on the ear an' went out and got drunker'n ever. When I
come home again they always had somethin' special nice cooked fur
me to eat. [*Puffing at his pipe.*] That's the on'y way to fix 'em when
they gits on their high horse. I don't s'pose you ever tried that?

SMITTY [*pompously*].   Gentlemen don't hit women.

THE DONKEYMAN [*placidly*].   No; that's why they has mem'ries when
they hears music. [SMITTY *does not deign to reply to this but sinks into a
scornful silence.* DAVIS *and the girl* VIOLET *come out of the forecastle and close
the door behind them. He is staggering a bit and she is laughing shrilly.*]

DAVIS [*turning to the left*].   This way, Rose, or Pansy, or Jessamine, or
black Tulip, or Violet, or whatever the hell flower your name is.
No one'll see us back here. [*They go off left.*]

THE DONKEYMAN.   There's love at first sight for you—an' plenty more
o' the same in the fo'c's'tle. No mem'ries jined with that.

SMITTY [*really repelled*].   Shut up, Donk. You're disgusting. [*He takes a
long drink.*]

THE DONKEYMAN [*philosophically*].   All depends on how you was
brung up, I s'pose. [PEARL *comes out of the forecastle. There is a roar
of voices from inside. She shuts the door behind her, sees* SMITTY *on the
hatch, and comes over and sits beside him and puts her arm over his
shoulder.*]

THE DONKEYMAN [*chuckling*].   There's love for you, Duke.

PEARL [*patting* SMITTY's *face with her hand*].   Ullo; pretty boy. [SMITTY *pushes her hand away coldly.*] What you doin' out here all alone by yourself?

SMITTY [*with a twisted grin*].   Thinking and—[*he indicates the bottle in his hand*]—drinking to stop thinking. [*He drinks and laughs maudlinly. The bottle is three-quarters empty.*]

PEARL.   You oughtn't drink so much, pretty boy. Don' you know dat? You have big, big headache come mawnin'.

SMITTY [*dryly*].   Indeed?

PEARL.   Tha's true. Ah knows what Ah say. [*Cooingly.*] Why you run 'way from me, pretty boy? Ah likes you. Ah don' like them other fellahs. They act too rough. You ain't rough. You're a genelman. Ah knows. Ah can tell a genelman fahs Ah can see 'im.

SMITTY.   Thank you for the compliment; but you're wrong, you see. I'm merely—a ranker. [*He adds bitterly.*] And a rotter.

PEARL [*patting his arm*].   No, you ain't. Ah knows better. You're a genelman. [*Insinuatingly.*] Ah wouldn't have nothin' to do with them other men, but [*she smiles at him enticingly*] you is diff'rent. [*He pushes her away from him disgustedly. She pouts.*] Don' you like me, pretty boy?

SMITTY [*a bit ashamed*].   I beg your pardon. I didn't mean to be rude, you know, really. [*His politeness is drunkenly exaggerated.*] I'm a bit off color.

PEARL [*brightening up*].   Den you do like me—little ways?

SMITTY [*carelessly*].   Yes, yes, why shouldn't I? [*He suddenly laughs wildly and puts his arm around her waist and presses her to him.*] Why not? [*He pulls his arm back quickly with a shudder of disgust, and takes a drink.* PEARL *looks at him curiously, puzzled by his strange actions. The door from the forecastle is kicked open and* YANK *comes out. The uproar of shouting, laughing and singing voices has increased in violence.* YANK *staggers over toward* SMITTY *and* PEARL.]

YANK [*blinking at them*].   What the hell—oh, it's you, Smitty the Duke. I was goin' to turn one loose on the jaw of any guy'd cop my dame, but seein' it's you—[*Sentimentally.*] Pals is pals and any pal of mine c'n have anythin' I got, see? [*Holding out his hand.*] Shake, Duke. [SMITTY *takes his hand and he pumps it up and down.*] You'n me's frens. Ain't I right?

SMITTY.   Right it is, Yank. But you're wrong about this girl. She isn't with me. She was just going back to the fo'c's'tle to you. [PEARL *looks at him with hatred gathering in her eyes.*]

YANK.   Tha' right?

SMITTY.   On my word!

YANK [*grabbing her arm*].   Come on then, you, Pearl! Le's have a drink
with the bunch. [*He pulls her to the entrance where she shakes off his
hand long enough to turn on* SMITTY *furiously.*]

PEARL.   You swine! You can go to hell! [*She goes in the forecastle, slam-
ming the door.*]

THE DONKEYMAN [*spitting calmly*].   There's love for you. They're all the
same—white, brown, yeller 'n' black. A whack on the ear's the
only thing'll learn 'em. [SMITTY *makes no reply but laughs harshly
and takes another drink; then sits staring before him, the almost empty
bottle tightly clutched in one hand. There is an increase in volume of the
muffled clamor from the forecastle and a moment later the door is thrown
open and the whole mob, led by* DRISCOLL, *pours out on deck. All of them
are very drunk and several of them carry bottles in their hands.* BELLA *is
the only one of the women who is absolutely sober. She tries in vain to
keep the men quiet.* PEARL *drinks from* YANK'S *bottle every moment or
so, laughing shrilly, and leaning against* YANK, *whose arm is about her
waist.* PAUL *comes out last carrying an accordion. He staggers over and
stands on top of the hatch, his instrument under his arm.*]

DRISCOLL.   Play us a dance, ye square-head swab!—a rale, Godforsaken
son av a turkey trot wid guts to ut.

YANK.   Straight from the old Barbary Coast in Frisco!

PAUL.   I don' know. I try. [*He commences tuning up.*]

YANK.   Ataboy! Let 'er rip! [DAVIS *and* VIOLET *come back and join the
crowd.* THE DONKEYMAN *looks on them all with a detached, indulgent
air.* SMITTY *stares before him and does not seem to know there is any one
on deck but himself.*]

BIG FRANK.   Dance? I don't dance. I trink! [*He suits the action to the
word and roars with meaningless laughter.*]

DRISCOLL.   Git out av the way thin, ye big hulk, an' give us some room.
[BIG FRANK *sits down on the hatch, right. All of the others who are not going
to dance either follow his example or lean against the port bulwark.*]

BELLA [*on the verge of tears at her inability to get them in the forecastle or
make them be quiet now they are out*].   For Gawd's sake, boys, don't
shout so loud! Want to git me in trouble?

DRISCOLL [*grabbing her*].   Dance wid me, me cannibal quane. [*Some
one drops a bottle on deck and it smashes.*]

BELLA [*hysterically*].   There they goes! There they goes! Captain'll hear
that! Oh, my Lawd!

DRISCOLL.   Be damned to him! Here's the music! Off ye go! [PAUL
*starts playing "You Great Big Beautiful Doll" with a note left out every
now and then. The four couples commence dancing—a jerk-shouldered
version of the old Turkey Trot as it was done in the sailor-town dives, made
more grotesque by the fact that all the couples are drunk and keep lurching*

into each other every moment. Two of the men start dancing together, intentionally bumping into the others. YANK *and* PEARL *come around in front of* SMITTY *and, as they pass him,* PEARL *slaps him across the side of the face with all her might, and laughs viciously. He jumps to his feet with his fists clenched but sees who hit him and sits down again smiling bitterly.* YANK *laughs boisterously.*]

YANK. Wow! Some wallop! One on you, Duke.

DRISCOLL [*hurling his cap at* PAUL]. Faster, ye toad! [*Paul makes frantic efforts to speed up and the music suffers in the process.*]

BELLA [*puffing*]. Let me go. I'm wore out with you steppin' on my toes, you clumsy Mick. [*She struggles but* DRISCOLL *holds her tight.*]

DRISCOLL. God blarst you for havin' such big feet, thin. Aisy, aisy, Mrs. Old Black Joe! 'Tis dancin'll take the blubber off ye. [*He whirls her around the deck by main force.* COCKY, *with* SUSIE, *is dancing near the hatch, right, when* PADDY, *who is sitting on the edge with* BIG FRANK, *sticks his foot out and the wavering couple stumble over it and fall flat on the deck. A roar of laughter goes up.* COCKY *rises to his feet, his face livid with rage, and springs at* PADDY, *who promptly knocks him down.* DRISCOLL *hits* PADDY *and* BIG FRANK *hits* DRISCOLL. *In a flash a wholesale fight has broken out and the deck is a surging crowd of drink-maddened men hitting out at each other indiscriminately, although the general idea seems to be a battle between seamen and firemen. The women shriek and take refuge on top of the hatch, where they huddle in a frightened group. Finally there is the flash of a knife held high in the moonlight and a loud yell of pain.*]

DAVIS [*somewhere in the crowd*]. Here's the Mate comin'! Let's git out o' this! [*There is a general rush for the forecastle. In a moment there is no one left on deck but the little group of women on the hatch;* SMITTY, *still dazedly rubbing his cheek;* THE DONKEYMAN *quietly smoking on his stool; and* YANK *and* DRISCOLL, *their faces battered up considerably, their undershirts in shreds, bending over the still form of* PADDY, *which lies stretched out on the deck between them. In the silence the mournful chant from the shore creeps slowly out to the ship.*]

DRISCOLL [*quickly—in a low voice*]. Who knoifed him?

YANK [*stupidly*]. I didn't see it. How do I know? Cocky, I'll bet. [*The* FIRST MATE *enters from the left. He is a tall, strongly-built man dressed in a plain blue uniform.*]

THE MATE [*angrily*]. What's all this noise about? [*He sees the man lying on the deck.*] Hello! What's this? [*He bends down on one knee beside* PADDY.]

DRISCOLL [*stammering*]. All av us—was in a bit av a harmless foight, sir—an'—I dunno—[THE MATE *rolls* PADDY *over and sees a knife wound on his shoulder.*]

THE MATE.   Knifed, by God. [*He takes an electric flash from his pocket and examines the cut.*] Lucky it's only a flesh wound. He must have hit his head on deck when he fell. That's what knocked him out. This is only a scratch. Take him aft and I'll bandage him up

DRISCOLL.   Yis, sor. [*They take* PADDY *by the shoulders and feet and carry him off left.* THE MATE *looks up and sees the women on the hatch for the first time.*]

THE MATE [*surprised*].   Hello! [*He walks over to them.*] Go to the cabin and get your money and clear off. If I had my way, you'd never— [*His foot hits a bottle. He stoops down and picks it up and smells of it.*] Rum, by God! So that's the trouble! I thought their breaths smelled damn queer. [*To the women, harshly.*] You needn't go to the skipper for any money. You won't get any. That'll teach you to smuggle rum on a ship and start a riot.

BELLA.   But, Mister—

THE MATE [*sternly*].   You know the agreement—rum—no money.

BELLA [*indignantly*].   Honest to Gawd, Mister, I never brung no—

THE MATE [*fiercely*].   You're a liar! And none of your lip or I'll make a complaint ashore tomorrow and have you locked up.

BELLA [*subdued*].   Please, Mister—

THE MATE.   Clear out of this, now! Not another word out of you! Tumble over the side damn quick! The two others are waiting for you. Hop, now! [*They walk quickly—almost run—off to the left.* THE MATE *follows them, nodding to* THE DONKEYMAN, *and ignoring the oblivious* SMITTY.]

[*There is absolute silence on the ship for a few moments. The melancholy song of the negroes drifts crooning over the water.* SMITTY *listens to it intently for a time; then sighs heavily, a sigh that is half a sob.*]

SMITTY.   God! [*He drinks the last drop in the bottle and throws it behind him on the hatch.*]

THE DONKEYMAN [*spitting tranquilly*].   More mem'ries? [SMITTY *does not answer him. The ship's bell tolls four bells.* THE DONKEYMAN *knocks out his pipe.*] I think I'll turn in. [*He opens the door to his cabin, but turns to look at* SMITTY—*kindly.*] You can't hear it in the fo'c's'tle— the music, I mean—an' there'll likely be more drink in there, too. Good night. [*He goes in and shuts the door.*]

SMITTY.   Good night, Donk. [*He gets wearily to his feet and walks with bowed shoulders, a bit, to the forecastle entrance and goes in. There is silence for a second or so, broken only by the haunted, saddened voice of that brooding music, and far-off, like the mood of the moonlight made audible.*]

CURTAIN

ARIA DA CAPO

Edna St. Vincent Millay

CAST OF CHARACTERS
PIERROT
COLUMBINE
COTHURNUS, Masque of Tragedy
THYRSIS } Shepherds
CORYDON }

Scene: A stage

[*The curtain rises on a stage set for a Harlequinade, a merry black and white interior. Directly behind the footlights, and running parallel with them, is a long table, covered with a gay black and white cloth, on which is spread a banquet. At the opposite ends of this table, seated on delicate thin-legged chairs with high backs, are* PIERROT *and* COLUMBINE, *dressed according to the tradition, excepting that* PIERROT *is in lilac, and* COLUMBINE *in pink. They are dining.*]

COLUMBINE.   Pierrot, a macaroon! I cannot *live* without a macaroon!
 PIERROT.   My only love,
      You are so intense! . . . Is it Tuesday, Columbine?—
      I'll kiss you if it's Tuesday.
COLUMBINE.   It is Wednesday,
      If you must know . . . . Is this my artichoke,
      Or yours?
PIERROT.   Ah, Columbine,—as if it mattered!
      Wednesday . . . . Will it be Tuesday, then, tomorrow,
      By any chance?
COLUMBINE.   Tomorrow will be—Pierrot,
      That isn't funny!
PIERROT.   I thought it rather nice.
      Well, let us drink some wine and lose our heads
      And love each other.

169

COLUMBINE.   Pierrot, don't you love
  Me now?
PIERROT.   La, what a woman!—how should I know?
  Pour me some wine: I'll tell you presently.
COLUMBINE.   Pierrot, do you know, I think you drink too much.
PIERROT.   Yes, I dare say I do. . . . Or else too little.
  It's hard to tell. You see, I am always wanting
  A little more than what I have,—or else
  A little less. There's something wrong. My dear,
  How many fingers have you?
COLUMBINE.   La, indeed,
  How should I know?—It always takes me one hand
  To count the other with. It's too confusing.
  Why?
PIERROT.   Why?—I am a student, Columbine;
  And search into all matters.
COLUMBINE.   La, indeed?—
  Count them yourself, then!
PIERROT.   No. Or, rather, *nay*.
  'Tis of no consequence. . . . I am become
  A painter, suddenly,—and you impress me—
  Ah, yes!—six orange bull's-eyes, four green pin-wheels,
  And one magenta jelly-roll,—the title
  As follows: *Woman Taking in Cheese from Fire-Escape.*
COLUMBINE.   Well, I like that! So that is all I've meant
  To you!
PIERROT.   Hush! All at once I am become
  A pianist. I will image you in sound. . . .
  On a new scale. . . . Without tonality. . .
  Vivace senza tempo senza tutto. . . .
  Title: *Uptown Express at Six O'Clock.*
  Pour me a drink.
COLUMBINE.   Pierrot, you work too hard.
  You need a rest. Come on out into the garden,
  And sing me something sad.
PIERROT.   Don't stand so near me!
  I am become a socialist. I love
  Humanity; but I hate people. Columbine,
  Put on your mittens, child; your hands are cold.
COLUMBINE.   My hands are *not* cold!
PIERROT.   Oh, I am sure they are.
  And you must have a shawl to wrap about you,
  And sit by the fire.

COLUMBINE. Why, I'll do no such thing!
    I'm hot as a spoon in a teacup!
PIERROT. Columbine,
    I'm a philanthropist. I know I am,
    Because I feel so restless. Do not scream,
    Or it will be the worse for you!
COLUMBINE. Pierrot,
    My vinaigrette! I cannot *live* without
    My vinaigrette!
PIERROT. My only love, you are
    So fundamental! . . . How would you like to be
    An actress, Columbine?—I am become
    Your manager.
COLUMBINE. Why, Pierrot, *I* can't act.
PIERROT. Can't act! Can't act! La, listen to the woman!
    What's that to do with the price of furs?—You're blonde,
    Are you not?—you have no education, have you?—
    Can't act! You underrate yourself, my dear!
COLUMBINE. Yes, I suppose I do.
PIERROT. As for the rest,
    I'll teach you how to cry, and how to die,
    And other little tricks; and the house will love you.
    You'll be a star by five o'clock . . . that is,
    If you will let me pay for your apartment.
COLUMBINE. *Let* you?—well, that's a good one!
    Ha! Ha! Ha!
    But why?
PIERROT. But why?—well, as to that, my dear,
    I cannot say. It's just a matter of form.
COLUMBINE. Pierrot, I'm getting tired of caviar
    And peacocks' livers. Isn't there something else
    That people eat?—some humble vegetable,
    That grows in the ground?
PIERROT. Well, there are mushrooms.
COLUMBINE. Mushrooms!
    That's so! I had forgotten . . . mushrooms . . . mushrooms. . . .
    I cannot *live* with . . . How do you like this gown?
PIERROT. Not much. I'm tired of gowns that have the waist-line
    About the waist, and the hem around the bottom,—
    And women with their breasts in front of them!—
    Zut and ehè! Where does one go from here!
COLUMBINE. Here's a persimmon, love. You always liked them.
PIERROT. I am become a critic; there is nothing

I can enjoy. . . . However, set it aside;
  I'll eat it between meals.
COLUMBINE.   Pierrot, do you know,
  Sometimes I think you're making fun of me.
PIERROT.   My love, by yon black moon, you wrong us both.
COLUMBINE.   There isn't a sign of a moon, Pierrot.
PIERROT.   Of course not.
  There never was. "Moon's" just a word to swear by.
  "Mutton!"—now *there's* a thing you can lay the hands on,
  And set the tooth in! Listen, Columbine:
  I always lied about the moon and you.
  Food is my only lust.
COLUMBINE.   Well, eat it, then,
  For Heaven's sake, and stop your silly noise!
  I haven't heard the clock tick for an hour.
PIERROT.   It's ticking all the same. If you were a fly,
  You would be dead by now. And if I were a parrot,
  I could be talking for a thousand years!

[*Enter* COTHURNUS.]

PIERROT.   Hello, what's this, for God's sake?—
  What's the matter?
  Say, whadda you mean?—get off the stage, my friend,
  And pinch yourself,—you're walking in your sleep!
COTHURNUS.   I never sleep.
PIERROT.   Well, anyhow, clear out.
  You don't belong on here. Wait for your own scene!
  Whadda you think this is,—a dress-rehearsal?
COTHURNUS.   Sir, I am tired of waiting. I will wait
  No longer.
PIERROT.   Well, but whadda you going to do?
  The scene is set for me!
COTHURNUS.   True, sir; yet I
  Can play the scene.
PIERROT.   Your scene is down for later!
COTHURNUS.   That, too, is true, sir; but I play it now.
PIERROT.   Oh, very well!—Anyway, I am tired
  Of black and white. At least, I think I am.

  [*Exit* COLUMBINE.]

Yes, I am sure I am. I know what I'll do!—
  I'll go and strum the moon, that's what I'll do. . . .

Unless, perhaps . . . you never can tell . . . I may be,
You know, tired of the moon. Well, anyway,
I'll go find Columbine. . . . And when I find her,
I will address her thus: "*Ehè*, Pierrette!"—
There's something in that.

[*Exit* PIERROT.]

COTHURNUS.   You, Thyrsis! Corydon!
   Where are you?

THYRSIS [*off stage*].   Sir, we are in our dressing-room!

COTHURNUS. Come out and do the scene.

CORYDON [*off stage*].   You are mocking us!—
   The scene is down for later.

COTHURNUS.   That is true;
   But we will play it now. I am the scene.
   [*Seats himself on high place in back of stage.*]

[*Enter* CORYDON *and* THYRSIS.]

CORYDON.   Sir, we are counting on this little hour.
   We said, "Here is an hour,—in which to think
   A mighty thought, and sing a trifling song,
   And look at nothing."—And, behold! the hour,
   Even as we spoke, was over, and the act begun,
   Under our feet!

THYRSIS.   Sir, we are not in the fancy
   To play the play. We had thought to play it later.

CORYDON.   Besides, this is the setting for a farce.
   Our scene requires a wall; we cannot build
   A wall of tissue-paper!

THYRSIS.   We cannot act
   A tragedy with comic properties!

COTHURNUS.   Try it and see. I think you'll find you can.
   One wall is like another. And regarding
   The matter of your insufficient mood,
   The important thing is that you speak the lines,
   And make the gestures. Wherefore I shall remain
   Throughout, and hold the prompt-book. Are you ready?

CORYDON-THYRSIS [*sorrowfully*].   Sir, we are always ready.

COTHURNUS.   Play the play!

[CORYDON *and* THYRSIS *move the table and chairs to one side out of the way, and seat themselves in a half-reclining position on the floor.*]

THYRSIS.   How gently in the silence, Corydon,
      Our sheep go up the bank. They crop a grass
      That's yellow where the sun is out, and black
      Where the clouds drag their shadows. Have you noticed
      How steadily, yet with what a slanting eye
      They graze?
CORYDON.   As if they thought of other things.
      What say you, Thyrsis, do they only question
      Where next to pull?—Or do their far minds draw them
      Thus vaguely north of west and south of east?
THYRSIS.   One cannot say. . . . The black lamb wears its burdocks
      As if they were a garland,—have you noticed?
      Purple and white—and drinks the bitten grass
      As if it were a wine.
CORYDON.   I've noticed that.
      What say you, Thyrsis, shall we make a song
      About a lamb that thought himself a shepherd?
THYRSIS.   Why, yes!—that is, why,—no. [I have forgotten my line.]
COTHURNUS [*prompting*].   "I know a game worth two of that!"
THYRSIS.   Oh, yes. . . . I know a game worth two of that!
      Let's gather rocks, and build a wall between us;
      And say that over there belongs to me,
      And over here to you!
CORYDON.   Why,—very well.
      And say you may not come upon my side
      Unless I say you may!
THYRSIS.   Nor you on mine!
      And if you should, 'twould be the worse for you!

[*They weave a wall of colored crêpe paper ribbons from the centre front to the centre back of the stage, fastening the ends to* COLUMBINE'S *chair in front and to* PIERROT'S *chair in the back.*]

CORYDON.   Now there's a wall a man may see across,
      But not attempt to scale.
THYRSIS.   An excellent wall.
CORYDON.   Come, let us separate, and sit alone
      A little while, and lay a plot whereby
      We may outdo each other.

[*They seat themselves on opposite sides of the wall.*]

PIERROT [*off stage*].   *Ehè,* Pierrette!
COLUMBINE [*off stage*].   My name is Columbine!
   Leave me alone!
THYRSIS [*coming up to the wall*].   Corydon, after all, and in spite of
   the fact
   I started it myself, I do not like this
   So very much. What is the sense of saying
   I do not want you on my side the wall?
   It is a silly game. I'd much prefer
   Making the little song you spoke of making,
   About the lamb, you know, that thought himself
   A shepherd!—what do you say?

[*Pause.*]

CORYDON [*at wall*].   (I have forgotten the line.)
COTHURNUS [*prompting*].   "How do I know this isn't a trick?"
CORYDON.   Oh, yes. . . . How do I know this isn't a trick
   To get upon my land?
THYRSIS.   Oh, Corydon,
   You *know* it's not a trick. I do not like
   The game, that's all. Come over here, or let me
   Come over there.
CORYDON.   It is a clever trick
   To get upon my land. [*Seats himself as before.*]
THYRSIS.   Oh, very well! [*Seats himself as before.*]
   [*To himself.*] I think I never knew a sillier game.
CORYDON [*coming to wall*].   Oh, Thyrsis, just a minute!—all the
   water
   Is on your side the wall, and the sheep are thirsty.
   I hadn't thought of that.
THYRSIS.   Oh, hadn't you?
CORYDON.   Why, what do you mean?
THYRSIS.   What do I mean?—I mean
   That I can play a game as well as you can.
   And if the pool is on my side, it's on
   My side, that's all.
CORYDON.   You mean you'd let the sheep
   Go thirsty?
THYRSIS.   Well, they're not my sheep. My sheep
   Have water enough.
CORYDON.   *Your* sheep! You are mad, to call them
   Yours—mine—they are all one flock! Thyrsis, you can't mean

To keep the water from them, just because
They happened to be grazing over here
Instead of over there, when we set the wall up?
THYRSIS.   Oh, can't I?—wait and see!—and if you try
To lead them over here, you'll wish you hadn't!
CORYDON.   I wonder how it happens all the water
Is on your side. . . . I'll say you had an eye out
For lots of little things, my innocent friend,
When I said, "Let us make a song," and you said,
"I know a game worth two of that!"
COLUMBINE [*off stage*].   Pierrot,
D'you know, I think you must be getting old,
Or fat, or something,—stupid, anyway!—
Can't you put on some other kind of collar?
THYRSIS.   You know as well as I do, Corydon,
I never thought anything of the kind.
Don't you?
CORYDON.   I *do* not.
THYRSIS.   Don't you?
CORYDON.   Oh, I suppose so.
Thyrsis, let's drop this,—what do you say?—it's only
A game, you know . . . we seem to be forgetting
It's only a game ... a pretty serious game
It's getting to be, when one of us is willing
To let the sheep go thirsty for the sake of it.
THYRSIS.   I know it, Corydon.

[*They reach out their arms to each other across the wall.*]

COTHURNUS [*prompting*].   "But how do I know—"
THYRSIS.   Oh, yes. . . . But how do I know this isn't a trick
To water your sheep, and get the laugh on me?
CORYDON.   You can't know, that's the difficult thing about it,
Of course,—you can't be sure. You have to take
My word for it. And I know just how you feel.
But one of us has to take a risk, or else,
Why, don't you see?—the game goes on forever! . . .
It's terrible, when you stop to think of it. . . .
Oh, Thyrsis, now for the first time I feel
This wall is actually a wall, a thing
Come up between us, shutting you away
From me. . . . I do not know you any more!
THYRSIS.   No, don't say that! Oh, Corydon, I'm willing
To drop it all, if you will! Come on over

And water your sheep! It is an ugly game
I hated it from the first. . . . How did it start?
CORYDON.   I do not know . . . I do not know . . . I think
I am afraid of you!—you are a stranger!
I never set eyes on you before! "Come over
And water my sheep," indeed!—They'll be more thirsty
Than they are now before I bring them over
Into your land, and have you mixing them up
With yours, and calling them yours, and trying to
keep them!

[*Enter* COLUMBINE]

COLUMBINE [*to* COTHURNUS].   Glummy, I want my hat.
THYRSIS.   Take it, and go.
COLUMBINE.   Take it and go, indeed. Is it my hat,
Or isn't it? Is this my scene, or not?
Take it and go! Really, you know, you two
Are awfully funny!

[*Exit* COLUMBINE]

THYRSIS.   Corydon, my friend,
I'm going to leave you now, and whittle me
A pipe, or sing a song, or go to sleep.
When you have come to your senses, let me know.
[*Goes back to where he has been sitting, lies down and sleeps.*]

[CORYDON, *in going back to where he has been sitting, stumbles over bowl of colored confetti and colored paper ribbons.*]

CORYDON.   Why, what is this?—Red stones—and purple stones—
And stones stuck full of gold!—The ground is full
Of gold and colored stones! . . . I'm glad the wall
Was up before I found them!—Otherwise,
I should have had to share them. As it is,
They all belong to me. . . . Unless—
[*He goes to wall and digs up and down the length of it, to see if there are jewels on the other side.*]
None here—
None here—none here—They all belong to me!
[*Sits.*]

THYRSIS [*awakening*].   How curious! I thought the little black lamb
Came up and licked my hair; I saw the wool
About its neck as plain as anything!

It must have been a dream. The little black lamb
Is on the other side of the wall, I'm sure.
[*Goes to wall and looks over.* CORYDON *is seated on the ground,
tossing the confetti up into the air and catching it.*]
Hello, what's that you've got there, Corydon?

CORYDON.   Jewels.

THYRSIS.   Jewels?—And where did you ever get them?

CORYDON.   Oh, over here.

THYRSIS.   You mean to say you found them,
By digging around in the ground for them?

CORYDON [*unpleasantly*].   No, Thyrsis,
By digging down for water for my sheep.

THYRSIS.   Corydon, come to the wall a minute, will you?
I want to talk to you.

CORYDON.   I haven't time.
I'm making me a necklace of red stones.

THYRSIS.   I'll give you all the water that you want,
For one of those red stones,—if it's a good one.

CORYDON.   Water?—what for?—what do I want of water?

THYRSIS.   Why, for your sheep!

CORYDON.   My sheep?—I'm not a shepherd!

THYRSIS.   Your sheep are dying of thirst.

CORYDON.   Man, haven't I told you
I can't be bothered with a few untidy
Brown sheep all full of burdocks?—I'm a merchant.
That's what I am!—And if I set my mind to it
I dare say I could be an emperor!
[*To himself.*] Wouldn't I be a fool to spend my time
Watching a flock of sheep go up a hill,
When I have these to play with?—when I have these
To think about?—I can't make up my mind
Whether to buy a city, and have a thousand
Beautiful girls to bathe me, and be happy
Until I die, or build a bridge, and name it
The Bridge of Corydon,—and be remembered
After I'm dead.

THYRSIS.   Corydon, come to the wall,
Won't you?—I want to tell you something.

CORYDON.   Hush!
Be off! Be off! Go finish your nap, I tell you!

THYRSIS.   Corydon, listen: if you don't want your sheep,
Give them to me.

CORYDON.   Be off! Go finish your nap.

A red one—and a blue one—and a red one—
And a purple one—give you my sheep, did you say?—
Come, come! What do you take me for, a fool?
I've a lot of thinking to do,—and while I'm thinking,
The sheep might just as well be over here
As over there. . . . A blue one—and a red one—

THYRSIS. But they will die!

CORYDON. And a green one—and a couple
Of white ones, for a change.

THYRSIS. Maybe I have
Some jewels on my side.

CORYDON. And another green one—
Maybe, but I don't think so. You see, this rock
Isn't so very wide. It stops before
It gets to the wall. It seems to go quite deep,
However.

THYRSIS [with hatred]. I see.

COLUMBINE [off stage]. Look, Pierrot, there's the moon.

PIERROT [off stage]. Nonsense!

THYRSIS. I see.

COLUMBINE [off stage]. Sing me an old song, Pierrot,—
Something I can remember.

PIERROT [off stage]. Columbine.
Your mind is made of crumbs,—like an escallop
Of oysters,—first a layer of crumbs, and then
An oystery taste, and then a layer of crumbs.

THYRSIS [searching]. I find no jewels . . . but I wonder what
The root of this black weed would do to a man
If he should taste it.... I have seen a sheep die,
With half the stalk still drooling from its mouth.
'Twould be a speedy remedy, I should think,
For a festered pride and a feverish ambition.
It has a curious root. I think I'll hack it
In little pieces. . . . First I'll get me a drink;
And then I'll hack that root in little pieces
As small as dust, and see what the color is
Inside. [Goes to bowl on floor.]
    The pool is very clear. I see
A shepherd standing on the brink, with a red cloak
About him, and a black weed in his hand. . . .
    'Tis I. [Kneels and drinks.]

CORYDON [coming to wall]. Hello, what are you doing, Thyrsis?

THYRSIS. Digging for gold.

CORYDON.   I'll give you all the gold
    You want, if you'll give me a bowl of water.
    If you don't want too much, that is to say.
THYRSIS.   Ho, so you've changed your mind?—It's different,
    Isn't it, when you want a drink yourself?
CORYDON.   Of course it is.
THYRSIS.   Well, let me see ... a bowl
    Of water,—come back in an hour, Corydon.
    I'm busy now.
CORYDON.   Oh, Thyrsis, give me a bowl
    Of water!—and I'll fill the bowl with jewels,
    And bring it back!
THYRSIS.   Be off, I'm busy now.
    [*He catches sight of the weed, picks it up and looks at it, unseen by*
    CORYDON.]
    Wait!—Pick me out the finest stones you have . . .
    I'll bring you a drink of water presently.
CORYDON [*goes back and sits down, with the jewels before him*].   A bowl
    of jewels is a lot of jewels.
THYRSIS [*chopping up the weed*].   I wonder if it has a bitter taste.
CORYDON.   There's sure to be a stone or two among them
    I have grown fond of, pouring them from one hand
    Into the other.
THYRSIS.   I hope it doesn't taste
    Too bitter, just at first.
CORYDON.   A bowl of jewels
    Is far too many jewels to give away
    And not get back again.
THYRSIS.   I don't believe
    He'll notice. He's too thirsty. He'll gulp it down
    And never notice.
CORYDON.   There ought to be some way
    To get them back again. . . . I could give him a necklace,
    And snatch it back, after I'd drunk the water,
    I suppose. . . . Why, as for that, of course a necklace. . . .

[*He puts two or three of the colored tapes together and tries their strength by
pulling them, after which he puts them around his neck and pulls them, gently, nodding to himself. He gets up and goes to the wall, with the colored tapes
in his hands.* THYRSIS *in the meantime has poured the powdered root—black
confetti—into the pot which contained the flower and filled it up with wine
from the punch-bowl on the floor. He comes to the wall at the same time,
holding the bowl of poison.*]

THYRSIS.   Come, get your bowl of water, Corydon.

CORYDON.   Ah, very good!—and for such a gift as that
I'll give you more than a bowl of unset stones.
I'll give you three long necklaces, my friend.
Come closer. Here they are. [*Puts the ribbons about* THYRSIS' *neck.*]

THYRSIS [*putting bowl to* Corydon's *mouth*].   I'll hold the bowl
Until you've drunk it all.

CORYDON.   Then hold it steady.
For every drop you spill I'll have a stone back
Out of this chain.

THYRSIS.   I shall not spill a drop.

[CORYDON *drinks, meanwhile beginning to strangle* THYRSIS.]

THYRSIS.   Don't pull the string so tight.

CORYDON.   You're spilling the water.

THYRSIS.   You've had enough—you've had enough—stop pulling
The string so tight!

CORYDON.   Why, that's not tight at all ...
How's this?

THYRSIS [*drops bowl*].   You're strangling me! Oh, Corydon!
It's only a game!—and you are strangling me!

CORYDON.   It's only a game, is it?—Yet I believe
You've poisoned me in earnest! [*Writhes and pulls the strings
tighter, winding them about* THYRSIS' *neck.*]

THYRSIS.   Corydon! [*Dies.*]

CORYDON.   You've poisoned me in earnest. . . . I feel so cold. . . .
So cold . . . this is a very silly game. . . .
Why do we play it?—let's not play this game
A minute more . . . let's make a little song
About a lamb. . . . I'm coming over the wall,
No matter what you say,—I want to be near you. . . .
[*Groping his way, with arms wide before him, he strides through the
frail papers of the wall without knowing it, and continues seeking for
the wall straight across the stage.*]
Where is the wall? [*Gropes his way back, and stands very near*
THYRSIS *without seeing him; he speaks slowly.*]
There isn't any wall, I think.
[*Takes a step forward, his foot touches* THYRSIS' *body, and he falls down
beside him.*]
Thyrsis, where is your cloak?—just give me
A little bit of your cloak! . . .

[*Draws corner of cloak over his shoulders, falls across* Thyrsis' *body, and
dies.*]

[COTHURNUS *closes the prompt-book with a bang, arises matter-of-factly, comes down stage, and places the table over the two bodies, drawing down the cover so that they are hidden from any actors on the stage, but visible to the audience, pushing in their feet and hands with his boot. He then turns his back to the audience, and claps his hands twice.*]

COTHURNUS.   Strike the scene! [*Exit* COTHURNUS.]

[*Enter* PIERROT *and* COLUMBINE.]

PIERROT.   Don't puff so, Columbine!
COLUMBINE.   Lord, what a mess
　　This set is in! If there's one thing I hate
　　Above everything else,—even more than getting my feet wet—
　　It's clutter!—He might at least have left the scene
　　The way he found it ... don't you say so, Pierrot?

[*She picks up punch bowl. They arrange chairs as before at ends of table.*]

PIERROT.   Well, I don't know. I think it rather diverting
　　The way it is.
　　[*Yawns, picks up confetti bowl.*]
　　Shall we begin?
COLUMBINE [*screams*].   My God!
　　What's that there under the table?
PIERROT.   It is the bodies
　　Of the two shepherds from the other play.
COLUMBINE [*slowly*].   How curious to strangle him like that,
　　With colored paper ribbons.
PIERROT.   Yes, and yet
　　I dare say he is just as dead. [*Pauses. Calls.*]
　　　Cothurnus!
　　Come drag these bodies out of here! We can't
　　Sit down and eat with two dead bodies lying
　　Under the table! ... The audience wouldn't stand for it!
COTHURNUS [*off stage*].   What makes you think so?—
　　Pull down the tablecloth
　　On the other side, and hide them from the house,
　　And play the farce. The audience will forget.
PIERROT.   That's so. Give me a hand there,
　　Columbine.

[PIERROT *and* COLUMBINE *pull down the table cover in such a way that the two bodies are hidden from the house, then merrily set their bowls back on the table, draw up their chairs, and begin the play exactly as before.*]

COLUMBINE.   Pierrot, a macaroon,—I cannot *live* without a macaroon!
PIERROT.   My only love,
   You are *so* intense! ... Is it Tuesday, Columbine?—
   I'll kiss you if it's Tuesday.

[*Curtains begin to close slowly.*]

COLUMBINE.   It is Wednesday,
   If you must know.... Is this my artichoke
   Or yours?
PIERROT.   Ah, Columbine, as if it mattered!
   Wednesday. . . . Will it be Tuesday, then, tomorrow,
   By any chance? . . .
                    CURTAIN

THE KNAVE OF HEARTS
Louise Saunders

CAST OF CHARACTERS

The Manager
Blue Hose
Yellow Hose
1st Herald
2nd Herald
Pompdebile the Eighth, King of Hearts
  [*pronounced Pomp-dibiley*]
The Chancellor
ρ The Knave of Hearts
Ursula
The Lady Violetta
Six Little Pages

[The Manager *appears before the curtain in doublet and hose. He carries a cap with a long, red feather.*]

The Manager [*bowing deeply*].   Ladies and gentlemen, you are about to hear the truth of an old legend that has persisted wrongly through the ages, the truth that, until now, has been hid behind the embroidered curtain of a rhyme, about the Knave of Hearts, who was no knave but a very hero indeed. The truth, you will agree with me, gentlemen and most honored ladies, is rare! It is only the quiet, unimpassioned things of nature that seem what they are. Clouds rolled in massy radiance against the blue, pines shadowed deep and darkly green, mirrored in still waters, the contemplative mystery of the hills—these things which exist, absorbed but in their own existence—these are the perfect chalices of truth.

But we, gentlemen and thrice-honored ladies, flounder about in a tangled net of prejudice, of intrigue. We are blinded by conventions, we are crushed by misunderstanding, we are distracted by violence, we are deceived by hypocrisy, until only

184

too often villains receive the rewards of nobility and the truly great-hearted are suspected, distrusted, and maligned.

And so, ladies and gentlemen, for the sake of justice and also, I dare to hope, for your approval, I have taken my puppets down from their dusty shelves. I have polished their faces, brushed their clothes, and strung them on wires, so that they may enact for you this history.

[He parts the curtains, revealing two PASTRY COOKS *in flaring white caps and spotless aprons leaning over in stiff profile, their wooden spoons, three feet long, pointing rigidly to the ceiling. They are in one of the kitchens of* POMPDEBILE THE EIGHTH, *King of Hearts. It is a pleasant kitchen, with a row of little dormer windows and a huge stove, adorned with the crest of* POMPDEBILE—*a heart rampant, on a gold shield.]*

You see here, ladies and gentlemen, two pastry cooks belonging to the royal household of Pompdebile the Eighth—Blue Hose and Yellow Hose, by name. At a signal from me they will spring to action, and as they have been made with astonishing cleverness, they will bear every semblance of life. Happily, however, you need have no fear that, should they please you, the exulting wine of your appreciation may go to their heads—their heads being but things of wire and wood; and happily, too, as they are but wood and wire, they will be spared the shame and humiliation that would otherwise be theirs should they fail to meet with your approval.

The play, most honored ladies and gentlemen, will now begin.

[He claps his hands. Instantly the two pastry cooks come to life. THE MANAGER *bows himself off the stage.*

BLUE HOSE. Is everything ready for this great event?

YELLOW HOSE. Everything. The fire blazing in the stove, the Pages, dressed in their best, waiting in the pantry with their various jars full of the finest butter, the sweetest sugar, the hottest pepper, the richest milk, the—

BLUE HOSE. Yes, yes, no doubt. *[Thoughtfully]* It is a great responsibility, this that they have put on our shoulders.

YELLOW HOSE. Ah, yes. I have never felt more important.

BLUE HOSE. Nor I more uncomfortable.

YELLOW HOSE. Even on the day, or rather the night, when I awoke and found myself famous—I refer to the time when I laid before an astonished world my creation, "Humming birds' hearts soufflé, au vin blanc"—I did not feel more important. It is a pleasing sensation!

BLUE HOSE. I like it not at all. It makes me dizzy, this eminence on which they have placed us. The Lady Violetta is slim and fair. She does not, in my opinion, look like the kind of person who is capable of making good pastry. I have discovered through long experience that it is the heaviest women who make the lightest pastry, and *vice versa*. Well, then, suppose that she does not pass this examination—suppose that her pastry is lumpy, white like the skin of a boiled fowl.

YELLOW HOSE. Then, according to the law of the Kingdom of Hearts, we must condemn it, and the Lady Violetta cannot become the bride of Pompdebile. Back to her native land she will be sent, riding a mule.

BLUE HOSE. And she is so pretty, so exquisite! What a law! What an outrageous law!

YELLOW HOSE. Outrageous law! How dare you! There is nothing so necessary to the welfare of the nation as our art. Good cooks make good tempers, don't they? Must not the queen set an example for the other women to follow? Did not our fathers and our grandfathers before us judge the dishes of the previous queens of hearts?

BLUE HOSE. I wish I were mixing the rolls for tomorrow's breakfast.

YELLOW HOSE. Bah! You are fit for nothing else. The affairs of state are beyond you.

[*Distant sound of trumpets.*]

BLUE HOSE [*nervously*]. What's that?

YELLOW HOSE. The King is approaching! The ceremonies are about to commence!

BLUE HOSE. Is everything ready?

YELLOW HOSE. I told you that everything was ready. Stand still; you are as white as a stalk of celery.

BLUE HOSE [*counting on his fingers*]. Apples, lemons, peaches, jam— Jam! Did you forget jam?

YELLOW HOSE. Zounds, I did!

BLUE HOSE [*wailing*]. We are lost!

YELLOW HOSE. She may not call for it.

[*Both stand very erect and make a desperate effort to appear calm.*]

BLUE HOSE [*very nervous*]. Which door? Which door?

YELLOW HOSE. The big one, idiot. Be still!

[*The sound of trumpets increases, and cries of "Make way for the King." Two Heralds come in and stand on either side of the door.* THE KING OF HEARTS *enters, followed by ladies and gentlemen of the court.* POMPDEBILE *is in full regalia, and very imposing indeed with his red robe bordered with ermine, his crown and sceptre. After him comes the* CHANCELLOR, *an old man with a short, white beard. The* KING *strides in a particularly kingly fashion, pointing his toes in the air at every step, toward his throne, and sits down. The* KNAVE *walks behind him slowly. He has a sharp, pale face.*]

POMPDEBILE [*impressively*].   Lords and ladies of the court, this is an important moment in the history of our reign. The Lady Violetta, whom you love and respect—that is, I mean to say, whom the ladies love and the lords—er—respect, is about to prove whether or not she be fitted to hold the exalted position of Queen of Hearts, according to the law, made a thousand years ago by Pompdebile the Great, and steadily followed ever since. She will prepare with her own delicate, white hands a dish of pastry. This will be judged by the two finest pastry cooks in the land. [BLUE HOSE *and* YELLOW HOSE *bow deeply.*] If their verdict be favorable, she shall ride through the streets of the city on a white palfrey, garlanded with flowers. She will be crowned, the populace will cheer her, and she will reign by our side, attending to the domestic affairs of the realm, while we give our time to weightier matters. This of course you all understand is a time of great anxiety for the Lady Violetta. She will appear worried—[*To* CHANCELLOR] The palfrey is in readiness, we suppose.

CHANCELLOR.   It is, Your Majesty.

POMPDEBILE.   Garlanded with flowers?

CHANCELLOR.   With roses, Your Majesty.

● KNAVE [*bowing*].   The Lady Violetta prefers violets, Your Majesty.

POMPDEBILE.   Let there be a few violets put in with the roses— er—We are ready for the ceremony to commence. We confess to a slight nervousness unbecoming to one of our station. The Lady Violetta, though trying at times, we have found—er—shall we say—er—satisfying?

KNAVE [*bowing*].   Intoxicating, Your Majesty?

CHANCELLOR [*shortly*].   His Majesty means nothing of the sort.

POMPDEBILE.   No, of course not—er—The mule—Is that—did you—?

CHANCELLOR [*in a grieved tone*].   This is hardly necessary. Have I ever neglected or forgotten any of your commands, Your Majesty?

POMPDEBILE.   You have, often. However, don't be insulted. It takes a great deal of our time and it is most uninteresting.

CHANCELLOR [*indignantly*].   I resign, Your Majesty.

POMPDEBILE.   Your thirty-seventh resignation will be accepted to-morrow. Just now it is our wish to begin at once. The anxiety that no doubt gathered in the breast of each of the seven successive Pompdebiles before us seems to have concentrated in ours. Already the people are clamoring at the gates of the palace to know the decision. Begin. Let the Pages be summoned.

KNAVE [*bowing*]. Beg pardon, Your Majesty; before summoning the Pages, should not the Lady Violetta be here?

POMPDEBILE. She should, and is, we presume, on the other side of that door—waiting breathlessly.

[*The* KNAVE *quietly opens the door and closes it.*]

KNAVE [*bowing*]. She is not, Your Majesty, on the other side of that door waiting breathlessly. In fact, to speak plainly, she is not on the other side of that door at all.

POMPDEBILE. Can that be true? Where are her ladies?

KNAVE. They are all there, Your Majesty.

POMPDEBILE. Summon one of them.

[*The* KNAVE *goes out, shutting the door. He returns, following* URSULA, *who, very much frightened, throws herself at the* KING's *feet.*]

POMPDEBILE. Where is your mistress?

URSULA. She has gone, Your Majesty.

POMPDEBILE. Gone! Where has she gone?

URSULA. I do not know, Your Majesty. She was with us a while ago, waiting there, as you commanded.

POMPDEBILE. Yes, and then—speak.

URSULA. Then she started out and forbade us to go with her.

POMPDEBILE. The thought of possible divorce from us was more than she could bear. Did she say anything before she left?

URSULA [*trembling*]. Yes, Your Majesty.

POMPDEBILE. What was it? She may have gone to self-destruction. What was it?

URSULA. She said—

POMPDEBILE. Speak, woman, speak.

URSULA. She said that Your Majesty—

POMPDEBILE. A farewell message! Go on.

URSULA [*gasping*]. That Your Majesty was "pokey" and that she didn't intend to stay there any longer.

POMPDEBILE [*roaring*]. *Pokey!!*

URSULA. Yes, Your Majesty, and she bade me call her when you came, but we can't find her, Your Majesty.

[*The* PASTRY COOKS *whisper.* URSULA *is in tears.*]

CHANCELLOR. This should not be countenanced, Your Majesty. The word "pokey" cannot be found in the dictionary. It is the most flagrant disrespect to use a word that is not in the dictionary in connection with a king.

POMPDEBILE. We are quite aware of that, Chancellor, and although we may appear calm on the surface, inwardly we are swelling, *swelling,* with rage and indignation.

KNAVE [*looking out the window*]. I see the Lady Violetta in the garden. [*He goes to the door and holds it open, bowing.*] The Lady Violetta is at the door, Your Majesty.

[*Enter the* LADY VIOLETTA, *her purple train over her arm. She has been running.*]

VIOLETTA. Am I late? I just remembered and came as fast as I could. I bumped into a sentry and he fell down. I didn't. That's strange, isn't it? I suppose it's because he stands in one position so long he—Why, Pompy dear, what's the matter? Oh, oh! [*Walking closer*] Your feelings are hurt!

POMPDEBILE. *Don't* call us Pompy. It doesn't seem to matter to you whether you are divorced or not.

VIOLETTA [*anxiously*]. Is that why your feelings are hurt?

POMPDEBILE. Our feelings are not hurt, not at all.

VIOLETTA. Oh, yes, they are, Pompdebile dear. I know, because they are connected with your eyebrows. When your feelings go down, up go your eyebrows, and when your feelings go up, they go down—always.

POMPDEBILE [*severely*]. Where have you been?

VIOLETTA. I, just now?

POMPDEBILE. Just now, when you should have been outside that door waiting *breathlessly.*

VIOLETTA. I was in the garden. Really, Pompy, you couldn't expect me to stay all day in that ridiculous pantry; and as for being breathless, it's quite impossible to be it unless one has been jumping or something.

Pompdebile. What were you doing in the garden?

VIOLETTA [*laughing*]. Oh, it was too funny. I must tell you. I found a goat there who had a beard just like the Chancellor's—really it was quite remarkable, the resemblance—in other ways too. I took him by the horns and I looked deep into his eyes, and I said, "Chancellor, if you try to influence Pompy—"

POMPDEBILE [*shouting*]. Don't call us Pompy.

VIOLETTA. Excuse me, Pomp—[*Checking herself.*]

KNAVE. And yet I think I remember hearing of an emperor, a great emperor, named Pompey.

POMPDEBILE. We know him not. Begin at once; the people are clamoring at the gates. Bring the ingredients.

[*The* PASTRY COOKS *open the door, and, single file, six little boys march in, bearing large jars labeled butter, salt, flour, pepper, cinnamon, and milk. The* COOKS *place a table and a large bowl and a pan in front of the* LADY VIOLETTA *and give her a spoon. The six little boys stand three on each side.*]

VIOLETTA. Oh, what darling little ingredients. May I have an apron, please?

[URSULA *puts a silk apron, embroidered with red hearts, on the* LADY VIOLETTA.]

BLUE HOSE. We were unable to find a little boy to carry the pepper, My Lady. They all *would* sneeze in such a disturbing way.

VIOLETTA. This is a perfectly controlled little boy. He hasn't sneezed once.

YELLOW HOSE. That, if it please Your Ladyship, is not a little boy.

VIOLETTA. Oh! How nice! Perhaps she will help me.

CHANCELLOR [*severely*]. You are allowed no help, Lady Violetta.

VIOLETTA. Oh, Chancellor, how cruel of you. [*She takes up the spoon, bowing.*] Your Majesty, Lords and Ladies of the court, I propose to make [*impressively*] raspberry tarts.

BLUE HOSE. Heaven be kind to us!

YELLOW HOSE [*suddenly agitated*]. Your Majesty, I implore your forgiveness. There is no raspberry jam in the palace.

POMPDEBILE. What! Who is responsible for this carelessness?

BLUE HOSE. I gave the order to the grocer, but it didn't come. [*Aside*] I knew something like this would happen. I knew it.

VIOLETTA [*untying her apron*]. Then, Pompdebile, I'm very sorry—we shall have to postpone it.

CHANCELLOR. If I may be allowed to suggest, Lady Violetta can prepare something else.

KNAVE. The law distinctly says that the Queen-elect has the privilege of choosing the dish which she prefers to prepare.

VIOLETTA. Dear Pompdebile, let's give it up. It's such a silly law! Why should a great splendid ruler like you follow it just because one of your ancestors, who wasn't half as nice as you are, or one bit wiser, said to do it? Dearest Pompdebile, please.

POMPDEBILE. We are inclined to think that there may be something in what the Lady Violetta says.

CHANCELLOR. I can no longer remain silent. It is due to that brilliant law of Pompdebile the First, justly called the Great, that all members of our male sex are well fed, and, as a natural consequence, happy.

KNAVE. The happiness of a set of moles who never knew the sunlight.

POMPDEBILE. If we made an effort, we could think of a new law—just as wise. It only requires effort.

CHANCELLOR. But the constitution. We can't touch the constitution.

POMPDEBILE [*starting up*]. We shall destroy the constitution!

CHANCELLOR. The people are clamoring at the gates!

POMPDEBILE. Oh, I forgot them. No, it has been carried too far. We shall have to go on. Proceed.

VIOLETTA. Without the raspberry jam?

POMPDEBILE [*to* KNAVE]. Go you, and procure some. I will give a hundred golden guineas for it.

[*The little* BOY *who holds the cinnamon pot comes forward.*]

BOY. Please, Your Majesty, I have some.

POMPDEBILE. You! Where?

BOY. In my pocket. If someone would please hold my cinnamon jar—I could get it.

[URSULA *takes it. The* BOY *struggles with his pocket and finally, triumphantly, pulls out a small jar.*]
There!

VIOLETTA. How clever of you! Do you always do that?

BOY. What—eat raspberry jam?

VIOLETTA. No, supply the exact article needed from your pocket.

BOY. I eat it for my lunch. Please give me the hundred guineas.

VIOLETTA. Oh, yes—Chancellor—if I may trouble you.

[*Holding out her hand.*]

CHANCELLOR. Your Majesty, this is an outrage! Are you going to allow this?

POMPDEBILE [*sadly*]. Yes, Chancellor. We have such an impulsive nature!

[*The* LADY VIOLETTA *receives the money.*]

VIOLETTA. Thank you. [*She gives it to the* BOY.] Now we are ready to begin. Milk, please. [*The* BOY *who holds the milk jar comes forward and kneels.*] I take some of this milk and beat it well.

YELLOW HOSE [*in a whisper*]. Beat it—milk!

VIOLETTA. Then I put in two tablespoonfuls of salt, taking great care that it falls exactly in the middle of the bowl. [*To the little* BOY] Thank you, dear. Now the flour, no, the pepper, and then—one pound of butter. I hope that it is good butter, or the whole thing will be quite spoiled.

BLUE HOSE.   This is the most astonishing thing I have ever witnessed.

YELLOW HOSE.   I don't understand it.

VIOLETTA [*stirring*].   I find that the butter is *not* very good. It makes a great difference. I shall have to use more pepper to counteract it. That's better. [*She pours in pepper. The* BOY *with the pepper pot sneezes violently.*] Oh, oh, dear! Lend him your handkerchief, Chancellor. Knave, will you? [YELLOW HOSE *silences the* BOY'*s sneezes with the* KNAVE'*s handkerchief.*] I think that they are going to turn out very well. Aren't you glad, Chancellor? You shall have one if you will be glad and smile nicely—a little brown tart with raspberry jam in the middle. Now for a dash of vinegar.

COOKS [*in horror*].   Vinegar! Great Goslings! Vinegar!

VIOLETTA [*stops stirring*].   Vinegar will make them crumbly. Do you like them crumbly, Pompdebile, darling? They are really for you, you know, since I am trying, by this example, to show all the wives how to please all the husbands.

POMPDEBILE.   Remember that they are to go in the museum with the tests of the previous Queens.

VIOLETTA [*thoughtfully*].   Oh, yes, I had forgotten that. Under the circumstances, I shall omit the vinegar. We don't want them too crumbly. They would fall about and catch the dust so frightfully. The museum-keeper would never forgive me in years to come. Now I dip them by the spoonful on this pan; fill them with the nice little boy's raspberry jam—I'm sorry I have to use it all, but you may lick the spoon—put them in the oven, slam the door. Now, my Lord Pompy, the fire will do the rest.

[*She curtsies before the* KING.]

POMPDEBILE.   It gave us great pleasure to see the ease with which you performed your task. You must have been practising for weeks. This relieves, somewhat, the anxiety under which we have been suffering and makes us think that we would enjoy a game of checkers once more. How long a time will it take for your creation to be thoroughly done, so that it may be tested?

VIOLETTA [*considering*].   About twenty minutes, Pompy.

POMPDEBILE [*to* HERALD].   Inform the people. Come, we will retire. [*To* KNAVE.] Let no one enter until the Lady Violetta commands.

[*All exit, left, except the* KNAVE. *He stands in deep thought, his chin in hand—then exits slowly, right. The room is empty. The cuckoo clock strikes. Presently both right and left doors open stealthily. Enter* LADY VIOLETTA *at one door, the* KNAVE *at the other, backward, looking down the passage. They turn suddenly and see each other.*]

VIOLETTA [*tearfully*].   O Knave, I can't cook! Anything—anything at all, not even a baked potato.

KNAVE.   So I rather concluded, My Lady, a few minutes ago.

VIOLETTA [*pleadingly*].   Don't you think it might just happen that they turned out all right? [*Whispering.*] Take them out of the oven. Let's look.

KNAVE.   That's what I intended to do before you came in. It's possible that a miracle has occurred.

[*He tries the door of the oven.*]

VIOLETTA.   Look out; it's hot. Here, take my handkerchief.

KNAVE.   The gods forbid, My Lady.

[*He takes his hat, and, folding it, opens the door and brings out the pan, which he puts on the table softly.*]

VIOLETTA [*with a look of horror*].   How queer! They've melted or something. See, they are quite soft and runny. Do you think that they will be good for anything, Knave?

KNAVE.   For paste, My Lady, perhaps.

VIOLETTA.   Oh, dear. Isn't it dreadful!

KNAVE.   It is.

VIOLETTA [*beginning to cry*].   I don't want to be banished, especially on a mule—

KNAVE.   Don't cry, My Lady. It's very—upsetting.

VIOLETTA.   I would make a delightful queen. The fêtes that I would give—under the starlight, with soft music stealing from the shadows, fêtes all perfume and deep mystery, where the young—like you and me, Knave—would find the glowing flowers of youth ready to be gathered in all their dewy freshness!

KNAVE.   Ah!

VIOLETTA.   Those stupid tarts! And wouldn't I make a pretty picture riding on the white palfrey, garlanded with flowers, followed by the cheers of the populace—Long live Queen Violetta, long live Queen Violetta! Those *abominable* tarts!

KNAVE.   I'm afraid that Her Ladyship is vain.

VIOLETTA.   I am indeed. Isn't it fortunate?

KNAVE.   Fortunate?

VIOLETTA.   Well, I mean it would be fortunate if I were going to be queen. They get so much flattery. The queens who don't adore it as I do must be bored to death. Poor things! I'm never so happy as when I am being flattered. It makes me feel all warm and purry. That is another reason why I feel sure I was *made* to be a queen.

KNAVE [*looking ruefully at the pan*]. You will never be queen, My Lady, unless we can think of something quickly, some plan—

VIOLETTA. Oh, yes, dear Knave, please think of a plan at once. Banished people, I suppose, have to comb their own hair, put on their shoes, and button themselves up the back. I have never performed these estimable and worthy tasks, Knave. I don't know how; I don't even know how to scent my bath. I haven't the least idea what makes it smell deliciously of violets. I only know that it always *does* smell deliciously of violets because I wish it that way. I should be miserable; save me, Knave, please.

KNAVE. My mind is unhappily a blank, Your Majesty.

VIOLETTA. It's very unjust. Indeed, it's unjust! No other queen in the world has to understand cooking; even the Queen of Spades doesn't. Why should the Queen of Hearts, of all people!

KNAVE. Perhaps it is because—I have heard a proverb: "The way to the heart is through the—"

VIOLETTA [*angrily, stamping her foot*]. Don't repeat that hateful proverb! Nothing can make me more angry. I feel like crying when I hear it, too. Now see, I'm crying. You made me.

KNAVE. Why does that proverb make you cry, My Lady?

VIOLETTA. Oh, because it is such a stupid proverb and so silly, because it's true in most cases, and because—I don't know why.

KNAVE. We are a set of moles here. One might also say that we are a set of mules. How can moles or mules either be expected to understand the point of view of a Bird of Paradise when she—

VIOLETTA. Bird of Paradise! Do you mean me?

KNAVE [*bowing*]. I do, My Lady, figuratively speaking.

VIOLETTA [*drying her eyes*]. How very pretty of you! Do you know, I think that you would make a splendid chancellor.

KNAVE. Her Ladyship is vain, as I remarked before.

VIOLETTA [*coldly*]. As I remarked before, how fortunate. Have you anything to suggest—a plan?

KNAVE. If only there were time my wife could teach you. Her figure is squat, round, her nose is clumsy, and her eyes stumble over it; but her cooking, ah—[*He blows a kiss*] it is a thing to dream about. She cooks as naturally as the angels sing. The delicate flavors of her concoctions float over the palate like the perfumes of a thousand flowers. True, her temper, it is anything but sweet— However, I am conceded by many to be the most happily married man in the kingdom.

VIOLETTA [*sadly*].   Yes. That's all they care about here. One may be, oh, so cheerful and kind and nice in every other way, but if one can't cook nobody loves one at all.

KNAVE.   Beasts! My higher nature cries out at them for holding such views. Fools! Swine! But my lower nature whispers that perhaps after all they are not far from right, and as my lower nature is the only one that ever gets any encouragement—

VIOLETTA.   Then you think that there is nothing to be done—I shall have to be banished?

KNAVE.   I'm afraid—Wait, I have an idea! [*Excitedly*] Dulcinea, my wife—her name is Dulcinea—made known to me this morning, very forcibly—Yes, I remember, I'm sure—Yes, she was going to bake this very morning some raspberry tarts—a dish in which she particularly excels—If I could only procure some of them and bring them here!

VIOLETTA.   Oh, Knave, dearest, sweetest Knave, could you, I mean, would you? Is there time? The court will return.

[*They tiptoe to the door and listen stealthily.*]

KNAVE.   I shall run as fast as I can. Don't let anyone come in until I get back, if you can help it.

[*He jumps on the table, ready to go out the window.*]

VIOLETTA.   Oh, Knave, how clever of you to think of it. It is the custom for the King to grant a boon to the Queen at her coronation. I shall ask that you be made Chancellor.

KNAVE [*turning back*].   Oh, please don't, My Lady, I implore you.

VIOLETTA.   Why not?

KNAVE.   It would give me social position, My Lady, and that I would rather die than possess. Oh, how we argue about that, my wife and I! Dulcinea wishes to climb, and the higher she climbs, the less she cooks. Should you have me made Chancellor, she would never wield a spoon again.

VIOLETTA [*pursing her lips*].   But it doesn't seem fair, exactly. Think of how much I shall be indebted to her. If she enjoys social position, I might as well give her some. We have lots and lots of it lying around.

KNAVE.   She wouldn't, My Lady, she wouldn't enjoy it. Dulcinea is a true genius, you understand, and the happiness of a genius lies solely in using his gift. If she didn't cook she would be miserable, although she might not be aware of it, I'm perfectly sure.

VIOLETTA.   Then I shall take all social position away from you. You shall rank below the scullery maids. Do you like that better? Hurry, please.

KNAVE. Thank you, My Lady; it will suit me perfectly.

[*He goes out with the tarts.* VIOLETTA *listens anxiously for a minute; then she takes her skirt between the tips of her fingers and practises in pantomime her anticipated ride on the palfrey. She bows, smiles, kisses her hand, until suddenly she remembers the mule standing outside the gates of the palace. That thought saddens her, so she curls up in* POMPDEBILE'S *throne and cries softly, wiping away her tears with a lace handkerchief. There is a knock. She flies to the door and holds it shut.*]

VIOLETTA [*breathlessly*]. Who is there?

CHANCELLOR. It is I, Lady Violetta. The King wishes to return.

VIOLETTA [*alarmed*]. Return! Does he? But the tarts are not done. They are not done at all!

CHANCELLOR. You said they would be ready in twenty minutes. His Majesty is impatient.

VIOLETTA. Did you play a game of checkers with him, Chancellor?

CHANCELLOR. Yes.

VIOLETTA. And did you beat him?

CHANCELLOR [*shortly*]. I did not.

VIOLETTA [*laughing*]. How sweet of you! Would you mind doing it again just for me? Or would it be too great a strain on you to keep from beating him twice in succession?

CHANCELLOR. I shall tell the King that you refuse admission.

[VIOLETTA *runs to the window to see if the* KNAVE *is in sight. The* CHANCELLOR *returns and knocks.*]

CHANCELLOR. The King wishes to come in.

VIOLETTA. But the checkers!

CHANCELLOR. The Knights of the Checker Board have taken them away.

VIOLETTA. But the tarts aren't done, really.

CHANCELLOR. You said twenty minutes.

VIOLETTA. No, I didn't—at least, I said twenty minutes for them to get good and warm and another twenty minutes for them to become brown. That makes forty—don't you remember?

CHANCELLOR. I shall carry your message to His Majesty.

[VIOLETTA *again runs to the window and peers anxiously up the road.*]

CHANCELLOR [*knocking loudly*]. The King *commands* you to open the door.

VIOLETTA. Commands! Tell him—Is he there—with you?

CHANCELLOR. His Majesty is at the door.

VIOLETTA.   Pompy, I think you are rude, very rude indeed. I don't see how you can be so rude—to command me, your own Violetta who loves you so. [*She again looks in vain for the* KNAVE.] Oh, dear! [*Wringing her hands*] Where *can* he be!

POMPDEBILE [*outside*].   This is nonsense. Don't you see how worried we are? It is a compliment to you—

VIOLETTA.   Well, come in; I don't care—only I'm sure they are not finished.

[*She opens the door for the* KING, *the* CHANCELLOR, *and the two* PASTRY COOKS. *The* KING *walks to his throne. He finds* LADY VIOLETTA'S *lace handkerchief on it.*]

POMPDEBILE [*holding up handkerchief*].   What is this?

VIOLETTA.   Oh, that's my handkerchief.

POMPDEBILE.   It is very damp. Can it be that you are anxious, that you are afraid?

VIOLETTA.   How silly, Pompy. I washed my hands, as one always does after cooking; [*to the* PASTRY COOKS] doesn't one? But there was no towel, so I used my handkerchief instead of my petticoat, which is made of chiffon and is very perishable.

CHANCELLOR.   Is the Lady Violetta ready to produce her work?

VIOLETTA.   I don't understand what you mean by work, Chancellor. Oh, the tarts! [*Nervously.*] They were quite simple—quite simple to make—no work at all—A little imagination is all one needs for such things, just imagination. You agree with me, don't you, Pompy, that imagination will work wonders—will do almost anything, in fact? I remember—

POMPDEBILE.   The Pastry Cooks will remove the tarts from the oven.

VIOLETTA.   Oh, *no*, Pompy! They are not finished or cooked, or whatever one calls it. They are not. The last five minutes is of the greatest importance. Please don't let them touch them! *Please*—

POMPDEBILE.   There, there, my dear Violetta, calm yourself. If you wish, they will put them back again. There can be no harm in looking at them. Come, I will hold your hand.

VIOLETTA.   That will help a great deal, Pompy, your holding my hand.

[*She scrambles up on the throne beside the* KING.]

CHANCELLOR [*in horror*].   On the throne, Your Majesty?

POMPDEBILE.   Of course not, Chancellor. We regret that you are not yet entitled to sit on the throne, my dear. In a little while—

Violetta [*coming down*].   Oh, I see. May I sit here, Chancellor, in this seemingly humble position at his feet? Of course, I can't *really* be humble when he is holding my hand and enjoying it so much.

Pompdebile.   Violetta! [*To the* Pastry Cooks] Sample the tarts. This suspense is unbearable!

[*The* King's *voice is husky with excitement. The two* Pastry Cooks, *after bowing with great ceremony to the* King, *to each other, to the* Chancellor— *for this is the most important moment of their lives by far—walk to the oven door and open it, impressively. They fall back in astonishment so great that they lose their balance, but they quickly scramble to their feet again.*]

Yellow Hose.   Your Majesty, there are no tarts there!

Blue Hose.   Your Majesty, the tarts have gone!

Violetta [*clasping her hands*].   Gone! Oh, where could they have gone?

Pompdebile [*coming down from throne*].   That is impossible.

Pastry Cooks [*greatly excited*].   You see, you see, the oven is empty as a drum.

Pompdebile [*to* Violetta].   Did you go out of this room?

Violetta [*wailing*].   Only for a few minutes, Pompy, to powder my nose before the mirror in the pantry. [*To* Pastry Cooks] When one cooks one becomes so disheveled, doesn't one? But if I had thought for one little minute—

Pompdebile [*interrupting*].   The tarts have been stolen!

Violetta [*with a shriek, throwing herself on a chair*].   Stolen! Oh, I shall faint; help me. Oh, oh, to think that any one would take my delicious little, my dear little tarts. My salts. Oh! Oh!

[Pastry Cooks *run to the door and call.*]

Yellow Hose.   Salts! Bring the Lady Violetta's salts.

Blue Hose.   The Lady Violetta has fainted!

[Ursula *enters hurriedly bearing a smelling-bottle.*]

Ursula.   Here, here—What has happened? Oh, My Lady, my sweet mistress!

Pompdebile.   Some wretch has stolen the tarts.

[Lady Violetta *moans.*]

Ursula.   Bring some water. I will take off her headdress and bathe her forehead.

Violetta [*sitting up*].   I feel better now. Where am I? What is the matter? I remember. Oh, my poor tarts!

[*She buries her face in her hands.*]

CHANCELLOR [*suspiciously*].   Your Majesty, this is very strange.

URSULA [*excitedly*].   I know, Your Majesty. It was the Knave. One of the Queen's women, who was walking in the garden, saw the Knave jump out of this window with a tray in his hand. It was the Knave.

VIOLETTA.   Oh, I don't think it was he. I don't, really.

POMPDEBILE.   The scoundrel. Of course it was he. We shall banish him for this or have him *beheaded*.

CHANCELLOR.   It should have been done long ago, Your Majesty.

POMPDEBILE.   You are right.

CHANCELLOR.   Your Majesty will never listen to me.

POMPDEBILE.   We *do* listen to you. Be quiet.

VIOLETTA.   What are you going to do, Pompy, dear?

POMPDEBILE.   Herald, issue a proclamation at once. Let it be known all over the Kingdom that I desire that the Knave be brought here dead or alive. Send the royal detectives and policemen in every direction.

CHANCELLOR.   Excellent; just what I should have advised had Your Majesty listened to me.

POMPDEBILE [*in a rage*].   Be quiet. [*Exit* HERALD.] I never have a brilliant thought but you claim it. It is insufferable!

[*The* HERALDS *can be heard in the distance.*]

CHANCELLOR.   I resign.

POMPDEBILE.   Good. We accept your thirty-eighth resignation at once.

CHANCELLOR.   You did me the honor to appoint me as your Chancellor, Your Majesty, yet never, never do you give me an opportunity to chancel. That is my only grievance. You must admit, Your Majesty, that as your advisers advise you, as your dressers dress you, as your hunters hunt, as your bakers bake, your Chancellor should be allowed to chancel. However, I will be just—as I have been with you so long; before I leave you, I will give you a month's notice.

POMPDEBILE.   That isn't necessary.

CHANCELLOR [*referring to the constitution hanging at his belt*].   It's in the constitution.

POMPDEBILE.   Be quiet.

VIOLETTA.   Well, I think as things have turned out so—so unfortunately, I shall change my gown. [*To* URSULA] Put out my cloth of silver with the moonstones. It is always a relief to change one's gown. May I have my handkerchief, Pompy? Rather a pretty one, isn't it,

Pompy? Of course you don't object to my calling you Pompy now.
When I'm in trouble it's a comfort, like holding your hand.

POMPDEBILE [*magnanimously*].   You may hold our hand too, Violetta.

VIOLETTA [*fervently*].   Oh, how good you are, how sympathetic! But
you see it's impossible just now, as I have to change my gown—
unless you will come with me while I change.

CHANCELLOR [*in a voice charged with inexpressible horror*].   Your
Majesty!

POMPDEBILE.   Be quiet! You have been discharged! [*He starts to descend, when a* HERALD *bursts through the door in a state of great excitement. He kneels before* POMPDEBILE.]

HERALD.   We have found him; we have found him, Your Majesty. In
fact, *I* found him all by myself! He was sitting under the shrub-
bery eating a tart. I stumbled over one of his legs and fell. "How
easy it is to send man and all his pride into the dust," he said, and
then—I saw him!

POMPDEBILE.   Eating a tart! Eating a tart, did you say? The scoundrel!
Bring him here immediately.

[*The* HERALD *rushes out and returns with the* KNAVE, *followed by the six
little* PAGES. *The* KNAVE *carries a tray of tarts in his hand.*]

POMPDEBILE [*almost speechless with rage*].   How dare you—you—
you—

KNAVE [*bowing*].   Knave, Your Majesty.

POMPDEBILE.   You Knave, you shall be punished for this.

CHANCELLOR.   Behead him, Your Majesty.

POMPDEBILE.   Yes, behead him at once.

VIOLETTA.   Oh, no, Pompy, not that! It is not severe enough.

POMPDEBILE.   Not severe enough, to cut off a man's head! Really,
Violetta—

VIOLETTA.   No, because, you see, when one has been beheaded, one's
consciousness that one has been beheaded comes off too. It is
inevitable. And then, what does it matter, when one doesn't
know? Let us think of something really cruel—really fiendish. I
have it—deprive him of social position for the rest of his life—
force him to remain a mere Knave, forever.

POMPDEBILE.   You are right.

KNAVE.   Terrible as this punishment is, I admit that I deserve it, Your
Majesty.

POMPDEBILE.   What prompted you to commit this dastardly crime?

KNAVE.   All my life I have had a craving for tarts of any kind. There
is something in my nature that demands tarts—something in my
constitution that cries out for them—and I obey my constitution

as rigidly as does the Chancellor seek to obey his. I was in the garden reading, as is my habit, when a delicate odor floated to my nostrils, a persuasive odor, a seductive, light brown, flaky odor, an odor so enticing, so suggestive of tarts fit for the gods——that I could stand it no longer. It was stronger than I. With one gesture I threw reputation, my chances for future happiness, to the winds, and leaped through the window. The odor led me to the oven; I seized a tart, and, eating it, experienced the one perfect moment of my existence. After having eaten that one tart, my craving for other tarts has disappeared. I shall live with the memory of that first tart before me forever, or die content, having tasted true perfection.

POMPDEBILE. M-m-m, how extraordinary! Let him be beaten fifteen strokes on the back. Now, Pastry Cooks to the Royal Household, we await your decision!

[*The* COOKS *bow as before; then each selects a tart from the tray on the table, lifts it high, then puts it in his mouth. An expression of absolute ecstasy and beatitude comes over their faces. They clasp hands, then fall on each other's necks, weeping.*]

POMPDEBILE [*impatiently*]. What on earth is the matter?
YELLOW HOSE. Excuse our emotion. It is because we have at last encountered a true genius, a great master, or rather mistress, of our art.

[*They bow to* VIOLETTA.]

POMPDEBILE. They are good, then?
BLUE HOSE [*his eyes to heaven*]. Good! They are angelic!
POMPDEBILE. Give one of the tarts to us. We would sample it.

[*The* PASTRY COOKS *hand the tray to the* KING, *who selects a tart and eats it.*]

POMPDEBILE [*to* VIOLETTA]. My dear, they are marvels! marvels! [*He comes down from the throne and leads* VIOLETTA *up to the dais.*] Your throne, my dear.
VIOLETTA [*sitting down, with a sigh*]. I'm glad it's such a comfortable one.
POMPDEBILE. Knave, we forgive your offense. The temptation was very great. There are things that mere human nature cannot be expected to resist. Another tart, Cooks, and yet another!
CHANCELLOR. But, Your Majesty, don't eat them all. They must go to the museum with the dishes of the previous Queens of Hearts.

YELLOW HOSE.   A museum—those tarts! As well lock a rose in a money-box!

CHANCELLOR.   But the constitution commands it. How else can we commemorate, for future generations, this event?

KNAVE.   Your Majesty, please, I will commemorate it in a rhyme.

POMPDEBILE.   How can a mere rhyme serve to keep this affair in the minds of the people?

KNAVE.   It is the *only* way to keep it in the minds of the people. No event is truly deathless unless its monument be built in rhyme. Consider that fall which, though insignificant in itself, became the most famous of all history, because someone happened to put it into rhyme. The crash of it sounded through centuries and will vibrate for generations to come.

VIOLETTA.   You mean the fall of the Holy Roman Empire?

KNAVE.   No, Madam, I refer to the fall of Humpty Dumpty.

POMPDEBILE.   Well, make your rhyme. In the meantime let us celebrate. You may all have one tart. [*The* PASTRY COOKS *pass the tarts to* VIOLETTA.] Are you willing, dear, to ride the white palfrey garlanded with flowers through the streets of the city?

VIOLETTA.   Willing! I have been practising for days!

POMPDEBILE.   The people, I suppose, are still clamoring at the gates.

VIOLETTA.   Oh, yes, they must clamor. I *want* them to. Herald, tell them that to every man I shall toss a flower, to every woman a shining gold piece, but to the babies I shall throw only kisses, thousands of them, like little winged birds. Kisses and gold and roses! They will surely love me then!

CHANCELLOR.   Your Majesty, I protest. Of what possible use to the people—?

POMPDEBILE.   Be quiet. The Queen may scatter what she pleases.

KNAVE.   My rhyme is ready, Your Majesty.

POMPDEBILE.   Repeat it.

KNAVE.   The Queen of Hearts
              She made some tarts
              All on a summer's day.
              The Knave of Hearts
              He stole those tarts
              And took them quite away.

              The King of Hearts
              Called for those tarts
              And beat the Knave full sore.
              The Knave of Hearts
              Brought back the tarts
              And vowed he'd sin no more.

VIOLETTA [*earnestly*].   My dear Knave, how wonderful of you! You shall be Poet Laureate. A Poet Laureate has no social position, has he?

KNAVE.   It depends, Your Majesty, upon whether or not he chooses to be more laureate than poet.

VIOLETTA [*rising, her eyes closed in ecstasy*].   Your Majesty! Those words go to my head—like wine!

KNAVE.   Long live Pompdebile the Eighth, and Queen Violetta!

[*The trumpets sound.*]

HERALDS.   Make way for Pompdebile the Eighth, and Queen *Vi*-oletta!

VIOLETTA [*excitedly*].   *Vee*-oletta, please!

HERALDS.   Make way for Pompdebile the Eighth, and Queen *Vee*-oletta—

[*The* KING *and* QUEEN *show themselves at the door—and the people can be heard clamoring outside.*]

CURTAIN

Biographies
of the
Playwrights

ARISTOPHANES (C. 448 B.C.E.–C. 385 B.C.E). Aristophanes' eleven ex-
tant plays are the only complete examples of Greek Old Comedy,
a mixture of fantasy, farce, and satire. In his plays, Aristophanes attacks
the mores and morals of Athens, demagogues, social reformers, politics,
and sophists. His first surviving play, *The Acharnians*, is considered to be
the world's first anti-war comedy, a theme he continued with *Peace* and
with *Lysistrata,* in which the women of Athens deny their husbands
their marital rights until they make peace with Sparta. Little is known
of his life, but his family was no doubt well-to-do, since he was obvi-
ously well-educated, as evidenced by the wide knowledge of both literature and philosophy shown in his plays.

JAMES M. BARRIE (1860–1937). Barrie was born in Kirriemuir in
Scotland, the ninth of ten children. He attended Dumfries Academy
and the University of Edinburgh and received an M.A. in 1882. He
moved to London in 1885, where he supported himself as a free-
lance writer. His first successful book, *Auld Licht Idylls,* a book of
sketches of Scottish life, was published in 1888. In 1891, he published *The Little Minister,* which became a huge success. In 1897, *The
Little Minister* was produced for the stage, after which Barrie wrote
primarily for the theater. His most famous character, Peter Pan,
made his first appearance in 1902 in *The Little White Bird.* Although
Peter Pan was produced for the stage in 1904, it was not printed in
a definitive version until 1911. Other plays include *Quality Street*
(1902), *The Admirable Crichton* (1902), *What Every Woman Knows*
(1908), and *Dear Brutus* (1917).

ANTON CHEKHOV (1860–1904). The grandson of a serf, Anton
Chekhov was born in the seaport town of Taganrog in the Crimea.
He attended the University of Moscow, receiving a degree in medi-
cine in 1884. He began to publish short stories while in school in
order to support himself. He published his first novel in 1882 and, by
1886 was widely known as a writer. Although he maintained a medi-
cal practice for eight years, he eventually turned all his energies to his
writing. He started writing one-act plays early in his career and produced a number of masterful examples of the genre, including *The
Bear* (1888), *The Proposal* (1888–89) and *The Wedding* (1889). His early
full-length plays were less successful, and it was not until the 1897
production of *The Seagull* by the Moscow Art Theater that he had his
first critical success. This success was followed by *Uncle Vanya* (1899),
The Three Sisters (1901) and *The Cherry Orchard* (1904). Chekhov died
of tuberculosis in Germany in 1904.

Susan Glaspell (1876–1948). During her long career, Susan Glaspell wrote numerous stories, articles and essays, fourteen novels, and thirteen plays, including the Pulitzer Prize-winning, *Alison's House,* loosely based on Emily Dickinson's biography. Born and raised in the Midwest, Glaspell received her B.A. from Drake University in Des Moines, and attended one semester at the University of Chicago. After college, she worked as a reporter for the *Des Moines News,* and also contributed stories to various women's magazines. Her first novel, *The Glory of the Conquered,* was published in 1909. After her marriage, she and her husband, George Cram Cook, moved to Provincetown, Massachusetts. In 1915, together with friends, they founded the Provincetown Players, a group that fostered the career of several important American playwrights, including Eugene O'Neill. In her seven years with the Players, Glaspell served as actor and director as well as playwright. *Trifles,* inspired by a trial that she covered as a reporter, is her most anthologized play.

Edna St. Vincent Millay (1892–1950). Edna St. Vincent Millay, the first woman to win a Pulitzer Prize for poetry (1923, for *The Harp Weaver and Other Poems*), wrote plays, short stories, and political articles as well as over two hundred sonnets and poems. She was born in Rockland, Maine, one of three daughters born to Cora and Henry Millay. Millay began writing early in life, and, by the age of 15, had had several poems published. She received a scholarship to Vassar College, where she became involved in theater and began to write plays as well as poetry. Her first book, *Renascence and Other Poems,* was published in 1917. After college, she moved to New York and lived in Greenwich Village, where she became involved with the Provincetown Players, for whom she wrote and directed *Aria da Capo* in 1919. In 1927, she wrote the libretto for a highly successful American opera, *The King's Henchman,* composed by Deems Taylor. Throughout her life, she was passionately interested in social issues and was involved in the defense of Sacco and Vanzetti, two Italian anarchists who were accused, many believed falsely, of robbery and murder.

Molière [Jean-Baptiste Poquelin] (1622–1673). Molière was born in Paris, the son of a furniture merchant and upholsterer to the king. He was educated at the College de Clermont in Paris and was familiar with the royal court due to his father's work. At the age of 23, Jean-Baptiste fell in love with Madeleine Béjart, a young actress.

Together with her family, he founded the the Illustrious Theater. It was around this time that he changed his name to Molière. Having little success in Paris, the troupe toured the provinces, where they remained for twelve years. Molière began to write plays for the company that enjoyed great success. In 1658, they returned to Paris and performed at the court of Louis XIV. The King granted the troupe the use of the Hôtel du Petit Bourbon, and later, the Théâtre du Palais Royal. Among Molière's best-known plays are *The School for Husbands* (1661), *The Misanthrope* (1666), *The Miser* (1668) and *The Imaginary Invalid* (1673).

EUGENE O'NEILL (1888–1953). Winner of three Pulitzer Prizes and the 1936 Nobel Prize for Literature, Eugene O'Neill is unquestionably one of the foremost dramatists America has produced. The son of actor James O'Neill, he was born in New York City, and spent the first seven years of his life traveling with his father on tour. He was educated at boarding schools, and spent one year at Princeton. He then prospected gold in Honduras, worked in the theater as an actor and stage manager, was a reporter, and a sailor. In December 1912 he was diagnosed with tuberculosis and spent six months in a sanatorium. While in the sanatorium, he began to read both classic and modern drama and decided that he wanted to write plays. He studied play-writing at Harvard in 1914–15 with George Pierce Baker and in 1916 became associated with the Provincetown Players. This group produced his one-act play, *Bound East for Cardiff*, in Provincetown, then later in New York. In 1920, his first full-length play, *Beyond the Horizon*, was produced on Broadway and his fame was assured. After the demise of the Provincetown Players, he became the main playwright for the Theatre Guild. His popularity diminished somewhat in the years after he won the Nobel Prize. His later plays, some not published until after his death, definitively restored his reputation. His autobiographical *A Long Day's Journey into Night*, would win him a fourth, posthumous Pulitzer.

LOUISE SAUNDERS (1893–1965). Wife of Scribner's legendary editor, Max Perkins, Louise Saunders was a socialite, amateur actress and director, mother of five daughters and the author of a number of stories and plays. The Perkins were friends and neighbors of famed illustrator Maxfield Parrish and in 1916, Parrish designed the set for a production of Saunders' play *The Woodland Princess*. Their most famous collaboration, however, is the lavishly illustrated edition of *Knave of Hearts*, published by Scribner's in 1924.

AUGUST STRINDBERG (1849–1912). August Strindberg is considered to be one of the fathers of the modern theater. Although he is best known outside of Sweden as a dramatist; within Sweden, his stories, novels, poetry, and autobiographical works are equally well-known. Born in Stockholm, Strindberg was the third of ten children. He attended Uppsala University, where he first began writing plays. *Master Olaf,* written in 1872, is considered by some to be Sweden's first great drama, although it was originally rejected by theater managers and not produced until six years after it was written. He had his first great literary success with the novel, *The Red Room,* a social satire that brought him both scandal and fame. He married three times, each marriage ending in divorce. His early plays, such as *Miss Julie* and *The Father,* were written in the Naturalistic style, and are sometimes compared with the plays of Henrik Ibsen. Later in his career he turned to Expressionism, producing such plays as *The Dance of Death* and *A Ghost Sonata.*

JOHN MILLINGTON SYNGE (1871–1909). John Millington Synge was born near Dublin, one of eight children. He originally wanted to be a musician, and studied music at Dublin's Trinity College, then later in Germany. He moved to Paris, where he decided to become a literary critic. He also tried his hand at essays and poetry, albeit unsuccessfully. W.B. Yeats, recognizing his talent, convinced him to return to Ireland to study and write about Irish life and culture. In 1903, his first one-act play, *In the Shadow of the Glen* was produced by the Irish Literary National Theater. Synge, together with Yeats and Lady Gregory, became codirector of the theater when it became the Abbey Theater in 1904. Sadly, his dramatic output was small, cut short by his death in 1909. His best-known play was *The Playboy of the Western World,* written in 1907.

OSCAR WILDE (1854–1900). Dublin-born poet, author and playwright Oscar Wilde was a versatile and prolific writer, producing fairy tales, fiction, poetry, essays, and of course, the plays for which he is best remembered. He was educated at Trinty College in Dublin, then studied the classics at Magdalen College, Oxford. During the 1890s, he produced a number of popular plays, including *A Woman of No Importance, An Ideal Husband,* and *The Importance of Being Earnest,* that established his importance as a playwright and that are still widely performed today. In 1891 he began a homosexual relationship with English poet Alfred Douglas. Douglas's father disapproved, and eventually managed to have Wilde charged with "gross indecency." Wilde was convicted of the charges and sentenced to two years hard labor. While in prison he wrote "De Profundis," and *The Ballad of Reading Gaol* after his release, but never regained his former popularity. *A Florentine Tragedy* was never completed by Wilde. The first public presentation of the play was in 1907.

WILLIAM BUTLER YEATS (1865–1939). Although today Yeats is best remembered as a poet, he was equally adept as a dramatist. Born in Dublin, Yeats was educated in Dublin and London. His work shows a fascination with Irish legends and folklore and a strong interest in mysticism. In 1889 he met and fell in love with Irish actress and revolutionary Maude Gonne. Although his love was unrequited, she remained an importance influence on his work. He was deeply involved with Irish national politics and served as a member of the Irish senate from 1922 until his retirement in 1928. Together with Lady Gregory and others, in 1899 he became one of the founders of the Irish Literary Theater, which later became the Abbey Theater. In 1912, Yeats met Ezra Pound who introduced him to the Japanese Noh play, which became a major influence on his later work. Some of Yeats's finest work was produced after he received the Nobel Prize for Literature in 1923.